CHAPTER 1

The front doorbell rang, and went on ringing. I sighed. My brother must have forgotten his key again. Still clutching the spoon with which I'd been stirring the bolognaise sauce, I went out of the kitchen and along the narrow hallway. A glance at my reflection in the hall mirror showed me that my face looked much as it always did, if a little pale. Reassured that none of my family would suspect I'd been crying, I opened the front door.

A fairy-tale princess, wearing a long white dress embroidered with a scattering of green leaves, was standing on the doorstep. I started in surprise, and then, for the first time that day, I smiled.

'Lucy?' The princess was staring at me.

'Hi, Cassie,' I said.

'Lucy! Oh, it's so lovely to see you.' The star of *The Adventures of Princess Snowdrop* flung her arms around me. It was only with difficulty that I managed to avoid smearing bolognaise sauce all over her voluminous white skirts.

'It's great to see you again too,' I said. 'It must be – what? At least twelve years. Of course, I've seen you on TV since then.'

Cassie laughed, and reached up to straighten the crown of white flowers that perched somewhat precariously on top of her blonde curls. She'd grown up extraordinarily beautiful. It was no wonder that Prince Oak and Prince Ash obeyed her every whim.

'I've been doing a *Snowdrop* publicity gig just a few miles from here,' she said, 'and I decided to take a detour on my way back to London and pay you all a visit. May I come in? If it's convenient.'

'Oh… That's what you always used to say…' For a moment, it was as though we were children again, Cassie walking home from school with me and my stepfather, taking a turn at pushing my brother in his buggy, and when we reached our gate, asking very politely if she might come in, if it was convenient… Back then, it had never occurred to me to wonder why she spent so little time in her own family home, across the road from ours. Suddenly, my throat felt a little tight.

'Come in Cassie,' I said. 'Everyone except me is at work right now, but they'll be home very soon, and I know they'd love to see you.'

'I'll just speak to my driver.'

'You have a driver?' For the first time, I noticed the white limo with the blacked-out windows parked in the road outside. Cassie darted along our garden path and spoke to someone inside the car, which then drove off.

'I've told him to amuse himself for a couple of hours,' she said. 'I'll phone him when I want picking up.'

Cassie Clarke is a TV star now, I thought. Of course she has a limo and a driver. I stood aside to let her into the hall, and she headed straight for the kitchen.

'Oh, it's just the same.' Her gaze travelled

delightedly around the room. 'I *so* used to love coming here and playing with you and your brother.' She sat down at the kitchen table and ran her hands over its wooden surface. 'I remember sitting right here in this chair and helping Dylan do a jigsaw. He was such a cute little boy. How old is he now?'

'He's nineteen. And six foot tall. He's still considered cute though.'

'He used to draw me such lovely pictures. Does he still paint and draw?'

'Yes, he does,' I said. 'He's off to art college next year. He takes after his father.'

'And what about you, Lucy? Do you have a job?'

'Not yet.' At this reminder of the pointlessness of my existence, my face began to grow hot. 'I-I only left uni a month ago.'

Cassie's green eyes widened. 'You went to university? But that's wonderful. I'd have loved to go to university. What did you study?'

'I have a degree in English Literature.'

'You've done so well.'

The famous actress thought I'd done well. 'You've not done so badly yourself.'

Cassie smiled. 'Things have turned out pretty good for me.' She glanced down at her dress. 'Even if I do have to open shopping malls in a puff-sleeved frock with flowers in my hair.'

'Is that what you've been doing today?' I said. 'Opening a shopping mall?'

'No, today was a book signing. I quite like book signings. I get to sit down. I do have to be careful to remember to sign my books 'Snowdrop' though. One time, I signed a book 'Cassie' and nearly traumatised a six year old girl.'

I laughed. 'I'm sure if Princess Snowdrop had been around when I was six, I'd have read her books – and played with Snowdrop dolls.'

'The hours we spent playing with your dolls house,' Cassie said. 'Do you still have it?'

'I think it's somewhere up in the loft.'

The slam of the front door and heavy footsteps in the hall told me that Dylan was back – and for once he did have his key.

'Dyl,' I called. 'Come in here. We have a visitor.'

The expression on my brother's face when he saw Cassie Clarke sitting in her old place at the kitchen table was a joy to behold. To be fair, he recovered very quickly.

'Hey, Cassie,' he said. 'Long time no see.'

'You remember me then?' Cassie said.

'Of course I do,' Dylan said, lowering his lanky frame into a chair.

'Do you really? You were so little when I moved...' Cassie's voice trailed off, as the front door slammed again. The sound of voices reached us from the hall. An instant later, my mother came into the kitchen, back from the garage where she spent her days telling burly mechanics how to mend cars. She was followed by my stepfather, Stephen, his amiable face suntanned from an afternoon sketching in the park. Their reaction to Cassie's unexpected presence was to gape at her, in much the

4

same way as Dylan had done.

Her voice scarcely above a whisper, my mother said, 'Cassie?'

'Hello, Laura,' Cassie said, rising from her chair. 'Stephen.'

'It's been *such* a long time...' My mother shook her head as though to clear it. 'I can hardly believe that you're here, standing in front of me. Oh, I'm so glad to see you...'

'So am I,' Stephen said, smiling broadly. 'So very glad to see you here again in this house.'

Cassie looked from one of my parents to the other. 'It's wonderful to be back. I know I should have phoned, rather than just turn up on your doorstep, but -'

'No need for phone calls,' my mother said.

'You're always welcome here,' Stephen added.

And then, as she had done so often before, my mother said, 'It's time we ate. Would you like to have dinner with us, Cassie?'

'I'd like that very much,' Cassie said, just as she always had in the past.

Fifteen minutes later, we were all sitting around the kitchen table eating spaghetti bolognaise, while Cassie, wearing a borrowed sweatshirt over her white dress, her floral headdress tossed aside, told us anecdotes about the filming of her TV show. My mother asked lots of questions about who did what on a film set, wondering what exactly is a *Best Boy* and is there a *Best Girl?* Dylan remarked that the flame-haired actress who played Snowdrop's friend, Princess Poppy, reminded him of a pre-Raphaelite model, and that he'd like to paint her. Stephen told some truly appalling jokes. I remembered how much I'd missed Cassie that first summer after her family had moved out of the area - until I'd found myself a new best friend, as children do.

We'd reached the coffee stage, when my mother said, 'Cassie, I have to ask, how are your parents? Are they well?'

Cassie shrugged. 'I don't have any contact with either of them now.'

'Oh, I'm sorry –' I said.

'Don't be,' Cassie said. 'It's for the best.'

There was a long silence, broken by mother saying, 'In all honesty, Cassie, I have to agree with you. Given the way things were...'

'Nothing ever changed,' Cassie said. 'As soon as I could - once I'd turned sixteen and left school - I struck out on my own.'

'That can't have been easy,' Stephen said. 'Not at such a young age.'

'Oh, it wasn't so bad,' Cassie said. 'I always managed to find work of some sort and keep a roof over my head.'

'You were an independent young woman earning your own living,' my mother said proudly. She was big on financial independence. Only that morning she'd told me in no uncertain terms that I needed to find myself gainful employment. ('It's not that I don't appreciate your help with the household chores, Lucy, but I do think you could be doing something a little more challenging and remunerative with your time than cleaning my kitchen floor.') She was right, of course.

'I did all sorts of jobs back then,' Cassie said. 'Retail, waitressing, selling popcorn in my local cinema...'

'And now you're every little girl's favourite TV character,' I said.

Cassie laughed. 'I so am.'

The conversation moved on. My mother suggested that as it was growing late, Cassie might like to stay the night. Cassie phoned her driver and sent him back to London with instructions to pick her up the next day. We talked and laughed, and it struck me that despite the years that had passed, and everything that had happened since we'd last sat together at my mother's table, it was as though Cassie had never gone away.

It must have been after midnight when my mother and Dylan remembered that they both had to get up early for work in the morning. With many exhortations to Cassie to stay in touch and to visit us again very soon, they took themselves off to bed. Stephen stayed up a little longer, talking to Cassie about the artwork in *The Adventures of Princess Snowdrop* picture books, but then he too said goodnight.

'This has been such a fantastic evening,' Cassie said to me when Stephen had gone and we were having one last cup of coffee.

'Almost as good as all those showbiz parties that you get to go to.'

'I do get to go to some fabulous parties,' Cassie said. 'But it's not like I'm out every night, knocking back the mojitos. I get a whole lot of invites, but I have to be a bit picky about which events I attend, and who I hang out with. Princess Snowdrop is a role model for young girls. The tabloids would love it if she was caught on camera falling drunk out of a taxi and flashing her knickers at the paparazzi. As for *relationships*... I'm not seeing anyone right now, but I have to be very sure that any man I date knows how to be discreet.'

'Such is the price of fame.'

'Oh, I'm not complaining,' Cassie said. 'Without Snowdrop, I'd still be pulling pints or selling ice-cream and popcorn. I much prefer what I do now.'

'I read in a magazine that the show's casting director discovered you when you sold him some popcorn. Did the press make that up?'

'No, it's true,' Cassie said. 'More or less. At the time, I thought he was asking me to star in a porn movie. I nearly threw the popcorn over his head. Fortunately, he was very persistent. I had to do an audition, of course.'

'That must have been nerve-wracking,' I said.

'It wasn't, strangely enough.' Cassie smiled. 'Remember how you and I used to sing and dance around in your bedroom?'

'Ooh, yes.'

'That's what I did at the audition. I just pranced about in front of the camera. I had fun. I still do.'

After a moment of silence while we both sipped

our coffee, Cassie said, 'I've done nothing but talk about myself all night. I want to hear about you.'

'There's not much to tell.'

'I'm sure there is. Have you decided what you're going to do now you've left university?'

'Not really. I – I -' For the first time since I'd opened the front door to Cassie in her long white dress, the events of my final weeks at university crowded into my head. 'I need to get my act together and find a job.' *And forget what happened. Forget Lawrence.* Without thinking, I added, 'I'm not going to let that man ruin my life.'

'What man?' Cassie asked.

A leaden weight of misery settled in my chest. 'I'd rather not talk about it...him.'

'Princess Snowdrop is a very good listener.' Cassie leant forward, elbows on the table, and rested her chin on her steepled fingers. Her eyes met mine, and held my gaze.

As if from a distance, I heard myself say, 'I was... in a relationship. I ended it.'

'Why?'

'It's complicated... he's... unavailable.'

'You mean he's married?' Cassie said.

'He's *very* married.' I realised I'd just told Princess Snowdrop that I'd had an affair with a married man. 'Please don't judge me, Cassie. I honestly didn't know that he was married when I started sleeping with him. He let me think he was single. When I found out he had a wife, I fell apart.' To my shame and embarrassment, my eyes brimmed with tears. I dashed them away with the back of my hand. I was *not* going to cry. I'd done enough crying that day over Lawrence. 'I know I had to finish with him – but it still hurts.'

Cassie regarded me silently for a moment, and then she said, 'I could tell you that you did the right thing, that you're better off without him, blah, blah, blah... but I'm guessing that wouldn't make you feel any less unhappy.'

'Probably not.' A thought occurred to me. 'Please don't mention any of this to my mum or Stephen. Or Dylan.'

'You haven't told them?' Cassie said.

'I haven't told anybody – except you.' Telling my family that the reason I'd abandoned my post-grad studies and my promising academic career was because breaking off a sordid liaison with a married man had left me devastated and with my life in ruins, had never been an option. 'I've been so s*tupid*.'

Cassie put her hand on my arm. 'Don't beat yourself up. You're not the first girl to fall for a smooth-talking, lying, cheating *bastard*. And however much you're hurting right now, you *will* get over him.'

'That's what I keep telling myself, but I can't seem to get him out of my head.'

'A change of scene might help,' Cassie said. 'You said you needed to get a job –'

I nodded.

'Why don't you look for work in London?' Cassie

said. 'You can stay at my place while you get yourself sorted.'

What? My mouth actually fell open. 'Do you mean that?'

'Pack a case and travel back with me tomorrow.'

'Seriously?'

'I practically lived in your house when I was a child,' Cassie said. 'Come and live in mine for a while – as my guest. Stay as long as you like.'

'But… do you have space for me to come and stay?'

A smile flickered across Cassie's face. 'My house has five bedrooms. I have one, and my PA, Nadia, has one, but that still leaves three for you to choose from. Erin, my housekeeper, doesn't live in.'

I reminded myself that for a celebrity like Cassie, a five-bedroom house, a PA and a housekeeper were simply part of the package.

'I'm very tempted,' I said, 'but I can't just take off for London.'

'Why not? It's only forty miles down the motorway. It's not like you'd be moving to Outer Mongolia.'

'Well, I –' I could think of absolutely no reason why I couldn't go to London and stay with Cassie Clarke until I found myself a job and a place of my own. A memory came to me, Cassie and I swapping friendship bracelets, I'd been six, so she must been about eight…

'Are you sure about this?' I asked. You might regret it in the morning.'

Cassie laughed. 'I've done a few things at night that I've regretted in the morning, but I'm sure that inviting you to stay with me in London isn't going to be one of them.'

CHAPTER 2

I came up out of the crowded tube station into Piccadilly Circus. Edging my way through the throng of tourists taking photos of the statue of Eros and the illuminated advertising screen, I crossed the road, and headed up Shaftesbury Avenue, passing the theatres and bars that lined this famous thoroughfare in the heart of London's Theatreland, and turning into a narrow, cobbled side-street. I walked quickly along the pavement, until I came to the tall, red-brick building that was my new workplace. On the wall in front of me was a brass name-plate that read: *Reardon Haye – Theatrical Agents*.

From today, I thought, if anyone asks me what I do, I can say I'm a theatrical agent. I smiled, delightedly.

It had turned out to be much harder to find myself work in London than I'd anticipated. Since coming to live in Cassie's house, I'd set up my lap top on the dining table each morning, scrutinised the on-line recruitment sites and emailed my CV to likely employers, applying for anything from Advertising Executive to Zoo Administrator (well, I did once own a goldfish). I didn't get one interview. I'd used my enforced leisure to explore the city, and had discovered that I could happily while away an afternoon watching performance artists in Covent Garden or visiting an art gallery. What I couldn't do was rid myself of the feeling that until I started working, my life was on hold. Then, six weeks after I'd moved to London, Cassie had come back from a meeting with her agent, and told me that she might have found me a job…

'Good morning, Lucy.'

At the sound of my name, I swung around and found myself face to face with Eleanor Haye, my new boss.

'Oh, hello, Eleanor,' I said. 'I was just…'

'Going inside, I hope.'

'Yes, of course,' I said, following Eleanor through the revolving doors that led into a brightly-lit reception area. A girl of about my age, sitting behind a desk, looked up from the magazine she was reading and smiled.

'This is Lucy, who is starting at Reardon Haye today,' Eleanor announced as she headed towards the lift that would carry us up to the third floor. 'Lucy – Ruby, our building's receptionist.'

I just had time to mutter a quick 'Hi' to Ruby before hurrying after Eleanor, who was already stepping into the lift.

Once the lift doors had closed, Eleanor took her mobile out of her bag and began scrolling through her messages. I decided that now was not the time to try and impress her with my sparkling conversation. Instead, I studied her surreptitiously. In her late-thirties, a little taller than my five foot five, slim and elegant in a linen dress, with a scarf knotted loosely about her neck, her dark hair carelessly tousled, she looked every inch a professional. I was very glad that

14

I'd accepted Cassie's offer to lend me a designer shirt and black cropped trousers to wear on my first day at work. The lift shuddered to a halt, and Eleanor strode across the landing and into Reardon Haye's offices, with me scurrying in her wake.

When she'd interviewed me the previous week, it had been late in the day, and everyone else who worked at the agency had already left for home. Now, I saw that two of the three desks in the large, open-plan outer office were occupied, one by a girl tapping away at a keyboard, and the other by a boy speaking animatedly into a phone.

'Good morning all,' Eleanor said to the room at large.

'Morning Eleanor,' the girl replied.

The boy raised a hand in welcome.

'I'd like to introduce you to Lucy Ashford,' Eleanor said, when the boy had ended his call, 'the newest member of our team. Lucy, meet Adrian Barry and Maria Coleman.'

There was the usual exchange of greetings and pleasantries.

'For today,' Eleanor said to me, 'you can shadow Maria so she can show you what we do. Now, I have to make some calls…' She vanished into her own office, leaving me with my new co-workers.

'No need to look so terrified,' Adrian said. 'We don't bite.' He was older than I'd first thought, about thirty, a thin guy with sand-coloured hair, stubble that had almost made up its mind to be a beard, and glasses. He got up and wheeled a chair from my desk to Maria's. I smiled my thanks and sat down.

'Who were you with before Reardon Haye?' Maria asked. She was just a couple of years older than me, in her mid-twenties, and her shoulder length hair was dyed an intense black. She was wearing a short purple dress and a lot of eyeliner.

'I've not worked in a theatrical agency before,' I said.

'You've never worked in an agency?' Maria repeated. 'Then you're in for an interesting time.'

'Not to worry,' Adrian said. 'If you survive your first month, you'll be fine.'

'Don't take any notice of him,' Maria said, just as her desk phone started ringing.

'Let the madness begin,' Adrian said.

For the rest of the morning I sat with Maria while she took call after call from directors and producers looking to cast anything from feature films to radio plays to TV adverts. What were called 'breakdowns' of roles also flooded into the office by email, and it was Maria and Adrian's job (and now mine) to put forward the actors on our books who were suitable for the part.

'Casting directors will only audition a certain number of actors for each role,' Maria said to me. 'We have to persuade them that it's *our* clients that they really need to see.'

'Luckily,' Eleanor said, appearing in the outer office clutching a sheet of paper, 'I can be very persuasive.' She handed the paper to me. 'Lucy, I'd like you to phone everyone on this list. Let them know they have an audition at the BBC tomorrow. I've written down all the details.'

'I'll do that, Eleanor.' I got to my feet and pushed my chair back to my own desk.

'And Lucy,' Eleanor said, 'make sure you tell them they're auditioning for a gritty crime series set in Newcastle. We don't want anyone talking like a luvvie.'

Eleanor went back into her office, leaving the door open this time. Adrian showed me how to access the actors' contact details on my computer.

'Hi, my name is Lucy Ashford and I'm calling from Reardon Haye,' I said to the first name on my list. 'We've got you an audition tomorrow...'

The middle-aged actor, best known for playing an aristocratic landowner in a historical drama, listened to me rattle off the time and place of his audition.

'That's fabulous, darling,' he drawled. 'Always a pleasure to audition for the Beeb.'

'The character you'd be playing is from Newcastle,' I said quickly. 'You need to do the audition in a Geordie accent.'

'Alreet, pet,' the actor said. 'Divvint worry, I can dee that. Ye have a canny day.'

I decided that I was going to like working with actors.

By lunchtime, I'd rung most of the male actors on my list and had started on the actresses. I was also starving. When Maria and Adrian began discussing who was going to make the daily run to the nearest sandwich bar, I was glad to volunteer.

Maria grinned. 'I do like having a new girl in the agency. The new ones are always so keen to make a good impression.'

'Yeah, we should make the most of it,' Adrian said, handing me the money for a ciabatta. 'After a month they won't even make you a coffee. If they last that long.'

The sandwich bar was only a couple of hundred yards down the road, and I wasn't gone for more than fifteen minutes, but when I returned to Reardon Haye, the door to Eleanor's office was firmly closed again.

'Should I take this in to her?' I said to Maria, holding up the paper bag containing Eleanor's lunch order.

'Absolutely not,' Adrian said. 'If Eleanor closes her office door, it means that unless one of our clients has won an Oscar, she's not to be disturbed.'

'You sit down and eat your lunch, Lucy,' Maria said. 'Just keep watching that door.'

'OK,' I said, uncertainly.

Half an hour later, Eleanor's office door swung open, and Daniel Miller came out (yes, *that* Daniel Miller). What with… everything that had happened to me, I'd not seen *Fallen Angel*, the summer blockbuster that had made him a star, but as his photo was all over the internet (and on advertising hoardings all over London), I recognised him instantly.

He's *beautiful*, I thought.

Daniel was tall, just over six feet, and impossibly

handsome, with those chiselled cheekbones that always look so good on screen, a full, sensual mouth, and a square jaw. His face was framed by lustrous waves of dark-brown hair that cried out for a girl to run her fingers through it. For the first time in a long while, I felt a delicious fluttering low in my stomach - he was simply the most attractive man I'd ever seen.

'You must be Eleanor's new recruit,' he said, walking up to my desk and leaning across to shake my hand. 'I'm Daniel Miller.'

Somehow, I managed to ignore the effect Daniel's warm, brown, gold-flecked eyes and honeyed voice were having on my unruly insides, and give him a firm handshake.

'Lucy Ashford.' I took back my hand, which was tingling from his touch.

He smiled at me and then at Maria and Adrian. 'Well, I'll say goodbye for now.'

'See you soon, Daniel,' Maria said.

'Bye,' Adrian said, apparently unconcerned whether he saw Daniel sooner or later.

Daniel sauntered out of the office which gave me the opportunity of checking out his denim-clad rear. My stomach lurched. His jeans were very tight.

'He is *so* hot.' Maria picked up an actor's headshot from her desk and fanned her face. 'And that's my expert opinion as a theatrical agent.'

'What do you think, Lucy?' Adrian said. 'Do you agree with Maria that Daniel Miller is God's gift to womankind?'

'He's certainly very good-looking,' I said. 'I expect most women would find him attractive.'

'Particularly actresses, models and TV presenters,' Adrian said, 'according to the tabloids.'

'He's irresistible,' Maria said. 'He has the lust gene.'

'The what?' I said.

'The lust gene. If you're born with the lust gene, you only have to walk into a room and everyone starts salivating.'

'More importantly,' Eleanor said, coming out of her office, 'he can act and the camera loves him. As I keep telling him, if he chooses the right projects, there's every chance he'll have a highly successful career.' She turned to me and held out a sealed envelope addressed to a television production company. 'This is a copy of Daniel Miller's signed contract for a TV mini-series. It's only a few weeks filming, so he'll be able to fit it in before *Fallen Angel II,* which starts shooting early next year. If you run it down to reception now and hand it to Ruby, she'll make sure it catches the post.'

I took the envelope.

'This is the best part of being a theatrical agent,' Eleanor continued. 'Sharing our client's success, and knowing that we helped to make it happen.'

'And the worst part is when one of our actors gets right down to the final cut for their dream role, and then they don't get cast,' Adrian said.

'When that happens,' Eleanor said, 'they need us to hold their hands.' Her phone rang, and she went back into her office to answer it, taking her baguette with her.

'I agree about the handholding,' Maria said. 'Most actors come across as supremely self-confident, but underneath a lot of them are very insecure.'

'We call them clients,' Adrian said, 'but our relationship is more of a partnership. We're not just their *agent,* we're their confidante, their guru...'

'Their cheerleader,' Maria said.

'Their therapist.'

'Their friend?' I said.

'I don't know about *friend,'* Maria said. 'Let's not get carried away.'

I remembered that I needed to get Daniel Miller's contract in the post. I had a feeling that Eleanor didn't expect to tell her employees to do something more than once.

'I should take this downstairs,' I said, flourishing the envelope.

As I left the office, I heard Adrian say to Maria, 'Do I have the lust gene?'

'You're a lovely guy, Adrian,' Maria answered. 'But no, the lust gene isn't in your DNA. Sorry.'

I took the lift down to reception and handed Daniel Miller's contract to Ruby.

'Well, you certainly chose the right moment to start at Reardon Haye,' she said to me.

'I did?'

'It's not every day that the Fallen Angel himself drops by the offices,' Ruby said. 'Unfortunately.' She gestured towards the magazine she'd been

21

reading, and I saw that it had a picture of Daniel Miller on the cover. 'That bad boy sure is easy on the eye.'

I laughed. 'I guess my new job does have its advantages.'

Back in the lift, travelling up to the third floor, I relived the moment when Daniel Miller had reached across my desk and taken my hand in his. I wondered if *Fallen Angel* was still showing in London, or if I'd have to wait for the DVD to come out before I could see it. I really ought to see Daniel's film. It was surely part of my job to take an interest in his work. I could have seen *Fallen Angel* a dozen times by now if I hadn't wasted the summer crying a river over Lawrence.

Lawrence. Instead of the familiar wave of misery that broke over me whenever I thought of him, suddenly I felt... nothing. It occurred to me that I hadn't thought about him in weeks. I stood in the lift, and said his name aloud. 'Professor Lawrence Elliot.' Still, nothing. No pain, no anger... just indifference. I'd loved him once, and then I'd despised him, but now... Now I had no feelings left for him at all.

The lift opened and shut again. Quickly, I pressed the button to re-open the doors before I was carried back down to the ground floor, and stepped out onto the landing. I took a deep breath. I was twenty-three, I was living in London, and I had a job I was pretty sure I was going to like. And I was over Lawrence. I squared my shoulders, and went back into the agency.

* * *

That evening, I leapt up the front steps of Cassie's white stuccoed, three-storey house two at a time. Pausing only to re-set the burglar alarm, I ran across the hallway, with its original black and white Victorian tiles, and flung open the door to the large, airy reception room that took up half the ground floor. The room was empty, but the French windows that led onto the terrace were open, the white voile curtains stirring in a faint breeze, so I went outside. Except for the sound of birdsong, the garden was silent and still. I smelt new-mown grass and the heavy scent of full-blown roses. Cassie was lying on a lounger, under an umbrella on the lawn, one arm behind her head, her hair shining like burnished gold in the early evening light. For a moment, I thought she was asleep, but then she sat up and took off her sunglasses.

'Lucy!' she said. 'How was your first day at work?'

'It was great.' I sat down on the sun-lounger next to hers. 'I honestly don't think it could have gone any better.'

'Tell me *everything*.'

I described to her the events of my first day as a theatrical agent, up to the point when Daniel Miller had strolled out of Eleanor's office.

'I've never met him,' Cassie said, 'but when I saw *Fallen Angel*, I thought he had tremendous screen presence. He certainly makes a very handsome leading man.'

'He's *ridiculously* attractive,' I said. 'I wonder if he really has been with as many women as the press make out.'

'Let's think about that,' Cassie said. 'A young, single, straight, extraordinarily good-looking, charismatic actor who shot to fame after starring in a hugely successful film – has he slept with a lot of women?'

'Point taken.' I told myself very firmly that I needed to stop thinking about Daniel Miller, even if he was the first man who'd made my pulse race since… 'Actually, Cassie' I said, 'there's something else I want to tell you – nothing to do with work - something I realised today –' I broke off as Nadia, Cassie's PA, came out of the house, carrying a jug of lemonade and two glasses on a tray. Not for the first time, I thought how much she resembled Cassie, with the same long blonde hair, although her eyes were blue and Cassie's were green. She actually looked more like Cassie than the girl who was her stand-in on her TV show. Not that Cassie would have objected, but the star of *The Adventures of Princess Snowdrop* wasn't expected to wait around on set while a scene was lit or the camera crew planned shots.

'It's still so hot out here,' Nadia said, 'I thought you might like a cold drink.'

'Thanks, Nadia,' Cassie said. 'You're a mind reader.' She added, 'Lucy started work at Reardon Haye today.'

'Oh, I'd quite forgotten,' Nadia said. 'I'm so sorry

24

- I've been so busy.' She smiled at me. 'How long is it that you've been living here with us?'

'Just over six weeks.'

'*Six weeks*? I didn't realise it was that long. You must be *so* relieved to have a job to go to at last.'

I smiled back at her. 'I'm ecstatic.'

'It's very brave of you to take on a role you know so little about,' Nadia went on, 'but I'm sure you'll rise to the challenge. You won't let Cassie down.' She poured two glasses of lemonade.

'Won't you join us?' Cassie said.

'It's very sweet of you to ask me, but I've a few more emails I need to send before I go out.' Nadia turned on her heel and went back into the house.

And what, I thought, did she mean about me not letting Cassie down?

'Cassie,' I said, 'did you, by any chance, ask Eleanor to offer me the job at Reardon Haye?'

'No, I didn't,' Cassie said. 'I told you what happened. She mentioned that one of her agents had left, and she was looking for a replacement. All I said was that you might be interested.'

'It's not that I'm ungrateful, but I'd hate to think the only reason she took me on was because you're one of her most important clients.'

'My recommendation may have got you through the door, but if Eleanor didn't think you were right for the agency, she wouldn't have hired you, believe me.'

'That's good to know.' I said. 'Thanks, Cassie.'

'No worries. Now, what was it you were about to

25

tell me before Nadia interrupted you?'

'It was about Lawrence,' I said.

'Who?'

It occurred to me that I'd never told Cassie his name. 'Lawrence is the married guy who I – well, you know what I did. Anyway...' I took a deep breath. 'I'm over him. I think I've been over him a while, I just hadn't realised it. I haven't thought about him in weeks.'

Cassie's face broke into a smile. 'I'm very pleased to hear it,' she said, 'but I knew you'd get there. Everyone who goes through a break-up thinks they'll never recover, but they do.'

'I can't believe I was ever stupid enough to fall for him. I'm supposed to be *clever*.'

'I guess even the smartest of women can make mistakes when it comes to men.' Cassie stretched out on the sun-lounger. Then immediately sat up again. 'We should do something to celebrate your successful first day as a theatrical agent. Let's order in pizza - my treat.'

'Ooh, yes, please,' I said. 'Shall we watch a DVD as well?'

'As soon as I've learnt tomorrow's script, we can go wild,' Cassie said. 'Never let anyone tell you that Princess Snowdrop doesn't know how to live a glamorous showbiz life.'

CHAPTER 3

'I'm going to have to be very careful where I walk,' Dylan said.

'Why?' Yawning, I sat up in bed. It was good to talk on the phone with my brother (our sporadic communications more usually took the form of texts or comments on Facebook), but at ten o'clock on a Sunday morning, I was still half asleep.

'I wouldn't want to step on any of those names you keep dropping,' Dylan said.

I realised that my sole topic of conversation for the entire call had been my job at Reardon Haye. 'I need to stop going on about the actors I meet at work, don't I?'

'That's OK,' Dylan said. 'If I were hanging out with celebrities like the Fallen Angel, I'd want to tell you about it.'

'I've only met Daniel Miller once,' I said. 'And I don't exactly *hang out* with any of Reardon Haye's clients – apart from Cassie. Obviously the agency does a certain amount of entertaining, and we get invites to after-parties.'

'Invites to what?'

'After-show parties,' I said. 'Networking is very important in showbusiness. A few nights ago I got to go to a premiere in Leicester Square which was *amazing*.'

'Are we talking red carpet and flashing lights?'

'You kind of have to walk along the red carpet to

get into the cinema when you're attending a premiere. Sadly, not one paparazzi took our photo. They were too busy photographing the star of the film and his model girlfriend.'

'Who did you go to the premiere with?'

'The other agents, Maria and Adrian,' I said. 'They've really made an effort to welcome me to Reardon Haye. Ruby, the receptionist, is nice as well. She invited me to her house party and - Oh, I'm doing it again. Talking about work.'

'I don't mind,' Dylan said. 'There is something I want to ask you, though. That's why I called.'

'You can ask me anything, Dyl,' I said in a rush of sisterly affection.

'Now that you're living in London,' he said, 'can I have your old room? It's so much bigger than mine…'

Having established that I relinquished all claims to my childhood bedroom (it seemed only fair, now that I had my own spacious room in Cassie's house), Dylan went off to start moving clothes, books and furniture. My thoughts strayed back to my job, and more precisely to the delectable Daniel Miller, now off on location filming his mini-series. And shagging his co-star – photos of her leaving his hotel in the early hours were on every showbiz website, much to the chagrin of the actress who'd been photographed coming out of his London flat the morning he'd left for Ireland. Not that it was ever likely to happen, I thought, but if that bad boy ever showed any interest in me, I'd run a mile.

My rumbling stomach told me that even though it was Sunday, it was time I got up. I slid out of bed, and immediately felt a chill in the air. London had been basking in a late heatwave, but autumn appeared to have arrived overnight. I showered quickly in my gleaming en-suite bathroom, pulled on my jeans and a jumper, and went out onto the landing. The house was very quiet. I walked softly down the broad sweeping staircase, crossed the black and white tiled hallway, and went into the kitchen - where I found Ryan Fleet, wearing just a pair of football shorts, frying bacon and eggs.

A couple of months ago, if I'd come downstairs in search of breakfast and discovered that a premiership footballer had got there before me, I would have been speechless. But in the last few weeks my life had changed dramatically. I'd moved into a TV star's house, and at work I met actors who were household names on a daily basis. A shirtless Ryan Fleet wielding a spatula wasn't going to throw me.

'Hi,' I said, 'I'm Lucy Ashford. I'm a friend of Cassie's.'

'Hi, Lucy,' he said. 'I'm Ryan Fleet. I'm… with Cassie.'

He was, I thought, a good-looking guy, with tousled light brown hair and a friendly smile.

'I know who you are,' I said. 'I mean, I know you're Ryan Fleet, not that you're Cassie's...' *Boyfriend? Lover? Friend-with-benefits?* 'Cassie's footballer – oh, that sounds wrong. Not what I intended.'

Ryan grinned. 'Cassie's footballer. I like it. I am Ryan Fleet, Cassie's footballer. I shall always introduce myself like that in future.' He started to dish up the eggs and bacon. 'I made fresh coffee. Help yourself.'

'Did someone mention coffee?'

Ryan and I both spun around to see Nadia framed in the kitchen doorway.

'Hello, Nadia,' Ryan said.

'Ryan,' Nadia said. 'How lovely to see you. And how unexpected.'

'I was only ever going to be in Spain for six months,' Ryan said.

'I know that was the plan,' Nadia said, advancing into the kitchen, 'but I did wonder if you'd be able to tear yourself away from all that sun, sangria and... football.'

'It wasn't so hard to leave,' Ryan said. 'I missed Cassie the whole time I was there.'

'Well, you've come back to England at the worst time of year. When I got up this morning, I noticed how cold it was. You must be freezing, standing there without a shirt.' Nadia walked over to Ryan and laid a hand on his bare chest. 'No, you're not at all cold. You're hot.'

There was nothing flirtatious in the tone of Nadia's voice, and she touched Ryan only for a few seconds, but her words, and the way she stood so close to him, made me feel distinctly uncomfortable. I gave myself a firm mental shake. What was I thinking? Nadia couldn't possibly be coming on to

Ryan. Even if she wanted to, she wouldn't do it in front of me. Besides, she had a steady boyfriend, Leo, who I'd met a couple of times when he'd come to pick her up from Cassie's house. She'd been out with him only last night.

'I never feel the cold.' Ryan took a step backwards. 'Can you find me a tray please, Nadia?'

'Of course.' Nadia opened a cupboard and produced a wicker tray.

Ryan loaded the tray with the plates of eggs and bacon and two steaming mugs of coffee. 'I must take this up to Cassie. I'll see you guys later.'

'Laters,' Nadia said.

'Good to have met you,' I said.

Ryan smiled at me and walked out of the kitchen. I heard his footsteps going up the stairs.

'He is *such* a sweetie.' Nadia poured two cups of coffee, one for her and one for me, and settled herself on a chair at the kitchen table. 'I'm so glad he's back. Although I'm very surprised.'

'I'm a bit confused,' I said. 'Are Cassie and Ryan Fleet together? I mean, are they a couple?' I was sure Cassie had told me she wasn't seeing anyone right now.

'They *were* a couple,' Nadia said. 'They met when they were both guests on the same late night chat show and dated for several months. Then, six months ago, he went off to play for some football team in Madrid. I thought that would be him and Cassie finished, but now he's back... Has Cassie never talked to you about Ryan?'

'No, she's never mentioned him.'

'How strange,' Nadia said. 'She talks about him to me all the time. But then, Cassie and I are very close. Still, she can hardly stop you finding out about him if you're living in her house.'

'Why wouldn't she want me to know about him?' A thought struck me. 'He's not married is he?'

'What a fertile imagination you have, Lucy. Of course Fleet Feet, as the tabloids call him, isn't married. Why would you think that?'

'No reason,' I said, quickly. 'Do the press know that he and Cassie are together?'

'No, that's about the one thing they don't know about Fleet Feet.' Nadia put her head to one side and regarded me thoughtfully. 'Maybe that's why Cassie didn't tell you about him. Maybe she thought you wouldn't be able to keep their relationship private, the way they like it. It can put a terrible strain on a couple if photos of their intimate moments are posted on the internet or they feature in the gossip columns.'

'I'm Cassie's *friend*,' I said, annoyed by what Nadia was implying. 'There's no way I'd talk to the press about her love life.'

'I'm not suggesting you'd do it on purpose, but the tabloids can be very cunning. There was this one time when a guy who chatted me up in a bar turned out to be a journalist digging for dirt on Princess Snowdrop.'

I gasped. 'That's awful.'

'That's showbusiness. Fortunately, as Cassie's PA, I'm used to dealing with the media, but you should be very careful who you talk to while you're living in Cassie's house. Although, I suppose you won't be staying much longer.'

I was taken aback by this remark. 'I've not got any plans to move out.'

'Really? I was under the impression that your staying here was just a temporary arrangement until you found yourself a job and could afford a place of your own.'

'Well, yes, it was but -'

'I'm sure Cassie won't mind, however long you stay. Although it might be a bit awkward for you now that Ryan's back. After all, two's company. It's different for me. I *work* for Cassie. And I stay over at Leo's half the time. More coffee?'

'Please.'

Nadia was right, of course. I couldn't carry on as Cassie's house-guest forever. She'd invited me to stay with her *until I'd sorted myself out*. Which I had done. I had a job that I was already good at, and which paid me an ample salary to rent a room in a shared flat. There was no reason why I shouldn't start looking for a place of my own. Except that I liked sharing Cassie's house. With her working long hours at the studio, and having to be available for photo shoots and other events at weekends, and now my job at Reardon Haye, we didn't see that much of each other, but we'd still managed to fall into an easy-going friendship, cemented by long conversations late into the night, and a mutual fondness for rom coms. And I'd started to think of her house as my home.

'Toast?' Nadia's voice broke in on my thoughts.

'What? Oh, yes, please, Nadia.'

Nadia put two slices of bread in the toaster. 'If you ever do decide to move out, I'd be very happy to help you look for somewhere suitable to live. I've lived in London since I was eighteen, so I know it very well.'

'That's very kind of you, Nadia,' I said.

'In the meantime, you can do what I do, and try and keep out of Cassie and Ryan's way.'

'That shouldn't be too hard,' I said. 'It's a large house.'

'You'd think so wouldn't you?' Nadia said. 'But I remember coming home late one night last year and walking in on them in the living room. On the sofa. Apparently he'd scored a winning goal that afternoon, and they were celebrating and got rather carried away. Cassie and I joked about it afterwards, but at the time I was *so* embarrassed.' Nadia laughed. I smiled feebly. Even if they weren't given to ravishing each other on the living room sofa, every couple needed their own space. I could hardly expect to go on living in Cassie's house now that her footballer was back in her life.

I need to speak to Cassie and tell her that I've decided to move out, I thought.

Not surprisingly, as he'd been away for six months, neither Ryan nor Cassie reappeared for the rest of Sunday, so I didn't get a chance to tell her of my decision. On Monday night, Cassie came in much

34

later than usual (Prince Ash had kept forgetting his lines and the day's shooting had overrun) and went straight to her room with a sandwich and the next day's script. On Tuesday, I accompanied Eleanor to see one of our clients in a production of *Cat on a Hot Tin Roof*, and didn't get in until long after Cassie had gone to bed. On Wednesday, Thursday and Friday, Ryan was back, and although he was very charming, offering me coffee every time we came across each other in the kitchen, I really didn't want to discuss my moving out of Cassie's house in front of him. On Saturday, he went out very early as he had an away match, but Cassie slept in, and in any case I'd planned to go shopping on Oxford Street with Maria and Ruby.

It was the first time I'd been clothes shopping since I'd started earning, and I staggered back home laden with carrier bags stuffed full of outfits for work, outfits for going out, and shoes to go with them. I'd laid out my purchases on my bed, and was trying them on again in front of my full-length mirror when Cassie knocked on my door and asked if she could come in.

'Oh, yes, do come in, Cassie,' I said.

'Looks like you've had a successful shopping trip.' She moved aside a pencil skirt so that she could sit on my bed.

'I decided that now I'm not a student any more, now that I'm a professional working woman, I need a more sophisticated wardrobe.'

'You look amazing in that dress. Are you going

out somewhere special?'

'Oh, no, I'm not going anywhere tonight. I was just trying on the dress one more time before I hang it up in the wardrobe.'

'That dress deserves to go out,' Cassie said. 'Let's take it to a nightclub. Somewhere upmarket, and with a VIP area.'

'Tonight?'

'Why not? You and I haven't had a proper night out together in all the time you've been in London.'

'Aren't you seeing Ryan?'

'No. He's going out with some of his team tonight. It's the goalkeeper's thirtieth birthday.'

'Boys' night out?'

'Yep. So are you up for clubbing?'

'Me and my new dress are definitely up for clubbing.'

'I'll start getting ready then.' Cassie stood up.

'No, wait, Cassie. There's something I need to tell you.'

Cassie sank down again. 'You sound very serious, Lucy. Is something wrong?'

'No. Nothing's wrong. It's just that... I think it's time I moved into a place of my own.'

There was a long, heavy silence.

'Aren't you happy living here?' Cassie asked eventually.

'I'm very happy here,' I said, 'but I don't want to outstay my welcome.'

'As if you could do that. I like having you share my house. It's far too big for one person. I don't know why I bought it. Actually, that's not true, I do know why I bought it...'

I waited for Cassie to go on, but when she didn't, I said, 'I love living here, really I do, but I don't want to intrude on your privacy.'

Cassie raised her eyebrows. 'Is this to do with Ryan?'

'Not entirely.'

'I should have told you about Ryan. You must think it really weird that I never said anything about his coming back from Spain.'

'No, of course not.' I smiled. 'OK, maybe it is a little weird.'

'The thing is,' Cassie said, 'I never talk about Ryan. I was with him for two months before he went to Spain, but apart from my staff and the guys at Reardon Haye, hardly anyone knew. He and I kept a very low profile, never appearing together at any showbiz or sporting events, and luckily the press never discovered we were a couple. If it had come out that Princess Snowdrop was dating Ryan Fleet Feet – disaster!'

'I don't see why. The tabloids love a romance.'

'Princess Snowdrop doesn't do boyfriends, Lucy. She has *never ever* had sex.'

'OK. So you and Ryan kept your relationship out of the gossip columns. And then he went to Spain?'

Cassie nodded. 'His club did a deal that meant he was lent to Real Madrid for six months. He didn't want to be away from me for that long and was going to turn the transfer down, but I told him he had to go.'

'But why? If he wanted to stay with you...'

'It was a terrific career opportunity for him. I wasn't going to let him miss out on it because of me. He'd only come to resent me for it.'

I wasn't sure that I agreed with Cassie's line of reasoning, but I didn't argue with her.

'So Ryan went to Spain,' Cassie said. 'And I told myself we were over. What were the chances that a girl could have a long-distance relationship with a *footballer?* Think about it. The hot Spanish nights. The adoring female fans. The impossibility of his keeping his trousers on.'

'Couldn't you have flown out to Spain to visit him?'

'It wasn't that easy. Ryan and I both had busy schedules. We talked on the phone a lot, and Skyped when we could, but we never managed to visit each other.' Cassie drew up her legs and hugged her knees. 'Before Ryan went to Spain, I wasn't even sure how I felt about him or how he felt about me. I had no idea what would happen to us when he came back to England. Of if there even was an *us*. That's another reason why I didn't tell you about him. If we weren't a couple any more there didn't seem to be much point.'

'And how do you feel about him now?'

Cassie's smile lit up her whole face. 'I'm not sure what either of us is feeling right now. But there's definitely an *us*.'

'I *so* need to move out of your house and give you

guys some space,' I said.

'You really don't.'

'Maybe you should check with Ryan.'

Cassie's eyes locked on mine. 'Ryan is very important to me. But if it came to me having to choose between him and you or Dylan or Stephen or your mother, I'd choose you and your family over Ryan every time.'

I stared at her, disquieted by the intensity with which she spoke.

'Sorry,' Cassie said. 'I didn't mean to freak you out.'

'You didn't,' I said, remembering that she was an actress and naturally disposed to be overdramatic. 'And I would really like to stay on living in your house. But now that I have a job, I should start paying you rent.'

'I don't want your money,' Cassie said. 'And without meaning to sound arrogant, I don't need it.'

'But I need to feel that I'm paying my way. At least let me contribute to the housekeeping.'

'Is it really that important to you?'

'It really is.'

'Well, all right. I'll have a word with Nadia – she handles the household accounts – and we'll sort something out. But no more talk of moving out. *Mi casa es tu casa,* as they say in the movies. My house is your house. My home is your home. It's settled.'

'What's settled?' Nadia came into my room, and I found myself irritated that she hadn't bothered to knock, even though the door was half-open.

'Lucy had this mad idea that she was going to move into her own place,' Cassie said. 'But I talked her out of it. She's staying.'

'Oh, Lucy, I did tell you that Cassie wouldn't want you to leave just because Ryan's back on the scene,' Nadia said. 'You should have listened to me.'

That wasn't quite how I remembered Nadia's and my conversation, but I couldn't think of a way to say this without sounding like a petulant teenager. So I smiled and said nothing.

'Lucy and I are going clubbing tonight,' Cassie said, breaking the silence. 'Would you like to come, Nadia, if you've not got other plans?'

'Oh, yes, I'll come,' Nadia said immediately. 'I'm not doing anything I can't cancel.'

'In that case,' Cassie said, 'the three of us can have a girls' night out.'

CHAPTER 4

'We should have stayed in the VIP area,' Cassie wailed. 'If we'd stayed in the VIP area, it would never have happened. Here, take a look.' She passed me her laptop.

Balancing the laptop on my knees, I clicked through the on-line showbiz gossip and news sites that she'd brought up on her screen. Every one of them featured pictures of Ryan leaving West End nightclub BarRacuda and getting into a car with a 'mystery blonde.' The girl was Cassie, but she was holding her hand over her face, and was unrecognisable. I was also in some of the photos, but I was looking away from the camera, and you couldn't really tell it was me. Ryan's friend, his team's goalkeeper whose birthday we'd been celebrating, was in one photo, and in the picture it looked as though his hand was on my rear. I was fairly sure it hadn't been.

'My bum looks big in that photo,' I said.

'That's really not my main concern right now,' Cassie said.

'Yes. I know. Sorry.'

The previous evening had started well. Cassie's hired limo had dropped her, Nadia and me off at BarRacuda, the bouncers had ushered us to the front of the queue, and once we were inside, a smiling hostess had escorted us into the VIP area. This was a new experience for me, and I have to admit that I enjoyed it. (If you'd been turned away from your local nightclub when you were seventeen because your fake ID couldn't cut it, you'd enjoy it too.) The VIP area was packed, but Cassie and I squeezed onto a couch with Rochelle Thorne (yes, *that* Rochelle Thorne – the tall one from the girl band, the Thorne Sisters) who she introduced as a good friend, and who was, I discovered, a really nice, down-to-earth girl, and an actor from one of the soaps. Nadia went off to talk to a guy she knew. I didn't recognise him, but Cassie told me he was an up-and-coming film director named Sam Hurst. I made a mental note to Google him when we went home. If I was going to be a successful agent, I needed to know about these people.

Another guy had joined us for a while, young, very well-spoken, and buying champagne like it was going out of fashion. I'd no idea who he was either, but I knew he must be rich or famous or both, because of the champagne - and because of the number of rich and famous people I did recognise who were so eager to stop by and talk to him. Somehow, I got the idea that he was an actor on Cassie's show, and asked him if he ever got to ride a unicorn.

'He must have thought I was very odd,' I said to Cassie, once the young man, who'd listened so politely while I'd enthused about fairy dust and mermaids had gone, and Cassie had informed me that he was the drummer from the heavy metal band,

Feral.

'Don't worry about it,' Cassie said. 'I didn't recognise him the first time I met him. He looks very different without all that leather gear and make-up he wears on stage.'

Then Nadia re-appeared, full of the news that Ryan and some of his team mates had been spotted on the dance floor in the main area of the club.

'We should go downstairs and join him,' I said to Cassie.

Cassie frowned. 'No, I don't think so. I'd never have suggested we come to BarRacuda if I'd known he was going to be here. We should leave.'

'I'd rather go and join Ryan and his friends,' I said. 'My new dress doesn't want to leave. My dress will sulk if she has to leave.' By then, I'd drunk rather more than my share of the drummer's champagne.

Suddenly, Cassie's mood changed and she smiled. 'Far be it from me to deprive you of a chance to show off your new dress. We'll go downstairs. Are you coming, Nadia?'

'No, I think I'll stay here. Call me on my mobile when you decide to go home, and I'll come down and find you.' She went back to the film director and they were soon once again deep in conversation.

Leaving Nadia in the VIP area, Cassie and I made our way downstairs and onto the club's main dance floor. Ryan's team mates were easy enough to spot amongst the crowd as they were surrounded by a large proportion of BarRacuda's female clientele, all

43

dancing in a way designed to attract the attention of a footballer out on the prowl.

'Where's Ryan?' I said.

'Over there.' Cassie pointed to the bar where Ryan was drinking a beer and talking to a couple of lads who gazed back at him in speechless admiration.

'He's doesn't care much for nightclubs,' Cassie remarked.

'He certainly doesn't seem to be having as good a time as his mates,' I said, glancing over to where two of the footballers were performing a break dance in the middle of a circle of squealing girls. 'Shall we go and join him?'

'Oh, no, we can't do that,' Cassie said. 'We have to be more subtle. We have to pretend we don't know him.'

'What?'

'I told you. Ryan and I have to be very careful. We need to keep our relationship private.'

'Oh,' I said. 'Listen, Cassie, I know I said I didn't want to leave the club, but maybe we should just go back up to the VIP area.'

'No, it's OK. Now that we're down here, we may as well dance.' Cassie headed determinedly out onto the dance floor, and after some hesitation, I went after her. As soon as she reached the middle of the crowd, she began dancing, moving sinuously in perfect time to the music, every step taking her closer to where Ryan was propping up the bar. I did my best to copy her, but I'm not much of a dancer. Her body rippled and her hips swayed suggestively. My hips

44

just swayed awkwardly. Ryan didn't appear to have noticed us, but I felt sure he was watching Cassie. Plenty of other men were.

The music stopped. Before the next track started, Ryan had abandoned his admirers and was standing in front of me, with his back to Cassie.

'Would you like to dance?' he said.

It was all done very smoothly. No-one watching would have guessed that Ryan and Cassie knew each other, let alone that they were in a relationship. I wondered if they'd acted out this scene before.

'I'd love to dance,' I said. The music started again and Ryan and I danced together, while Cassie danced by herself. When the next track came on, he danced with her, and then he danced with both of us.

When the track changed, Cassie said, 'We have to go now.' She linked her arm in mine and started to walk off the dance floor.

'Don't go yet,' Ryan said. 'I've not even introduced myself.'

Cassie turned back to him.

'I'm Cassie's footballer,' Ryan said.

Well that did it, of course. There was no way Cassie was going to leave Ryan all alone on the dance floor when he was looking at her with those big soulful eyes and telling her that he was *hers*. We spent the rest of the night dancing and drinking with him. And with his team mates. Cassie had only had one glass of the drummer's champagne, but she moved on to fruit juice. I was less restrained. I blame the tequila (and the jägerbombs) for the fact that I snogged the goalkeeper in a dark corner of the club. He had some interesting suggestions about some other things we could do, starting with my going home with him, but I had to tell him it wasn't going to happen. With the possible exception of Ryan Fleet, I reckoned that a footballer who was all over a girl in a nightclub was unlikely to be looking for a meaningful relationship.

At five o'clock in the morning the music stopped. The lights came on to reveal scenes of devastation and destruction, smudged make up, beer-stained shirts, incipient hangovers, and ill-advised liaisons. Cassie got out her phone to call Nadia, but she'd already left a voice mail, saying that she'd decided to take a cab over to Leo's house in Battersea. Ryan draped his arm over Cassie's shoulders, the goalkeeper said he would share our taxi, and the four of us lurched out into the dawn. Where we were greeted with enthusiasm by the paparazzi…

I had a good time last night,' I said. 'My new dress was a social triumph.'

'Don't,' Cassie said. 'I know you're only trying to cheer me up, but don't.'

'It's really not so bad,' I said.

'How do you figure that out? *How* is it not so bad?' Cassie had been lying on her back on the sofa, but now she sprang to her feet. 'If the press find out that the mystery blonde who went home with Ryan Fleet was Princess Snowdrop, I could be fired.'

To me it seemed very unlikely that the actress

who played Princess Snowdrop could be fired for getting into a cab with a footballer, but Cassie had been working in showbusiness a lot longer than I had.

'Where is Ryan, anyway?' I said.

'He went out for a run.'

'We didn't get in until half past five. It's now ten o'clock. And Ryan's gone for a run?'

'He's an athlete. He has a *lot* of energy.'

'Lucky you.' I decided that the next guy I dated was going to have to agree to take part in at least one physical activity on a weekly basis. Apart from the obvious.

Cassie was still studying the laptop. 'Oh. My. God. On this page, there's actually a phone number for people to ring if they know Ryan Fleet's mystery girl.'

At that moment both of us started as Ryan rapped on the French windows. Cassie let him in.

'Why have you come in through the garden?' She tilted her face up towards him for his kiss.

Looking far too lively for a man who'd been dancing and drinking in a nightclub 'til dawn, Ryan kissed her lightly on the mouth. 'I saw a car with a guy who could have been a journalist parked just a couple of doors down from your house, so I ran straight past him and came in the back way.'

'Please tell me he didn't recognise you.'

Ryan grinned. 'Cassie, I'm kidding. I rang the front door bell, but it doesn't seem to be working. I was knocking for ages before I decided to try around the back.'

'Not funny.' Cassie flung herself back onto the sofa. 'It's not just about *us*, Ryan. If someone who saw me at BarRacuda tells the press that I'm the mystery blonde in the photos, it could mean the end of Princess Snowdrop as a role model for young girls.'

'I hate to break it to you,' Ryan said, 'but twenty and thirty-something clubbers are unlikely to be hard-core members of Princess Snowdrop's fan base. They probably failed to realise that Her Highness was gracing BarRacuda with her presence.'

'Everyone in the VIP area knew I was there.'

'I know a lot of celebrities,' Ryan said. 'And not one of them would leak a name to the press.'

'That's so nice,' I said.

'Not really,' Ryan said, 'they're all desperate to get their own names in the papers. They're not going to give free publicity to someone else.'

'What about your friends, Ryan?' Cassie said. 'Not all of them have had media training. They could easily let slip my name without even meaning to.'

'I don't think they realised who you were,' Ryan said. 'They were all pretty much hammered. And you did look very different last night to the way you look on TV. That backless dress you wore was *hot*.'

Cassie smiled happily at the compliment. 'Thank you.'

'Yeah, I'm sure my friends didn't recognise you,' Ryan said. 'They just thought I'd scored with a hot chick.'

Cassie's eyes narrowed. 'Are you saying that dress makes me look like the sort of trashy girl who picks up footballers in clubs?'

'No,' Ryan said. 'You looked sexy and classy, and I'm the luckiest guy alive because I got to take you home.'

Cassie's face glowed with pleasure. Ryan smiled adoringly at her. Then he turned to me.

'I got a text from Fabio this morning,' he said. 'It says, "Do you know the girl I kissed? Can you get me her mobile number?"'

'Fabio?'

'Fabio Rossi. The goalkeeper. The very drunk guy who shared our cab last night, and was so disappointed when you insisted on staying in the car when we dropped him off at his flat.'

'Oh. I didn't catch his name. Will you text back "No" and "No."'

'Are you sure?'

'Yes, Ryan, I'm sure.'

'OK. I'll text him now. Then I'm going to jump in the shower. And then I'll take a look at the doorbell and see if I can fix it.'

'You can leave the bell, Ryan,' Cassie said. 'When Nadia gets in, I'll have her call an electrician.'

'It probably just needs a new battery,' Ryan said, as he headed out of the living room. 'Find me one while I'm in the shower.'

When he had gone, Cassie said, 'Do we have any spare batteries?'

'I don't know,' I said. 'I'll go and see. Where do we keep the spare batteries if we have them?'

'I have absolutely no idea. Nadia takes care of that sort of thing.'

I started to laugh.

'What's so amusing?' Cassie asked.

'You don't know where anything's kept in your own home.'

'Yes, I do.'

'So where would I find a light bulb?'

'Somewhere in the kitchen maybe?'

'Not good enough. Candles? Matches?'

'Don't know where they're kept either,' Cassie said. 'Sorry. If the lights go out when Nadia's not here, we'll be sitting in the dark.'

'You're such a *celebrity*,' I said. 'You're completely dependent on your PA.'

Cassie shrugged. 'What can I say? I shouldn't have to bother myself with the mundane details of household management. I'm a *star*.'

'You're *Princess Snowdrop*.'

'I'm on *television*. But I'm still Cassie from the block.'

We were both laughing now, and suddenly neither of us could stop. It was just like when we were kids and Stephen told us stupid jokes until we were doubled up with laughter. And then my mother would come in and complain that men always got children wound up and overexcited, before she started laughing too.

'Cassie, where are you?' Nadia burst into the

living room.

'Hi, Nadia.' Cassie controlled her laughter with difficulty. 'We were just talking about you.'

'Have you seen the photos on the internet?' Nadia caught sight of Cassie's laptop. 'Oh, you have. Have you had the TV on? There were more photos of you on the early morning news.'

Cassie groaned.

'You've been so careful,' Nadia said, 'and now this. Ryan must feel terrible this morning.'

Cassie looked puzzled. 'He seems fine.'

'Not that I'm suggesting for a moment that this situation is his fault,' Nadia continued, 'but it's only natural if he blames himself for ruining your career.'

'Cassie's career isn't ruined,' I said.

Ignoring me, Nadia read aloud from the laptop screen. '"He moves so Fleet, and not just with his feet." Who writes this stuff? At least your name hasn't been mentioned. *Yet.*'

'It will be, though, won't it?' Cassie said. 'It's only a matter of time. There's even a phone number for people to call if they can identify Ryan Fleet's mystery blonde.'

'If it comes out in the media that Princess Snowdrop is involved with a footballer...' Nadia shook her head. 'Cassie, you should ring your publicist. Maybe she can do some damage limitation.'

'For goodness' sake,' I said. 'Cassie, you're *not* Princess Snowdrop. You don't live in a white castle in a magic kingdom. You're an actress. No-one is going to care if you have a boyfriend.'

Nadia put her hand on my arm. 'I know you mean well, Lucy, but you don't have any media experience. Cassie Clarke is so closely identified with the role of Princess Snowdrop, that in the minds of the public she is one and the same person.'

I started to protest that this was ridiculous, but then remembered how another actor, one of Reardon Haye's clients, had received death threats when his character in a long-running soap had beaten up his screen wife. Maria had told me that he'd hired a bodyguard.

'This is awful. Why was I so stupid?' Cassie put her hands over her face.

'It's all very unfortunate,' Nadia said, 'but I do have a solution.'

Cassie looked up hopefully.

'The girl in the pictures,' Nadia said, 'Ryan's 'mystery blonde.' She could be me.'

'Pass me my laptop.' Cassie studied the photos on the screen. 'You're right. She could be you.'

Nadia did have a point. All that could be seen of the 'mystery' girl was that she was small and slim, had great legs, and long blonde hair. Her face wasn't visible in any of the shots.

'I really don't care if the world and his wife think that *I* slept with Ryan Fleet last night,' Nadia said. 'I suggest that one of us rings that number and leaves my name.'

'Oh, Nadia, that's so kind of you,' Cassie said, 'but it wouldn't be fair to throw you to the mercy of the paparazzi. And if they got hold of your name and found out where you lived, they'd still be camped on *my* doorstep.'

'Well, the offer stands,' Nadia said. 'Does anyone want coffee?'

'Please,' Cassie said.

Nadia went off to the kitchen.

'Batteries!' I said. 'I'll go and ask Nadia...'

Leaving Cassie still trawling through the internet, I went along the hallway to the back of the house. The kitchen door was open, and I heard Nadia's voice from within.

'That girl could be me. That girl *should* be me.'

I stopped walking. Nadia's phone rang.

'Oh. Leo,' she said. 'Yes, I got your voice mails. All ten of them... No, I couldn't ring you back... I told you... OK, I texted you. I had to go out with Cassie to BarRacuda... You know why. It's part of my job. I have to be available 24/7. I don't work nine to five like you... I know I said I'd come over to your place last night, but I couldn't get away... Cassie insisted I stay at the club... You know how *needy* she is...'

There was a long pause, presumably while Leo was talking, during which I stood in the hall, rooted to the spot.

'If you log onto the internet, Leo,' Nadia carried on, 'you'll see exactly what I was doing. I was acting as Cassie's decoy. I left BarRacuda with Ryan, so that *I* got papped with him and not her... There are photos on every news site... Yes, I expect they'll be

53

in the papers tomorrow... Oh, yes, Cassie's still determined to keep her and Ryan's relationship out of the press... I agree with you, she's being ridiculous, but what can I do? Lucy only encourages her... We didn't leave the club until five. I really don't think there would have been any point in coming to your place at five o'clock in the morning...'

I listened in growing disbelief. Nadia had seemed so concerned for Cassie, selflessly offering to out herself as the 'mystery blonde,' but what she really wanted was to set up her own alibi. She was lying to Leo, and at the same time badmouthing Cassie and me. If Nadia wasn't at Leo's last night, I thought, where was she? And who was she with?

When Cassie and I had gone downstairs to dance, Nadia had been sitting at the bar with the well-known director. Had she gone home with him? Or some other guy she'd met at the club?

Poor Leo, I thought. That Nadia would cheat on her boyfriend and lie about it with such apparent ease, appalled me, but I told myself I had no right to be judgemental. For all I knew, she may have woken up that morning in a stranger's bed and realised she'd made the worst mistake of her life. Could I blame her if she was twisting what happened last night to stop Leo finding out?

I could no longer hear Nadia talking. I waited a few minutes until I was sure she had ended the call, and then I went into the kitchen.

It was only after she'd found the batteries and I

was taking them and the coffee back to the living room, that I remembered what Nadia had said just before her phone had rung. *That girl could be me. That girl should be me.* I told myself that I'd imagined the bitterness in her voice.

CHAPTER 5

'I'm still surprised that no-one told the press the name of the *other* girl in the photos,' Adrian said.

'Me too,' I said. 'I'm actually quite insulted that none of my friends recognised my rear view. I've had my fifteen minutes of fame and nobody even noticed.'

'You should stick the pictures in a scrapbook to show your grandchildren,' Adrian said. 'They'll be well impressed that you partied with TV stars and footballers in your wild youth.'

'I don't think my youth has been particularly wild.'

'But you did sleep with Fabio Rossi, didn't you?' Adrian said. 'Come on, Lucy, you can tell us.'

'I did *not* sleep with the goalkeeper,' I said. 'All I did was share a taxi with him. I believe I've told you this before, Adrian. Like every day for the past month.'

Maria laughed. 'Ignore him, Lucy. He's just trying to wind you up.'

My phone rang.

'That could be *him*,' Adrian said.

I glared at Adrian and picked up the phone. It was Ruby to tell me that my eleven o'clock appointment had arrived in reception.

'Send him up,' I said.

The speculation as to the identity of Ryan Fleet's 'mystery blonde' had continued for over a week, both on the internet and in the newspapers. Several tabloids had run articles featuring girls (mostly unknown actresses and glamour models) who claimed to have met him at BarRacuda and spent the night with him. Most of the articles were accompanied by photos of said girl, naked except for a pair of football boots. Headlines like 'Fleet Scores' and 'A Fleeting Night of Passion' irritated Cassie, but amused Ryan. The only article that annoyed him was one in which the girl proclaiming herself the 'mystery blonde' described him as hopeless in bed. He refused all requests for interviews unless they were about football. A mildly hysterical Cassie came into the agency and told Eleanor *exactly* what had happened on our disastrous girls' night out (a lot of famous actors have a tendency to over-share with their agents – who else can they trust?), and everyone at Reardon Haye was ready to deny *everything* if they were ambushed by the press.

Then the lead singer of boyband Silver Dollar announced his engagement to a backing dancer, and the 'I Am Ryan's Fleet's Mystery Blonde' kiss and tell stories were old news. Except at Reardon Haye, where Adrian continued to tease me mercilessly about the goalkeeper, refusing to believe that I hadn't at least been *tempted* to go home with him.

Adrian said, 'If I promise not to mention the goalkeeper ever again, will you do the sandwich run today?'

'Tell him "no,"' Maria said. 'It's his turn.'

'I can't do the sandwich run,' I said, 'I'm auditioning all day.'

There was a knock on the office door.

'And that's my next auditionee.' I picked up a CV from my desk and read the name aloud. 'Owen Somers. Aged twenty-four. Trained in acting, singing and dancing. Here's hoping he's a star in the making.'

I'd been surprised and ridiculously pleased when, earlier in the week, Eleanor had handed me a pile of young, male actors' CVs and told me that I was to interview them, on my own, for a place on the agency's books – until then I'd only conducted auditions under the watchful eye of Maria or Adrian. I was convinced that I was going to discover the next Daniel Miller. Sadly, none of the actors I'd seen so far were likely to set screen or stage alight. Only a couple of them could actually *act*.

My first thought when I opened the door to Owen was that he was a good-looking guy. Not devastatingly *beautiful* like the Fallen Angel, but definitely attractive, tall and broad-shouldered. When he pushed back the untidy, dark blond hair that had fallen over his forehead, I saw that he had the most extraordinary blue eyes. His headshot didn't do him justice.

'Hi,' I said, 'I'm Lucy Ashford.'

'Owen Somers,' he said.

I showed him into the small room adjacent to the main office, where we interviewed prospective clients, and gestured to him to take a seat.

58

'I see from your CV that you graduated from drama school in June,' I began, 'but you've not yet had any professional acting work.' Inwardly I cringed, thinking how patronising this sounded, but Owen didn't appear to mind.

'No, not yet,' he said. 'I've found that it's almost impossible to get work if you don't have an agent. At drama school they warned us that acting is an overcrowded profession and that only a few of us would make it as successful actors. What I didn't realise was quite how hard it would be to get my first job.'

Me neither, I thought. If it hadn't been for Cassie... 'You could always give up acting and try something else,' I said.

'No, I really couldn't,' Owen said. 'The only thing I've ever wanted to do with my life is act.' His face broke into a disarming smile. 'That sounded more intense than I intended.'

I smiled back. 'So what sort of roles do you see yourself playing? Do you want to perform in the theatre or in film or TV?'

'What I *want* is to play leads in the West End, the National Theatre, feature films and prestigious BBC dramas. Unfortunately, I have to eat and pay the rent, so I'll take whatever acting work I can get.'

I nodded encouragingly. 'If an unknown actor takes a minor part in a TV advert, it gets them into a film studio, and they start making contacts in the industry.' This was something I'd heard Maria and Adrian say many times, and it seemed to me that it made a lot of sense.

'If I had a walk-on role in *anything,*' Owen said, 'it would mean I was acting. And it could lead onto other things.'

'Absolutely.' I liked Owen's attitude. Too many of the other guys I'd interviewed had told me that they would only accept a major role. 'Can you show me your audition pieces now?'

'Sure.' Owen got to his feet, and stepped into the centre of the room. 'I've a speech from *Iago* ...'

The play, a modern version of *Othello,* with the story told from the villainous Iago's point of view, had been one of my set texts at uni, so I knew it well.

'Whenever you're ready, Owen,' I said.

Suddenly the boy with the winning smile was gone and in his place was a brutal sadist, taking vicious pleasure in describing exactly how he was going to destroy Othello, the master he hated. I watched, mesmerised, as he paced back and forth across the room like a caged animal, venom dripping from his voice as he spoke. His eyes were hard and cold like blue steel. When he stopped speaking, I realised that I'd been holding my breath.

'That was really good,' I said.

'Thank you.' Owen was once again himself, his voice calm, his eyes warm and friendly.

I had him perform another speech, this time from a comedy, and he succeeded in making me laugh. Then I listened to him sing. I'm no musician, but I can hear if someone's singing in tune, and I could tell that he had a good voice. I felt a rising excitement –

this guy had *real talent*. We talked some more about his ambitions for his career, and whilst he was confident, he certainly wasn't up himself. I liked him for that as well.

'Well that's all I need for today,' I said. 'Unless you've any questions...'

'I've only one question,' Owen said. 'Are you going to take me on?'

I do hope so, I thought. Aloud, I said, 'I can't tell you that right now. The final decision is made by the head of the agency. But I'll call and let you know either way.' I stood up to show Owen that the audition was over, shook his hand, and opened the office door.

'For what it's worth,' I said, 'I think you're an extremely good actor. If giving you a place on the agency books was just up to me... But it isn't.' I realised that I'd spoken rather too freely, even unprofessionally, but I couldn't unsay it.

'Thank you,' Owen said, quietly. 'I appreciate your telling me that.'

'You're welcome.'

We smiled at each other, and I thought, I have never seen eyes that blue before. I watched him walk to the lift, and went back into the main office.

'So, was he any good?' Maria asked. 'Can he act?'

'Yes, he can act,' I said. 'He's very talented.'

Eleanor appeared in the doorway to her office. 'Who's very talented?'

'Owen Somers,' I said. 'The guy I just interviewed.'

Eleanor held out her hand for Owen's CV, and studied his headshot.

Without thinking, I said, 'He's better looking than his photo. He has the most amazing blue eyes.'

Eleanor arched one eyebrow.

'But it's his acting that impressed me,' I said quickly. 'He sent shivers up my spine.'

'Reardon Haye isn't a large agency,' Eleanor said. 'Every day, we receive dozens of CVs and showreels from actors looking for an agent, but we can only handle a limited number of clients. Are you saying that Owen Somers should be one of the very few young actors we take on this year?'

'Yes,' I said.

'You have to be *sure*. If we put him on the agency's books, will we be able to get him work and further his career as an actor? Will he make us money?'

I'd been ready to answer Eleanor's questions about Owen's acting, but it hadn't occurred to me that she'd ask me if I was certain he'd make the agency money. It seemed wrong to be deciding an actor's future on that basis. Then I remembered what Owen had said about having to eat and pay the rent.

'Yes, he will,' I said confidently.

'In that case, we'd better have him sign a contract,' Eleanor said, much to my relief. 'Congratulations, Lucy, you have your first client.' She swept back into her office, leaving me with the distinct feeling that I'd passed some sort of initiation test.

CHAPTER 6

'So, I called the actress and told her that she'd better pack her suitcase – she's got the part, and next week, she's off on tour.' I was sitting cross-legged on my bed, recounting the highlights of my day to Cassie, while she sat at my dressing table, painting her nails. She looked up and smiled.

'You're really loving your work, aren't you, Lucy?'

'Yes, I am,' I said. 'When I heard that Owen Somers – *my* client – had been cast in a new play, I think I was more excited than he was - Oh no! I'm doing it *again*. Talking about the agency. It's all I ever talk about. I'm so boring.'

'No you're not. It's great that you enjoy what you do. And it seems like you're pretty good at it.'

'I *am* good at my job,' I said. 'Even if I say it myself. When I see Owen tonight, I'll know that it was me who suggested him for the role to the director and –'

'You're seeing him tonight? Aha! I knew it!'

'You knew what?'

'All those charming young men on Reardon Haye's books. One of them was bound to ask you out. It was only a matter of time.'

I laughed. 'I'm sorry to disappoint you, but none of them have asked me out, charming or otherwise.'

'You're not going on a date with this Owen guy?'

'No, I'm really not. My interest in Owen is purely

professional. Tonight, I'm going to watch him act in *Siblings* at the Wardour Street Theatre. Tomorrow, I'm going to watch another actor in another play.'

'I don't know very much about live theatre,' Cassie said. 'Even though I call myself an actress –' Her phone vibrated, and she broke off to answer it. 'You did? Oh, well done, that's amazing… I'm *so* proud of you… Yes, I'll be right down.' She ended the call. 'Ryan's outside in the car – I'll probably stay at his place for the rest of the weekend.' She stood up to leave.

'OK,' I said. 'See you Monday.'

'His team were two-one down at the start of the second half, and then he scored twice.'

'That's great.' I knew very little about football, but I was fairly sure that this was a matter for congratulations. 'Tell him congrats from me.'

'I will.' She opened the door, but then shut it again. 'Ryan asked me to watch him play from the stands with the other wives and girlfriends today. Obviously, I couldn't, but I do feel bad that I didn't see him score those goals.'

I felt a vague sense of unease, without quite knowing why. 'Did Ryan mind that you wouldn't go and watch him?'

'Oh, no. Well, we had a few words, but I reminded him that it was me who would lose my job if our relationship became public, and he apologised. And we're fine now.' She smiled. 'Ryan is just so… so…'

I pushed my feelings of disquiet away. 'The perfect boyfriend?'

Cassie laughed. '*No* man is perfect, but Ryan comes pretty close.' She opened the door and stepped out onto the landing. Over her shoulder, she said, 'I think I may be just a little bit in love with him.'

'Oh, Cassie! And does Ryan feel the same?'

'He's told me that he does.' She smiled at me, and without another word, closed the door.

There was no-one to see me, but I also smiled, happy for my friend. If only I could meet a guy as nice as Cassie's footballer, I thought. Not that I was *desperate* to become half of a couple again, but if the *right* man happened to come along...

I reached for my laptop, and spent an hour or so catching up with some of my uni friends on Facebook, before it was time for me to leave for the theatre. I inspected myself in my mirror. A quick comb of my hair and a touch-up of my lipstick and I was good to go.

On the landing outside my room, I met Nadia coming out of her bedroom, which was opposite mine. She was wearing a black satin dress that was cut almost as low at the front as the back, and she was carrying a fur coat and a sequined clutch bag.

'You look very glam tonight,' I said. 'Where are you off to?'

'Only a birthday party,' Nadia said.

'Whose birthday is it?'

'No-one important. Just some friend of Leo's. But I do feel that a girl should always make an effort.' Nadia looked me up and down, but evidently decided that my off-the-shoulder jumper, skinny jeans and

65

boots were unworthy of comment. 'And how are you spending the evening? Do you have a date?'

'No,' I said. 'I'm going out on my own to see a play.'

'On your own? On a Saturday night? Oh, Lucy, what are we going to do with you?'

Not for the first time, I found Nadia's condescending tone intensely irritating. 'I'm *working* tonight. I'm going to watch a client.'

'Anybody famous?'

'No,' I said. 'He's not famous. Not yet. But he may be one day. His name's Owen Somers.'

'Owen Somers?' Nadia said. 'Is he tall with fair hair? Does he have blue eyes?'

'He is. He does. Do you know him?'

'I used to know him,' Nadia said. 'I haven't seen him in years.'

'He's a very talented actor.'

'Really?' Nadia sounded incredulous. 'You think that gawky boy has talent? He must have changed a great deal since I knew him.'

'Owen Somers is going to be a star,' I said. 'I'm certain of it. It was me who persuaded Eleanor Haye to take him on as a client.'

'I see.' Nadia smiled sweetly. 'Well, I hope that you're right about Owen. It won't do your reputation at the agency much good if he turns out to be a failure as an actor.' She added, 'I must get going. Leo's outside in his car – did I tell you he's just got a new Porsche? Can we give you a lift to the tube?'

At that moment, furious that Nadia had cast

doubts on my ability to do my job, there was a part of me that wanted to tell her to go screw herself. There was another part of me that knew it was raining hard outside, and that of the three girls who lived in Cassie's house, I was the one who did not have a boyfriend picking her up that evening in an enviably luxurious motor. On balance, I think it was probably a wise decision to grit my teeth and have Leo drive me to the station, even though it meant that I had to listen to his pontificating on the state of the economy the whole way. It was, I reflected, the longest time I'd spent in his company, and it wasn't an experience I was eager to repeat.

'Enjoy the play,' Nadia said to me as I made my escape from the car. 'Remember me to Owen. I do hope you're not disappointed by his performance.'

A delay on the underground meant that I arrived at the Wardour Street Theatre later than I'd intended. Like a lot of small studio theatres, the seats weren't numbered, and most of the audience had already taken their places in the auditorium. I thought I'd have to squeeze in at the back, but when I presented my comp ticket to the guy working front of house, he asked me if I was Owen Somer's agent, and then showed me to a reserved seat in the front row.

I thought, *I* have a theatre seat specially reserved for me by one of *my* clients. Check me out.

Almost as soon as I sat down, the house lights went out, the stage lights came on, and the play, a serious drama about brothers and sisters fighting over an inheritance, began. Owen, playing the youngest brother, had only a small part, but from his first appearance I knew that I'd been right about his talent. He was extremely good, more than holding his own with the other actors, who were all experienced performers. In the interval, I didn't go to the bar but stayed in my seat and read my programme. It had photos of the entire cast, with a list of their credits and the names of the people they wanted to thank for supporting them in their acting career. Owen's photo was much better than the one he'd sent into the agency. I'd have to tell him to get some new headshots, I thought. I read his credits, which listed the parts he'd played at drama school and mentioned that his role in *Siblings* was his professional debut. I was flattered, if somewhat surprised, when I saw the only person he'd thanked for supporting him was 'Lucy Ashford.'

By the final scene of the play, none of the characters in *Siblings* were on speaking terms, one sister had tried to shoot the other, and the youngest brother was setting fire to the ancestral home. As flames engulfed the scenery, the audience, who had watched the previous scenes in shocked silence, let out a collective gasp of breath. When the actors filed on stage to take their bow, they were greeted with respectful, if not rapturous, applause. The clapping that greeted Owen, I noticed, was louder than the rest - which must have been annoying for the actor who was playing the lead role of the eldest son, but was very gratifying for me.

Meeting a client after a show to congratulate them on a good performance was another part of my job that I loved. As soon as the actors had vanished off the stage into the wings, I grabbed my coat and dashed out of the theatre ahead of the crowd. Thankfully, it had stopped raining. I made my way down the alley at the side of the building that led to the stage door and waited for Owen to appear. After a few minutes I was joined by three middle-aged women clutching autograph books, and an elderly couple, who from their conversation, were the grandparents of one of the cast.

The first actor to come out the stage door was the leading man. He quickly signed his autograph for the middle-aged women. They were eager to talk to him about the play, but he muttered something about having a train to catch and headed down the alley towards the street. The actress who'd played the gun-toting daughter came out next. The middle-aged women eagerly held out their autograph books, but the actress ignored them and took off at a run. The middle-aged women looked most put out.

Then Owen came out the stage door. Before I could say anything to him, the autograph-hunters had pounced on him, thrusting their books into his hands, telling him he was the best actor in the play. He signed his name, chatted amiably, and even posed for a photograph with each of the women in turn. Then, extricating himself with a charming smile, he walked over to me.

'Lucy!' He was smiling broadly now. 'Thank you

so much for coming to see me. Did you enjoy the play?'

'I don't know if *enjoy* is exactly the right word for a play that dark,' I said. 'But it's certainly a powerful piece of drama. And you gave a riveting performance. Congratulations, Owen. You were terrific.'

'That's so good to hear.'

'How do you like appearing on stage six nights a week?'

'Lucy, it's incredible. I can't begin to tell you...' Owen hesitated, and then he said, 'It's freezing out here and there's a wine-bar just round the corner. Shall we go and get a drink?'

'Sure,' I said. 'But I'm buying. I can claim it back as *entertaining a client* on my expenses.'

'No, I'm buying,' Owen insisted. 'Money spent *entertaining my agent* is tax deductible.'

The wine-bar was packed, but I spotted a couple of girls leaving and bagged their table while Owen fought his way through the crowd to fetch us drinks. He was obviously a man who was good at getting a bartender's attention, because he returned in minutes with a bottle of white wine and two glasses. He set the wine down on the table and took the chair across from mine. One of the barmaids put a candle on the table and lit it. It occurred to me that she thought Owen and I were a couple.

'This is nice wine,' I said, sipping my drink. 'I so much prefer white to red.'

Owen picked up the bottle and studied the label.

'It was a good year.'

'Do you know about wine?'

'A little,' Owen said. 'I used to work for a wine merchant. One of the many jobs I did to fund my drama school training.'

'You paid your own way through drama school?'

Owen nodded. 'I was eighteen. I was determined to go to drama school and become an actor, but my parents were totally against it. I couldn't ask them for money. So I stacked supermarket shelves, drove a fork-lift truck, cleaned offices, dug the roads... Anything to earn enough to pay my fees.'

'That must have been hard,' I said.

'I didn't know what hard work meant until I'd been a road digger. In the rain.'

'But now you're an actor.'

'Yes, I am. Thanks to *you*, Lucy.'

'Thank *you*, for thanking me in the programme.'

'You took me on at Reardon Haye. You sent me to the audition that's got me my first professional role. You believe in me. Unlike my parents, to whom I'm a continual disappointment. Sorry, I won't bore you by going on about my dysfunctional family – you've already seen quite enough of that sort of thing tonight on stage.'

'Oh, I don't mind,' I said. 'I'm your agent. You can tell me anything.' I drained my wine. 'Have your parents seen you in the play?'

'They're not interested in coming to see me.'

My face must have registered my shock. 'But why not?'

Owen re-filled my glass. 'They still don't approve of my choice of career. My father is a very successful businessman who expected me to follow him into the family firm. When I told him I'd enrolled at drama school, he went ballistic. After a *lot* of shouting about the thousands of pounds he'd wasted on my education, he threw me out of the house and didn't speak to me for months. My mother, whose main purpose in life is to spend my father's money, took his side. Even now, three years later, on the rare occasions I visit my parents, the atmosphere isn't great.'

'That has to hurt.' I thought back to the previous summer. However exasperated my mother had been by my inability to find myself a job, she would never *ever*, under any circumstances, have turned me out of her house. It would have been inconceivable to either of us.

Owen shrugged. 'My parents and I have never been close. I get on well with my sister though. She's coming to see the play next week.'

'The play ends its run the week after that, I think?'

'Yep. And I'll be a *resting* actor again.'

'Not for long, I'm sure. There's not much work around in December - except for pantomimes and they're already cast - but I've got you a couple of auditions for shows that open in the New Year.'

'I seem to have found myself a really good theatrical agent.'

'And I've discovered a really talented actor,' I said.

72

Owen's mouth lifted in a lazy smile. He poured out the last of the wine and raised his glass.

'To a long and successful partnership,' he said.

We clinked glasses, and his fingers brushed lightly against mine. It seemed to me that they lingered a little too long for the touch to have been entirely accidental.

'I know how important it is for an actor to work closely with their agent,' he said. I'm looking forward to working with mine.'

I thought, *is he flirting with me*? And how do I feel about that? To cover my confusion, I drank some more wine. I looked across the table at Owen. His startlingly blue eyes gazed steadily back. My heart began to beat just a little bit faster.

A female voice called out, 'Owen!'

Owen glanced round and waved to a dark-haired girl who was making her way towards us through the crowded bar. When she reached our table he stood up and kissed the side of her face, and she hugged him. I saw that she was very beautiful. Stunning, in fact.

'Hey, Julie,' Owen said.

'I was hoping I'd find you in here after the show,' the girl said. 'I wanted to tell you that I've got a day's holiday on Monday, so I can come and watch you in *Siblings*.'

'That's fantastic,' Owen said. 'I'll get you a comp.' He added, 'Lucy, this is Julie Diaz. We often meet up here after we've finished work. Julie, this is my agent, Lucy Ashford'.

'Your agent?' Julie said. 'Oh, I'm sorry, I didn't

realise –' To me, she said, 'You must think me so rude, barging in on you like this.'

'No, of course not.' I said.

'I'm just so pleased that I'm going to be able to see Owen in his first professional role. I didn't think I'd be able to get the time off.' Julie smiled up at Owen and he smiled back at her with obvious affection. I decided that another part of my job as an agent was to know when a client had things on his mind other than his acting career. I made a show of checking the time on my watch.

'It's later than I thought,' I said, pushing back my chair and standing up. 'I need to get going.'

Owen looked concerned. 'Are you OK to get home? Would you like to share a cab?'

'Oh, no, you stay here. I'll be fine on the tube and it's only a short walk the other end.'

I said my goodbyes, promised to call Owen first thing on Monday with the details of the auditions I'd arranged for him, and made my way out of the still crowded bar. When I was outside, I looked back in through the window and saw that he and Julie were now sitting next to each other, their heads very close together. As I watched, she put her hand on his arm. Feeling rather foolish, because there had been a moment when I really had thought he'd been about to come on to me, I turned away and started walking to the station.

CHAPTER 7

'What do you think?' I stood in the centre of the living room, and twirled around so that Cassie could admire my latest purchase: an oyster-coloured silk dress with cut-away lace panels and a very short skirt.

'You look stunning,' Cassie said.

'Thanks,' I said. 'I was planning to wear that sequinned dress I wore to BarRacuda, but then I thought most girls treat themselves to a new outfit for their work's Christmas party.'

'And this isn't just *any* office party –' Cassie said. 'It's the *Reardon Haye* Christmas party. Oh, there's the doorbell.'

I heard footsteps in the hall, the front door opening, and Nadia's voice. A moment later, she put her head round the living room door.

'Your car's here,' she said. 'I've told the driver you'll be a few minutes.'

'Thanks, Nadia.' Cassie got to her feet and picked up her coat. 'Where's my bag?'

I gathered up my own coat and bag and followed her out into the hall.

'I can't see it,' Cassie said. 'I must have left it in my bedroom.' She ran off up the stairs. Instead of going back to whatever it was she'd been doing before she'd answered the door, Nadia remained standing with me in the hall.

'Another new dress, Lucy?' she said. 'Anyone

would think it was *you* who was the celebrity rather than Cassie.' She laughed uproariously, and I made myself laugh too, although I didn't find her remark particularly amusing. Having got her hilarity under control, she continued, 'I suppose there'll be casting directors from all the major film and TV companies at this 'do' you're going to tonight?'

'I expect so,' I said.

'So the party isn't just for the actors on Reardon Haye's books?'

'Not as far as I know.' The conversation lapsed into silence, but Nadia remained hovering at the foot of the stairs. I thought, is she angling for a last minute invitation? Not that I had any say in who was invited to the agency's Christmas party, but standing there with Nadia, I felt very uncomfortable. I was very glad when Cassie re-appeared, brandishing her bag, and we were able to go out to the car.

The stark meeting room on the ground floor of the Reardon Haye building had been transformed into a winter wonderland of holly, ivy and fake snow. A white tree, untraditional but very striking, decorated with white lights, took up one corner of the room. In another corner, three girls in white satin dresses trimmed with white fur belted out Christmas number ones, accompanied by piano and guitar.

Cassie and I were amongst the first to arrive at the party, (as a Reardon Haye employee, I'd been obliged to arrive unfashionably early), but soon the event was in full swing. With the notable exception of Daniel Miller, who was still filming in Ireland, almost all of the agency's clients put in an appearance, including those who arrived late after appearing in pantomime, and those who had to leave early because they had to be in make-up at five o'clock the next day. I chatted to the stars of sit coms, West End shows, and feature films, a young actress who had just landed a part in a soap and was *very* excited about it, and a world-weary older actor who was totally blasé about his forthcoming role in a National Theatre production of *King Lear.* Half-way through the evening Owen Somers arrived. Cassie, who'd been impressed by my description of his performance in *Siblings,* was eager to meet him, so I introduced them, and left them talking animatedly about the differences between acting on stage and on screen.

The level of conversation in the room grew ever louder. The singer finished her set and was replaced by show tunes played over the meeting room's state-of-the art sound system. Cassie came and found me to let me know that she was leaving to go and meet up with Ryan. She told me that she thought Owen was a lovely guy. When I thought about how easy it was to work with him, how pleased he always sounded when I rang to tell him I'd found him an audition, even if it was only for a walk-on part, I had to agree with her.

Towards midnight, hoarse from talking to so many people, my feet beginning to protest at the height of my heels (oyster coloured stilettos that perfectly matched my dress), I found myself standing next to Adrian.

Leaning close so that I could hear him above the noise of the music, the chatter and the clink of glasses, he said, 'All these actors knocking back the mulled wine, and only one sent home in a taxi because they're tired and emotional. I think we can say that it's all going very well.'

'Eleanor will be pleased,' I said.

'She'll be relieved,' Adrian said. 'At last year's Christmas party, two soap stars came to blows over a mince pie, and a Bafta-winning actress had to be prevented from doing an impromptu striptease.'

'You're making that up,' I laughed.

'Would I lie to you?'

'Yes.'

Adrian grinned. 'So what are your plans for Christmas, Lucy? Who are you going to be kissing under the mistletoe?'

'As I'm spending Christmas with my family,' I said, 'I don't think kissing under the mistletoe is going to be a huge part of my Yuletide celebrations.'

'The goalkeeper still hasn't called you then?'

'No, he hasn't, strangely enough.'

'I'd try to forget him, if I were you,' Adrian said. 'You don't need him. Not now that other guy is after you.'

'And what guy would that be?' I asked.

'Your favourite client,' Adrian said. 'Owen Somers.'

'Don't be ridiculous.'

'You must have noticed how often he's been coming into the agency to see you.'

'You're right,' I said. 'He came into the agency twice last week. To collect a script. And to go over a contract.'

'He's hardly taken his eyes off you all evening,' Adrian said.

I glanced around the room and spotted Owen amongst a group of younger actors. He saw me at the same time as I saw him, and his face broke into a smile.

'He wants you, Lucy,' Adrian said.

'No he doesn't,' I said. 'He has a girlfriend.'

'And your point is?'

'Owen's not like that,' I said. 'He's nice.'

'You think he's *nice*? That poor guy.'

'You're very lucky that it's the season of good will to all men, Adrian, or I'd be really annoyed at you right now.'

Across the room, Owen left the group he was with and started to wend his way through the mildly inebriated crowd towards me and Adrian.

'Five pounds says he asks you out before the New Year,' Adrian said.

'Not listening, Adrian.' Helping myself to two glasses of wine from the tray of a passing waitress, I left Adrian alone with his over-active imagination, and went and joined Owen.

'I've decided I like being an actor,' Owen said by way of greeting.

'Why's that?' I handed him a glass of wine.

'I get invited to showbiz parties. I meet all these famous people…'

I laughed. 'Sometimes you even get to do some acting.'

'Oh, yes, there is that,' Owen said. 'Seriously, Lucy, I've enjoyed this party. It's been great to talk to so many actors who've been in the business a lot longer than I have. Cassie Clarke gave me some really useful advice about acting for television.'

'Cassie's a good friend of mine,' I said. 'We've know each other since we were children. I live in her house.'

'Yeah, she said.'

Suddenly the image of Nadia telling me that she knew Owen floated into my head. 'I forgot to tell you when I came to see your play, Cassie's PA is actually an old friend of yours. Nadia Pincher.'

Owen's face became expressionless. 'I wouldn't exactly describe Nadia as a friend.'

'Oh. Right.'

'I used to work with her,' Owen said. 'Handing out advertising flyers in the street. One of the worst jobs I did before I went to drama school. The only good thing about it was that everyone else was a resting actor and I got to talk to them about acting.'

I pictured the girls and guys who stood around in Covent Garden, Leicester Square and Piccadilly Circus handing out flyers advertising bars, clubs and West End shows. Most of them were out-of-work actors. Like waitressing, bartending or working in a call centre, flyering was a job that let you take time off to go to auditions.

'I'd no idea that Nadia used to be an actress,' I said.

'She was always reading scripts and talking about parts she'd played,' Owen said. 'Although now that I think about it, I do remember that she left the flyering job because she'd taken a job as a PA. It was supposed to be temporary.'

'I wonder why she's never gone back to acting,' I said.

'I wouldn't know. Like I said, we weren't friends.'

Owen doesn't much care for Nadia, I thought. I cast my mind back over the months I'd lived in Cassie's house, remembering all the things Nadia had said that had irritated me, and how she'd probably cheated on her boyfriend and bad-mouthed me and Cassie to cover it up. And I admitted to myself that I didn't much like Nadia either.

In an abrupt change of subject, Owen asked, 'Have you done all your Christmas shopping?'

'I've done most of it,' I said. 'But I still have to get something for my brother. Boys are so much harder to buy for than girls.'

'I disagree,' Owen said. 'I still have to get Julie's present and I've no idea what she'd like.'

'Every girl likes perfume.'

'I was hoping to get her something a little more original,' Owen said. 'She's invited me to spend Christmas Day with her family, and I want to give

81

her something that shows how much I appreciate the invitation.'

I thought for a moment. 'What does Julie do?'

'She's an actress. Musical theatre.'

Of course Owens's exquisitely beautiful girlfriend was an actress. 'Then why don't you get her some jewellery with a theatrical theme?'

Owen looked doubtful. 'Maybe. Though she does own a lot of jewellery.'

At that moment, over Owen's shoulder, I noticed the door of the room opening to admit a late-arriving guest. The late-comer, dressed all in black, his dark hair delectably tousled, was Daniel Miller.

Even in that room full of successful actors, the arrival of the Fallen Angel did not go unremarked. I saw a number of West End leading ladies glancing sideways at him while whispering conspiratorially to their companions. The excitable soap actress's mouth actually dropped open, while the faces of the young actors Owen had been talking to earlier expressed admiration and envy in equal measure. Seemingly oblivious of the stir his entrance had caused, Daniel stood in the doorway and let his gaze travel over the crowd. When he saw me, he smiled. I felt a sinuous warmth low in my stomach.

Only half-listening to what Owen was saying about his girlfriend's taste in music and whether a CD might make a suitable present, I watched as Daniel joined the group of actors gathered around Eleanor. He stayed with her for just a few minutes before going over to Adrian and shaking his hand.

After a short conversation, he left Adrian and went to talk to a woman who cast guest stars for a popular BBC drama series. I lost sight of him then, as other people obscured my view. The next time I saw him, he was talking to Maria.

Owen broke in on my thoughts. 'So, do you really think jewellery would be OK?'

With an effort, I tore my attention away from Daniel, and made myself focus on Owen and his Christmas shopping. Having listened to him agonising over what to buy his girlfriend, I only hoped she was as fond of him as he seemed to be of her.

'Hello again, Lucy.' Suddenly, Daniel Miller was standing next to me, close enough for me to smell his aftershave. My stomach turned itself inside out.

'Daniel,' I said. 'I thought you were filming in Ireland.'

'I was,' Daniel said, 'but we wrapped early. I flew back to England this evening and came here straight from the airport. I couldn't miss the legendary Reardon Haye Christmas party.'

With Daniel's brown eyes boring into mine, it was difficult to think straight, but I remembered my manners long enough to say, 'Daniel, this is Owen.'

'Owen Somers,' Daniel said, 'how the devil are you?'

'Not so bad,' Owen said. 'How's life treating you?'

'Oh, I get by.'

'I gather you two know each other?' I said.

'We went to the same drama school,' Owen said.

'I was two years ahead of Owen,' Daniel said, 'but we were in some student shows together.'

'Were you rivals for the lead?' I'd talked with enough drama school graduates by now to know that even while actors were still in training, competition for parts was fierce.

'We'll never be rivals,' Daniel said. 'We're really not the same casting type.'

'No, of course, not,' I said. How could I think they'd ever be up for the same part? Daniel was sex on legs, and Owen was... nice.

Daniel and Owen embarked on a conversation about other actors they'd trained with, and how well (or not) they were doing in their chosen career. I should leave them to it, I thought. I should go and circulate. Instead, I just stood there, gawping at Daniel's handsome profile and thinking entirely unprofessional thoughts about his lean, muscular body.

At around one o'clock, the music stopped playing and the lights in the meeting room became noticeably brighter. If that was not enough to convince the guests that the party was well and truly over, the waitresses stopped handing out drinks and started collecting up empty glasses. Taking the hint, people began to gravitate towards the door and head out into the night.

Daniel glanced at his watch. 'It's still so early,' he said to me and Owen. 'Why don't we all go on to a club?'

'I can't,' Owen said, 'I have to be somewhere.'

He's probably going to spend the night with his girlfriend, I thought.

'Looks like it'll just be me and you then, Lucy,' Daniel said.

Just me and you. My heart started beating very fast. 'Sounds good, Daniel.'

He smiled. 'I'll wait outside while you finish up here.'

Owen cleared his throat. 'I'll say goodnight, then. Have a good Christmas, Lucy.'

'You too, Owen.'

He and Daniel were amongst the last guests to leave. Eleanor rounded up the stragglers, wished them a Merry Christmas, and ushered them out of the building and into one of the taxis waiting by the kerb. Leaving the caterers to clear up the party's debris, and the night security guard to lock up after them, she congratulated her staff on a job well done, and told us she didn't expect to see any of us in the office before noon.

'I only booked the one car to get us all home,' Eleanor said when we were standing outside on the pavement. 'We'll have to work out who needs to be dropped off first.'

I looked up and down the street, and saw Daniel leaning casually against a taxi parked on the opposite side of the road.

'Thanks, Eleanor,' I said, 'but I have a lift. I... I'll see you all tomorrow.' Leaving my colleagues staring after me, I darted across the road to Daniel.

He opened the door of the taxi so that I could get into the back seat, and slid in next to me.

'Is Mojave OK with you?' he said.

For a moment I couldn't think what he was talking about, but then I realised that Mojave was the name of a club.

'I've never been there,' I said, 'but I don't mind trying out somewhere new.'

Ten minutes later, the cab deposited us in a side street in Mayfair, outside a gracious Georgian townhouse, with a garish neon sign above the door that proclaimed it to be London nightclub Mojave. There was a small queue, hunched up and shivering in the cold night air, but the Fallen Angel was waved straight past by the bouncers, without even the need to stop and identify himself. Once through the doors, we were welcomed with great enthusiasm (well, he was at any rate) by not one but two hostesses, whose greatest pleasure in life was apparently to take charge of our coats.

The interior of the club could best be described as late 1960s retro, the low lighting provided by lava lamps. Directly in front of us was a bar area, with glass tables, and white leather sofas occupied by couples and groups of young men and women. Most of them, from what I could see, were very fashionably and expensively dressed. The background music wasn't loud enough to drown out their shouted conversations, or the occasional outbreak of braying laughter.

Daniel said, 'There's dancing in the basement. Or

would you rather get a drink first?'

Having no desire to show him my dubious dance skills, I said, 'A drink would be lovely.'

Already, the other people in the bar had become aware of the Fallen Angel's presence. As I followed Daniel to one of the leather sofas, I was aware of faces turning towards us, the sudden absence of talk as we approached, and renewed chatter once we'd walked past. With so many eyes on me, I was relieved that I made it to the sofa without falling over my feet. Conscious of my short skirt, I was particularly careful of how I positioned my legs when I sat down. Daniel sat next to me, leaving very little space between us. A waiter immediately materialised beside us and asked what we'd like to drink. Daniel promptly ordered champagne.

'Did you notice everyone looking at you?' I said to him when the waiter had gone.

Daniel shrugged. 'Since *Fallen Angel* came out, I get recognised all the time.'

'Having total strangers watching your every move must take some getting used to.'

'I'm an actor,' Daniel said. 'Being the centre of attention kind of goes with the territory.'

I thought of the numerous articles about Daniel's amorous exploits in Ireland that I'd read in the gossip columns. And the photos of him glued to his co-star's face.

'But you must find it irritating to be continuously stalked by the paparazzi,' I said.

Daniel smiled. 'I don't mind them. I rather enjoy

seeing photos of myself in the tabloids. It's free publicity.'

The waiter returned with our champagne, poured two glasses, and left the bottle within easy reach in a bucket of ice.

When we were alone again, Daniel said, 'I waited a long time to become famous. Now that I've had a taste of what it means to be a star, I want more. I want the Hollywood mansion and the Malibu beach house. I want the private jet and the yacht in the south of France. And if getting them means I have to pose for a few photographs outside a nightclub, I really don't see it as a problem. But I'm glad there weren't any paparazzi outside Mojave tonight. It would've been hard to make you run a gauntlet of flashing cameras when we're only on our first date.'

'Is this a date?' I said.

'Well, there's you, me, and a bottle of champagne,' Daniel said. 'I'd call that a date.'

I was on a date with film star Daniel Miller. The thought made me feel light-headed.

'What would that actress you dated in Ireland think about you being here with me?' I said.

Daniel looked taken aback. 'She wouldn't think anything. I was never in a relationship with her. DCOL.'

'What?'

'Doesn't Count On Location.'

'I see.'

We drank our champagne. Daniel talked about the auditions for *Fallen Angel* and how he'd felt when

Eleanor phoned him to tell him he'd got the lead. It was warm in the club, and he took off his suit jacket and undid a couple of buttons on his shirt. I found it increasingly difficult to hold up my end of the conversation. It was an effort to stop myself from undoing the rest of his buttons, and ripping the shirt from his back.

Then the champagne bottle and our glasses were empty.

'Shall I order us another?' Daniel asked.

'No more for me.' I'd acquired a taste for champagne since I'd been working in showbusiness, but I knew when I'd had enough.

Daniel inched closer to me, so that his thigh was touching mine. He gazed at me through hooded eyes.

'Will you sleep with me tonight, Lucy?' he said, softly.

My heart actually skipped a beat. What had I expected? The Fallen Angel could have any woman he wanted. He wasn't going to take me to a club and *not* ask me to sleep with him. And I wanted to, I really did. I wanted *him.* But I wasn't some starstruck girl who'd jump into bed with a guy just because he was famous. And I'd never put out on a first date.

Through a haze of champagne and lust, I heard myself say, 'I don't think so, Daniel.'

Daniel's face didn't give away any of the shock he must be feeling at being turned down. Instead, his mouth lifted in a slow, seductive smile.

'I want you to come back to my place,' he said. 'I want to kiss you and undress you, and make love to you in my bed.'

'Daniel, I'm not going to sleep with you.'

'Not tonight maybe,' Daniel said. 'But you will. Right now, I'll take you home – your home. And I'll go back to mine.'

Daniel paid for our drinks and then, one of Mojave's extremely efficient and helpful staff having returned our coats, we got up to go. Daniel put a hand on the small of my back to guide me out of the bar. When he helped me on with my fake fur, his fingers brushed my bare shoulders. My whole body tingled pleasurably at his touch.

Outside, it had started to snow.

CHAPTER 8

I tilted my head up to the sky and let the flakes settle on my face. Daniel laughed and did the same.

'Much as I like looking at your legs in that dress, you must be freezing. Let's get in the taxi.' He gestured to the black cab parked a few yards down the road.

He was right, of course. My short dress and waist-length jacket were not designed to be worn in the snow. He held out his hand. I took a step towards him. My high heels slipped on the wet pavement, my right ankle twisted under me, and I landed on my knees at Daniel's feet.

'Lucy! Are you all right?' His strong arms lifted me up, and held me close against his chest.

'I think so,' I said, embarrassed. I tried putting my weight on my ankle, and it seemed OK. 'I'm fine.' Apart from the fact that I've just made a complete fool of myself, I thought. 'I guess you're used to having women throw themselves at you.'

Daniel didn't say anything. Instead, he bent his head and kissed me. Gently at first and then suddenly passionately, his tongue sliding between my lips and exploring my mouth. I felt such a strong desire for him, to have him inside me, that I shocked myself. My legs were shaking, and if it wasn't for him holding me tight within the circle of his arms, I would have fallen at his feet once again.

'You're shivering,' Daniel said. 'We should go.'

91

We walked to the taxi and clambered into the back seat.

'Where to, mate?' the driver asked.

'What's your address, Lucy?' Daniel said.

I thought, I can go home alone to my empty bed or I can go home with the hottest guy on the planet and have a night of torrid passion.

'Daniel, what I said earlier, I've changed my mind.' I lowered my voice so that the taxi driver couldn't hear. 'I will sleep with you tonight.'

For a moment Daniel didn't say anything. Then he gave the cab driver an address in Chiswick. The taxi sped off through the dark London streets. Daniel put an arm around my shoulder. He smiled at me, and stroked my face. Then he kissed me again. He went on kissing me the whole time we were in the taxi. The driver kept his eyes on the road. I figured he'd probably seen worse in the back of his cab in any case.

By the time we reached the block of flats where Daniel lived, it was snowing hard. There was no-one about and no other cars, and everything was silent and still. Daniel paid the taxi driver, and the cab pulled away from the kerb and was soon lost to sight in the swirling snowflakes. Daniel took my hand and led me along the snow-covered path to his building's communal front door. He kissed me again, before producing the key fob that would let us in. Still kissing me, he walked me to the lift, and pressed the button for the first floor. In the lift, he slid his hand inside my coat and cupped my breast. I thought I was going to faint.

The lift doors opened and we stumbled out, our mouths still locked together. Daniel let us into his flat, slamming the front door shut behind us.

'This way,' he said hoarsely, and together we staggered into his bedroom. I shrugged off my coat and he did the same.

'How does this come off?' He was fumbling at the back of my dress.

'Zip. Side.'

'What?'

I unzipped my dress, pulled it off over my head and kicked off my shoes. Daniel had already stripped off down to his boxers. He pulled me to him and kissed me on the mouth hard, the neck, the top of my breasts above my bra, and my stomach. He rolled my tights down my legs, and I gasped as he kissed my thighs.

'Jeez, Lucy, you've got an awful cut on your leg.'

I glanced down and saw that my right knee was grazed and bloody from my fall. At that moment, I really didn't care.

'It's nothing' I said. 'Doesn't hurt at all.'

Daniel stood up, and there was more frenzied kissing as he rid me of my underwear and I tugged his boxers over his hips. We fell together onto his bed, and then he was rooting in his nightstand for a condom, and I was opening my legs, and he was lying on me, and thrusting into me and… and it felt *sooo* good.

* * *

When I woke up the next morning, I found myself alone in Daniel's bed. The previous night, what with the hot naked guy doing incredible things to my body, I hadn't taken much notice of my surroundings. Now I sat up and looked around. Despite the amount of action that was alleged to take place inside it, Daniel's bedroom was unremarkable, with a king-size bed, fitted wardrobes and a chest of drawers. A poster, a scene from *Fallen Angel,* hung on one wall, and a flat-screen TV on the other. Directly opposite the bed was a mirror, which showed me the reflection of a girl with mussed hair and smudged mascara. I smiled and the girl smiled back. She had obviously just woken up after a night of amazing sex.

The door to the bedroom opened and Daniel, still minus his clothes, came in carrying two mugs of tea. The sight of him, his naked body bathed in the pale winter sunlight streaming through the bedroom window, took my breath away.

'Morning,' Daniel said.

'Hi, Daniel.'

He passed me a mug of tea and sat down on the bed.

'I was watching the news on TV in the other room,' he said. 'It snowed all night, and now half the country's ground to a halt.' He reached out and touched my mouth, which was still swollen from his kisses. I thought about snow, public transport and my journey to work. Daniel's hand strayed from my face to my breast

'Daniel,' I said, 'Last night was lovely, but I have to go.'

'Last night was great.' His hand stole under the duvet and stroked my thigh. 'Don't go yet, Lucy.'

'I must. I have to be at Reardon Haye by mid-day, and I need to go home first and sort myself out.'

Daniel looked disappointed, but he took his hand off my thigh. I pushed back the duvet and got out of bed, feeling just a little self-conscious as his gaze travelled up and down my body.

'Your leg looks very sore,' he said. 'You might want to clean it before you go.'

The cut on my knee, which I had thought a slight graze, was now red and angry, and the knee itself was badly bruised.

'Can I use your shower?' I asked.

'Sure. I'll show you where it is.'

As Daniel's flat consisted of three rooms off a hallway, I could probably have found my own way to the bathroom, but he seemed to want to make certain I was happy with the soap and that I had enough towels. He even handed me a toothbrush in an un-opened packet, which, for me, was a morning-after-the-night-before first. I was touched, until I realised that a guy who has a supply of new toothbrushes for overnight guests obviously expects to get lucky. As soon as he'd gone out, I rifled through his bathroom cabinet for signs that any one girl was staying over on a regular basis. He owned more pots of moisturiser and tubes of fake tan than I did, but there were no lipsticks or bottles of nail varnish remover.

However many women Daniel Miller had brought back to his flat, none of them seemed to have marked it as her territory. At that moment, it occurred to me that I was behaving like the worst sort of tabloid reporter. I closed the cabinet and climbed in the shower.

When I went back to the bedroom, Daniel was dressed in jeans and a sweatshirt. I put on my clothes, and he produced a roll of sticking plaster for my knee. I sat on the bed, enjoying the touch of his cool, gentle fingers on my skin while he covered the cut, and the feeling of being looked after.

I don't want last night to be the only time I sleep with Daniel Miller, I thought. And I don't just want to have sex with him, I want to get know him, the guy not the film star.

'I really need to get home now, Daniel. How do I get to the underground from here?' I willed him to ask if he could see me again, preferably that night.

'I'm not about to let you go limping through the snow to the train station,' Daniel said. 'Actually, even if you hadn't hurt your leg, I don't think you could walk in the snow in those shoes.'

'You're right.' I'd not get very far in my satin stilettos. And my knee, while not desperately painful, had become very stiff. I was also bare-legged, as my tights were in shreds from my fall. I got out my mobile to call a minicab.

Daniel put his hand over mine. 'I'll drive you home. I'll wait there while you get changed, and then I'll drive you to Reardon Haye.'

Outside, snow covered the buildings and the pavements, but the roads were clear. London seemed to have escaped the worst of the blizzards. Daniel's car was a Ferrari, and he was obviously very pleased with it. He also assumed that a female would have no knowledge of cars, and spent most of the journey explaining what made it such a superior vehicle. I didn't have the heart to tell him that having had a Saturday job in my mother's garage throughout my teens, I probably knew a lot more about cars than he did. I wondered if he'd believe me if I told him how my mother had met Stephen when she'd stopped to help him change a flat tyre. I wished that Daniel would stop talking about cars and ask to see me again.

We turned into Cassie's road, and I told Daniel where to pull up outside her house.

'You live *here*?' Daniel said. 'What a fabulous place.'

'Oh, it's not mine. It belongs to my friend Cassie. Cassie Clarke the actress.'

'Princess Snowdrop,' Daniel said. 'Well, she certainly lives in a palace.' He was still staring admiringly at Cassie's house when the front door opened and Ryan came out, brandishing a garden spade. He started to clear the snow off the front steps. Daniel and I got out of the car. Ryan proceeded to watch with unabashed interest as I did my walk of shame across the slush-covered pavement.

'Hey, Ryan,' I said, 'this is Daniel. Daniel – Ryan.' I didn't bother with their surnames. The

97

Fallen Angel and Fleet Feet obviously recognised each other.

Leaving Ryan manfully shovelling snow, Daniel and I went into the house and shut the front door. Nadia, wearing a loosely tied silk dressing gown that revealed way too much of her cleavage, was in the hallway.

'Good morning, Lucy,' she said. Then she saw who I was with, and her eyes widened with surprise.

'Nadia – Daniel – Daniel – Nadia Pincher,' I said.

'Hello, Daniel,' Nadia said. 'It's a *real* pleasure to meet you. I absolutely adored *Fallen Angel*. I've seen it five times.'

I noticed that as well as being almost as short as my dress, Nadia's gown was very thin, and her nipples were clearly visible through the silk. If she was aware of this, she apparently didn't care.

'Thank you, Nadia,' Daniel said. 'It's always good to hear that someone likes my work.'

Nadia put her head on one side and twirled a strand of hair round her finger. 'I hope you don't mind my saying, but you're much better looking in the flesh than on screen. Don't you agree, Lucy?'

I stared at her. Did she actually think that flirting with Daniel Miller, when it was pretty obvious that I'd just spent the night with him, was entirely appropriate?

Without thinking, I said, 'I don't know. I've not seen *Fallen Angel*.'

'You've not seen it?' Daniel sounded shocked.

I felt my face grow hot. 'Not yet.'

Nadia couldn't hide her astonishment. 'I can't believe that you've not seen *Fallen Angel*. It's one of those films that everyone simply *has* to see.' Shaking her head at yet another example of my hopeless incompetence, she continued on her way, past Daniel and myself, and disappeared into the kitchen.

Go screw yourself, Nadia, I thought.

'Have you really not seen *Fallen Angel*?' Daniel said.

'No, I haven't,' I said. 'Despicable of me, I know. I missed it when it came out - I've been meaning to buy the DVD.' I felt terrible. I should have watched that film.

'So it wasn't my charismatic screen presence that got you into my bed?' Daniel said.

'No. Sorry. I was only after your body.'

Daniel laughed, and immediately I felt a lot better. We walked upstairs.

'Ryan? Nadia? I tried to run a bath, but there's no water. I think the pipes are frozen –' Cassie, loosely wrapped in a towel, came out of her bedroom on the floor above, and started to walk down the stairs. When she saw me and Daniel on the first floor landing, she gave a little shriek, and clutched the bath towel tight about her.

'Cassie – Daniel,' I said.

'Hello, Cassie,' Daniel said. 'I can't believe we haven't met before. I'm sure we're on a lot of the same guest lists.'

'Er, yes, I expect we are,' Cassie said.

To break the awkward silence which followed this

exchange, I said, 'Are you not working today?'

'I was supposed to be,' Cassie said, 'but most of the crew, including the director, are snowed in. Filming was cancelled.'

'Oh, right.' There was another awkward silence.

'Well, er, I guess I should…' Cassie scurried back inside her bedroom. Before we could be accosted by any more half-naked women, I dragged Daniel into my room and closed the door.

'What an interesting household,' Daniel said. 'An international footballer and three gorgeous girls. Which one of you does he belong to?'

'He's Cassie's footballer,' I said. 'They've been dating for a while, but they value their privacy, so keep it to yourself.'

'What about the other girl? The one whose tits are scared of the dark. Is she a friend of Cassie's like you?'

'She's Cassie's PA.'

'She and Cassie are very alike,' Daniel said. 'In looks, I mean. Not in their reaction to strange men seeing their tits. '

'You're right,' I said. 'They do look alike, but their personalities are very different.' Cassie is my friend, I thought, and Nadia most certainly isn't.

Daniel watched with an appreciative glint in his eyes while I stripped off my night before clothes, but made no attempt to dissuade me from putting on my jeans, a warm jumper and my boots. Neither did he say anything that made me think he was going to ask to see me again. I managed to get him out of the house without another encounter with Nadia's breasts, and he drove me to Reardon Haye.

'Thanks for the lift, Daniel,' I said, when we drew up outside the agency. 'I really appreciate it.' If he wants to see me again, I thought, he'll say so now. If he doesn't, then last night was just a one-night-stand.

Daniel kissed me. It was just a brush of his lips, but it was on my mouth. Ask to see me again, I thought. *Ask to see me again.*

'I'll call you,' he said.

I'll call you. Those words men say when they have absolutely no intention of phoning you *ever*.

That's that then, I thought. I smiled at Daniel, got out of his car, and went into Reardon Haye's building. Riding up in the lift to the third floor, I thought about my night with the Fallen Angel. The sex had been amazing. Despite my disappointment that there wasn't going to be a repeat performance, I wasn't sorry that I'd slept with him. Apart from anything else, it had been a while. It was good to know that I was back in the saddle, so to speak. It was only when I was unlocking the door to Reardon Haye's outer office that it occurred to me to wonder if shagging one of the agency's most important clients had been a wise move for my career.

Eleanor came into the agency soon after I did. I felt slightly sick when she stopped by my desk, but all she talked about was the party, not about anything that might have happened afterwards, before going into her own office. I reminded myself that all she, Maria and Adrian knew was that I'd shared a taxi with Daniel, they didn't *know* I'd spent the night with him, even if they may have suspected it. Thank goodness, I thought, there were no paparazzi outside Mojave last night.

Adrian arrived next. I steeled myself for his inevitable teasing, but he seemed strangely subdued. Apart from a couple of comments about the inclement weather, he sat at his computer, absorbed in whatever he had up on the screen. Last night he'd seemed perfectly sober, but I wondered if he had a hangover. An hour or so passed before Maria appeared, cursing trains that couldn't cope with a few inches of snow.

'It's the architects-next-door's Christmas party tonight,' she said. 'Shall we gatecrash like we usually do? They never seem to mind.'

'I can't,' Adrian said. 'I've been out every night this week, and my girlfriend is *not* very happy. If I go to another Christmas party, I'll be sleeping on the sofa.'

'Oh. Right,' Maria said. 'What about you, Lucy?'

'I'll come,' I said. 'Why not?' It's not like I'm doing anything else, I thought.

Eleanor's phone rang. Her door was open, and her voice carried clearly into the outer office.

'Hello, Daniel… You enjoyed the party?… I'm so glad… Yes… Yes, she's available… I'll put you through.'

Daniel. The ringing of the phone on my desk made me jump out of my chair. With a shaking hand, I picked up and held it to my ear.

'Lucy, I have Daniel Miller for you,' Eleanor said.

I heard a click as Eleanor transferred the call. 'Daniel?'

'Hey, Lucy. I said I'd call.'

'You did,' I said. I just didn't believe you, I thought.

'I've booked us a table at Quattro's for nine tonight – I hope you like Italian food. Can you meet me there?'

Can I meet Daniel Miller at one of London's most fashionable restaurants? 'Yes, I like Italian food. Yes, I can meet you there.'

'I'll see you later, then. Bye, lovely.'

'See you later.'

Daniel rang off. My hand was still shaking as I put down my phone.

'So, Lucy, am I right in thinking that you won't be coming to the architects' party?' Maria asked.

'Yes. I mean, no. I won't be coming to the party. Sorry.' I felt bad leaving Maria to gatecrash the party on her own. For about two seconds. My mother, who has a very low opinion of women who cancel on their female friends the moment a man asks them out, would have been horrified.

From behind his computer screen, Adrian said, 'Sounds like the goalkeeper is out of luck again tonight.'

CHAPTER 9

Cassie hung the tiny wooden reindeer on the six-foot high Christmas tree that almost obscured the living room window.

'Now for the star,' she said. 'Can you reach?'

'Just about.' Balancing on tip-toe, I placed the silver star on the topmost branch, and stepped back to admire Cassie's and my handiwork. The dark green tree, festooned with the painted wooden ornaments that we'd found just a few days ago in the Christmas market on the South Bank, looked wonderful, and infused the living room with the scent of pine. A Christmas garland hung over the fireplace, and sprays of holly with bright red berries decorated the mirror and picture frames. Cassie's music system was playing carols.

Cassie went to the dimmer switch, turned the main light down low, and switched on the coloured lights we'd strung around the tree amongst the pine needles. We both gasped with delight as the tree lit up.

'Now it's really starting to feel like Christmas,' I said. 'Ooh, I do love this time of year.' I gazed at the tree, and my mind drifted back to Christmas Eve when I was five years old. While my mother was reading me a bedtime story, Stephen had gone across the road to Cassie's to deliver her present. I'd been so excited when he'd returned with Cassie herself, and told me that she would be spending Christmas

Day and Boxing Day with us. My parents obviously hadn't known that she would be joining us – not until Stephen had discovered that in her parents' house, Christmas was no different to any other day of the year - but they'd managed to improvise gifts for their unexpected guest (sweets, paints, a miniature doll very like the dolls in my new dolls house), and had made the day as magical for her as it always was for Dylan and me.

Breaking in on my thoughts, Cassie said, 'I'm pleased Ryan wants me there with him and his parents and brothers at Christmas, really I am, but I'm so nervous about meeting them all.'

'Are you?' I said. 'But why?'

'What if they don't like me?' Cassie said. 'Ryan says they make a big deal out of Christmas. I don't want to ruin it for them.'

I tried, and failed, to imagine how Cassie's presence could have any adverse effects on the Fleet family's seasonal celebrations.

'Well, as long as you don't neck all the Bucks Fizz and fall asleep face down in the brandy butter,' I said, 'I expect you'll get along with them just fine.'

Cassie's smile was a little tight, but she did smile. She said, 'Is Daniel visiting his family for Christmas?'

'No,' I said, 'he's spending Christmas and New Year in Switzerland, skiing with friends.'

'So you won't be seeing much of him over the holidays?'

'He said he'd call me when he gets back.' This

time, I was reasonably sure he would call me. I'd watched him key my mobile number into his phone. And he'd given me his number to put in mine.

'Just so that I know I've got this clear,' Cassie said. 'Are you *with* Daniel Miller? Are you an item?'

'I – I'm not sure...'

When I'd arrived at Quattro's for my second date with Daniel, the restaurant had been packed. I was aware of sidelong glances from the other diners as I joined him for a drink in the bar, and when we were shown to our table, but Quattro's affluent clientele were too sophisticated to stare at us for any length of time. The wine waiter had mentioned that he'd enjoyed *Fallen Angel* immensely, and the maitre d' had asked us if we were happy with the food rather more times than I imagined was usual, but generally we were left alone like any twenty-something couple on a date. After our meal, Daniel's stellar status ensuring that the doorman hailed us a cab, we'd gone back to his flat. We'd had sex that night, and again in the morning, and I'd almost been late for work.

I said, 'I've been out with Daniel twice. And I've slept with him both times. Does that make us an *item*? Probably not, but I'd like it if we were.'

Cassie hesitated, and then she said, 'Daniel Miller may be *hot*, but is he boyfriend material?'

I shrugged. 'I don't know, Cassie. But I'm sure going to enjoy finding out.'

* * *

106

From what my friends tell me, my mother must be the only woman in England who, when her adult daughter comes home for Christmas, doesn't interrogate her about her love life, asking if she's seeing anyone, if she's met any nice men, if she has a *boyfriend*. Instead, the topics of conversation around my family's festive dinner table ranged from my job, to Stephen's latest commission, to the new apprentice at my mother's garage, who had an uncanny ability to restore old motors. Which suited me just fine. Until I knew where I stood with Daniel, I had no wish to discuss him with my relatives.

After the turkey, the Christmas pudding and the crackers, we adjourned to the living room for a game of charades, a tradition at Christmas from as far back as I could remember, and then we opened our presents. Stephen and my mother gave me a leather jacket. It was a beautiful pale biscuit colour, and fitted me perfectly, and I suspected that Stephen had chosen it because my mother, who is happiest in the overalls she wears for work, is hopeless at shopping for clothes. Having thanked my parents profusely, I unwrapped my present from Dylan, and found myself holding a DVD of *Fallen Angel*. My brother was surprised at how delighted I was with his gift, and suggested that we all watch the film together. I couldn't think of a way to get out of it that wouldn't hurt his feelings. Which meant that the first time I saw Daniel Miller on screen, the circumstances were not ideal. There is something totally cringe-worthy about watching a guy you've slept with playing a

107

sex-scene on the TV in the corner of your family's living room. With your mother, step-father and brother watching too. I loved the film, though. And Daniel's performance - when I managed to forget that my family were also viewing his tastefully lit musculature - took my breath away. (In the unlikely event that there is anyone who *still* hasn't seen *Fallen Angel*, I won't give away the plot, but I will say that a tear ran down my face in the final reel.)

As the end credits rolled, Stephen said, 'I'm actually quite surprised at how good an actor that Daniel Miller is. I assumed it was his face that got him work.'

'Because he's beautiful, you didn't think he'd be able to act?' I said.

My mother muttered, 'Handsome is as handsome does.'

'People do get cast just on looks, though,' Dylan said. 'Isn't that right, Lucy?'

'It has been known to happen.' So much for not talking about Daniel. 'But not in his case. He's very talented. And very charming.' *And very good in bed.*

'You've met him?' Stephen asked.

'Yes, I've met him several times.' *I've had hot sex with him in three different positions.* 'He's one of my agency's most important clients.'

'It must be weird meeting celebrities all the time,' Dylan said.

'It's not all the time,' I said. 'And I'm used to it.'

'I guess you must be,' Dylan said, 'since you live with Princess Snowdrop.'

We talked about Cassie then (I told them that she was dating Ryan Fleet. And swore them to secrecy, which they found faintly ridiculous), and for the moment, as far as my family was concerned, the Fallen Angel was forgotten.

Sometime later, my mother announced that she couldn't keep her eyes open any longer. She and Stephen headed off upstairs. Dylan and I did some sibling bonding over the last of the mince pies, and then he too said goodnight. I waited until I judged the others would be asleep, and then I watched *Fallen Angel* again, with the scenes that Daniel wasn't in on fast forward. I also watched the DVD Extras, the deleted scenes and the interviews with the director and the cast, including Daniel's interview (although I knew most of what he was saying about the shooting of the movie because he'd already told me to my face). Then, deciding that I was behaving more like a deranged obsessive fan than a girl who worked in showbusiness, I switched off the DVD player and went upstairs to the bedroom that had been Dylan's before I'd moved to London.

I'd just climbed into the single bed that took up half the floor-space, when my phone vibrated with a text: *Are you still awake? Cassie xx*

I texted back that I was indeed, and almost immediately, she rang me.

'I know it's late,' she said, breathlessly, 'but now that Ryan's asleep, I simply had to talk to you.'

'Is everything OK?' I said.

'Oh, yes,' Cassie said. 'Everything's *wonderful*.

I'm calling because I wanted to tell you that I've had the most amazing day. Ryan's family are lovely – they made me feel so welcome.'

I smiled. 'That's good to hear, Cassie.'

'I don't know why I was so worried about meeting them,' Cassie continued. 'Ryan's mother was so kind to me. She told me she was really happy to have another woman in the house.'

'I guess with a husband and four sons she must feel a little outnumbered at times.'

Cassie laughed. 'That's what she said.' After a short silence, she added, 'today reminded me of the Christmases I spent with your family. Ryan's lot even played charades after lunch – just like your family used to do when we were children.'

'We played charades today too,' I said. 'It wouldn't be a proper Christmas without a game of charades.'

'I want a large family,' Cassie said. 'Not right now, obviously, but one day I'd like to see my own children gathered around my table for Christmas lunch.'

'Oh, me too,' I said, 'but not for years. Not for decades.'

Cassie laughed again. Then she said, 'I suppose I'd better let you go to sleep – and get to bed myself. I want to be up early tomorrow to have breakfast with Ryan before he goes to football.'

'Goodnight, then,' I said. 'I'm glad your first meeting with Ryan's family went so well. Not that there was ever any reason why it shouldn't.'

'Goodnight, Lucy. Merry Christmas.'
'Merry Christmas, Cassie.'

CHAPTER 10

Daniel came out of Eleanor's office where he'd been discussing the last-minute changes to the script of *Fallen Angel II* (more nudity required) that were going to make his already considerable fee even more considerable, and walked over to my desk.

'How long are you going to be?' he said. 'Shall I wait?'

'I'll be another hour at least,' I said. 'Why don't you go home and start packing, and I'll come straight over once I've finished here.'

Eleanor put her head round her office door. 'Go with him now, Lucy. Make sure that he's got everything he needs for tomorrow. Like his passport.'

'The thing with the passport wasn't really my fault, Eleanor,' Daniel said with a flash of white teeth.

The previous week, he'd phoned Reardon Haye and announced that his passport had been stolen from his jacket (Eleanor assumed he'd lost it). Which was not good, as *Fallen Angel II* was due to start filming in a few days' time. In New York. Fortunately, he was enough of a VIP to be fast-tracked at the passport office. (No, it's not fair that A-listers get special treatment, but such is life.)

'Lucy, I'm counting on you to see that he's on that plane.' Eleanor, immune to the charm of Daniel's boyish grin, ducked back inside her office.

'Looks like I'm coming home with you,' I said to Daniel.

'Have a good trip, Daniel,' Maria said.

'Yeah, hope the shoot goes well,' Adrian added.

'See you guys in two months,' Daniel said.

I fought a rising panic. Two months. Daniel was going off on location for a whole two months. And I had no idea if our fledgling relationship was strong enough to survive.

I'd been dating him for six weeks now. After Christmas, I'd stayed on with my family, celebrating New Year's Eve in our local pub, with Dylan and a crowd of our old school friends. On New Year's Day, I'd headed back to London, and spent a quiet evening at home with Cassie and Ryan. On 2nd January, I went back to work, and scoured the internet for news of Daniel. There wasn't any. On 3rd January, he'd called me.

We didn't go out that night. Instead, I'd gone to his flat and he'd cooked (well, he'd micro-waved a ready-meal and lit a couple of candles), and we'd eaten and drunk wine, and then he taken me to his bed...

Since then we'd seen each other several times a week. The majority of our dates had been in fashionable bars and restaurants, but so far we'd managed to avoid the paparazzi, and the name of the Fallen Angel's latest squeeze had not appeared in the press. I'd got used to being half of a couple, to sleeping next to Daniel's toned, muscular body. To having him stop by my desk and kiss my cheek whenever he came into the agency (if Eleanor had

113

any issues with my dating a client, she'd kept them to herself). To hearing him say to a radio interviewer that yes, he was seeing someone, but it was a very new relationship, so he'd rather not talk about it in case he jinxed it, and to know that he meant me. I didn't want it all to end with him shagging his co-star in a New York hotel. Which, given his track record, was not entirely unlikely.

From inside her office, Eleanor said, 'Mr Miller, why are you still here?'

Daniel laughed. 'Bye then,' he said to Adrian and Maria. 'Keep an eye on Lucy for me while I'm in the States.'

'We will,' Maria said.

I grabbed my bag and my coat, and with Daniel's hand resting on the small of my back, we headed out of the office.

Just as I was closing the door, I heard Maria say to Adrian, 'He seems very keen on her.'

Daniel's warm brown eyes met mine. 'He is. She's his girlfriend.'

'Oh, Daniel...' A warm glow spread through me as I realised it was the first time he'd called me his *girlfriend* to my face. I thought, maybe it'll be OK. Maybe in two months he'll come back to me.

We got into the lift, and he kissed me all the way down to the ground floor.

'Are you sure you don't want me to come with you to the airport?' I said to Daniel the next morning.

'No, I hate airport goodbyes,' Daniel said. 'And

there are always photographers hanging round the entrance to the VIP lounge. I don't want us splashed across the tabloids just when I'm leaving the country. It wouldn't be fair on you to have to deal with the press on your own.'

'Oh. I forgot about the paparazzi.' I put the idea of a romantic farewell at the airport (with me kissing my boyfriend in departures, before heading up to the viewing area to wave to his plane and maybe shed a few tears), out of my mind.

The ring of the front door bell told us that Daniel's car had arrived. He pressed the intercom and told the driver he'd be down in five.

'Have you got your passport?' I asked.

'Shhh.' Daniel stood in front of me and put a finger on my lips. Then he kissed me, his tongue in my mouth, one arm about my waist, a hand entwined in my hair. I pressed myself against him, and felt him grow hard. With an effort I lifted my mouth from his, and stepped away from him. Both of us were gasping.

'Daniel, you have to go,' I said. 'You'll miss your plane.'

He ran a hand through his hair. 'Right now, I don't care.'

Fighting the urge to tear off Daniel's clothes, I opened the front door. With a sigh, he picked up the two suitcases that I'd packed for him (he'd turned out to be hopeless at packing) and headed towards the lift. I followed with his hand-luggage.

Outside, standing on the pavement, while the

driver was stashing the suitcases in the boot, Daniel kissed me again. It was a tender, gentle kiss. Which was just as well – if he'd kissed me in the street the way he'd kissed me in the flat, we'd have been arrested. Then, without saying a word, he got into the car. I stood by the kerb, blinking back tears, as the car drove off. Daniel looked back once. Then he was gone. For two long months.

I went back into his flat, with the intention of tidying away the detritus of last night's take-away (and having a good cry), before taking myself back to Cassie's house. There, on the dining table, was Daniel's passport.

CHAPTER 11

'Oh, no,' Cassie said. 'What did you do?'

'I called his mobile,' I said. 'And told him to have the car turn around and come back for it. Fortunately, he hadn't gone very far.'

'He still made his flight?'

'Just. Thank goodness. Or I'd never have been able to face Eleanor on Monday.' We were drinking coffee in Cassie's living room. It was still only mid-morning, but it seemed ages since Daniel had kissed me and said goodbye.

'And are you all right, Lucy?' Cassie said. 'I remember when Ryan went to Spain, I felt *awful*.'

'I'm OK now,' I said. 'When Daniel left for the airport, I was ready to *howl*. But then, when I found his passport, I had to pull myself together. I'll miss him while he's away, but I'm not about to start wallowing on your sofa all day in my pyjamas.'

'I should think not,' Cassie said. 'Besides, you can always fly out and visit him. I'm sure Reardon Haye can manage without you for a few days. Take some leave when Daniel's halfway through the shoot.'

'I thought of that.' Unfortunately Daniel hadn't thought of it. Or if he had thought of it, he hadn't mentioned it. 'But he's going to be working six days a week.'

'That still leaves one day when he can be with you. And the nights.'

Nights spent in Daniel's bed, I thought. Yes

117

please. Aloud I said, 'Plane tickets to New York are expensive.'

'I'll pay,' Cassie said.

'I couldn't let you do that.'

'Why not?'

'It wouldn't feel right.'

'I would very much like to pay for your plane tickets so that you get to visit Daniel while he's away on location,' Cassie said. 'Look on it as my way of paying back a little of what I owe your family.'

'You don't *owe* my family anything. We all loved having you spend time with us – we missed you when you moved away.'

Cassie's eyebrows drew together in a frown. 'You really don't get it, do you, Lucy?'

'Get what?'

'Come with me,' Cassie said.

Bemused, I got up and followed her out of the living room, along the hallway and out the front door. She crossed the road and stood on the opposite kerb, facing her house. I stood next to her.

'Why do you think I bought this place?' she said to me.

I thought, I have absolutely no idea. 'Because it's the sort of house a TV star would live in?'

'Look at it more carefully.'

I studied the house, but nothing came to me.

Cassie said, 'I bought it because it reminded me of your dolls house.'

I was taken aback. 'I suppose it does look like it. A bit. If it were pink and not white -'

Cassie was striding back across the road. Mildly alarmed by her erratic behaviour, I hurried after her.

Back in the living room, seated on the sofa, her legs curled up under her, she said, 'You probably think I'm crazy.'

'No I don't. Well, maybe just a little. But I'm sure you're crazy in a good way. I mean, why not buy a house because it looks like a dolls house you played with when you were a child?'

'I want you to understand how important you and your family are to me.'

'I get that.'

'I don't think you do.' For a moment, Cassie stared off into the distance, and then she said, 'How much *exactly* do you know about my parents?'

'I know they more or less left you to fend for yourself.' Even when we were children, I'd known that Cassie's parents didn't look after her the way my parents looked after me and Dylan. I'd accepted, without question, my mother's explanation that Cassie's parents were 'too tired' to take her to school or go to work, even while sensing her disapproval. Back then, I'd been too young to understand words like 'feckless' and 'neglect.'

'My father,' Cassie said, 'was a drug addict and a thief who was in and out of prison. My mother was an alcoholic who brought men back to our house and went with them for money. The reason we upped and left the area when I was thirteen was because my father couldn't pay his dealer what he owed and it wasn't safe for us to stay. We moved around a lot, and ended up living in a squat. A few months later, I was taken into care. I haven't seen my parents since. Thank God.'

There was a long silence while I absorbed what she had told me.

Eventually I said, 'I'd no idea. I - I'm so sorry.' My words sounded hopelessly inadequate.

'No-one knew quite how bad things were for me at home. Not even Laura and Stephen.'

'But... why didn't you tell them?'

'I was a child,' Cassie said, 'and children don't see things the same way as adults. I got it into my head that your parents wouldn't like me anymore – or let me play with you and Dylan – if they knew.'

'Oh, Cassie, that would never have happened.' A memory surfaced of me and my mother surveying the racks of newly-arrived *Princess Snowdrop* DVDs in our local supermarket, not long after the first series had been shown on TV. Having exclaimed with pleasure over her success as an actress, my mother had told me how concerned she and Stephen had been for the neglected Cassie, and how they'd often wondered if they could – or should – have done more for her. 'My parents would have wanted to help you,' I said.

'They did help me,' Cassie said. 'If it hadn't been for their welcoming me into their home, I'd have no idea how normal, decent people live or how they care for their children, no idea what it's like to be part of a loving family. If it wasn't for Stephen helping me with my homework and lending me books, I'd be illiterate, and even more ignorant than I am now. If Laura hadn't fed me, I'd have gone hungry. If she hadn't told me that a woman can do anything, be anything, if she puts her mind to it, I'd have probably ended up on the street.'

'I don't know what to say...' My throat constricted, and my eyes pricked with tears.

'I've never told anyone else about my parents,' Cassie continued. 'Not even Ryan. I don't want sympathy, and I certainly don't want sob-stories about my childhood in the press – it really wouldn't fit Snowdrop's image. So please keep what I've just told you to yourself.'

'Of course.'

'Don't look so sad, Lucy. I had a rough start, and a few tough years after I left care, but it was all a long time ago. When I'm filming my TV show, or at some glitzy showbiz event, or even when I look around this house, I have to say that I think I'm doing all right.'

'You've made a good life for yourself,' I said.

'But I wouldn't have any of it,' Cassie said, 'I wouldn't be Princess Snowdrop, if your parents hadn't been so kind to me when I was a child. So please let me have the pleasure of treating you to a plane ticket now that I can.' She smiled, and I found myself smiling back.

'Thank you,' I said. 'I really appreciate the offer. But I'm still not flying to New York.'

Cassie rolled her eyes. 'Why ever not?'

'Daniel hasn't invited me.'

'He hasn't?' Cassie said. 'Then invite yourself.'

'I can't,' I said. 'I don't want him to think I'm clingy.'

'It's hardly being clingy to –' Cassie's voice broke off. 'Nadia. Hi.'

I turned my head to see Nadia standing just outside the living room. I wondered how long she'd been there. For reasons I couldn't readily explain, even to myself, the thought that she might have overheard Cassie's and my conversation made me feel vaguely uneasy.

'Cassie, you need to change and do your hair and make-up,' Nadia said. 'The car will be here in an hour.'

'What? Oh, yes, Princess Snowdrop is opening a children's centre this afternoon. I'd completely forgotten.' Cassie got to her feet. 'Duty calls.'

She went out, and Nadia came into the living room and took her place on the sofa.

'I know you don't mean to be irresponsible Lucy,' Nadia said, 'but when Cassie has a PR gig, you do need to keep an eye on the time. It wouldn't look good if Princess Snowdrop kept her young fans waiting.'

Gritting my teeth, I said, 'I'm sure you'd never let her be late for a gig, Nadia.'

'Well, I do pride myself on my exceptional organisational skills,' Nadia said. 'But don't fret, Lucy, I do understand if you're a little distracted right now. With Daniel out of the country, you must be worried sick.'

'What do you mean?' I said.

'We all know what actors are like. It's only natural to be concerned. But you have to remember DCOL. Have you heard that expression before? Doesn't Count On Location.'

'I know what DCOL stands for.' Daniel had told me.

'Then you'll also know that even if Daniel sleeps with another girl while he's off filming, it probably won't mean anything. I'm sure you two will be able to pick up where you left off once he's back in England.'

I gaped at her. 'That is so wrong on so many levels.'

'Oh, Lucy, you are such an innocent.' Nadia smiled sweetly. 'Then again, maybe Daniel is so besotted with you that he won't even *look* at other women while he's away. It's odd that he didn't ask you to go to New York with him, though… Will you be visiting him during the shoot?'

'I don't think so.' As you know very well, I thought, because you were obviously listening while I was talking to Cassie.

'How long is he away?' Nadia asked.

'Two months.'

'That long?' Nadia raised her eyebrows. Then she stood up, smoothing down her skirt, checking her reflection in the glass of the French windows that led to the garden, smiling at what she saw. 'Anyway, I must crack on. I need to print out Cassie's schedule for next week. Try not to worry too much, Lucy.'

With another sickly sweet smile, she walked out of the room.

That was when I decided that Nadia was a complete and utter bitch.

CHAPTER 12

Eleanor held up two pieces of thick cream card, and said, 'I have here two tickets for the Star Gazer Gala, which is one of my favourite events in the showbiz calendar. As my sister has very selfishly decided to get married this weekend, my husband and I can't go. So you three can fight or toss a coin over who gets to go in my place. Or if you've made other plans for Saturday night, I'll give them to one of our clients.'

'I went to the gala a couple of years ago,' Adrian said.

'I remember,' Eleanor said. 'I'd just given birth, so I couldn't go that time either.'

'So if Maria or Lucy would like the tickets,' Adrian went on, 'that's fine by me.'

'See you on Saturday, Lucy?' Maria said.

'Great,' I said. I'd never actually heard of the Star Gazer Gala, but given Eleanor's enthusiasm, I decided it was definitely an event that a theatrical agent like myself should be keen to go to.

'Enjoy.' Eleanor handed Maria and me a ticket and disappeared inside her office.

'It's a fundraiser,' Maria said to me before I could scrutinise my ticket. 'And yet another one of those networking opportunities that you'll have heard so much about since you started working at Reardon Haye.'

'It's also a good night out,' Adrian said. 'You get a meal and a cabaret performed by the stars of a West

End musical. They give their services for free because it's for charity. There's also dancing at some point.'

'Everyone really dresses up,' Maria said. 'We're talking ball gowns for the girls and DJs for the guys.'

'Yeah, it's full on glitz,' Adrian said. 'The year I went, one woman wore a tiara.'

'It sounds fabulous.' I wondered if I'd be able to avoid the dancing.

'It'll do you good to get out of the house, Lucy,' Adrian said. 'You can't be sitting at home every night pining for Daniel.'

I shot Adrian a withering glance. While I obviously missed Daniel, wished he would call more often, and couldn't wait for him to be back in England, I hadn't sat around moping and waiting for him to phone. Instead, I'd used my boyfriend's absence to put in extra hours at work, to pay another visit to my family, and to spend some time with Cassie, whom I'd rather neglected in the six weeks that Daniel and I had been together. The fact that there had been no stories in the press or on the internet about the Fallen Angel doing the dirty with any of the film's cast or crew had been a plus.

'Thank you for your concern, Adrian,' I said, 'but I can assure you that I'm not pining away. The shoot's half over, and I'm sure I can survive another month.'

From inside her office, Eleanor said, 'You can pine for Daniel all you want, Lucy. As long as you do it in your own time.'

Saturday afternoon found me standing in front of my bedroom mirror looking at my reflection in despair. As none of the dresses in my London wardrobe could possibly be described as a ball gown, I'd bought myself a new ankle-length dress, pale coral in colour and vaguely Grecian in style. When I'd tried it on in the shop I'd loved it, but now that I'd got it home, I realised that while it would have been ideal for a beach wedding on a Greek island, it wasn't nearly formal enough for a charity gala attended by the great and good of the British stage and screen.

My mobile rang. Still looking at my reflection in the mirror, I picked it up and hit the answer key.

'Lucy. Hi. It's Maria.'

'Hi, hun,' I said, making an effort to sound considerably more upbeat than I felt. 'I'm glad you phoned because I'm having a bit of a crisis over my dress –'

'Lucy, listen,' Maria said. 'I'm sorry but I'm not going to be able to make it tonight.'

What? 'But why not? I mean, are you OK?'

'No, actually I'm totally not OK. I have the worst migraine ever. Pounding head. Flashing lights. Throwing up.'

'Poor you. Would you like me to come over?' I'd never been to Maria's flat, but I knew she lived in Swiss Cottage. 'I can easily get a train.'

'That's very sweet of you, but all I want to do is go to bed and sleep it off. I'm sure you'd be fine going to the gala on your own tonight...'

'Oh, yes, don't worry,' I said, willing myself to stay calm. In just a few hours, I'd be representing Reardon Haye at a prestigious, high profile event all on my own. No pressure there.

'…But I've arranged for a courier to bring you my ticket,' Maria continued. 'He should be with you within the next half hour. I know it's late notice, but I thought you might like to invite a friend to go with you…' Maria's voice faltered, and then she said, 'Sorry, Lucy, I really do need to go and lie down.' She rang off.

I studied my reflection gloomily. Maybe I'd look OK if I wore enough jewellery.

Twenty minutes later, every necklace, bangle and pair of earrings that I owned tried on and rejected, I heard a knock on my door, followed by Cassie saying, 'Lucy? Are you there?'

I opened the door so that she could come in.

'A motorcycle courier just delivered this for you,' she said. 'I signed for it.'

'Thanks.' I took the envelope containing Maria's ticket and tossed it onto my bed. 'Cassie, are you doing anything tonight?'

'Yes, I am. Ryan's team are playing at home this week. I'm meeting him after the game, and we're going for a meal with the team's manager and his wife. Why do you ask?'

I gestured towards the envelope. 'I have a spare ticket for the Star Gazer Gala. Maria and I were going together, but she has a migraine.'

'Oh, if I hadn't agreed to go for this meal, I'd

have definitely come with you. I bought tickets last year. It's a great night and such a good cause... Lucy, I don't mean to be rude, but are you thinking of wearing that dress to the gala? You look lovely, but it's a little informal.'

'Welcome to my world. No-one to go out with on a Saturday night and nothing suitable to wear. I don't suppose you have a tiara you could lend me?'

'I think I can do a bit better than that.' Cassie put her hands on her hips and looked me up and down. 'OK. This is the plan. You start making phone calls. You must know someone who'd be up for a free meal. I'll start going through my evening dresses. I've so many, there must be one that's perfect for you.' Tucking her hair determinedly behind her ears, Cassie swept out of my bedroom. I picked up my mobile and opened my address book.

The obvious person to have Maria's ticket was Adrian, so I called him first. His phone rang several times before he answered.

'Hi Adrian,' I said. 'It's Lucy –'

He interrupted me to say, 'Could you call back later? It's not such a good time for me right now.'

'I'll talk quickly. Maria's not well and can't make the gala tonight.'

'What's wrong with her?'

'Migraine. Would you like her ticket?'

Before Adrian could answer, I heard an angry female voice say, 'Who are you talking to? Get off your frickin' phone and come here.'

Definitely not a good time for me to have called, I

thought. 'I'm guessing you don't want Maria's ticket.'

'Er, no. Why don't you offer it to Ruby? You know how starstruck she is. I'm sure she'd love to go to a showbiz event.'

The female voice shrieked, 'Adrian! Get off your phone or I'm out that door.'

'I have to go.' Adrian ended the call.

I rang Ruby's mobile. Her phone went straight to voicemail. I trawled through my address book. If any of my uni friends were at a loose end this Saturday, they lived too far away from London for me to invite them to an event that was due to start in just a few hours. Then I saw Owen Somers' number. For a moment I couldn't understand why I had it in my own phone rather than my work phone, but then I remembered I'd added it before I'd gone to see his play. He'd had several minor roles since then, a walk-on in a TV series, a speaking part (but with only one line) in a film, and an advert. I'd still not managed to get him seen for a lead on stage or screen, but I was working hard on it. I was convinced it was only a matter of time.

I could invite Owen to the gala, I thought. Maria had said it was good for networking. Eleanor had talked about giving the tickets to a client. I pressed the call button on my phone, and he answered straight away.

'Hey, Lucy. I don't usually hear from Reardon Haye on a Saturday.' He obviously thought I was phoning him about a job.

'Before you get your hopes up,' I said, 'I'm not calling about an audition. I'm representing the agency at the Star Gazer Gala tonight, and I find myself with a spare ticket. I wondered if you'd like to come with me.' To my embarrassment, I realised that it sounded like I was asking him out on a date. Quickly, I added, 'As long as your girlfriend wouldn't mind, of course. If you've not got other plans for tonight. And if you have a dinner jacket.'

'I can borrow a dinner jacket. I don't have a girlfriend.'

'Oh, did you and Julie break up?' I felt my face grow hot. 'I'm sorry.'

'Julie?'

'You introduced me to her in the wine bar after I came to see you in *Siblings.'*

'You thought Julie Diaz was my *girlfriend*?' Owen sounded incredulous. 'Whatever made you think that?'

'You seemed like you were close. You talked about her at the Reardon Haye party. You said she'd invited you for Christmas.'

'She's a close friend of mine,' Owen said. 'She knew I wouldn't be spending Christmas with my family, so she invited me to spend it with hers. But I've never dated her. Or even thought about dating her.'

'You're just good friends?'

'Yep.' After a pause, Owen said, 'So you didn't recognise her.'

'Should I have?'

'Her full name - her stage name – is Julie Farrell Diaz. She's married to the actor Zac Diaz, who is also a good friend of mine. They're quite a famous showbiz couple.'

'I'm sorry, but I've not heard of them. A fine theatrical agent I am.'

Owen laughed. 'There's no need to apologise. I don't expect my agent to know *everyone* in showbusiness. Actually, a while back, Julie mentioned something about the Star Gazer Gala. She and Zac may be going. If they're there, I'll introduce you properly.'

'You'll come with me then?'

'I'd be delighted to escort you to the Star Gazer Gala,' Owen said. 'As long as your boyfriend doesn't mind, of course.'

'My boyfriend's out of town,' I said. 'He won't even know about it.'

Cassie came back into my bedroom, holding something behind her back. I told Owen the time of the gala, said that I'd meet him outside the Hyde Park Hotel where it was being held, and rang off.

'All sorted?' Cassie said.

'Yes. I'm taking a client. Owen Somers. You met him at the Reardon Haye Christmas party.'

'Tall, blond and cute? With extraordinary blue eyes?'

'That's him.'

'I didn't talk to him for very long, but he seemed like a nice guy.'

'He is. So now all I need to worry about is my dress.'

'I believe I have that covered.'

With a flourish, from behind her back, Cassie produced a long evening dress. It had a plunging halter-neck and a high waist, and it was made of midnight blue silk, so dark as to be almost black, with a gossamer-fine overskirt that shimmered silver in the light.

'It's gorgeous,' I said. 'But do you think it'll look good on me? I don't usually suit dark colours.'

'Try it on and see.'

I took off the dress I was wearing and stepped carefully into the dress that Cassie held out to me. She helped me with the halter tie and the zip. I turned to face the mirror.

'Oooh.' A smile spread across my face. 'I look…'

'Beautiful? Sophisticated? Hot? All of the above?'

'I'm not going to lie to you,' I said. 'I feel amazing in this dress.'

'Good. Let me get the tags off it.'

'It's still got the tags on? Haven't you worn it? Are you sure you don't mind me borrowing it?'

'You can keep it.' Cassie ripped off the price tags before I could see how much the dress had cost. 'Wait here.'

She raced out of my room and came back brandishing a pair of silver shoes and a matching clutch bag.

'It's so lucky we're the same size,' she said. 'Now, how are you going to do your hair?'

'Well, I thought up rather than down.'

'How about up but with lots of loose curls?'

Cassie said. 'Would you like me to style it for you? Princess Snowdrop is rather good at that sort of thing. She goes to a lot of balls and parties.'

'Why, thank you, Your Highness.'

Cassie danced a few steps around my room. 'Don't you just adore getting ready for a date?' She looked and sounded much younger than her twenty-five years.

'I do,' I said. 'But tonight isn't a date.'

'No. No, of course not. I don't know why I said that.'

'I have a boyfriend,' I said. 'His name is Daniel Miller.'

'That's the name of the guy you're dating?' Cassie said, smiling. 'I think I've heard that name before. Is he an actor?'

'He's done a bit of acting.'

'OK, Lucy,' Cassie said. 'Pass me your straighteners, and I'll fix your hair for your not-a-date with Owen Somers.'

CHAPTER 13

The Mercedes edged slowly through the Park Lane traffic, and drew up outside the Hyde Park Hotel. The driver sprang out and opened the rear passenger door.

'Thank you,' I said, climbing out of the car and onto the pavement in what I hoped was a suitably elegant manner for a girl wearing a designer dress and a faux fur coat.

'You're very welcome, Miss Ashford,' the driver said. 'I'll be back at one a.m to pick you up. You have a good night.'

'Thanks,' I said again. When I'd told Cassie I was intending to travel to the Star Gazer Gala by tube she'd been horrified, and had insisted on booking me a car, and charging it to her account. I did appreciate not having to negotiate the Saturday night crowds and the escalators in a floor-length gown.

The car drove off. I looked around for Owen. The pavement outside the hotel was crowded with people in evening dress heading into the gala, but I spotted him standing by the entrance. He scrubbed up rather well, I thought, even if his borrowed DJ was a little tight across the shoulders. He was talking to a girl wearing a red dress, who I recognised as Julie Diaz, and a tall, dark-haired man, who since he had his arm around her waist, I assumed was Julie's husband, Zac. They were a strikingly good-looking couple. And according to Owen, they were well-known in showbusiness. Feeling slightly intimidated, I went and joined my client.

'Lucy. Hi.' Owen greeted me with a kiss on each side of my face. 'You've met my friend Julie…'

Julie and I smiled and nodded at each other.

'This is her husband, Zac Diaz,' Owen went on. 'Zac, this is Lucy Ashford, my agent.'

'Good to meet you,' I said.

'And you,' Zac said.

'Julie and Zac have been asked to sing for us tonight,' Owen said.

'I'll look forward to that.' If Owen's friends are performing at the Star Gazer Gala, I thought, they must have played leads in the West End. I decided to Google Zac and Julie Diaz at the first opportunity.

'I hope you don't mind, Lucy,' Zac said, 'but when Owen told me that you and he were coming tonight, I phoned my aunt and had her put us all on the same table. She's on the Star Gazer fundraising committee.'

'Of course I don't mind,' I said, happy to sit with Owen's friends. Besides which, I was pretty sure that sharing a table with the relatives of one of the gala's organisers counted as good networking.

Julie said, 'Shall we go in? I'd like to check out the stage.'

We went into the hotel where an army of hostesses, all wearing slinky black evening gowns, stood ready to relieve us of our coats, and usher us into a flower-bedecked, candle-lit ballroom. Our table was one of many placed around a small dance floor, and we were sharing it with an actress friend of Julie's and her lawyer husband, and a young up-and-coming comedian and his scriptwriter (I was quite unable to tell if their relationship was anything other than professional). Looking round at the people sat at the other tables, I saw many famous faces, actors I recognised from TV, several of Reardon Haye's clients, a politician who was known to be a generous patron of the arts and a couple of casting directors. Then, as my gaze wandered over the tables on the far side of the room, I found myself looking directly at Nadia.

She was sitting with a group of people I didn't know. I did, however, recognise the man sitting next to her. Sam Hurst, the film director. The last time I'd seen them together had been at BarRacuda. The night Ryan had been photographed with a mystery blonde. The night I was convinced that Nadia had cheated on her boyfriend Leo. Who was not amongst the people sitting at Nadia's table.

Owen, sitting next to me and noticing who I was looking at, said, 'Isn't that Nadia Pincher?'

Before I could answer, Julie Diaz, who was sitting on the other side of Owen, said, 'Yes, it is.'

'Oh, do you know Nadia?' I said.

'Not really,' Julie said. 'Not any more. I used to work with her, but I haven't seen her in years. Is she a client of yours?'

I shook my head. 'She's my friend Cassie Clarke's PA.'

At that moment, Nadia looked up and saw the

three of us staring at her. For an instant she looked startled, but then she smiled and waved. I waved back. She said something to Sam Hurst, and then she got to her feet and walked across the dance floor to our table. She was wearing a gold dress that clung to her in all the right places, and however much I disliked her, I had to admit she looked good in it.

'Julie!' Nadia exclaimed as she reached our table. 'Zac! How lovely to see you both. It's been an *age*.'

'Hello, Nadia,' Julie said, with considerably less enthusiasm.

Zac, who was talking to the scriptwriter, nodded at Nadia, but didn't interrupt his conversation. Nadia positioned herself behind my chair.

'I wasn't expecting to see *you* here tonight, Lucy,' she said. 'If you'd told me you were coming, we could have shared a cab.'

I felt compelled to say, 'You can travel home with me, if you like. I've a car booked for one o'clock.'

Ignoring my grudging offer of a lift, Nadia said, 'You look different tonight, Lucy. Not at all your usual style. That dress you're wearing... Is it Cassie's?'

'Yes, it is. Well, it was. She gave it to me.'

'And I see you have one of her bags as well. She's so generous to you.'

'She certainly is.' You patronising cow, I thought.

Nadia turned to Owen. 'And here's another blast from the past. Long time no see, Owen. I hear you're an actor these days. How's that working out?'

'It's working out just fine.' Owen smiled at me.

'Thanks to my amazing agent.'

'Lucy is doing well, isn't she?' Nadia said. 'Particularly for someone so young and in her first job. Did you know that before she started at Reardon Haye she'd never worked in showbusiness?'

'No I didn't know that,' Owen said.

'Oh yes, if it wasn't for Cassie Clarke persuading Eleanor Haye to take her on,' Nadia continued, 'Lucy wouldn't have had a chance of becoming a theatrical agent. She knows very little about the industry.'

'Is that so?' Owen said.

'But you mustn't worry that having Lucy as your agent will hold you back in your career. I'm sure her hard work makes up for her lack of experience.'

Nadia has just told Owen that I'm not fit to represent him, I thought. My face grew hot. I opened my mouth to say something in my own defence, but no words came out, so I shut it again. Mortified, I glanced at Owen. His expression was unreadable. Next to him, Julie Diaz, visibly embarrassed, shifted uncomfortably in her chair. Fortunately, the others at the table, engrossed in their own conversations, hadn't heard what Nadia had said. Or if they had, they were pretending they hadn't.

Owen said, 'Lucy does work hard on my behalf. That's how she gets me so many auditions.'

I flashed Owen a grateful smile. Nadia, however, wasn't listening to him. Her attention was on her own table on the other side of the room, where Sam Hurst was talking to a curvaceous Shakespearean actress.

'Well it's been great catching up with you all,' Nadia said, 'but I mustn't abandon my other friends. I'll let you know if I need to come home in the car with you, Lucy.'

I gaped at her. Did she seriously expect me to give her a lift home when she'd deliberately humiliated me in front of a client?

Abruptly, Nadia turned on her heel and walked back across the dance floor to her own table. I watched as she slid into her seat next to the film director, touching his arm to get his attention, reaching up to brush his hair out of his eyes, and leaning close to whisper in his ear.

Poor Leo, I thought.

'That woman is a piece of work,' Owen said.

I took a deep breath. 'Owen, what Nadia said about me –'

Owen's blue eyes looked directly into mine. 'You're good at what you do, Lucy, I really don't care how long you've been doing it.' With a grin, he added, 'Anyway, from what I've seen of the agency, the extremely experienced Eleanor Haye keeps a pretty close watch on the rest of you.'

Our talk was interrupted at that point by the arrival of the first course of our five-course meal, and I made a conscious decision to put Nadia out of my mind for the rest of the evening. The food was delicious and exquisitely presented (and more than enough for me, although I noticed Owen eating his way through the bread basket), and the wine and the conversation flowed. Like most actors, Owen's friends were good company, with an endless supply of anecdotes about their chosen profession, and the comedian had us in fits of laughter with his jokes.

The waiters were bringing round the coffee when Julie said, 'Zac, we need to get backstage.'

'Yeah, time to sing for our supper,' Zac said.

'Break a leg guys,' Owen said to them.

A few minutes after they had gone, a piano was wheeled out onto the low stage at the far end of the ballroom. The lights dimmed and then went out altogether. The talk and laughter, which had been deafening until then, faded into silence. A spotlight came on to reveal Julie Diaz alone in the centre of the stage. Another spotlight shone on Zac Diaz sitting at the piano. He played a few bars of intro, and then Julie started to sing. I didn't recognise the song, but Julie's pure soprano voice literally made the hairs on the back of my neck stand on end. This girl is incredible, I thought.

Julie finished her song to rapturous applause. With a smile for her audience, she walked over to the piano, where Zac sat with his hands idling over the keys. As she reached him he started to play a tune I did recognise, the famous duet from the musical *A Tale of Two Cities*. He sang the first verse of the song, and Julie sang the second, and then they sang the last verse together, their voices blending perfectly.

Owen whispered, 'They're good, aren't they?'

I whispered back, 'They're outstanding.'

For the next half hour, Julie and Zac sang a

selection of solos and duets from musicals and contemporary pop ballads. Their performance ended with Zac singing a love song to Julie, him sitting at the piano and gazing up into her face, while she stood very still and gazed back at him, a smile playing about her mouth all the while. Zac sang with such emotion that it almost made me cry.

The last notes of the song faded. There was a moment of silence as the entranced audience came back to themselves, and then the applause began again, growing ever louder as Zac led Julie to the front of the stage and they took their bow. When he pulled her towards him and kissed her, the cheers were ear-splitting. Beside me, Owen stood up and clapped harder still, and the rest of the audience were quick to follow.

The clapping and cheering only stopped when Zac and Julie left the stage and started to make their way back to our table. As they were accosted by someone wanting to talk to them at every table they passed, this took them quite some time. They had barely sat down, when a four piece band started setting up on stage. The music began, and they were the first couple on the dance floor, their dancing as impressive as their singing.

'That last song Zac sang,' I said to Owen, 'is it from a musical?'

'No, it's not from a musical,' Owen said. 'It's called *Julie's Song*. Zac wrote it for her.'

'That is *so* romantic,' I said. 'I may be just a tiny bit envious of your friend Julie.'

'Isn't your boyfriend the romantic type?'

'Daniel?' I said. 'I've not been with him long enough to find out. You probably know him better than I do.'

Owen looked puzzled. 'How come?'

'You were at drama school with him.'

'You're dating *Daniel Miller*?' Owen said.

'I am,' I said. 'We got together at the Reardon Haye Christmas party.'

'I remember,' Owen said. 'I was there. Daniel wanted the three of us to go on to a club.'

'That's right,' I said. 'But you couldn't come. So I went to the club with Daniel. And now we're an item.' At least, I hope we are, I thought. Under the cover of the damask table cloth, I crossed my fingers.

'So what's it like to date a famous film star?' Owen said.

'No different from dating any other guy,' I said. 'Except for the fame.'

'And where is the famous Fallen Angel tonight?'

'In New York, on location for *Fallen Angel II.*'

'Oh, well, if Dan's off gallivanting in the Big Apple, he can't have any objection to my dancing with his girl.' Owen stood up and held out his hand.

'I can't dance, Owen.'

Owen grinned. 'Do you need to phone your boyfriend and ask his permission?'

I rolled my eyes. 'No. But I'm a *terrible* dancer. You might want to reconsider the invitation.'

For an answer, Owen took my hand and led me out onto the now crowded dance floor. He turned out to be a very good dancer, while I lurched from side to side in my usual awkward fashion, and tried not to step on his feet. When the music stopped, I thought I'd be able to make my escape, but before I could head back to our table, he caught hold of my arm.

'One more dance,' he said.

'Really? Haven't you suffered enough?'

The music started again, a slow dance this time. Owen rested his hands lightly on my hips. I stepped closer to him so that I could put my hands on his shoulders.

'Relax, Lucy,' he said. 'Let me lead.'

'If you must,' I said. Owen laughed and began to dance, moving easily with the music.

'Look at me,' he said.

I looked up into Owen's blue eyes, and let the gentle pressure of his hands guide my movements, and suddenly I realised that my body was moving in time to the music. I was *dancing*. I was sorry when the dance came to an end and Owen led me back to our table.

'I don't know how you did it,' I said to him, 'but I really enjoyed that.'

Owen smiled. 'If I don't make it as an actor, I guess I can earn a living as a dance instructor.'

'But you *are* going to make it as an actor,' I said.

Owen smiled again. 'Yes, I am.'

The evening went on. People moved from table to table, chatting to old friends, and making new ones. Zac introduced me to his aunt, who told me to be sure to remember her to Eleanor Haye. Nadia left the gala arm in arm with the film director. She did not come over to our table to say goodbye. The band announced the last dance. The comedian and the scriptwriter decided to call it a night, as did Julie's actress friend and her lawyer husband.

It was well after midnight when Owen and Zac went out to the bar to fetch one final round of drinks, leaving Julie and me sitting at the table.

Unexpectedly, she said, 'Nadia Pincher upset you tonight didn't she?'

'She did a bit,' I said. 'She doesn't seem to like me much. I don't know why.'

'Don't let her get to you, Lucy. She's like that with everybody. It's as though she can only feel good about herself when she's putting other people down.'

'It isn't just me then?'

'No it isn't.' Julie hesitated, and then she added, 'When I first graduated from drama school I couldn't get any work as an actress, and I took a job handing out flyers for a nightclub…'

'Is that how you met Owen? He told me he'd had a job handing out flyers.'

Julie nodded. 'Nadia worked there as well. I hadn't been dating Zac very long when she took great delight in *warning* me that he was the type who slept around, because she *didn't want me to get hurt*. He doesn't sleep around, by the way.'

'The way he sang to you,' I said, 'I'd kind of worked that out. Nadia is such a stirrer.'

'She's a bitch,' Julie said. 'I feel bad saying it, but that's what she is. My advice to you is to ignore her.'

'I will in future. It was just that tonight I was so *angry* about what she said to Owen.'

'You don't need to worry about that,' Julie said. 'Owen really rates you. Actually, I'm glad I've had a chance to talk to you, because I've been thinking about getting an agent. Would it be OK if I sent you my CV?'

A West End star was asking if I'd take a look at her CV!

'Yes, of course,' I said. 'Let me give you my card.' Thanking the patron saint of theatrical agents that I'd thought to stash a handful of Reardon Haye business cards in my bag before I'd left home that night, I passed one to Julie. 'Which agency are you with at the moment?'

'I'm not with anyone,' Julie said.

'That's very unusual,' I said. Very few performers managed to get work without an agent to introduce them to directors and producers. For a West End actress not to have an agent was virtually unheard of.

'I know,' Julie said, ruefully. 'I did try to get an agent when I first left drama school, but no-one seemed to be interested in yet another wannabe with stars in her eyes. And without an agent, I didn't get any performing work for a whole year. I nearly gave up acting. I was very lucky to get cast in my first role from an open audition. That really was the proverbial big break for me.'

'You're a successful actress.' At least, I thought, I'm pretty sure you are. Even if I've never heard of you. 'Why have you decided that you need an agent now?'

'That's the thing. I'm an *actress*. I want to spend my time acting, not negotiating contracts with production teams. Now that I'm getting so many offers of work, I need an agent to do the negotiating for me.'

I thought, I may just have found Reardon Haye another prestigious client. I felt a rising excitement.

Julie went on, 'I feel it's important that I'm not with the same agency as Zac. We do like working together, but we're not a double act.'

'OK,' I said. 'Email me your CV and give me a call on Monday. We'll arrange a time for you to come into the office to discuss whether Reardon Haye is the right agency for you.'

'Thank you so much.'

'My pleasure.' The successful West End actress is thanking me, I thought. Owen rates me. I am good at my job – whatever Nadia thinks.

Owen and Zac came back from the bar with four glasses of champagne.

'We decided that men who've spent an entire evening being strangled by bow ties deserve to drink champagne,' Zac said.

'As do women who've been dancing in high heels,' Owen added.

Julie said, 'Ooh, I love champagne. What shall we drink to, Lucy?'

I raised my glass. 'To showbusiness.'

Owen, Julie and Zac chorused, 'To showbusiness.'

We clinked glasses and drank.

CHAPTER 14

'So as soon as I got home,' I said, 'I Googled Zac and Julie Diaz, and it turns out they're showbiz royalty.'

'I'm very surprised you'd never heard of them,' Nadia mused. 'Zac's family are musical theatre *legends.*'

I walked straight into that one, I thought.

It was Sunday night. Ryan had gone out for a drink with his friend and team mate, goalkeeper Fabio Rossi. Cassie and I had eaten far too much of one of Erin's delicious home-made casseroles (as well as her other household duties, Cassie's housekeeper made sure the freezer was well-stocked), and we were still in the kitchen talking over the Star Gazer Gala when Nadia had arrived home. Joining us at the table, she'd been very quick to tell us that she'd gone straight from the gala to Leo's house, where she'd spent the rest of the weekend. Which convinced me she'd done nothing of the kind.

'I met Julie Farrel Diaz once,' Cassie said, suddenly, 'at an awards ceremony for women in the entertainment industry, but I've never heard her sing.'

'Personally, I've always thought she has a wonderful voice,' Nadia said. 'All those rumours that she only got her first lead role because she was shagging the famous Zac Diaz were so unfair.'

Spreading ugly gossip while denying it - that takes

some doing, I thought.

Through gritted teeth, I said, 'As she's been starring in West End musicals for the last three years, I think we can assume that her success is down to her talent, whatever the rumours.'

'Oh, I agree, but -' Nadia's phone rang, and she broke off mid-sentence to look at the screen. 'I need to take this. Remember your call time is an hour early tomorrow, Cassie.' She jumped up and hurried out of the kitchen. I wondered who it was she was so anxious to talk to in private. Probably not Poor Leo.

'I'd completely forgotten about that call time,' Cassie said. 'I don't know what I'd do without Nadia.'

I decided that telling Cassie I thought her PA was a two-faced cow was unlikely to contribute to domestic harmony. What I couldn't understand was why Cassie didn't see it for herself.

'Your favourite client, Owen Somers, must be pretty impressed with you, if he's recommending you to his famous friends,' Cassie said.

'I don't have a *favourite* client,' I said. 'But I do think Owen is a very talented actor. If you'd seen him on stage, you'd think so too.'

'You like him, don't you?'

'Yes, I do,' I said. 'Actually, I'm meeting him for a drink tomorrow after work.'

'Was that your idea or his?' Cassie said.

'I'm not sure.' The previous night, after we'd finished our champagne, the four of us had left the hotel together. Zac and Julie had taken a taxi, and I'd

149

invited Owen to share my hired car, dropping him off at his flat in South London. While we sped through the dark streets, we'd talked non-stop about the gala and about the theatre. But as to which of us had suggested continuing the conversation over a drink, I'd no idea. I said, 'I think it was me. I don't remember.'

Cassie gave me a long look. 'Lucy, tell me honestly. Is there something going on between you and Owen?'

'There honestly isn't,' I said, taken aback. Where was this coming from? 'We had a good time together last night, but I'm not attracted to him.'

'Does he know that?' Cassie said.

'Of course he does.' I said. 'He knows I'm with Daniel. He's a friend of Daniel's – an acquaintance. They went to the same drama school.'

'As long as you're sure you know what you're doing.' Cassie turned her head towards the door, as Ryan came into the kitchen, still in his outdoor coat.

'Hey, beautiful.' He dropped a kiss on the top of her head. 'What are you two talking about?'

'Men and relationships,' Cassie said.

'Any chance you'd like to talk about football?'

'Absolutely not.'

Ryan grinned. 'Then I'll leave you to it. 'Night, Lucy.'

'Goodnight,' I said.

'I should probably go up too,' Cassie said, after Ryan had left. 'I'm feeling rather tired.'

'Yes, with that early call tomorrow, you should get

some sleep,' I said. 'You're blushing, by the way.'

'I am not.' Cassie laughed, and headed upstairs to join her boyfriend.

Left on my own in the kitchen, my thoughts drifted to Daniel. I wondered what he was doing now. On impulse, I picked up my mobile and called his number. There was no reply. Telling myself firmly that this could have been for any number of reasons – even on a Sunday, he could be filming - I made myself a cup of hot chocolate, and took myself off to my lonely bed.

I met Owen in a bar in Soho. He'd got there before me, and had staked a claim for us at a table in the window. He'd also bought a bottle of white wine. I slid into the seat opposite him, and he poured me a glass.

'Are you hungry?' he said to me. 'They do a good seafood platter in here. Or we could go on somewhere else after we've finished our drinks.'

'I'm ravenous,' I said. 'And seafood would be great.'

So we drank our wine, and ate and talked about showbusiness, about uni and drama school, and what we wanted out of life apart from our (obviously) brilliant careers. We decided that earning a fortune wasn't a priority for either of us (as long as you have enough, you know, to do what you want).

'You haven't mentioned fame,' I said to Owen. 'Surely you want to be famous?'

'I wouldn't object to being famous,' Owen said,

'but that's not why I became an actor.'

'So what is the reason?'

Owen's face grew thoughtful. 'It's hard to explain. Do you really want to know?'

I nodded.

'The reason I became an actor,' Owen said gravely, 'was to meet girls.'

'Really?' He hadn't mentioned *that* when I auditioned him.

'You look shocked, Lucy.'

'I am a bit,' I said. 'Meeting women doesn't seem the best reason to go into acting. It's such a hard profession...'

Owen started laughing. I stared at him for a moment. Then I hit him on the shoulder.

'Ouch,' he said. 'That hurt.'

'Good. I thought we were having a serious conversation, but you...' I tried to keep a straight face, but found myself laughing as well.

'It's true,' Owen protested. 'I went to an all-boys school, and one of the few times we got to meet females was when the drama club put on a play with the girls' school down the road. Then, when I was about fifteen, I discovered *acting*. And that I was good at it. And that it was the only thing I wanted to do with my life.'

'Apart from meeting girls, of course,' I said. 'I have a younger brother, I know what fifteen year old boys are like.'

'Oh, I still like meeting girls,' Owen said. 'Sadly, my love life is a disaster.'

'Is it?' I said, surprised. 'Really? I mean, you're a good-looking guy...'

'Don't get me wrong,' Owen said. 'I'm not saying I – ah – don't get any action, but I've never dated any girl longer than a few weeks. When I look at friends who are in steady relationships like Zac and Julie, I find myself wanting what they have for myself.'

'Maybe you're dating the wrong girls,' I said.

'Perhaps I am,' Owen said. 'The last time I took a girl out, we found that we had absolutely nothing to say to each other. Until I accidently knocked a glass of red wine into her lap. She had quite a bit to say about that.'

I couldn't help laughing. 'Did you ask if you could see her again?'

'No, I didn't, strangely enough,' Owen said. 'Anyway, given my chronically single status, and the unlikelihood of me finding my soulmate in the next few days, are you free on Saturday?'

'I've not got anything planned. Why?'

'I was wondering if you'd like to come and see my friend's band playing in a pub in Camden? It won't be quite as glamorous an event as the Star Gazer Gala, but it should be a good night.'

Alarm bells went off in my head. In my mind's eye, I saw Cassie looking at me quizzically across the kitchen table. I thought, am I wrong about Owen? Maybe he does have the hots for me? I'm going to have to remind him that I'm already taken.

'I would like to come,' I said, hoping I didn't

153

sound as awkward as I felt. 'The only thing is, I'm in a relationship – a steady relationship - with Daniel Miller.'

'I know that.'

'He might be on another continent, but there's no way I'd ever cheat on him.'

'And you're telling me this because?'

'I wouldn't want you to think that anything was going to happen between us if I come out with you on Saturday.'

Owen raised his eyebrows. 'Lucy, you're a very attractive girl. I'm sure guys hit on you all the time. But I'm not interested in a leg over with the Fallen Angel's girlfriend. I'd like it if we were friends – not *friends with benefits*.'

'I'd like that as well.'

Owen's face broke into a smile. 'So you'll come to Camden on Saturday?'

'I'd love to,' I said.

CHAPTER 15

In London, on Saturday afternoon, reclining on my bed, I said, 'Everyone at work is very impressed with me right now.'

More than three thousand miles away in New York, where it was still early morning, Daniel said, 'Why's that then, babe?'

'I persuaded Julie Farrel Diaz to sign with Reardon Haye.'

'That's great.' Daniel sounded distinctly underwhelmed. 'She's mainly done musicals, right?'

'West End musicals,' I said. 'She came into the agency yesterday for a chat with me and Eleanor and we -'

'Hold on a sec,' Daniel said, 'there's someone knocking on the trailer... Come in... Now? OK, no worries... Yeah, I'll be right with you... Lucy, are you still there?'

'Yes, I'm still here.'

'Sorry, babe, I'll have to cut this call short. They need me on set.'

'Oh, I didn't realise you were in the middle of filming -'

'We're at a location in Central Park.'

'That sounds -'

'I've got to go, babe. I'll call you tonight, yeah? Your time.'

'I'm out tonight. I'm going to see a band - friends of *your* friend Owen Somers.'

'We'll talk tomorrow then, yeah?'

'Yeah – I mean, yes, I'll –' I realised that he'd already ended the call. I reached out and slowly ran my hand over the empty space next to me on my bed. Daniel's side of the bed. The place where he'd so often slept. I wished that he was lying there at that moment, that he was here with me in London instead of thousands of miles away in a different time zone. Suddenly, I was very glad that I was going to a gig with Owen that night. It would distract me from thinking too much about what the Fallen Angel might be doing in New York. In his private trailer. On location.

I took the tube to Camden Station, and walked along the High Street to the pub where Owen's friend's band, Viper, was playing. Owen was waiting for me outside, drinking beer from a bottle. Like me, he was wearing jeans and a T-shirt, but his T-shirt had the band's name emblazoned across the front. He greeted me with an air-kiss on each side of my face.

'I don't suppose you speak French?' he said.

'I do a bit,' I said. 'I'm far from fluent, but French was one of my A levels.'

'Oh, good,' Owen said. 'Michael, my flatmate, and his French girlfriend decided to tag along with me at the last minute, and she hardly speaks a word of English. Let's get a drink, and then you can meet them.'

Although Viper weren't due onstage for another hour, the pub was heaving with their fans, guys in leather and distressed jeans, and girls with kohl-lined eyes, short, fraying denim skirts, boots and ripped tights. There were a *lot* of chains, studs and piercings, and I was one of the very few people there who didn't have a visible tattoo. Owen and I fought our way through the crowd to the bar, where he bought beer for both of us. Drinking a bottle of beer instead of my usual white wine suited the general atmosphere.

'How come your flatmate has a French girlfriend?' I asked Owen.

'He met her when he spent a year in France as part of his degree,' Owen said. 'He's based in England now, doing a post-grad journalism course, and she lives in Paris, but they manage to meet up every few weeks.'

Tall enough to see over the heads of most of the people in the pub, Owen spotted Michael and his girlfriend standing with their backs to us near the stage. Again we forced our way through the crowd, and when we reached them, Owen tapped his flatmate on the shoulder, so that he spun around. When he saw me with Owen, he gave me a look that could only be described as appraising, but quickly followed it up with a smile.

'Michael – Lucy, my amazing agent,' Owen said.

'We meet at last,' Michael said. 'I've heard so much about you from Owen, I feel I know you already.'

'What has he been saying?' I asked.

'Only good things,' Owen interjected, before

Michael could reply. He indicated the girl standing at his flatmate's side, 'Lucy - Annette, also amazing, because she puts up with Michael.'

I smiled at the French girl, a tiny doll-like creature with short brown hair that fell into her eyes in a heavy fringe. She was wearing a floral dress clinched in with a wide leather belt that showed off her enviably small waist, and high-heeled lace-up ankle boots. Even with the heels, she barely came up to Michael's shoulder. I may be only five feet five, but next to her, I felt like a lumbering giantess.

'*Bonsoir,* Annette,' I said, '*Comment allez-vous?*'

Her face lit up. '*Vous parlez Francais?*'

'*Un peu.*' I said. 'A little.'

'*But this is wonderful,*' Annette said, still in French. '*I have found someone in England to talk to apart from Michael. I am learning English, but it is very hard.*'

For the rest of the evening I spoke to Annette in her own language, with Michael helping out when my French vocabulary failed me, and both of us translating what she said into English for Owen. Viper, three male musicians and a girl singer (who looked incredible in tight black leather jeans and a simple white vest top), came on stage and began their first set, heavy rock interspersed with lighter ballads, that went down really well with the crowd.

'They're really good,' I said to Owen. 'Which of them is your friend?'

'The singer,' Owen said. 'Her name's Jess.'

When Owen had asked me if I'd like to watch his

158

friend's band, I'd assumed his friend was a guy. But the singer was very definitely female. I wondered if she was an ex with whom he'd remained on good terms, or if, like Julie Diaz, she was another of his friends who just happened to be a girl. Before I could indulge my curiosity and find out, Viper launched into their next song, and Owen's attention was all on the stage.

When the band took a break, Michael went to the bar and came back with beer for all of us. Annette told me that she worked in a flower market in Paris. She asked me if I knew the city, and I confessed that I'd only been to France once, on a school trip to Calais. Viper returned to perform their second set. People were dancing now (well, jigging up and down, vaguely in time to the music), and Owen had to put his arm around my waist to steady me amongst the press of bodies in front of the stage. It grew very hot, so hot that I could feel sweat running down my back, and the floor became sticky with spilt beer. At an alcohol-fuelled gig, listening to rock music, I felt like a student again. I tried to tell Owen this, but the music was too loud for him to hear me.

Viper performed their last song and left the stage, and to no-one's surprise, came back on again in response to the audience's impassioned cries of *More! More!* (or in Annette's case *Encore! Encore!*) After several more songs, they really did leave the stage, and their roadies (the singer's boyfriend and the lead guitarist's dad, Owen informed me) started packing up their gear. The four members of the band came into the bar to mingle with their fans, many of whom they seemed to know by name. When she spotted Owen, the girl singer, Jess, rushed up to him and flung her arms around his neck.

'You came!' she said, somewhat unnecessarily.

Owen hugged her, lifting her up off her feet, before disentangling himself. 'Wouldn't have missed it. You were terrific.'

'We were, weren't we? We were brilliant.' Jess laughed, still on a high from her performance.

'I really like your sound,' I said.

'Thank you so much,' Jess said. 'That's all we want – for people to like our music. Of course, we wouldn't mind a record deal as well.'

Somewhat belatedly, Owen thought to introduce us all, mentioning that he and I had met when I'd auditioned him.

'How do you and Owen know each other?' I asked Jess.

'We used to wait tables in the same restaurant,' she said. 'You know what it's like when you're an out-of-work musician –'

'Or an out-of-work actor,' Owen said. 'You may be an *artiste*, but you have to eat.'

'You have to get a day job,' Jess said. 'I still do a bit of waitressing. When we've not had a gig in a while. It's not very rock'n'roll, but it pays the bills.'

Jess's boyfriend came over then, shaking Owen's hand, before telling Jess that their gear was packed up in the guitarist's dad's van and if they wanted a lift home, they needed to go now, because the guitarist's dad was on the early shift tomorrow at his real work.

Jess sighed. 'Again, not exactly rock'n'roll, but what can you do?' She kissed Owen goodbye, and then she and her boyfriend hurried off. I decided that I really should be getting home as well, but the others wouldn't hear of it. Owen went and fetched another round of drinks from the bar, and pretty soon I found myself agreeing that yes, it would be lovely to go back to his and Michael's flat for coffee.

Although it was gone midnight, Camden was as always, full of revellers, but once we were on the tube and travelling south of the river, the crowds began to peter out. Soon we were the only people in the carriage, and when we got off the train and came up out of the underground, the streets were deserted. A few days ago, when I'd dropped Owen home after the Star Gazer Gala, I'd been too intent on our conversation to take much notice of the area in South London where he lived. Tonight, as we left the main road and walked through the back streets, I saw that the terraced houses were small and run down, some of them had boarded up windows, and the tiny front gardens that separated them from the pavement were overgrown with weeds. We walked past a small parade of shops, their frontages hidden behind metal shutters covered with graffiti, a patch of wasteland, ominously dark where the street lights couldn't reach, and the rusting hulk of an abandoned car. I heard the wail of a police siren. My London, affluent Fulham where I lived with Cassie, Shaftesbury

Avenue with its bright lights and theatres, the tourists and mime artists of Covent Garden, the museums and parks, seemed very far away. When we passed a group of boys loitering at the entrance to an unlit alley, I instinctively moved closer to Owen.

'Are you OK?' he asked.

Feeling slightly foolish, I said, 'I wouldn't like to walk these streets alone.'

'You're not alone tonight.' Owen draped his arm across my shoulders and pulled me against him. And with a man's arm around me, I immediately felt safe. Dimly, I was aware that this feeling was entirely *wrong* on several levels (and that my mother would have raised a number of objections), but I didn't ask him to let go.

Owen and Michael's flat was on the second floor of what had once been a two-storey house. It had two bedrooms, a tiny bathroom, a galley kitchen and another room that they used as a communal living area, where we sat drinking coffee, and chatting in a mixture of English and French, mainly about Michael's journalism course. My love life was mentioned in passing, with Owen and Michael both teasing me mercilessly about my reasons for dating *film star* Daniel Miller. Annette and I swopped mobile numbers, and then she and Michael took themselves off to bed. Not long afterwards, Owen and I heard the unmistakable sound of a rhythmically creaking mattress.

Owen rolled his eyes. 'This flat has paper-thin walls. Shall we drink our coffee in my room? Give them a little privacy?'

In the next-door room, Annette cried out, '*Je t'aime, Michael, je t'aime.*'

'Absolutely,' I said to Owen, 'let's give them some space.'

We went across the hall to Owen's room where the sounds of unadulterated passion no longer reached us. His room was sparsely furnished with just a bed, a clothes rail, and a couple of storage boxes, one with a laptop balanced precariously on top. In a corner, there was a tottering pile of books, plays mostly, and a pile of sheet music. I sat crossed legged on Owen's bed, and he sat on the threadbare carpet, leaning back against the wall, his long legs stretched out in front of him.

He said, 'Jess sang so well tonight. If Viper ever do get a record deal, it'll be because of her voice.'

'Who writes their songs?'

'She does,' he said. 'She's an incredibly gifted musician. She looks good on stage. And she certainly knows how to work a crowd.'

'Did you and she ever date?' I said.

Owen shook his head. 'No. She was seeing the guy she's with now when I met her. Last year, she actually set me up with her cousin.'

'And?'

'Worst date *ever*,' Owen said. 'I took her to see a play. A mate of mine had already seen it, and he'd raved about it as a cutting edge contemporary drama, but it was awful. Two men and two women swearing at each other and rolling around on the floor in a tiny studio theatre. The audience sitting thigh to thigh on wooden benches. No air conditioning.'

I smothered a laugh. 'Sorry. It's not funny.'

'It gets worse,' Owen said. 'After the interval the actors took off their clothes and swore at the audience.'

'Not exactly a romantic evening.'

'No. Sitting on a hard wooden bench for two and a half hours, crushed up against a guy you've never met before, while a naked actor shouts obscenities at you, cannot in any way be described as romantic. Once the play ended, Jess's cousin couldn't get out of the theatre quick enough. I suggested we go on to a bar, but she said she thought not, and dived into a taxi.'

'I have to admit that I'd probably have done the same.'

'I can't say I'd blame you.' Owen smiled ruefully and drank some coffee.

It had been months since I'd thought of Lawrence, but suddenly I found myself remembering our last hideous evening.

'My worst date ever was last summer,' I said. 'The man I was in love with took me out to dinner. We ordered our meal and he put his hand over mine. And then he told me he was married – but we could still be good together and his wife need never know. When I told him we were over, and walked out of the restaurant, he seemed genuinely surprised.' I remembered that I'd managed not to cry until I'd got home. I was rather proud of myself for that.

164

'What a jerk,' Owen said.

'A total jerk. He was also my tutor at university.'

Owen raised one eyebrow. 'So he was a lot older than you?'

'He was young for a university professor,' I said, 'only thirty-six. He taught Nineteenth Century Romantic Poetry – ironically enough.' I remembered the first time I'd walked into Lawrence's book-lined study to find him sitting at his desk, writing in a leather-bound notebook, looking for all the world like a wild, romantic poet himself, with his long dark hair and piercing eyes. By the end of that first tutorial discussing Byron, Keats and Shelley, Lawrence gazing straight at me as he recited, 'She walks in beauty like the night,' I was already falling for him... I'd never once questioned his insistence that I tell no-one about 'us' (the university authorities didn't approve of relationships between lecturers and students) or wondered why he only ever took me to his studio flat, when I knew he owned other properties, including a large house on the far side of town. I'd imagined that once I'd finished my post-grad studies, I'd be able to tell all my friends that we were a couple... What a little idiot I'd been.

'I thought I'd found the man I was going to be with for the rest of my life,' I said, 'but for him, I was just a bit on the side.'

'Realising that must have hit you hard,' Owen said.

I nodded. 'I had an awful few months before I got over him – but I'm fine now. I have a great job, I'm in a new relationship, and I've some amazing friends. Old and new.' I smiled at Owen and he smiled back. 'I'm more than fine.'

'You go, girl,' Owen said. He pointed to my empty coffee cup. 'Can I make your life absolutely perfect by getting you a refill?'

'Thanks,' I said, 'but it's really late. Or do I mean early? Anyway, I should be making tracks.' I fished my mobile out of the back pocket of my jeans. 'I'll call a cab.'

Owen hesitated, and then he said, 'You can stay, if you like.'

CHAPTER 16

I woke up with a start. I was lying in a bed that was not my own, with absolutely no idea how I'd got there. Slowly, I sat up, trying to make sense of what I saw, the unfamiliar wallpaper, the tattered curtains, the rail of men's clothes.

This is Owen's room, I thought. Oh, no. What have I done? My heart thumping, I turned my head, fully expecting to see Owen lying in bed next to me. To my relief, I was alone. I reminded myself that I wasn't some slutty girl who drinks too much lager and cheats on her boyfriend. Of course I hadn't slept with Owen.

The events of the previous evening came flooding back to me. Camden. Michael and Annette. The band. Owen and I talking into the early hours. When he'd suggested I stay the night, I'd thought for a moment that he was asking me to have sex with him. The next moment, fortunately before I'd made a complete idiot of myself by reminding him that I'd no intention of cheating on Daniel, he'd said that I could have his room, and he'd sleep in the living room on the sofa.

Groggily, I clambered out of Owen's bed, peeled off the greying T-shirt that he'd lent me to sleep in (no-one would want to have sex with a girl wearing *that* T-shirt), and got dressed. In the clothes I'd been wearing the night before. Which is always a joy. Particularly when you've spent the previous evening in a crowded pub. I needed a drink of water. I needed to wash and clean my teeth. I also needed to go home and change my clothes. Not necessarily in that order. And I wouldn't mind another few hours' sleep. Not wanting to walk through Owen's neighbourhood to the station on my own even in daylight, I phoned for a minicab. Then, feeling like a total skank, I opened Owen's bedroom door and stepped out into the hall. And came face to face with Annette coming out of the kitchen, wrapped in a boy's – presumably Michael's – dressing gown, and carrying two mugs of tea and a plate of croissants. She didn't seem at all surprised to see me.

'*Bonjour*, Lucy,' she said. '*I hope you slept well.*' Her eyes strayed to Owen's bedroom door.

'I did,' I said, 'but not with Owen.' My face grew hot. I tried to remember the French words for what I wanted to say, but my mind went blank. Fumbling with the handle, I pushed Owen's door wide open to show the empty bed within. 'I wouldn't want you to think there was anything going on between me and him. He slept on the sofa.'

'*Je ne comprends pas.*' Annette was looking at me quizzically.

I tried again. 'Owen *et moi – non. I have a boyfriend.*'

'*I know. As you said, last night. Daniel Miller, the film star.*'

'Owen *and I are friends, but that's all.*'

'*Bien sûr.*' Annette said. '*Now, I must take my boyfriend his breakfast. Help yourself to croissants.*'

'*Merci*,' I said, '*but it's time I went home. I'll just say goodbye to Owen…*'

'*D'accord. Au revoir.*' Annette half-turned away, but then she said, '*It was good to meet you, Lucy. Maybe we could go for coffee the next time I'm in London?*'

'*Yes, I'd like that.*'

With a smile, Annette vanished into Michael's bedroom. After a brief detour to the bathroom to rid myself of yesterday's mascara, and raid Owen and Michaels's meagre supply of mouthwash, I went into the tiny kitchen, drank some water, and made a cup of tea. Then I knocked on the living room door, and when I didn't get a reply, opened the door just wide enough to look inside. Owen was lying with his back to me in a sleeping bag on the sofa.

'Owen?' I said.

When he didn't stir, I went and touched him lightly on the shoulder. He muttered something inaudible, and rolled over. Then his eyes fluttered open and he smiled.

'Hey, Lucy.'

'I made you tea,' I said. 'I wasn't sure if you took sugar…'

'I don't.' Owen took the mug and drank. 'Thanks, Lucy. Aren't you having any?'

'No, my cab will be here any minute. I just wanted to say goodbye. And to thank you for inviting me to the gig. It was a good night.'

'Yeah, it was.'

A thought occurred to me. 'Reardon Haye has

tickets for the premiere of *Hearts and Flowers* next week. Would you like to come?'

'Let me think about that. Would I like to go to a film premiere in Leicester Square? Most definitely.'

The front door bell rang.

'That'll be my cab.'

'I'll let you out.' Owen unzipped the sleeping bag, and stood up. Which is how I discovered that he slept naked.

My gaze travelled down from his tousled dark blonde hair to his face with its cute morning stubble, to the smooth planes of his sculpted chest, to the hard ridges of muscle and the line of darker hair on his wash-board stomach to… his erection. He has such a great body, I thought. And it certainly seems to be in working order. Realising that such thoughts were entirely inappropriate because (1) Owen was my *friend,* and (2) I was in a relationship with another guy, I tore my gaze away.

'Sorry, Lucy.' Owen grabbed a cushion off the sofa and covered his man bits. 'I forgot… I'm not properly awake yet.'

'Don't worry about it,' I said. 'Nothing I haven't seen before.'

'My clothes are here somewhere. If you'd turn around…'

I spun round on my heel.

After a moment, Owen said, 'OK. I'm decent.'

I turned back to face him, and saw that he'd put on a pair of tight, black boxers. They weren't *in*decent, but I wasn't sure that I'd describe them as decent either.

The doorbell rang again. Owen picked his keys up off the dining table, and strode out of the living room. I followed him along the hall, trying (unsuccessfully) not to look at his rear. He unlocked the front door.

'Bye, Owen,' I said. 'I'll call you about the premiere.'

'Thanks, Lucy, I'll look forward to it.' His very blue eyes met mine, and then he bent his head and kissed my cheek. I was quite unprepared for the shockingly pleasurable sensation that surged through me when his lips touched my face, and the stab of desire low in my stomach. Resisting a sudden urge to run my hands over Owen's abs, I planted a chaste kiss somewhere near his ear, before running downstairs and jumping into my cab.

I spent the first half of my journey home feeling incredibly guilty and disloyal to Daniel, but by the time I was north of the river, I'd decided that my reaction to Owen's naked body was merely the natural response of a healthy young woman at the sight of a superbly toned male physique. I wasn't about to tell my boyfriend that I'd allowed my gaze to linger on another guy's muscles, but I wasn't going to waste my time beating myself up about it. And I certainly wasn't going to let myself do it again.

Arriving back at Cassie's house, I was still gasping for water, so I headed straight for the kitchen. Where I found Ryan consulting a recipe book, Cassie chopping up vegetables, and Nadia sitting at the kitchen table reading a magazine.

Cassie and Ryan chorused 'Hi, Lucy.'

'Hi.' I took a glass out of a cupboard, went to the sink, and poured myself a drink.

Nadia looked me up and down, smiled sweetly, and said, 'Staying out all night, Lucy? People might get the wrong idea about you.' She laughed as though she had said something extremely funny.

I said, 'Stones and glass houses, Nadia.'

Nadia's smile didn't falter, but she returned her attention to her magazine. To my surprise, because he was always perfectly charming to Nadia, Ryan flashed a conspiratorial grin in my direction, and then turned away to put a tray of potatoes into the oven.

'Something smells good,' I said. 'What are you cooking?'

'A leg of lamb,' Cassie said. 'Fabio Rossi is coming to Sunday lunch. We decided to cook him a full roast.'

'Don't worry Lucy,' Ryan said, 'Fabio won't be renewing his attempts to seduce you. He's bringing a girl with him.'

'That's good to hear.'

'Would you like to join us for lunch?' Cassie said.

'Thanks, but after my wild night out, all I want to do is go to bed and fall asleep.'

'Was your night *very* wild?'

'Not particularly,' I admitted. 'I went to a gig in Camden, and crashed at a friend's flat. It was fun, though.'

'Cassie, I…' Nadia started to speak, but her voice trailed off.

Cassie paused in the act of slicing a carrot. 'What is it?'

Nadia sighed. 'I don't want to worry you, but after all the trouble you and Ryan have taken to keep your relationship private, do you think inviting Fabio Rossi and his girlfriend to your home was entirely wise?'

'How do you mean?' Cassie said.

'Well, I've never met either of them, of course,' Nadia said, 'but I can't help wondering if they know how to be *discreet.*'

Cassie looked anxious. 'Ryan, we talked about this. Are you sure Fabio never speaks to the press?'

'I am,' Ryan said. 'He had so much rubbish written about him when he first came over from Italy that he refuses to do interviews with English journalists. He's also a good mate of mine, so he's hardly likely to go running to the tabloids with stories about my love life.'

'You're very trusting, Ryan,' Nadia said. 'Everyone has their price.'

'As Fabio Rossi earns tens of thousands of pounds a week,' Ryan said, 'his price for betraying a friend is going to be pretty high.'

Nadia looked thoughtful. 'What about his girlfriend? Is she trustworthy?'

I said, 'I'm sure she's lovely. I've heard that Fabio Rossi has very good taste in women.'

Ryan and Cassie laughed. Nadia looked confused, but after a moment she decided to join in.

Cassie said, 'Ryan, would you mind finishing off

the carrots? They'll be here soon, and I'd like to go and get changed and put on some slap before they arrive.'

'Sure.'

'I won't be long.' Cassie passed her knife to Ryan, and went off to do her make-up. Not that she needed it, I thought. Even without make-up, and with her hair scragged back in a pony-tail, she was heart-stoppingly beautiful.

Ryan started slicing the carrots, and then cursed as he cut himself. I moved aside from the sink so that he could run his hand under the cold tap.

'You OK?' I said.

'Yeah. It's nothing.'

Nadia looked up from her magazine. 'You seem a little agitated, Ryan. Do you find entertaining stressful?'

'No,' Ryan said. 'I don't.'

'Is the table laid?' Nadia said. 'Would you like me to do it?'

'No,' Ryan said. 'It's all taken care of.'

'Would you like some help with the vegetables?'

'No,' Ryan snapped, 'what I'd like is for you to stop telling Cassie how to live her life. She doesn't need you to decide who she can or cannot trust.'

Nadia arched her eyebrows. 'I don't know what you're talking about.'

'Then let me make it simple for you. Who Cassie and I choose to invite into this house is nothing to do with you. In future, keep your opinion of our guests to yourself.'

'I'm Cassie's PA. It's part of my job to give her advice.'

'Actually, it isn't,' Ryan said. 'You need to back off.'

Nadia's face contorted with anger, but almost instantly she re-arranged her expression into a smile.

'After three years, I think I'm fully aware of what my job entails.' She glanced at the kitchen clock. 'Time for me to go and meet Leo.' She picked up her magazine and pushed back her chair. 'I know you're under a lot of pressure, and you're still upset about missing that penalty yesterday, but you really should try and put it out of your mind. Relax. Enjoy your lunch party.' She walked serenely out of the kitchen.

Ryan stared after her, his body rigid with suppressed rage. Then he looked at me, still standing by the sink, clutching my glass of water. The tension went out of him.

'I'm sorry you heard all that, Lucy,' he said. 'Now really wasn't the time to pick a fight with Nadia. I was just so angry. What she said about Fabio really worried Cassie. I could see the whole day being ruined.'

'Don't apologise,' I said. 'Nadia was completely out of order.'

'It wasn't just because of what she said today. Cassie thinks the world of Nadia, but I can't stand her.'

'Me neither,' I said. 'She is *not* a nice girl.'

'I agree with you,' Ryan said. 'Unfortunately,

Cassie can't seem to see it – she relies on Nadia far too much.'

'I suppose she's an efficient PA,' I said grudgingly.

Ryan shrugged. 'Cassie only gave her the job because she couldn't get any work as an actress. She'd had a bit part on *Princess Snowdrop* and they'd kept in touch. Working for Cassie was supposed to be a temporary arrangement, just until Nadia got her acting career back up and running.'

'Which hasn't happened.'

'Exactly,' Ryan said. 'Anyway, I need to crack on.' Returning his attention to his culinary duties, he filled a saucepan with water, and placed it on the hob.

I thought, maybe that's why Nadia's such a piece of work – she's a frustrated actress and she's taking it out on the rest of us. Then I remembered that for every Daniel Miller there were hundreds, maybe thousands, of actors who'd never make it. But they kept trying, or they gave up and got over it. They didn't all start behaving like Nadia.

Ryan said, 'Are you sure you won't join us for lunch, Lucy?'

'Thanks,' I said, 'but I'm almost asleep on my feet.'

'Maybe join us later? When you've slept it off?'

'I'm *tired*, Ryan, not hungover. Honestly.'

Ryan grinned. In the back pocket of my jeans, my phone started to vibrate. I fished it out and examined the screen.

'It's Daniel.' I hit the answer key. 'Hi, Daniel.'

'Hi, babe,' Daniel said. 'Sorry I had to cut you off yesterday.'

'Oh, that's OK.' Mouthing *see you later,* at Ryan, I left the kitchen, and took the rest of the call upstairs, lying on my bed. Daniel might not phone me very often, but when he did, and when he wasn't called away to a film set, the sort of things he said to me, and the things I said to him, could really only be said in the privacy of my bedroom.

CHAPTER 17

I let myself into Cassie's house, remembering to re-set the burglar alarm, before toeing off my high heels.

Cassie's voice came from the living room, 'Lucy? Is that you?'

I opened the living room door, and went inside. Cassie had been lying on the sofa, but now she sat up, yawned and stretched.

'I didn't expect to find you up this late,' I said, flopping down in a chair. 'Not on a school night.'

'I'm waiting for Ryan to come in,' Cassie said. 'He's at a fundraiser – a charity auction.' She rubbed her eyes. 'Have you had a good evening?'

'I have. Michael – Owen's flatmate – heard that he'd got the job he was after today, and we went out to celebrate.'

'Who is *we*?'

'Michael, his girlfriend Annette, Owen and me.'

'You've been seeing a lot of Owen lately,' Cassie remarked.

'We've had a drink together after work once or twice – as friends do.' I smiled. 'He has to be one of the nicest men I've ever met – so easy to talk to. Did I tell you that he and I are going to the zoo at the weekend?'

'The zoo?' Cassie said. 'I thought you were more a theatres-and-restaurants sort of girl.'

'Oh, I am,' I said, 'but it'll be fun to do something

different. I've never been to London Zoo, and Owen hasn't been since he was a child.'

Cassie looked thoughtful. 'Owen escorts you to showbiz events. You hang out in bars with him and his flatmate after work. And now you're going about with him at weekends. I can't help wondering if Daniel should be worried.'

I rolled my eyes. 'Owen and I are *friends*. I think I may have told you this.'

'Yes, but – ' Cassie broke off. 'Sorry. You did tell me.'

'Not that it's a big deal, but I do talk to Daniel on the phone about what I've been doing and who with. I'm sure he'd tell me if my friendship with Owen bothered him.'

'Maybe it's me who should be worried,' Cassie said.

'Why?'

Her voice quavering, Cassie said, 'I hardly dare ask... but have I been supplanted? Is Owen your new BFF?'

I laughed. 'Well, he did come round the other night so we could watch a DVD together.'

Cassie put her hand to her mouth in mock horror. 'Was it a rom com?'

'No,' I said. 'It was a thriller. His choice.'

'Hmm. Did you drink rosé? Did you eat chocolate?'

'No and no.'

'Oh, well that's all right then. You're still my best friend forever. I won't worry until you and Owen start going clothes shopping together.'

'Actually,' I said. 'I did go shopping with him last week. He needed a new shirt for an audition, and he wanted a woman's advice.'

'I guess I can allow you to help him buy a shirt,' Cassie said. 'But you are absolutely *not* to take him with you when you buy shoes.'

'Fair enough.' We both smiled.

Cassie said, 'So when exactly does Daniel get back to England?'

'Monday night.'

'Only a few more days.'

'Three days, eighteen hours and twenty minutes until his plane touches down at Heathrow. Not that I'm counting.'

'As if,' Cassie said. 'Are you going to meet him at the airport?'

'No,' I said, 'he's asked me to go to his flat and wait for him there. I thought I'd have a bottle of champagne ready on ice for when he arrives, and maybe light some candles. Or do you think that would be a bit much?'

'Well, if it was Ryan who'd just got off a long flight, I'd be offering him a cold beer. But then Ryan isn't a film star.'

'I'll compromise,' I said. 'I'll still get the champagne, but I'll make sure there's beer in the fridge.'

'What are you going to wear?'

'I can't decide. I want to look hot, obviously, but not slutty. I've treated myself to some gorgeous underwear, but I need to find an amazing dress to wear on top of it. I may have to take Owen shopping again.'

'In the circumstances, a man's opinion could be useful,' Cassie said. 'But I wouldn't worry too much about the dress. Your boyfriend's been away from you for two long months. Whatever you're wearing when he arrives home, I doubt you'll have it on for very long.'

'That's what I'm hoping,' I said. 'Maybe I won't bother shopping for something new.'

Three days, twenty hours and thirty-five minutes later, I was standing by the window in Daniel's flat, in his bedroom with the lights dimmed, when I saw his car draw up outside. He got out of the back seat, and stood in the pool of light from a street lamp, while his driver lifted his suitcases out of the boot. Darting away from the window, I lit the candles I'd placed around the room, switched off the electric light, quickly took off the bath-robe I was wearing over my new, pale pink lace bra and thong, and arranged myself in a seductive pose on Daniel's bed. Then, catching sight of myself in the mirror and deciding I looked like I was trying too hard, I leapt up, opened the bedroom door, and leant causally against the doorframe.

A few minutes later, the front door opened, and Daniel came in, pulling a suitcase behind him. Followed by his driver with the rest of his luggage. To his credit, the driver took one startled look at me in my barely-there lingerie, and immediately became extremely interested in the hall carpet, but I was horribly embarrassed.

In a strangulated voice, I said, 'Welcome home, Daniel.'

'It's good to be back,' Daniel said. To the driver he added, 'Thanks, mate, I'll take it from here. Goodnight.'

'Goodnight, Mr Miller.' Keeping his gaze firmly on the floor, the driver deposited the luggage at Daniel's feet, and hurried out of the flat.

'I'd no idea you'd have someone with you,' I wailed. 'I thought you'd be alone.'

Daniel grinned. 'Evidently.'

'I should have stuck with my original plan.'

'Which was?' He had just got home after a six hour flight. His clothes were crumpled, and his chin was dark with stubble. *He was beautiful.*

Instead of answering him, I backed slowly into the bedroom, and assumed my former pose on his bed. Daniel followed me into the room, his glance taking in the candles, the bottle of champagne in the ice bucket, and the two fluted glasses I'd placed on the chest of drawers. He looked at me reclining on his Egyptian cotton sheets, and his grin was replaced with a wolfish smile. He sat down next to me, flipping me over so that he could unhook my bra and take it off. I lay on my side resting my head on one elbow. Daniel trailed a finger between my breasts, and then he took off my thong. He reached for the champagne, but rather than pouring it into the glasses, he took a swig, and handed the bottle to me. Without saying a word, we passed the bottle back and forth between us. Lounging on a beautiful man's bed, naked and sharing a bottle of champagne, while he was fully clothed, was unexpectedly erotic. Despite the coldness of the champagne, my body felt like it was about to burst into flames.

When we'd drunk over half the bottle, Daniel replaced it in the ice bucket. He took off his shoes and socks, and then he stood up and reached behind his head to pull off his sweatshirt. The sight of him, with the candlelight flickering over his ripped torso, actually made me feel lightheaded with desire. For a long moment, he stood looking down at me, and then, a smile playing about his mouth, he unzipped his jeans, with agonising slowness, and let them drop to the floor, revealing a pair of tight boxers that did nothing to conceal his arousal. By now I was desperate to have him inside me, and he knew it. Kicking away his jeans, he stripped off his underwear, rummaged in a drawer for a condom, flung himself on top of me, and kissed me greedily on the mouth.

I was so ready for him, that he entered me with one smooth movement of his pelvis. I clung to him as he thrust into me, relishing the weight of his body on mine, my hips rising to meet his, my fingers digging into his back. We came at the same time, Daniel moaning and gasping and pushing into me so deeply that it was both pleasurable and painful all at once, and I felt so close to him, so glad that he had come back to me, that I almost cried.

For the second time, I said, 'Welcome home, Daniel.'

Still lying between my thighs, Daniel said. 'I could get used to a welcome like that.'

He slid out of me, and with a light kiss on my lips, he lifted himself off me and onto the bed.

'Would you like some more champagne?' he said.

'Please.'

He stood up and poured the remainder of the champagne into the glasses. Which gave me a delightful view of his butt. And the marks my nails had left on his back.

'Thanks,' I said, as he handed me my champagne flute. 'Er, do you have any more nude scenes to shoot on *Fallen Angel II?*'

'Only the one where I shag my leading lady. Why?'

'I got a bit carried away just now. Your back has scratches on it.'

Daniel laughed. 'Don't worry about it. My make-up artist is the best in the business. And she's very discreet.'

I drained my champagne, and tried not to imagine the sort of things Daniel Miller's make-up artist might need to be discreet about. Daniel had also finished his champagne. Sinking back onto the bed, he gave a sigh of contentment.

'Did you miss me a lot while I was away?' he said

'Yes, of course.' I had missed him – maybe not as much as I might have done if I hadn't had Owen to talk to, but I didn't need to tell Daniel that. 'Did you miss me?'

'I did.'

I wondered if he really *had* missed me while he was in America, or if he was just saying what he knew I'd want to hear. Then I told myself it really didn't matter, because he was back in England now, we'd just had the most amazing sex, and my fears that our relationship wouldn't survive the weeks we'd spent apart had proved groundless.

Daniel said, 'Lucy, there's something I need to say to you. Something I didn't want to bring up while I was in New York.'

'What is it, Daniel? You sound terribly serious.' My insecurities came rushing back. 'Is something wrong?'

'No. But you and I need to have a talk.'

'What about?' My voice sounded unnaturally shrill. I thought, please don't say that you've been sleeping with a glamorous Broadway actress while you were in New York. Or a rich, sophisticated Manhattanite. Or an American supermodel. Or anyone else. Because I don't think I could bear it.

Oblivious to my rising panic, Daniel said, 'How much do you know about my schedule for the next few weeks?'

'Not a lot,' I said. 'We're very flexible at the agency, and all of us try to get know every actor on our books, but we each have our own list of clients who we focus on. It's Eleanor who looks after our most important clients like you and Cassie.'

'Right,' Daniel said. 'Well, my schedule for the next few weeks is packed.'

'I know that you're going to be spending long hours on set.' Where was he going with this? Was he about to tell me he was going to be too busy to see me for the next few weeks?

'I don't just mean work. I've invites to a number of high profile events that I want to go to, and I'd like it if you'd be my plus one. And before you say anything, I will understand if you'd rather not.'

'Do I want to go with you to a showbiz party? Ooh, I don't know. I guess I could force myself.' He wants me to be his plus one. Yes, please, Daniel!

'Lucy, you need to think carefully about this. I have a very good relationship with the press – they don't hound me the way they do some celebrities - but the events I'm talking about are going to be magnets for the paparazzi. Photos of us together could be posted on the internet and in the tabloids. Are you ready for that sort of attention?'

My face broke into a smile. 'I've never been shy about having my photo taken.'

'I'm serious, Lucy. A lot of the women I've dated have been only too glad of the publicity, but you're not an actress. I don't want you getting upset if you get papped when you go out to buy a pint of milk with bed-hair and no make-up.'

'Daniel, I work as a theatrical agent. I live with Cassie Clarke. I've been to premieres in Leicester Square. I do know what the press can be like.'

'So you'll come with me to the Hedonists' Ball?

186

I've made it onto the guest list along with the Hollywood crowd again this year.'

I thought, that'll be A-listers only then – and me. What *am* I going to wear?

'I'll look forward to it,' I said, smiling.

CHAPTER 18

'Daniel warned me before we got out of the limo,' I said to Cassie the day after the Hedonists' Ball, while we were eating our lunch on the terrace, making the most of the spring sunshine, 'but I really didn't understand what it would be like to walk along a red carpet with the Fallen Angel. There were so many cameras flashing that half the time I literally couldn't see a thing, and all I could hear were the fans screaming and chanting his name.'

'That sounds rather alarming,' Cassie said.

'It was a bit disorientating at first,' I said, 'but I just clung onto Daniel, and I was fine. When he stopped walking and posed for the cameras, I did the same.' I pictured the scene on the red carpet. Daniel and I standing together in front of a bristling forest of long lenses. Blinding flashes of light. Daniel's dazzling smile. 'There are actually some quite good shots of us on the internet. Here, have a look.' I passed Cassie my mobile, and she scrolled through the photos of the ball's guests on *Goss* magazine's website.

'You look lovely, Lucy,' Cassie said. 'I *adore* your dress.'

'Daniel bought it for me when he was in New York.' He'd also bought me several more intimate articles of clothing which, although I was wearing them, weren't visible in the photographs.

'So did the Hedonists' Ball live up to its name?'

Cassie said. 'Was it hedonistic?'

'Not so that you'd notice,' I said. 'It wasn't that different to some of the student parties I used to go to. But with more champagne, more designer shoes, and a *lot* more botox.'

Cassie laughed. 'But you had a good time?'

'I did, actually. Your friend Rochelle Thorne was there. I ended up dancing on the bar with her and that TV presenter who shagged the politician.'

'Dancing on the bar! Scandalous!'

'Foolish, considering that I'm a hopeless dancer and I was in a room full of girls who sing and dance for a living. I don't know what got into me. Oh, yes I do. It was the vodka shots I did with the drummer from Feral and the lead guitarist from Silver Dollar.'

'What are you like!' Cassie said. 'Do tell me more.'

'Serena Davis was there,' I said.

'Who?'

'The skinny actress with the big breasts who's just joined the cast of *Family Matters*.'

'Oh, *her*. Please tell me she's not as gorgeous in the flesh as she is on TV, so I don't have to hate her.'

'She's not that stunning in real life. But feel free to hate her anyway.'

'You didn't bond with Ms Davis?'

'I did not,' I said. 'For one thing, however many times I told her my name, she kept calling me Lacy. And for the other thing, she was all over Daniel. She actually put her hand on his biceps and asked him how many times a week he worked out.'

'What a slut,' Cassie said. 'I bet her breasts are fake.'

I laughed, although I had actually been outraged at the actress's blatant interest in my boyfriend - and somewhat irritated that he hadn't seemed to notice how put out I was.

Cassie checked her watch. 'I'd better go in. I have an interview in ten minutes. A radio interview over the phone.' She gathered up our empty plates and went indoors. Almost immediately, my own phone rang, and I answered it without looking at the caller ID.

'Lucy? It's Emily.'

My mind raced through several girls I knew called Emily, before settling on the one who'd lived in the same hall of residence as me at uni. I hadn't seen or spoken to her in months – not since I'd moved to London.

'Hello, Em,' I said. 'How lovely to hear from you. I –'

'I've just seen you and *Daniel Miller* in *Goss* on-line,' Emily shrieked. 'Are you *dating* him?'

My heart sank. Before he'd dropped me back at Cassie's house earlier that morning, Daniel had reminded me that the photos of me and him at the Hedonists' Ball might well result in my being contacted by the press – any competent journalist could get my name from the ball's guest list. He'd also told me to be wary of calls from anyone I didn't know well, and if I was at all suspicious as to why they'd suddenly got in contact, to refer them to the

PR company who were handling the publicity for *Fallen Angel*. For an instant, I considered giving Emily the phone number. Then I recalled all the times we'd taken it in turn to make the coffee when we'd been studying late into the night or borrowed each other's lecture notes.

'Yes, I'm seeing him,' I said.

There was more shrieking from Emily. Then she said, 'Oh. My. Goodness. You're dating the Fallen Angel. I can hardly believe it.'

'Well, I am.' I said, thinking that she needn't have sounded quite so incredulous. Was it really so difficult to imagine that Lucy Ashford might be in a relationship with a ridiculously good-looking leading man?

'How did you meet him?' Emily asked.

'I met him through my work,' I said. 'I'm a theatrical agent – he's a client.'

'*Amazing*,' Emily said.

I wondered if she meant my job or my boyfriend. 'What about you, Em? What are you up to these days? Are you still with Robert?'

'Ooh, yes,' Emily said. 'We're going travelling together...'

To my relief, once she started talking about her and her boyfriend Robert's plans to back-pack round Australia, Emily stopped shrieking. For the next half hour, she and I had a satisfying conversation relaying the latest news about our mutual acquaintances (no-one else, as far as either of us knew, was dating a film star). By the time she rang off, I felt genuinely contrite that I'd allowed myself to think that her reasons for calling me might be anything worse than being completely starstruck over Daniel Miller.

My phone received a text from another university friend: *Just seen pic of you and Daniel Miller on TV!!!! WTF!!!! LOL ;) xx.* Several more texts, from other equally over-excited university and school friends followed.

I should, I supposed, have anticipated something like this. Most people who knew me before I started working in showbiz were naturally going to be surprised if they suddenly discovered that I was dating a celebrity. Including my family. Who never asked for details of my love life, but might feel somewhat aggrieved if they only found out that I was the Fallen Angel's girlfriend when they turned on the six o'clock news. Why hadn't I thought of this before? In a rising panic, knowing that I needed to give my relatives a heads up before photos of me and Daniel were plastered across every branch of the media, I snatched up my mobile and called my mother.

'Hi, Mum,' I said, when she picked up. 'How are you?'

'Lucy?' my mother said. 'Just a sec... Dylan, will you turn that music down, Lucy's on the phone and I can't hear a thing... Sorry, Lucy, your brother has developed a liking for heavy metal. I'm hoping it's just a phase. Like the eating mud phase he went through when he was two. Now what were you saying?'

'I asked how you were.'

'I'm fine.'

'And how's Stephen?'

'He's in excellent health,' my mother said. 'As is Dylan. Although I am a little concerned about his taste in music. Is everything OK with you, Lucy?'

'Oh, yes, I'm good,' I said. 'I'm actually phoning because, well, I wanted to talk to you about the guy I'm dating.'

'Oh lord, you're not ringing me for motherly advice, are you?' my mother said. 'Stephen's so much better at that sort of thing than I am. Shall I pass him the phone?'

'No, Mum,' I laughed. 'I just wanted to warn you that photos of me and my boyfriend have been posted on the internet, and there's every chance that we may be in the tabloids.'

'Why would you be in the papers, Lucy?' my mother said. 'Have you done something newsworthy?'

'Not exactly,' I said. 'It's just that the guy I'm seeing is famous. You know him.'

'I don't know anyone famous,' my mother said.

'I mean, you know of him,' I said.

'Who are you dating?'

'Daniel Miller.'

'Daniel Miller *the actor*?'

'Yes' I said. '*That* Daniel Miller.'

There was another long silence, and then my mother said, 'Lucy, these photos of you and Daniel Miller, are they… X-rated? Are there videos?'

'*What?*' My face flooded with heat as I realised my mother thought I'd made a celebrity sex-tape. '*Nooo*, Mum, nothing like that. They're photos of me and him at a party. I just thought I should let you know. In case one of your friends or someone at the garage saw them before you did.'

'That's very thoughtful of you, Lucy,' my mother said. 'Now, tell me, is he good to you, this young man that you're dating? I'm not interested in his fame. The important thing is, does he treat you right?'

'He's lovely, Mum.'

'Is he faithful to you?'

'Ye-es,' I said. *As far as I knew.* 'Yes, he is.'

'Then I'm happy for you,' my mother said. After a moment, she added, 'Are Stephen and I going to meet him?'

'It's early days,' I said, 'but maybe in a while.' Until then, I'd never thought about introducing Daniel to my family, but now I realised it was something I'd very much like to do. 'I think you and Stephen would get on well with him. You'd certainly like his car...' We chatted a while longer about Daniel's Ferrari, before my mother remembered that she was due to meet a friend for coffee, and ended the call.

Immediately my phone pinged with the arrival of another over-excited text.

CHAPTER 19

'My arms are aching,' I said to Owen. 'Would you like a turn at rowing?'

'Sure,' Owen said. 'Wait. Don't let go of the oars.'

'Oh – Sorry.' One of the oars was still firmly grasped in my hand, but the other was now floating in the Serpentine. Owen reached over the side of our small, hired, blue-painted vessel and retrieved it. We swopped seats. Owen pulled on the oars, and the boat skimmed smoothly and swiftly to the centre of the lake. My own efforts had left us going round in circles close to the shore, and I'd only narrowly avoided a collision with a pedalo. Owen had voiced the hope that I wouldn't get us banned from every boating lake in London for all time.

'You've done this before,' I said.

'I was on my school's rowing team,' Owen said. 'Didn't I tell you?'

'No, you forgot to mention that. Now I know why you were so keen to come to Hyde Park.' I let my fingers trail in the water. 'I'm glad you asked me to come with you, though. It's lovely out here.'

'My first choice for a Saturday afternoon's entertainment would always be a West End matinée,' Owen said, 'but sometimes it's good to do something different, I think.'

'Oh, *yes*,' I said. 'I think exactly the same.' I gazed out over the lake, raising a hand to shade my eyes against the sunlight reflected off the water. A refreshing breeze stirred my hair. A swan glided past the prow of the boat, and I watched it swim towards the tree-lined shore, where a number of young families were throwing bread to the ducks and other water birds.

Owen rested the oars, letting the boat drift. 'I've seen a *lot* of photos of you and Dan in the press the last few weeks,' he said. 'You're quite the celebrity couple.'

'We're a couple,' I said. '*He's* a celebrity. *I* am not.'

'But you are being stalked by the paparazzi everywhere you go, right?' Owen said. 'There are probably at least ten of them hiding behind the boathouse at this very moment.' He grinned. 'Just a suggestion, but if you were to *accidently* fall overboard, the photos of my heroic rescue of the Fallen Angel's girlfriend could be extremely advantageous for my career.'

'Sorry to disappoint you,' I said, 'but I only seem to attract the media's attention when I'm with Daniel.'

I cast my mind back over the previous month. By now, Daniel and I had left enough nightclubs together in the early hours that the flash of a camera no longer startled me, and I'd become adept at getting out of a limo in a short skirt, but so far the media had shown no interest in recording my every waking moment for posterity. I was still able to do the Reardon Haye lunchtime sandwich run without bothering to touch up my make-up. Which suited me just fine.

Owen said, 'You're not having to sneak out of Dan's flat in a hat and dark glasses?'

'Not as yet,' I said.

'Fame can be so fickle.'

We smiled at each other. The more time I spent with Owen, I thought, the more I liked him.

'I've really enjoyed this afternoon,' I said.

'Me too. It's good that you and I can still meet up now that your boyfriend's back from New York.'

'Why wouldn't we be able to meet up?' I said.

'I'd have thought the demands of dating an A-lister would be taking up all of your free time,' Owen said. 'Shouldn't you be having your nails done right now?'

I laughed.

Owen said, 'Seriously, Lucy, your friendship is important to me. I want you to know that.'

'I do know that,' I said, touching his hand briefly. 'And I'm glad we're friends.'

We fell silent. The boat rocked gently on the water. I tilted my face up to the sun.

'Lucy... I...'

'Mmm?' I turned back to Owen. His gaze met mine and held it. His eyes, I noticed, were the exact same blue as the sky.

'I... I need to get us back to dry land,' Owen said. He bent over the oars and started rowing again, his strong, muscular arms sending the boat flying across the lake towards the shore.

*　*　*

It really had been a lovely afternoon, I thought, an hour or so later, as I let myself into Cassie's house. Owen was such a nice guy. It was a shame he'd had to rush off to work (he was currently pulling pints in the same Camden bar where we'd seen Viper play) as soon as we'd returned our small craft to the boat keeper.

With both Cassie and Nadia away for the weekend (Cassie at Ryan's, Nadia allegedly at Leo's), the house was silent and still, and the sudden ringing of my phone made me start. I rummaged for it inside my bag, but by the time I'd found it, it had gone through to voice mail. It was a message from Daniel saying that shooting was running over, and not to expect him much before midnight, adding, 'we can still make an appearance at the Silver Dollar party, babe.'

Midnight. I'd seen his call sheet. The estimated wrap time had been six p.m. Suddenly my pulse was racing. Would a star like Daniel Miller really be expected to work long extra hours on a Saturday night? Was he really still on set – or was he somewhere else? With someone other than me...

I took a deep breath, and told myself very firmly to get my head together. It was hardly unknown for a day's filming to fail to finish on time. There were so many reasons why a scene might need another take. And not just on a feature film like *Fallen Angel II*. Cassie was late back from the TV studios at least once a week.

Deciding it was far too early to for me to start getting ready for the party to celebrate the launch of Silver Dollar's latest single, I went into the kitchen, helped myself to a glass of white wine from an open bottle in the fridge, and went out into the garden. One of the glossy magazines that Nadia liked to read was lying abandoned on the grass. I picked it up, sat down on a sun-lounger, and started flicking through it while I drank my wine.

On the left-hand centre page, I found a rather good photo of me and Daniel taken at a restaurant opening we'd been to the previous weekend. We were standing in front of a velvet curtain holding hands, and the camera had caught us just as he was planting a kiss on the side of my face. The picture was captioned 'The Girl who Tamed the Fallen Angel.' On the opposite page were several column inches of journalese confirming that Daniel Miller was no longer single (Sorry, ladies, that's another hot guy off the market), and in a steady relationship with theatrical agent Lucy Ashford (Our spies tell us that Daniel has been dating Lucy, 23, since the beginning of the year, and he is smitten. All of us here at *Celeb* think they make a cute pair).

I thought, *I* am the girl who tamed the Fallen Angel.

I wanted very badly to believe that it was true.

CHAPTER 20

Wearing one of Daniel's T-shirts, I lounged on his sofa, idly flicking through the channels on his new, state-of-the-art TV. Daniel, looking impossibly handsome in a worn pair of jeans, his hair flopping over his forehead, was sitting at the breakfast bar, his attention all on his laptop.

Yesterday, after four months of filming under hot studio lights, he'd shot his final scene. Last night he'd taken me to the wrap party, where he'd been the centre of attention, with everyone, cast and crew, telling him he'd done an amazing job, and any number of women flirting with him – which had annoyed me until I remembered that it was *me* he was taking home. Today, Sunday, he'd woken up with no scenes to learn for the next day's filming, no call sheet telling him he had to be in make-up by five thirty a.m, no rehearsals or costume fittings, no production assistant scurrying around to fulfil his every whim, and no private trailer. He would still be in demand for the normal celeb round of interviews, photos shoots, and publicity for the film but essentially he was out of a job.

Turning off the TV, I said, 'You must be feeling a bit down.'

Daniel looked up from his computer screen. 'No, I'm good. Why wouldn't I be?'

'I thought … Well, it's great that the film is finished, but won't you miss going to the studio each day?'

He shook his head. 'Hardly. I'm glad to have a break from work.'

'Really?' This was not a sentiment that I could share or even understand. The thought of not having a job to go to made me shudder.

'Don't get me wrong,' Daniel said. 'I'm not complaining, but filming twelve hours a day, six days a week isn't a joy ride.'

'Oh, I know that acting is both physically and emotionally draining,' I said. This was something Owen and I had talked about many times.

Daniel gave me an odd look. 'It's just a job with long hours, Lucy. But it's given me fame and a lot of money. What I want is some time off to enjoy it.'

I frowned, thinking of the number of casting directors calling Reardon Haye every day, all of them determined to secure Daniel as the star for their next project. The number of scripts piling up in the office for him to read. And he wanted to take some time off? The last time I'd taken a day off from work had been six months ago at Christmas.

Then I thought, all work and no play…

'Maybe we could both take a holiday,' I said. 'A short holiday. Go and lie in the sun by a swimming pool, read, drink wine…'

Daniel looked thoughtful. 'I'd like to go on holiday with you, babe. But before I do anything this summer, I want to find myself somewhere else to live.'

'You want to sell this flat?'

'As soon as I can. I bought it after my first film,

before I was earning big money. I can afford a place a lot more spacious now.'

I felt a pang of regret. Daniel's flat was compact (OK, by film star standards, it was tiny) but it was here that we'd spent our first night together.

Telling myself that it was ridiculous to be sentimental about bricks and mortar, I said, 'I take it you want to stay living in London?'

'Hell, yes. I'd never leave London. Well, not unless I was moving to LA to work in Hollywood.' He gestured towards his laptop. 'Come and have a look at this.'

I went and sat on a stool at the breakfast bar, and Daniel angled his laptop so that I could see the screen. I found myself looking at the website of an up-market estate agent. A slideshow of a large townhouse showed me a succession of white-painted rooms with wooden floors, bedrooms with walk-in wardrobes, opulent bathrooms, and a courtyard garden overflowing with tubs of flowers and shrubs.

'What do you think?' Daniel said. 'Do you like it?'

'It's a beautiful house,' I said. 'And I love the garden. Whereabouts in London is it?'

'Primrose Hill.'

'A lot of famous actors live in Primrose Hill.'

'Yeah, they do.'

I grinned. 'You'd feel right at home if you bought a house in that part of London.'

'My thoughts entirely,' Daniel said.

I looked back at the images of the house on

Daniel's laptop – and gasped when I saw the seven figure asking price. 'Have you seen how much they want for that place?'

Daniel shrugged. 'I can afford it.'

I realised I couldn't argue with that. He'd earned a small fortune on *Fallen Angel,* and the success of that film had meant that Eleanor had been able to negotiate him an enormous salary for the sequel.

Daniel said, 'You know all those actors who swear that fame won't change them in any way?'

'Yes,' I said. 'I can think of plenty of actors like that.'

'I'm not one of them,' Daniel said. 'I'm an A-list star. I have every intention of living an A-list lifestyle.'

'Well, Primrose Hill is definitely an A-list post code.'

Daniel turned back to his laptop and took another look at the slideshow of the house in Primrose Hill. I watched it over his shoulder.

'I'll phone the estate agent tomorrow and arrange a viewing,' Daniel said. 'Would you come with me? I'd like someone else to see the place before I put in an offer.'

On the website, the house was gorgeous. I wouldn't mind living there myself. My heart began beating very fast. I thought, does Daniel want me to go with him to see this house because he's planning to ask me to live with him? And, if he is, how do I feel about that? I realised that I didn't know the answer.

'Lucy?' Daniel said.

'Sure, I'll come with you to see the house. But it'll have to be in the evening, when I'm not at work.'

'Of course.' Daniel went back to surfing the net.

'I'll make us some coffee.' I slid off the barstool, went into the kitchen area and switched on the kettle. My hand was shaking as I spooned coffee into two mugs, and my head was all over the place. I liked Daniel. I liked him a *lot*. But as for living with him… Somehow I couldn't imagine us playing house together. I felt very confused.

The kettle boiled. I poured the hot water into the mugs and added milk to mine. I walked over to Daniel and handed him his coffee, black with no sugar, just the way he liked it. He raised his eyes from his laptop and smiled his thanks.

I thought, he is so beautiful. How can I *not* want to live with him? Then, I thought, get a grip, Lucy. He hasn't even asked you to live with him. Not yet. You don't have to think about this right now.

My phone announced the arrival of a text: *Last night. My worst date ever ☹ Owen xx*

Grateful for the distraction from my unsettling thoughts, I sat down on the sofa and called Owen's number.

'Worse date ever?' I said when he answered. 'Worse than the shouting naked man?'

'Well, maybe not the worst date *ever*,' Owen said. ' But pretty bad.'

'So you asked out the girl from the call centre?'

Unlike Daniel, Owen's last acting job, two day's

work on a gangster movie, hadn't paid him an A-list salary that would allow him to take time out until his next starring role. Temping in a call centre, his latest ghastly day job, had only been made bearable by the presence of the stunning (according to Owen) girl who sat at the next desk.

'Yes,' Owen said. 'I finally asked her out.'

'Tell me *everything*.'

'I took her to see a film, we went on to a bar, we went back to hers, I kissed her... And then her boyfriend turned up.'

'She has a *boyfriend*,' I said, 'but she lured you back to her place for sex? She sounds awful.'

'You're a bit judgemental,' Owen said. 'And I didn't have sex with her. I only kissed her.'

'I'm sure you were expecting to have sex with her,' I said.

'Given the state of my love life,' Owen said, 'I never *expect* to have sex with anybody. And before you say it, she isn't a slag.'

'She was cheating on her boyfriend!'

'No she wasn't,' Owen said. 'A month ago, they'd had a fight, and he'd told her it was over. And then, last night, he came back, banging on the front door, shouting through the letterbox that he'd been an idiot, begging her to forgive him and let him in.'

'And did she let him in?' I said.

'Yes.' Owen said. 'After she'd hidden me in the wardrobe.'

'She did *what?*'

'She panicked,' Owen said. 'She didn't want her

boyfriend to find her with another guy. So she shoved me into her wardrobe. Where I had to stay until her boyfriend left this morning.'

'You're making this up,' I said.

'I'm not.'

I started to laugh.

'I'm glad you think it's funny,' Owen said. 'You didn't just spend eight hours in a cupboard while a couple had enthusiastic and very loud make-up sex just a few feet away. It was a very uncomfortable night – literally and figuratively.'

'I can imagine.' I said. 'Actually, I don't think I will imagine it.'

'And then, when I got home,' Owen said, 'I found a letter from our landlord saying that he's sold the flat for development. Michael and I have to be out by the end of the month.'

'Oh, no!' Owen's flat might be in dire need of a face-lift, but for London, it had a very low rent. 'You're really not having a good weekend.'

'I'm having a shite weekend,' Owen said. 'To make it worse, Annette has decided that she's going to move to England, and her and Michael are going to get a place together, which means I need to find somewhere to live that I can afford on my own. So if you hear of anyone with a room to rent, let me know.'

'I'll ask around.'

Owen sighed. 'The way my life's going at the moment, I probably won't get either of the parts I'm auditioning for next week.'

'Your agent happens to think otherwise.'

'Well, that does make me feel a bit more confident.' Owen said. 'My agent is very good at her job.'

'She represents some very good actors,' I said.

'She does. And what sort of weekend is she having? How's her boyfriend coping with being a *resting* actor?'

'Oh, he's…' I decided that now was not the time to tell Owen that Daniel could take his pick from any number of offers of work, but that he wanted some time out to buy a stupidly expensive house. 'Oh, you know, he's waiting to see what comes up.'

'Yeah, I know what that's like,' Owen said.

I glanced over at Daniel. He was still absorbed in whatever was on his laptop screen. He hadn't told me what his plans were for the rest of the day, but I decided he could spare me for a couple of hours.

'Owen, would you like to meet up for a drink tonight? Drown your sorrows?'

'That's a very tempting offer,' Owen said, 'but an old school friend has invited me to a barbeque this afternoon, and it'll probably go on 'til late. What about a drink tomorrow night?'

'Meet me in our usual bar after work?'

'Will do.'

'See you tomorrow, then.'

'See you tomorrow, Lucy.' Owen rang off. I thought how easy it was to be friends with him. How uncomplicated.

'Was that Owen Somers you were talking to?' Daniel asked.

'Yes, it was,' I said.

'And you're seeing him tomorrow night?'

'Only for a drink after work. He needs cheering up.'

'Oh. Right. I see.' His face expressionless, Daniel turned back to his laptop.

After a few moments of silence, I said, 'Is there something wrong?'

'No. Why should there be?'

A stray thought, something Cassie had once said to me, drifted into my mind. 'Daniel,' I said, 'you do know that you have no reason to worry about Owen, don't you? He and I are good friends, but that's all we are. You don't need to be jealous.'

Daniel looked up from his laptop, his eyebrows arched in surprise. 'You think I'm jealous of Owen Somers?'

'Well, you don't seem entirely comfortable with my having a drink with him tomorrow night.'

'I was hoping that we'd be able to view the house in Primrose Hill tomorrow night, that's all.'

'Oh, I'm sorry,' I said. 'I wasn't thinking... I'll call him back. Let him know I can't see him tomorrow. I'll catch up with him later in the week.'

'You don't mind, do you?' Daniel said.

'Of course not. Seeing the house is important.' Especially if I might be living in it. 'I can have a drink with Owen anytime.'

'Me jealous of Owen Somers?' Daniel laughed. 'As if.'

I rang Owen back, but he didn't answer, so I left

him a voice mail. I did feel a little guilty cancelling on him, but then I reckoned he couldn't be all that down if he was going to a barbeque.

Daniel shut his laptop, and swivelled round on his barstool to face me.

'Do you want another coffee?' I said to him.

Daniel shook his head, and his warm brown eyes looked straight into mine. 'What I want is *you*.'

'Ooh.'

Grinning wickedly, Daniel said, 'Are you wearing anything under that T-shirt?'

'No.'

'Take it off.'

I stood up, pulled my T-shirt over my head, and dropped it on the floor.

Daniel's gaze travelled slowly over me, lingering on my breasts. He got off the barstool and stepped towards me. I thought he was going to kiss me, but instead he put a finger on my lips and traced the line of my mouth. Then he put his hand between my legs, and slid a finger inside me. My stomach clenched and a delicious heat spread throughout my whole body. I clung to him, gasping as he almost brought me to a climax, before taking his hand away.

'Come with me.' His voice was hoarse.

My knees felt decidedly weak, but somehow I managed to totter after Daniel into his bedroom.

'Lie on the bed,' he said.

In a haze of lust, I sank down onto the bed, while Daniel took off his jeans. He knelt over me and kissed me hard on my mouth. I felt his lips and his tongue on my neck and my breasts, and then his head was between my thighs, and I was writhing with pleasure and… again he stopped before I'd come.

'Daniel, please…'

'What's the hurry, babe? *Fallen Angel II* has wrapped, I don't have to learn a script for tomorrow's shooting. If we want, we can spend all day having sex.'

'Don't make me beg,' I said.

Daniel laughed, and lay down on his back. My eyes strayed to his erection.

'I'm all yours, babe.' he said.

I bent over him and took him in my mouth.

After some minutes, he groaned. 'Enough.'

I raised my head. 'Don't you like that?'

'You know I do. Very much. But you need to stop now.' He pulled open a bedside drawer and got out a condom. I straddled him, and he thrust himself inside me. His hands were on my waist and on my breasts, and I grinded my hips against him, gasping as he plunged into me again and again. When I came, it was so intense that I cried out. I felt his body shudder and rise towards me as he reached his own climax, before I collapsed on the bed beside him, breathless and slick with sweat. I rolled onto my stomach, resting my head on my folded arms. He lay on his side, his face close to mine and draped an arm across my back.

'You'd never cheat on me, would you, Lucy?' he said, quietly.

'I - I'd never cheat on anyone,' I said, wondering

why he would ask me a question like that.

'I want… never to hurt you.'

'Then don't.' My voice was scarcely above a whisper.

Daniel's mouth lifted in a satisfied smile, and he closed his eyes. Soon, his regular breathing and the weight of his arm told me that he had drifted into sleep. I lay very still so as not to wake him, and watched him while he slept.

And that was when I decided that I was in love with Daniel Miller, and when - or if - he asked me to live with him, I was going to say *yes*.

CHAPTER 21

'He actually stayed in the wardrobe the whole night?' Cassie, sitting next to me on my bed, struggled to keep a straight face. 'Your friend Owen doesn't have much luck with women, does he?'

'He told me once that he's never had a relationship that's lasted longer than a few weeks,' I said. 'I can't understand it. He's such a nice guy.'

'Maybe he's useless in bed,' Cassie said.

Without thinking, I said, 'That seems unlikely. He's got a great body, and everything appears to be in working order.'

'And you know this how?'

'Oh – one time, I accidently saw him without his clothes.'

'It happens,' Cassie said.

'Yeah. What can you do?' I was *not* going to start thinking about Owen's abs. 'So Owen's date ended badly, and he's about to be made homeless, but the good news is that he got one of the jobs he auditioned for last week. It's only a small part in a filler –'

'A what?' Cassie said.

'A filler. A play with a limited run that's put on to stop a house going dark.'

'Translation please, Lucy! I've only ever worked in TV, remember.'

'Sorry. When a long-running play closes, if there's a break before another production is due to

212

open, sometimes they put on a play for just a few weeks so that the theatre doesn't stand empty.'

'You love knowing all this stuff, don't you?' Cassie said. 'You should've done a degree in Theatre Studies, not English Literature.'

'I should,' I said. 'Anyway, Owen's play is only a filler, but it's in a theatre on Shaftsbury Avenue, which means he gets to make his West End debut. And he has a new, young, hot-shot director. There's been a lot of talk about this production in the industry.'

'I'm guessing that's not only good for Owen's career, but also for yours?'

'It certainly is,' I said.

Owen's first performance on the West End stage might not bring much money into Reardon Haye (if you think all West End actors earn fabulous salaries, you'd be wrong), but having one of our clients in such a prestigious show was extremely good for our reputation as a top theatrical agency. And for my reputation as a theatrical agent, as I'd put Owen up for the audition and handled his contract when he was offered the part.

'Owen's career may not be in the same league as Daniel's,' I said, 'but as a jobbing actor, he's doing fine.'

'And how is your film star boyfriend?' Cassie asked. 'Has he been behaving himself?'

'As far as I know,' I said. 'If he hasn't, I'm sure *Goss* or *Celeb* would have published the photographs by now.'

213

'So you and Daniel are doing OK?'

'We're good.'

'Which fab event is he taking you to tonight then?' Cassie said.

'It's the launch party for some WAG's perfume,' I said. 'I forget her name. Daniel gets invited to so many celeb parties.'

'And you get to be his arm candy!'

I smiled ruefully. 'I tag along with him when I can. When I'm available. I do have events of my own to attend on behalf of the agency.'

'Ryan and I find it hard to juggle our schedules at times,' Cassie said. 'It must be the same for you and Daniel.'

'It can be. No-one ever said that dating a *film star* was going to be easy. But Daniel's worth it.'

'Of course he is,' Cassie laughed. 'He's rich, famous, and hot.'

'He's also a very gifted actor.'

'So *that's* why you're dating him. It's nothing to do with his being hot.'

'I'm in love with him, Cassie.'

Cassie was silent for a moment, and then she said, 'Do you mean that you and Daniel are getting *serious*?'

'We... could be. He's decided to buy a house... and I'm pretty sure he's going to ask me to live with him.'

When we'd viewed the house in Primrose Hill, Daniel had asked my opinion on everything from the kitchen worktops ('Yes, Daniel, there's plenty of room for a microwave.') to the taps in bathrooms ('No, Daniel, I don't think gold ones would look better.'). He'd even invited me to inspect the wardrobe space in the master bedroom. The estate agent who'd showed us round, once she'd got over her completely unprofessional excitement when she first came face to face with Daniel Miller, had assumed that we were both moving into the house, and made a point of speaking to me as much as to him. He'd said nothing that might have disillusioned her. Afterwards, we'd gone for a walk on the Hill, and he'd kissed me and asked me if I liked the area. He hadn't actually asked me to move in with him, but it seemed to me that I had every justification in thinking that he was about to.

I'd expected Cassie to say that she was happy for me, but she just smiled rather tightly, and said, 'Living together – that's taking your relationship to a whole new level.'

'I realise that,' I said.

'Is it what you want?'

'I want to be with him. Of course I do.'

'But is Daniel ready for that sort of commitment? This is the Fallen Angel we're talking about. He's such a man-slut –' Cassie put her hand over her mouth. 'I shouldn't have said that. I'm sorry - I'm *so* sorry - really I am. But there's so much gossip in the industry – and I've seen so much stuff on the internet about Daniel shagging all those actresses. I know it was before he met you, but guys like him don't change. Sorry, I should probably stop talking now.

Don't be mad at me.'

'I'm not.'

'It's just that – last summer – I know how unhappy you were. I don't want you to get hurt again.'

'I'm not mad at you, Cassie. 'But you of all people should know that most of that rubbish on the internet is made up.'

'Some of it's true,' Cassie said.

'You don't need to worry about me.'

'He's a player, Lucy. Don't let that bad boy break your heart.'

'I won't.'

'Are you sure you're not mad at me?' Cassie said.

'Really, I'm not mad,' I said. 'You're my friend. I know you're just looking out for me. Now let's talk about something else.' I wasn't angry with Cassie, but I suspected that if she carried on reminding me about Daniel's track record with women, I would be. Daniel *had* changed since he'd been with me. I knew he had. I was the 'Girl who tamed the Fallen Angel.'

Cassie gave me a long look, but all she said was, 'This new play of Owen's – what's it about?'

'It's a comedy…' We talked about the play until Ryan arrived back from football and Cassie went off to hear all about the match - especially the goal he'd scored in extra time.

Realising that Daniel would be arriving in less than an hour to pick me up in a limo, I quickly showered, did my hair and make-up, and spent a happy ten minutes choosing what I was going to wear out of my growing collection of glitzy dresses. Once I was suitably glammed up, deciding that if I was going to be spending the rest of the night drinking free champagne, I probably ought to eat something, I went downstairs to make myself a sandwich.

Cassie and Ryan were sitting at the kitchen table demolishing a Chinese take-away. Ryan offered me a spring roll, which I accepted. He also offered me some beer, which I declined because of the champagne I intended to be drinking later.

'Where are you off to tonight?' Ryan asked me.

'Daniel has an invite to the launch of a WAG's new perfume,' I said. 'Is it dreadful of me not to remember her name when I'm going to her party?'

'Only if she knows *your* name,' Cassie said.

'Oh, well that's all right then. I'm sure she has more important things to do than memorise the name of Daniel Miller's girlfriend.'

'Her name's Zoe Dexter,' Ryan said. 'She's dating Thierry Belanger – he's one of the premiership's leading midfielders. She's a dancer.'

Cassie said, 'Ryan, have you been reading *Goss*?'

'No,' Ryan said, 'but I'm on the guest list for Zoe Dexter's perfume launch party. We can go, if you like.'

'Oh, I don't think so,' Cassie said.

'Why not?' Ryan said. 'It's Saturday night. Let's go out and party.'

'But you hate celebrity parties,' Cassie said. 'You're always telling me that football is a sport, not part of showbusiness.'

'I'd prefer to be known for the number of goals I've scored rather than the number of soap stars I've pulled, or the number of times I've been in rehab, but that doesn't mean I want to spend every night sat at home with a good book. Come out with me tonight, Cassie.'

I paused in the act of biting into my spring roll. 'You could come in the limo with me and Daniel. It'd be like a double date.'

'Princess Snowdrop doesn't go on dates with footballers,' Cassie said.

'Oh, for Chrissake!' Ryan snapped. 'You're not Princess frickin' Snowdrop. You're Cassie Clarke.'

The colour drained from Cassie's face. 'Please don't shout at me, Ryan.'

'I'm sorry. I apologise.' Ryan sprang up, almost knocking over his chair, and got a can of lager out of the fridge.

I swallowed my last bite of spring roll, and decided that I should probably make myself scarce.

'I have to be so careful, Ryan,' Cassie said. 'I have to think of my image. It's in my contract. And you know what the press are like.'

'You're twenty-five years old and you can't be seen out with a guy?' Ryan said incredulously.

'When you put it like that, it does sound a bit ridiculous.' Cassie put her elbows on the table, and rested her chin on her hands. 'Maybe it is time the media knew about our relationship. I'll speak to *Snowdrop's* producers and my publicist, and see how they think we could spin it.'

'We should get married,' Ryan said suddenly.

Now I knew I should definitely get out of that kitchen. I stood up and started to edge towards the door.

Cassie laughed. 'You and I are too young to get married.'

'I'm serious, Cassie.'

'You want to *marry* me?'

'Isn't that what happens in fairy tales?' Ryan said. 'The Princess marries her Prince and they live happily ever after. And the press are ecstatic.'

Cassie just stared at him.

'So, are we getting married?' Ryan said. There was a note of desperation in his voice.

I thought, come on, Cassie. Put the man out of his misery. Say *yes*. I stopped pretending that I was going to give them some privacy. I was rooted to the spot.

The kitchen door swung open. Nadia stood in the doorway, her hands on her hips.

'Didn't you hear the doorbell, Lucy?' she said. 'Daniel's arrived. I've left him in the living room talking to Leo.'

'I'll go and find him.' If Daniel's with Poor Leo, I thought, I'd better go and rescue him. I stayed in the kitchen.

Nadia looked at Cassie and frowned. 'You're very pale, Cassie. Are you OK?'

'I'm fine.' Cassie was still staring at Ryan. She gave an almost imperceptible nod of her head.

Ryan's face broke into the broadest smile *ever*.

219

'Cassie and I are getting married.'

I couldn't help shrieking aloud.

Cassie looked dazed. Ryan went to her, and she stood up so that he could put his arms around her.

'Congratulations!' I said. 'Many, many congratulations. I'm so happy for you!'

'That's… wonderful news,' Nadia said. 'I'm thrilled.'

I didn't think she sounded very pleased, but neither Cassie nor Ryan appeared to notice.

Daniel, looking particularly gorgeous that night, his dark hair curling over his ears, appeared in the kitchen doorway. At the sight of him, my stomach did its usual gymnastics.

'Hi, guys,' he said. 'Lucy, we're already fashionably late for this launch party. I'd like to get going. Are you ready?'

'Sorry, Daniel,' I said. 'I've been ready for a while, but I got a bit distracted. Cassie and Ryan have just got engaged.'

Daniel's smile was almost as broad as Ryan's. Everyone in the kitchen, with the exception of Nadia, was smiling. It was like we were auditioning for a toothpaste advert.

'Congratulations and well done mate,' Daniel said, shaking Ryan's hand. He gave Cassie a kiss on the cheek. 'Congratulations, lovely.'

'Thank you,' Cassie said. 'Thank you, all of you.'

'This needs a toast,' Ryan said. 'Do we have any champagne?'

'I don't think so,' Cassie said.

'There's champagne outside in my limo,' Daniel said. 'I'll fetch a bottle.'

'If you don't mind waiting another ten minutes while Ryan and I get changed, Daniel, we'd love to cadge a lift in your limo to Zoe Dexter's perfume launch. We could drink the champagne on the way.'

'Sounds good,' Daniel said.

'Is that OK with you, Ryan?' Cassie said.

For an answer, Ryan picked her up and swung her round in a circle before kissing her firmly on her mouth.

'It's *so* OK with me,' he said.

'But is it sensible?' Nadia said. 'I mean, if you want to keep your relationship private.'

'I don't,' Ryan said. 'I'm marrying Cassie Clarke, and I want to tell the world.'

Nadia turned to Cassie. 'Is this party the right sort of event for Princess Snowdrop to attend? Especially if she's planning to arrive in the same car as Daniel Miller – no offence, Daniel.'

'I'll be there as well,' I said. 'Cassie, you can't possibly come to the launch. Snowdrop's reputation will be irredeemably tarnished if she rocks up to a party with a girl who *isn't a celebrity*.'

'But you're an honorary celebrity, babe,' Daniel said. 'You're the Fallen Angel's girlfriend.'

'It's OK,' I said to Cassie. 'You can be seen in public with me. I'm famous for dating a famous person.'

'So let's go party,' Cassie said.

Cassie and Ryan changed into a dress and a suit

respectively and, leaving Nadia to give Poor Leo the good news about Princess Snowdrop's engagement, the four of us headed out of Cassie's house and piled into Daniel's limo. Daniel opened the champagne and poured us all a drink.

'To Cassie and Ryan,' he said, raising his glass. 'May you always be as happy as you are tonight.'

'Cassie and Ryan,' I said.

We clinked glasses and drank. Daniel slid along the seat so that his thigh was pressed against mine, and put his arm around my shoulders. I leant against him, and he kissed the top of my head.

'Should we have asked Nadia and Leo to join us, do you think?' Cassie said suddenly.

'No,' Ryan said. 'Nadia's your employee, not your friend.'

'I know,' Cassie said, 'but she enjoys coming with me to showbiz events, and I don't mind if she tags along.' She added, 'I actually feel rather sorry for Nadia.'

'Why?' Daniel said.

'She used to be an actress, but her career never took off. I met her when she had a walk-on part in *Snowdrop*, but she never had any other acting work after that.'

'You gave her a job,' Ryan said. 'You don't need to feel sorry for her.'

Cassie sighed. 'She says she likes working for me, but I know she misses acting. She's hinted a few times about me getting her more work on my show, but it's not something I can do for her. I may be the star, but I don't have that sort of influence with the casting team. I can't persuade them to hire someone who is totally wrong for a part.'

I said, 'Not even Eleanor Haye can do that.'

Ryan put a finger on Cassie's chin and turned her face towards his.

'You are the sweetest, kindest girl I've ever met,' he said. 'And I love you very much.'

He adores her, I thought.

'More champagne anyone?' Daniel said.

CHAPTER 22

'I didn't know if you'd make it in today,' Eleanor said to me when I arrived at work on Monday morning. 'I thought Cassie's house might be still besieged by photographers hoping to get a shot of the happy couple.'

'There was just one girl with a camera outside when I left this morning,' I said. 'She was extremely irritated when I told her that Cassie and Ryan weren't there. They went to Ryan's place last night – after the paparazzi had gone home.'

Eleanor frowned. 'How's Cassie coping with all the attention?'

'She's doing fine. She and Ryan stood on the doorstep and posed for a few photos, and the press were really kind to them. Of course, the fact that Ryan went round with a tray of glasses and offered them all celebratory champagne may have helped.'

'And how are you coping, Lucy?'

'Me?'

'You're getting quite a bit of attention yourself these days. And I don't just mean the media circus that went on yesterday outside Cassie's house.'

I shrugged. 'I only seem to get papped when I'm with Daniel, and I'm used to it by now.'

'Compared to Cassie and Ryan, you and Daniel have certainly had it easy,' Eleanor said. 'Even so, if you need to take some holiday to recharge your batteries you only have to ask.'

'I'm good, Eleanor, but thank you.'

In actual fact, at that moment, I was feeling exhausted. On Saturday night, we'd arrived *un*fashionably late at the club in Knightsbridge where the perfume launch was being held, but were still in time to be met with a barrage of flashing cameras as soon as we emerged from our limo. The party itself had been a mix of alcohol, A and B-list celebrities, alcohol, live music, air-kissing, queuing for the loos, and more alcohol. Unusually, for such an event, I didn't see anyone doing drugs. I chatted with friends like Rochelle Thorne, with other people who I only knew because they (or their current squeeze) were on the same guest lists as Daniel, and with people I didn't know at all, but whose famous faces I recognised. Rochelle introduced me to Zoe Dexter (who'd been a backing dancer for the Thorne Sisters on their UK arena tour), and we'd had an interesting conversation about ballet and contemporary dance. Daniel spent the night surrounded by salivating women. Ryan spent the night with his arm around Cassie's waist, telling everyone he spoke to that they were getting married, and the news of their engagement spread like wildfire through the party, from celebrity to celebrity, from dance floor to bar, and beyond. By the time the four of us stumbled from the club clutching our complimentary bottles of Zoe's perfume, the press outside were already speculating about the date of the wedding, the guests, and the honeymoon destination. The camera flashes were blinding. We'd got back to Cassie's at around three in the morning, and had managed just a few hours' sleep before the photographers and journalists started setting up camp (noisily) on the pavement in front of the house, and the phones started ringing. Louella, Cassie's enthusiastic publicist, and her assistant had arrived mid-morning. Nadia was in her element, liaising with Cassie's fan club, fielding calls from gossip columnists, and telling everyone else what to do:

'Lucy, you can see how busy we are, if you could make everyone coffee it'd be a great help to Cassie.'

I kept Eleanor updated with regular texts.

It had been Daniel's idea that Ryan should hand out glasses of champagne (liberated from our limo the previous night) to the press, and it proved a good move, as the atmosphere on the pavement became very good-humoured. Cassie and Ryan bowed to the inevitable and made several appearances on Cassie's doorstep, turning this way and that for photos and answering even the most intrusive questions with unfailing politeness. I was sure that Daniel wouldn't have objected to posing for a few photos, but it was Ryan and Cassie's moment, so we stayed inside and kept away from the windows. Nadia accidently managed to insert herself into one of the photo calls (wearing her best jeans and a lot of make-up, I noticed) when she'd taken another bottle of champagne outside to Ryan. It had been a very long day, and for the first time since I'd starting working at Reardon Haye it had been an effort for me to force myself out of bed on Monday morning and get to the office on time. But there was no way I was going to admit that to my boss.

Eleanor said, 'You're entitled to take a day off work now and then, Lucy. Actually, you're entitled to twenty five days off per annum plus public holidays. Check your contract.'

'Daniel and I are thinking about going on holiday,' I said. 'Once he's moved into his new house.' *And I'm living there with him. Hopefully.*

'Well, don't leave it too long, or he'll be starting another film.' With that, Eleanor swept into her office and closed her door.

Smothering a yawn, I turned on my computer and started replying to the numerous emails that had accumulated in my inbox since Friday (I swear that some actors spend their whole weekend emailing their agents).

Maria arrived, less interested in Cassie and Ryan's new status as the Nation's Sweethearts, than in the trouble she was having with her car. Adrian came in soon after, carrying a newspaper. A photo of Cassie and Ryan took up half of the front page.

'I broke up with Terri at the weekend,' he said, by way of greeting.

'Aw, Adrian, I'm sorry,' Maria said.

'I'm so sorry to hear that, Adrian,' I said. 'Are you OK? I mean, obviously you're not OK...'

'I'll get over it.' Adrian sat down at his desk and ran his hand through his hair. 'I feel like shit right now though.'

'When you've been with someone a long time,'

227

Maria said, 'even when you know the relationship has run its course, it's still hard to make that final break. It still hurts.'

'We've all been there,' I said. 'Even if you're the one who breaks it off because the man you're sleeping with turns out to be a lying, cheating love-rat, you still cry yourself a river.'

'But you get through it,' Maria said. 'And sometimes you realise that maybe it wasn't your boyfriend's fault that you drifted apart, it was just that he was the wrong guy at the wrong time in the wrong place. And you did have a good five years together.'

'Even when it's most definitely the guy's fault, you get through it,' I said. 'And when you're in a new relationship, you wonder what you ever saw in your sad loser of an ex.'

'I've had it with *relationships*,' Adrian said. 'It's strictly one night only for me from now on.'

'You don't mean that,' I said.

'I so do.' Adrian picked up his newspaper and studied the photo of Cassie and Ryan. 'The actress and the footballer. Is this for real or is it just a publicity stunt?'

'It's for real,' I said. 'Cassie and Ryan are crazy about each other.'

'It won't last.' Adrian chucked the newspaper in the bin.

CHAPTER 23

Two weeks later, Daniel signed the papers that made him the owner of the house in Primrose Hill. Ryan bought Cassie a diamond solitaire engagement ring. And Owen made his West End debut at the Aphra Behn theatre in *Live, Laugh, Love*.

'Are you sure you want me there?' Daniel said to me, as I put the finishing touches to my make-up, before we left for the theatre on Owen's opening night.

'Of course I do,' I said. 'Why wouldn't I?' I surveyed my reflection critically in my dressing table mirror. For a first night, I aimed to look elegant and sophisticated rather than glam. I decided that in my knee-length dress and vertiginously high-heeled court shoes, I'd managed to pull it off.

Daniel had been lounging on my bed, but now he came and stood behind me. 'You know what it's like when we go out, Lucy. If I come with you to see this play, I'll probably attract more attention sitting in the stalls than the actors performing on the stage.'

'When have you ever minded being stared at?'

'I was thinking of you,' Daniel said. 'You're supposed to be going to the play as Owen's agent, not the Fallen Angel's girlfriend.'

'I'm sure I can do both,' I said. 'Besides, once the play begins, everyone'll forget you're there.'

'No they won't,' Daniel said. 'I'm unforgettable.'

'You're so up yourself,' I said.

Daniel put his hands on my shoulders, turned me around to face him, and kissed me, a long languorous kiss that left me breathless.

'I think I've every right to be up myself,' he said.

'You do when you kiss me like that.' I smiled at him. He trailed a finger down the side of my face. He cleared his throat.

This is it, I thought. This is the moment when he tells me he loves me and asks me to live with him in his new house in Primrose Hill.

I tried not to mind when all he said was, 'Lucy, your lipstick's smudged.'

Arriving at the theatre by taxi, we made it across the pavement and through the doors before Daniel was inevitably recognised. Whispers followed us through the foyer and into the auditorium: 'Look, isn't that Daniel Miller?' and 'That's Daniel Miller - I think that's his girlfriend, Lucy What's-her-face,' and 'Oh my goodness, it's Daniel Miller.' Heads turned as we walked down the central aisle to the front of the stalls.

A few minutes after we'd found our seats, those next to us were taken by Owen's other guests, Michael and Annette. I introduced them to Daniel, and to my relief they displayed no signs of being starstruck. We all chatted easily until a disembodied voice reminded us to switch off our mobiles, the houselights went out, and the play, a dark, satirical, and extremely funny comedy, began.

Owen had told me once that he never suffered

from nerves before a performance, but as I sat waiting for him to walk out onto that West End stage, I found myself nervous for him. I needn't have worried. As soon as he made his entrance towards the end of Act I, and delivered his first line with perfect comic timing, he had the audience laughing out loud. In the interval, when we went to the bar, I heard his name mentioned more often than the play's leading man, if not quite as often as Daniel's.

'Owen's so good,' I said to the others, as we stood in a corner, drinking our interval drinks, and ignoring the sidelong glances from the people in the bar who had recognised my boyfriend.

'He's brilliant,' Michael said.

'I do not understand all the English words he says,' Annette said, 'but when he is acting you have to look at him, *non*?'

'Yes, you do,' I said. 'You're right. Owen has great stage presence.'

Daniel said, 'I was two years above him in drama school, and I have to admit that I never rated him as an actor, but tonight… Well, he's certainly got something.'

'I am so excited to see him in a famous theatre,' Annette said. 'Have you acted in the West End, Daniel?'

'No, I've no desire to perform live.'

Annette's English had improved a lot since I'd first met her, but now she looked confused.

'Daniel only acts in films and television,' I said to her in French. *'He doesn't want to work in the theatre.'*

231

'You like only the cinema, Daniel?' Annette said. 'But Owen says that all actors want to act in the West End. Even the stars of Hollywood.'

'Owen and I are very different,' Daniel said. 'He's passionate about *acting*. I'm only interested in roles that are going to make me a lot of money.'

I laughed. 'You are *so* shallow.'

'Yes, I am.' Daniel said.

Annette smiled a little uncertainly. 'Shallow?'

I said. '*Il est tres superficiel.*' Somehow, it sounded more damning in French.

'*Superficiel?*' Annette said. 'Ah, you are joking. *Pardonnez-moi.* I do not understand the English jokes.'

The second bell rang, signalling the end of the interval, so we drained our glasses and returned to our seats. Owen made only a brief appearance in Act II, but once again he had the audience in fits of laughter. The cheers when he took his bow at the curtain call were deafening.

'Are you sure you don't want to do live theatre?' I said to Daniel, as the audience got to its feet to give the cast a standing ovation. 'Wouldn't you like to stand on a stage and listen to an audience going wild?'

'Only if it's the stage at the Oscars and I'm making my Best Actor acceptance speech,' Daniel said.

A small-scale production like *Live, Laugh, Love* didn't have the budget for a lavish after-party, but once the paying audience had left the theatre, Daniel and I, Michael and Annette, and other invited guests crowded back into the bar to meet up with the cast for celebratory drinks. The young, hot-shot director and his actors made their entrance together, and were greeted by another tremendous round of clapping. The director made a short speech, thanking everyone who'd been involved in the production for all their hard work, and the leading man made a speech thanking the wonderful audience. And then, after more clapping, the actors were finally free to join their assembled friends, family and agents, bask in the warmth of their congratulations, and drink the cheap white wine provided by the theatre management.

Having spotted our group while the director was making his speech, Owen started to make his way through the crowd towards us, but was waylaid by a man I recognised as a theatre critic. Having extracted himself, he was immediately surrounded by the extended family of one of the other actors. I turned to Daniel to suggest that we go and join them, only to find him deep in conversation with the hot-shot director. I turned back to Michael and Annette, but they had vanished into the increasingly animated crowd. Then a man I knew slightly, the head of a rival theatrical agency, caught my eye and beckoned me over to where he was propping up the bar. Reminding myself that networking was part of my job, I went and sat on a bar stool next to him, and found myself bombarded with questions about whether I was happy working at Reardon Haye, and if I'd ever thought about moving to a larger agency, because he might have an opening for me. I'd have been flattered, if I hadn't suspected that he was only interested in hiring me because he thought I could bring Daniel Miller to his agency. I assured him that I had every intention of remaining at Reardon Haye for the foreseeable future, and dived back into the crowd in search of my friends.

'Hey, Lucy.' Suddenly Owen was standing in front of me, his blue eyes shining. He put his arms around me, pulling me close to give me a hug. I could almost feel the adrenaline still coursing through him.

'So how did I do?' he said.

'You did great, as if you didn't know that.' I smiled up at him. 'How does it feel to act in the West End?'

'Oh, Lucy, there's nothing like it –' Owen broke off abruptly as a girl, a tall, willowy blonde, stepped out of the crowd and put her hand on his arm.

'Hello, Owen,' she said.

'Vanessa!' Owen said. 'I'm so pleased you managed to get here.'

'I said I'd come if I possibly could,' the girl gushed in a cut-glass accent. 'And I'm very glad I did. You were *wonderful*, Owen. And so *funny*.'

All the while she was talking, the girl kept her hand possessively on Owen's arm. She was quite pretty, I decided, but there was something of the horse about her teeth.

'Thank you so much.' Owen beamed at the girl.

To me, he said, 'Lucy, this is Vanessa. When we were eighteen, she played Juliet to my Romeo – in a school play.'

'My one appearance on the stage,' Vanessa said.

'We hadn't seen each other in years,' Owen said. 'We met up again at that barbeque I went to the other week.'

'I was amazed when Owen told me he'd become an actor,' Vanessa said. 'I only did *Romeo and Juliet* because I was at an all-girls school and it was a joint production with the boys' school down the road. I thought it would be a good way to improve my social life.'

'I only took up acting to meet girls.' Owen laughed, and Vanessa joined in. She had a rather irritating laugh, I thought.

'Most of the cast of *Romeo and Juliet* were more interested in pulling than performing Shakespeare,' Vanessa said. 'Didn't you go out with the girl who played Lady Capulet?'

'Unfortunately, our relationship didn't last longer than a clinch at the cast party,' Owen said, 'but I seem to remember that you dated the boy who played Tybalt for a while?'

'I dated him for the whole of the summer term,' Vanessa said. 'We broke up when he went to Oxford, but I still run into him occasionally at parties. He works in the City now…'

Owen and Vanessa embarked on a long reminiscence about various people they both knew from their schooldays. Obviously, I couldn't join in the conversation, so I stood there in silence, trying to look interested, and wishing that Vanessa would go away so that I could talk to Owen about *Live, Laugh, Love* and his performance.

My gaze wandered around the room. I spotted Michael talking to the theatre critic, while Annette listened with an expression of intense concentration on her face as she tried to follow a discussion in English. And I saw Daniel sitting at the bar, talking to *Live, Laugh, Love's* leading actress, an attractive, vivacious woman in her thirties. The way she was looking at him and leaning towards him so that he couldn't avoid seeing down her top, I was pretty sure she was coming onto him. When she took a piece of paper out of her handbag and wrote something, presumably her phone number, on it before handing it to him, my suspicions were confirmed. I watched as Daniel read whatever she'd written, smiled, and put the paper in the back pocket of his jeans. Women came onto Daniel all the time, but that didn't make it any easier for me to see it. I fought a sudden impulse to pick up a glass of the theatre's disgusting wine and throw it in the actress's face. And over Daniel as well, because he didn't seem to be exactly discouraging her.

Vanessa said, 'Isn't that Daniel Miller over there at the bar?'

'Yes, it is,' Owen said.

'He is *so* hot,' she gushed. 'No wonder he's slept with so many women. Don't you agree, Lucy?'

'I - He's -' I really wasn't in the mood to discuss

236

my boyfriend's sexual prowess with this annoying school friend of Owen's.

'A good looking boy,' Owen said. 'It's a pity he's such a little whore.' Which was actually one of his lines from the play.

I glared at him, while Vanessa laughed her irritating laugh, as though he was some sort of comic genius.

'Owen, you are *hilarious,'* Vanessa said, when she'd managed to stop laughing. She added, 'I've had a really good time tonight, and I'd love to stay longer, but I have to go now and catch my train.'

'Are going to be OK going home on your own?' Owen asked. 'Would you like me to walk you to the station? Or maybe we could share a taxi?'

I remembered that he'd offered to share a taxi with me when I'd gone to see him in *Siblings.* I found myself even more irritated with this girl who'd monopolised his attention and was now going to drag him out of the theatre before I'd had a chance to have a proper talk with him.

'No, I'll be fine,' Vanessa said, 'I don't want to take you away from your friends.' Once again, she put her hand on his arm. 'It's been great seeing you, Owen.'

'Straight back at you,' Owen said. 'Maybe we could go for a drink sometime?'

I thought, is he asking her out on a date?

'Or how about lunch next week?'

He was asking her out on a date.

'That would be lovely,' Vanessa simpered.

'I'll call you.'

He'd asked her out on a date and she'd said yes. It struck me that while I'd been wishing Vanessa would go away and leave me alone with Owen, he'd most likely been wishing I'd push off and leave him alone with her. I thought, I am selfish, self-centred and a bad friend.

Vanessa said, 'Bye, Lucy. It was good to meet you.'

'You too.' I tried to sound like I meant it.

With several backward glances over her shoulder and a wave for Owen, Vanessa left the bar.

As soon as she'd gone, Owen said, 'Lucy, what I said to Vanessa about Daniel, I'm so sorry. It was just a line from the play.'

'I know. Don't worry about it.'

'And what she said –'

'It doesn't matter. Forget it.' I made myself smile. 'Besides, Daniel *is* hot, and he *has* slept with a lot of women.'

'She can't have recognised you, otherwise I'm sure she wouldn't have said anything like that.'

'It does seem rather unlikely.'

Suddenly, Owen's face broke into a grin. 'I remember being so nervous when I had to kiss her.'

I shot him a look. 'You *had* to kiss her?'

'In *Romeo and Juliet*,' Owen said. 'It was my first stage kiss, and I wanted it to look convincing. Especially as Tybalt was glaring at me from the wings.'

'The duel between Romeo and Tybalt in Act III

must have been interesting.'

Owen laughed. Then he said, 'Vanessa's lovely, isn't she?'

I thought, how would I know? I only met her half an hour ago. Aloud, I said, 'Yes, she seems very nice.'

Fortunately I was spared further discussion of Vanessa's inherent wondrousness by the arrival of Michael and Annette, and then Daniel, the three of them full of praise for both Owen and the play. When Daniel mentioned that he was surprised how old the leading lady was, I decided that my evening had improved considerably.

By now the crowd was thinning out as people started to leave the bar, and after one more glass of warm white wine, we left also. Daniel suggested we went on to a club, but the others weren't keen and none of us were dressed for clubbing. We ended up piling into a taxi and going back to Cassie's house, where Cassie and Ryan joined us as we sat around the kitchen table drinking coffee and eating biscuits. Michael and Annette did look a little wide-eyed as I introduced them to Princess Snowdrop and Ryan-he's-so-Fleet, but they recovered quickly, and Annette was soon admiring Cassie's engagement ring and wondering if she'd thought about flowers for her bridal bouquet. Michael, Daniel and Ryan talked about football before going on to cricket. I sat next to Owen, and we talked some more about *Live, Laugh, Love*, the cast of *Live, Laugh, Love* (the leading lady, Owen told me, was a right diva), and how Owen really needed to find a room to rent now that his landlord had chucked him out. He was currently living in Julie and Zac Diaz's spare bedroom, but didn't want to outstay his welcome.

It must have been after two in the morning when Michael got out his mobile and phoned for a minicab.

'It's all right for you actors to stay up all night,' he said to Owen, 'but some of us have real jobs to go to in the morning.'

'We actors have to get up early when we're filming,' Cassie said, 'but fortunately Princess Snowdrop has a day off tomorrow.'

'What is your job, Michael?' Ryan said.

'I'm a journalist,' Michael said.

Cassie shot Ryan a look of pure panic.

Oh, for goodness' sake, I thought.

'Relax, Cassie,' I said, 'Michael's not about to tell the world that Princess Snowdrop spent tonight in the company of the Fallen Angel – and forget to mention that her fiancé was there as well. He writes for a weekly newspaper not *Goss.*'

'You're not a showbiz journalist?' Cassie said. 'You don't write a gossip column?'

'Lord, no,' Michael said. 'I've no interest in writing about *celebrities* – no offence.'

Ryan laughed. 'None taken.'

'What do you write about?' Cassie said to Michael.

'I'm a political correspondent,' Michael said. 'Well, I will be one day. At the moment my assignments are mainly local council meetings and un-neighbourly disputes over parking. But I have to start somewhere, right?'

Cassie forced a smile.

'Am I right in thinking that you don't have a very high opinion of my noble profession?' Michael said.

Cassie flushed. 'I've not liked reading some of the rubbish journalists have written about me and Ryan.'

'It is different in France,' Annette said. 'We have the laws that protect the privacy of the famous people.'

'But why should they be protected?' Michael's eyes suddenly had an adversarial glint.

Rising to the challenge, I said, 'Surely people in the public eye are entitled to keep their *personal* lives private?'

'Not always,' Michael said. 'If a politician spends his evenings picking up underage rent boys, I think the people who voted for him have a right to know.'

'I'm not talking about corrupt politicians or shady financiers,' I said. 'I'm talking about people like my clients.'

'Your clients who employ publicists to keep their names in the papers?' Michael said.

'All I'm saying is that there's a difference between newsgathering and scandalmongering.'

The front door bell rang.

'Much as I'd like to debate the freedom of the press with you, Lucy,' Michael said, 'that's our cab.' He stood up and smiled at Cassie. 'Thank you for your hospitality. And I promise that anything you've said to me tonight is entirely off the record.'

'He will not write about you, Cassie.' Annette also got to her feet and picked up her bag. 'It is not good for him to write about his friends. I do not allow.'

'Just so you know, Michael,' Daniel said, 'you can write about me anytime. You can make it up, if you like. I don't mind.'

I rolled my eyes at Annette. '*Il est tres superficiel*,' I said.

'What you see is what you get,' Daniel said.

'Then it's lucky for you that I like what I see,' I said.

Daniel grinned wickedly and planted a kiss on the side of my face.

'I should get going as well,' Owen said. 'Michael, can I share your cab?'

'Of course,' Michael said. 'You can crash on our sofa tonight, if you like.'

After a short hiatus while we all hugged and air-kissed in true showbiz fashion, Michael and Annette, and Owen went out to their minicab. I waved them off, and re-joined the others at the kitchen table. Cassie and Ryan, who were openly yawning, drained their coffee mugs, said goodnight, and went to bed.

'Alone at last,' Daniel said.

In one sinuous movement, he sprang to his feet and pulled me off my chair. He grasped my upper arms and kissed me roughly, grinding his pelvis against mine, letting me feel how hard he was, how much he wanted me. A jolt of desire raced through me, and I kissed him back, my tongue in his mouth.

His hands slid down my body, and under my dress to caress my bare legs. Then he was hiking my dress up to my waist and tearing off my underwear, and I was unzipping his flies and tugging his jeans and boxers down over his hips.

He lifted me up and backed me onto the kitchen table, my arms around his neck, his hands under my thighs. There was a crash as a coffee mug fell off the table and shattered on the tiled floor. I wrapped my legs around him and he rammed himself inside me, in and out, hard and fast. I clung to him, abandoning myself to the intensity of sensations surging through my body, gasping and crying out as the torrent of passion crested and broke. He thrust into me more deeply, once, twice, and then he moaned, and his whole body shuddered and jerked as he pulled out of me and I felt him come, warm and wet on my thigh.

For a while we held each other as the beating of our hearts slowed and our breathing returned to normal. Then he stepped away from me and zipped up his jeans. I became aware that the edge of the kitchen table was digging uncomfortably into my backside and held out my hand so that he could help me to my feet.

I thought, we've just had sex on Cassie's kitchen table. Aloud I said, 'I can't believe what we just did.'

'It's OK, babe,' Daniel said. 'I was careful.' With a flourish, he handed me a kitchen towel.

I thought, I've had sex with Daniel on Cassie's kitchen table, and we didn't use a condom.

'I wasn't talking about *that*,' I said. I cleaned myself up. 'We're in the *kitchen*. Anyone could have come in.'

'Like who?' Daniel said. 'Cassie and Ryan are asleep and Nadia's out.' With a leer, he added. 'Once I've moved into my new house, I intend to have you in every room.'

'But this is *Cassie's* house. She *eats* at that table. We all do.'

'Yeah, next time we sit down to dinner together, all you and I are going to be thinking about is the incredible sex we had tonight.'

I couldn't help smiling. 'It was pretty incredible. You should put 'sex' under 'special skills' on your CV.'

'I might just do that. Now come to bed.'

I raised my eyebrows.

'Come to bed to sleep, Lucy. Don't tell the press, but I'm really not capable of a repeat performance right now.'

'You go on up. I'll follow you as soon as I've hidden the evidence of our incredible sex life.' I gestured at the pieces of broken coffee mug. Although I'd been living in Cassie's house for almost ten months, I still felt slovenly if I left the kitchen in a state overnight for Erin the housekeeper to deal with in the morning.

'Don't be long. By the way – your knickers are over there by the door.' Looking very pleased with himself, Daniel swaggered off upstairs.

We'd had sex and we hadn't used a condom. I

retrieved my knickers from the floor where Daniel had tossed them, and put them on. I swept up the shards of crockery.

I'm supposed to be clever, I thought. I have a First Class Degree. I'm twenty-three years old. I'm not some naive teenager who believes her boyfriend when he says he'll take it out in time. I put the other mugs in the dishwasher and the remaining biscuits away in a tin.

First thing tomorrow, I thought, before I go to work, I have to visit a pharmacy. I knew that it was actually fairly unlikely that I'd just conceived Daniel's child, but I wasn't taking any chances.

But how could he have been so irresponsible? Not that I'd exactly fought him off. How could *I* have been so irresponsible? It was as though the sensual touch of Daniel's hands on my body obliterated my ability to think.

After opening several drawers and cupboards, I found where Erin kept her cleaning products, and blushing furiously, although there was no-one there to see me, I washed the kitchen table. It just seemed like the right thing to do.

I surveyed my handiwork. The kitchen was immaculate. Except for a small piece of paper lurking by the fridge. I picked up the paper, unfolded it, and read the name of *Live, Laugh, Love's* leading lady and a mobile number. It must have fallen out of Daniel's pocket while we were banging away, oblivious to anything except each other. It wasn't that I didn't trust Daniel, not exactly, but I couldn't think of any good reason why he would need that woman's phone number.

I tore the paper to shreds and threw it in the rubbish bin.

I might have let my feelings for my Fallen Angel overcome my intelligence and my common sense to such an extent that I'd had irresponsible, unprotected sex with him on a kitchen table, but I wasn't *completely* stupid.

CHAPTER 24

'Hey, Cassie.' I sat on Daniel's bed, my laptop balanced on my knees. Cassie smiled back at me from my computer screen, courtesy of Skype.

'Hey, yourself,' she said. 'How's it going in Primrose Hill? Have you opened the celebratory champagne?'

The previous day, Daniel had picked up the keys to his new house – or rather, the removal company he'd hired had picked them up for him. Specialists in house moves for the rich and famous, they'd orchestrated the whole thing. Daniel had left them to pack up everything at his old flat, he and I'd spent the night at Cassie's, and when we arrived at his new house this morning, everything was unpacked, ready and waiting for us.

'The champagne's on ice, I'm afraid,' I said. 'We just about had time to look over the place and find out how everything works before Daniel had to go out. He's appearing on a chat show for the BBC.' I glanced at my watch. Ten o'clock. 'I promised him I'd watch it, but it's not on for another hour. So we've time for the virtual guided tour. If you like.'

'I wouldn't mind a tour of the famous movie star's mansion.'

I laughed. 'It's not a mansion. It's a desirable modern townhouse in a highly sought-after area. This is the master bedroom...'

Carrying my laptop, I went from room to room,

pointing out to Cassie all the features that had attracted me to the house when Daniel had first shown me the photos on the estate agent's website. We ended up in the long through-room that took up most of the ground floor, where she was suitably admiring of the contemporary design of the fireplace. I sat down on Daniel's new L-shaped sofa.

'I'm impressed,' Cassie said. 'It's a beautiful house.'

'It is,' I said. 'I just wish Daniel would get his act together and ask me to live in it.'

'He hasn't said anything about you moving in?'

'Not yet. But he's always talking to me about the house – asking me where I think furniture should go and that sort of thing – so I'm sure it's only a matter of time.'

'Well, there's no hurry, is there?' Cassie said. After a moment, she added, 'Lucy – don't rush into anything you might regret.'

'I won't,' I said. But inwardly I thought, I'd move in with Daniel tomorrow if he asked me.

'And how is the other man in your life?' Cassie asked.

'Owen?' I said. 'I've not seen much of him lately. Actually, I've not seen him at all since the first night of his play. His new girlfriend seems to take up all of his spare time.'

'He has a girlfriend?' Cassie said. 'Have you met her?'

'Very briefly,' I said. 'Her name's Vanessa. She looks a bit like a horse.'

'Oh. So you don't like her.'

'I never said I don't like her.'

'Well, that's good,' Cassie said, 'because it could be very awkward if Owen was dating a girl you didn't like. What with you and him being so close.'

'It doesn't matter to me who he's dating,' I said. It shouldn't matter, but it did. 'Anyway, I told you, I've not seen him in a while.'

'Maybe his girlfriend doesn't want him hanging out with you,' Cassie said. 'Some girls get very possessive, even when they've only been with a guy a few weeks. She might be worried that you and he are more than just good friends.'

'Then she's going to be one very worried woman,' I said, 'because a lot of Owen's friends are female.'

'Or maybe,' Cassie said, 'he's one of those people who drop their friends the moment they're *in a relationship*.'

I shrugged. 'I wouldn't know.'

'Still, you must be pleased that he's met someone.'

'Of course,' I said.

Since the night of his West End debut, engraved on my mind for ever as Kitchen Table Night (oh, the relief when I knew for sure that I wasn't pregnant – I was never going to let myself get carried away like that again), I'd spoken on the phone to Owen just once. I'd asked how things were going with Vanessa, but all he'd said was that they'd had lunch, that he was seeing her again, and then he'd abruptly changed the subject. I'd texted him the following Sunday, the one day of the week he wasn't at the theatre, suggesting we meet for a drink, but he texted back that he was taking Vanessa out to dinner. The day after *Live, Laugh, Love* closed, I got a text from him saying they were going to Paris for a few days, and he'd be in touch. That had been two weeks ago, and I hadn't heard from him since. I wasn't at all pleased that he was devoting all his time and attention to Vanessa. I missed him. Desperately.

'Of course I'm pleased for him.' I checked the time. 'Cassie, I'm going to have to go. Daniel's chat show starts in five minutes.'

'No worries,' Cassie said.

'I'll be home tomorrow after work.'

'See you then.' She ended the call.

I switched on the TV. The chat show had already started, but Daniel wasn't the first guest, and I found myself watching a supermodel plugging her book of make-up tips. She was followed by a soap star plugging her exercise DVD. Bored, I picked up my mobile and scrolled through my messages, deleting most of them until I came to the text Owen had sent me two weeks ago: *We're off to Paris for a few days. Will call u when I get back. Owen xx*

Why hadn't he called me? I'd have liked to have heard about his trip. Closing my text messages, I went into Facebook and brought up Owen's page. I wasn't stalking him, I told myself. I was just going to look at his holiday photos. Annoyingly, he hadn't posted anything since *Live, Laugh, Love* had opened, but the lack of a photographic record didn't stop me picturing him holding hands with the wonderful Vanessa as they strolled along the banks of the Seine.

So what if he's seeing Vanessa, I thought, he's still my friend.

I brought up Owen's number on my phone, and hit the call button. He answered straight away.

'Lucy. Hang on a sec.' He was almost inaudible above the sound of loud excited chatter and piano music. 'I'll just go into another room.'

There was a pause, and then the music faded.

'Are you OK to talk? I don't want to interrupt anything'

'I'm good,' Owen said. 'I'm only at Zac and Julie's place.'

'It sounds like they're having a party.'

'No, it's just a few friends drinking too much wine and playing Zac's piano rather badly. Lucy, are you all right?'

'Yes, I'm fine' I said. 'Why wouldn't I be?'

'No reason. But eleven thirty at night is an unusual time for you to call me.'

'It's just that I realised we haven't spoken in a while,' I said. 'I didn't really think about the time.'

'Hey, I'm not complaining. And you're right. It's been too long. It's good to hear from you.'

I could tell by the tone of his voice that he was smiling.

I said, 'So how was your trip to Paris?'

'Paris was great. We did all the tourist stuff: the Eiffel Tower, the Louvre, Notre Dame, the Museé D'Orsay. And in the evenings, Annette took us to the

251

bars and restaurants the tourists don't know about.'

'Oh... I didn't realise you went to Paris with Michael and Annette.'

'I wasn't with them the whole time. I did do some exploring on my own while they visited her parents.'

He'd explored Paris on his own? 'Didn't Vanessa go with you?'

'Er, no, she didn't.'

'That's a shame.'

There was a silence and then Owen said, 'Lucy, I'm not dating Vanessa. We're not an item.'

'But I thought...' Fortunately Owen couldn't see my blushing face. 'I'm sorry to hear that.'

'There's no need for you to be sorry. It's not like I'm cut up about it.'

'What happened?'

'Nothing dramatic,' Owen said. 'I took her out a couple of times, but we soon found out that apart from our privileged education, we have absolutely nothing in common -' He broke off. I heard a burst of music, laughter, and someone shouting drunkenly for him to 'come and play the piano.' Other voices joined in, chanting his name.

'You should get back to the party.'

'It's not a party. But I should get back to it. As it's my turn to play the piano. Apparently.'

We both laughed.

'Let's continue this conversation tomorrow after you've finished work,' Owen said.

'Sure,' I said. 'Tomorrow's good for me. Shall we go to our usual bar?'

'Yeah, I'll see you there. Goodnight, Lucy.'

'Night, Owen.'

I rang off.

So Owen isn't dating that dreadful girl, I thought. I knew I should be sad that things hadn't worked out for him and Vanessa, but I wasn't. If a male friend dates a girl you can't stand, it puts a terrible strain on your friendship.

I returned my attention to the television – to see Daniel looking back at me. I watched as he shook hands with the chat show host, and left the set to the applause of the studio audience.

Oh, no, I thought. I've missed Daniel's interview!

With a renewed appreciation for twenty-first century technology, I hit rewind on the TV remote.

CHAPTER 25

Cassie came out of the house carrying two glasses of white wine. She was wearing a gold bikini that would have looked trashy on most girls, but somehow on her looked glamorous. Ryan, cooking steaks on the barbeque, noticed her immediately, and his eyes followed her as she walked towards me across the grass.

Daniel, who despite the heat, was playing an energetic game of tennis with Owen, whistled and called out, 'Nice swimsuit, Cassie.'

I glanced down at my gingham bikini top and cut-off denim shorts. Clearly I still needed to work on my honorary-celebrity wardrobe.

Ryan grinned and said, 'Are you flirting with my fiancée?'

'Yep,' Daniel said.

I smiled through gritted teeth. I knew he didn't mean anything by it, but Daniel's compulsion to flirt with every attractive woman in his vicinity was *so* irritating.

'I've made the salad,' Cassie said, handing me a glass of wine. 'So now all you and I have to do is wait for the barbeque.' She lowered herself onto the lounger next to mine, which was shaded by a beach umbrella.

'Don't you want to get a tan?' I asked.

'Princess Snowdrop can't get a tan,' Cassie said. 'It's in her contract.'

'Oh. Right.' I sipped my wine. It was deliciously cold. Placing it carefully on the grass within arm's reach, I turned onto my stomach and undid my bikini so I wouldn't get strap marks.

From the far end of the garden, there was a shout of triumph from Daniel as he won another point.

'That's thirty-love to me,' Daniel said. 'I hope you're keeping score, Lucy.'

My earlier irritation faded. He was my Fallen Angel. I couldn't stay annoyed at him for very long.

'Don't worry,' I said, 'my score-keeping skills are legendary.'

Daniel and Owen resumed their game. Their court might be a small patch of Cassie's sun-scorched lawn, and their net strung between two garden stakes, but from the expressions of concentration on their faces, they could have been at Wimbledon.

Daniel missed a shot, and Owen called out, 'That's thirty–fifteen.'

Lowering my voice so that only Cassie could hear, I said, 'Thanks again for letting Owen rent a room in your house.'

'There's no need to thank me,' Cassie said. 'It's lovely for Ryan and Daniel to have another little boy to play with.'

I laughed.

'Seriously, Lucy,' Cassie said. 'I know how hard it is to find somewhere affordable to live in London, and it's not like we don't have the space.'

A week ago, not wanting to wear out his welcome in Zac and Julie Diaz's spare bedroom, Owen had taken over a room in a shared house from a Canadian friend-of-a-friend (who was moving back to Toronto). I'd helped him transport his few possessions to his new address. When I'd told Cassie about the mould growing on his ceiling and the cockroaches in the communal kitchen, she'd gone very quiet, before telling me that my description reminded her of a place she'd lived in when she first came to London. Then she'd asked me to phone Owen and offer him a room in her house in Fulham at the same rent as he was paying to live in what the newspapers call a 'socially deprived area.' He'd moved in the next day.

Daniel sent a ball straight into the net.

Owen called out, 'Thirty all.'

Cassie said, 'I wouldn't want to let a room to just anybody, but Owen is such a nice guy. And he's certainly easy on the eye.'

My gaze slid sideways to the far end of the garden. Neither of the boys was wearing shirts, and I found myself transfixed by the rippling muscles in Owen's back as he raised his racket to hit the ball.

Cassie giggled. 'Have you seen those abs?'

I thought, I will not think about Owen's abs. 'Yes, I have. And that cute butt.'

We were both giggling now like a couple of schoolgirls.

'This conversation is so wrong on so many levels,' Cassie said.

'It is,' I agreed. 'Particularly as our boyfriends might hear us.'

'On the other hand, men have conversations like this about women all the time.'

'But women are so much more evolved than men. We should know better.'

Cassie lay back and shut her eyes. 'I love summer days like this. Just lazing around in the garden with friends.'

'There's no better way to spend a Saturday.'

'Ryan might not agree though,' Cassie said. 'He can't wait for the new football season to start.'

Owen called out,' Thirty-forty!'

He'd certainly fitted seamlessly into Cassie's household. Already, I'd grown used to meeting him in the kitchen each morning as we both downed a quick cup of coffee before leaving for work. And it'd been good to have his company in the evenings when I wasn't going out with Daniel. Who, despite having given me a spare key to the house in Primrose Hill, still hadn't invited me to move in with him. He hadn't asked for it, but after checking that Cassie didn't mind, I'd given him a key to her house as well.

Owen shouted, 'Game and set to me' and punched the air.

'That's one set each.' Daniel said. 'Best of three?'

'If you like,' Owen said. 'But only after I've had a beer.'

'Now that's a plan.'

They both headed off into the house, reappearing a few minutes later armed with ice-cold beers from the fridge. Daniel came and sat on the end of my sun lounger, while Owen took a can to Ryan, before stretching out on the grass.

'I think I'm going to like my new theatrical digs,' he said to Cassie.

Cassie smiled. 'Well, I want to be a good theatrical landlady, so if there's anything you need, just let me know.'

'Actually, I was going to ask you a favour. Lucy, my amazingly gifted and hard-working agent, has got me an audition for a role in a new TV series about a family of werewolves, working title *Alpha Male*. I've learnt the script, but it's a scene for two people, a man and a woman, and I was wondering if you'd read in the other part while I rehearsed.'

'I'd be delighted,' Cassie said. 'When's your audition?'

'It's on Monday.'

'Then we'll run through the scene straight after lunch,' Cassie said. 'And if you feel you need more practice, we'll rehearse it again tomorrow.'

'Thanks, Cassie, I'd really appreciate it.'

'Is it a lead role you're going for?' Daniel said to Owen.

'No,' Owen said. 'I'm being seen for the part of the main character's werewolf brother, who gets killed by a silver bullet in the first episode. But I do get to howl at the moon.'

I smiled. 'Is howling something you studied at drama school?'

'Indeed it is,' Owen said. 'I got an 'A' in that class.'

'I think you should give us a demonstration,' Cassie said.

'I would,' Owen said, 'but I don't want to upset your neighbour's very large dog.'

Daniel said, 'Was that the front doorbell?' We all turned our heads towards the house.

'I'll go and check.' Owen rose to his feet.

'Oh, don't worry, Nadia'll get it,' Cassie said.

A few moments later, Cassie's PA stepped out into the garden through the open French windows. To my surprise, because my employer was not in the habit of calling on her clients uninvited, she was followed by Eleanor Haye, looking enviably cool in white linen trousers and a pale blue, sleeveless, cotton shirt.

'Hello, Cassie,' Eleanor said, as she and Nadia reached us.

'Eleanor!' Cassie sprang to her feet, and she and Eleanor exchanged air-kisses. Daniel and Ryan greeted her in the same fashion, while Owen fetched her a deckchair. I contented myself with saying 'Hi' from my sun-lounger because (1) it would have been weird to air-kiss my boss and (2) I was having trouble doing up my bikini top and risked a costume malfunction if I stood up.

'I'm sorry to burst in on you all like this,' Eleanor said. 'I can see I'm interrupting your weekend.'

'Not at all,' Cassie said. 'Can I interest you in a glass of wine?'

'No.' Eleanor perched on the edge of her chair. 'No, thank you.' She looked pointedly at Owen, Daniel and Nadia. 'Guys, I don't mean to be rude, but I really need to have a private word with Cassie

259

and Ryan. If you'd give us a minute.'

'Ready for another game, Daniel?' Owen said. Without waiting for an answer, he strode off down the garden.

Daniel picked up his tennis racket and followed after Owen. Cassie and Ryan sat next to each other on a sun-lounger.

'Perhaps I could fetch you a non-alcoholic drink?' Nadia said to Eleanor.

'No, I'm fine,' Eleanor said.

'Well, I'll be in my office if you need me.' Nadia smiled graciously at Eleanor and went back inside the house.

By now I'd managed to fasten my bikini. I half-rose from my sun longer, but a frown from Eleanor made me sit back down. I felt a sudden chill, as though the sun had gone behind a cloud.

'You're looking very grim, Eleanor,' Ryan said. 'What is it you need to tell us?'

'Nothing bad, I hope.' Cassie sounded scared.

Eleanor sighed. 'There's no easy way to break this to you, so I'll just come straight out with it.'

Please don't say that Ryan's cheated on Cassie, I thought. Please don't say that Ryan's cheated on Cassie.

'This morning,' Eleanor said, 'I had coffee with a friend of mine who happens to be one of the producers on *Princess Snowdrop*. She told me, in strictest confidence, that the show has been cancelled. The current series is the last.'

Cassie stared at her. 'I don't understand.'

'You film the final episode of *Snowdrop* next week. Your contract isn't going to be renewed.'

'No...' Cassie's voice was scarcely above a whisper.

'I'm sorry, Cassie,' Eleanor said.

Cassie shook her head. 'They can't cancel the show.'

'There's going to be an official announcement to the cast and crew, and a press release, on Monday, but I thought it best to come here and tell you myself. To warn you.'

'Thank you, Eleanor,' Ryan said. 'That was kind of you.' He turned to Cassie, and took hold of her hand. 'I'm so sorry, my darling. I know how much *Snowdrop* means to you.'

'I'm sorry, too,' I said, but Cassie didn't appear to hear me. I did feel incredibly sorry for her, but at the same time I was relieved that Eleanor hadn't discovered some awful story about Ryan on the internet. Which probably said more about me than Cassie and Ryan's relationship.

'Why?' Cassie said. 'Why have they cancelled the show?'

For the first time since I'd started working for her, Eleanor Haye looked distinctly uncomfortable.

'According to my producer friend,' she said, 'Princess Snowdrop just isn't as popular as she used to be. Viewing figures for the current series are way down. The merchandise isn't selling. The production company feels that children want TV characters they can identify with more closely. Characters who are nearer their own age.'

'Princess Snowdrop is too *old?*' Cassie said.

'No TV show lasts forever,' Eleanor continued. 'Tastes change. You must have noticed that you've been getting far fewer bookings for public appearances.'

'No, I hadn't noticed.' Cassie had gone very pale. Ryan put his arm around her. Seeing the look of concern in his eyes, I felt guilty that I'd imagined for one *second* that he could *ever* have cheated on her.

'I know this has come as a great shock to you,' Eleanor said, 'and you're bound to be upset, but very few actors spend years playing the same character. Very few would want to.' Eleanor paused, but Cassie didn't say anything. 'You've one more week of filming on *Snowdrop,*' Eleanor went on. 'After that, I suggest you take a break, give yourself time to think about what you want to do next.'

'I agree,' Ryan said. To Cassie, he added, 'Apart from anything else, we have to start planning our wedding. The media are calling it the 'Wedding of the Year,' and we haven't even set a date yet.'

'That's an excellent idea,' Eleanor said. 'Finish *Snowdrop,* take some time to focus on your wedding arrangements, and when you're ready, you can come into the agency and we'll have a talk about your future career.'

Cassie nodded distractedly.

'I'm going to go now, Cassie,' Eleanor said. 'I'll speak to you on Monday once S*nowdrop's* production team have made their official announcement. No, don't get up, Ryan, Lucy can see me out.'

'Goodbye, Eleanor,' Ryan said. 'It was good of you to take the trouble to come here this afternoon. Thank you.'

Cassie didn't say a word. To my amazement, because she was not a demonstrative person, Eleanor patted Cassie on the shoulder, before marching off towards the house. I hurried after her.

'I knew she'd take it badly,' Eleanor said to me once we reached the hallway. 'It's always hard for an actor when a long-running show comes to an end, and Cassie's been in *The Adventures of Princess Snowdrop* since she was seventeen.'

'She'll bounce back,' I said. 'She's a strong, capable woman – even if she does look like a fairy-tale princess.'

'You think so?' Eleanor said. 'To me she's always seemed rather vulnerable. I'm just glad I was able to break the news to her myself while Ryan was with her, and she didn't have to hear it at the studios on Monday when she was on her own.'

The door of the office opened and Nadia came out into the hall.

'Oh, are you leaving, Eleanor?' she said.

'Yes, Nadia, I'm just going.'

Nadia smiled her sickly-sweet smile, turned on her heel, and made for the garden.

'I don't know why Cassie employs that woman,' Eleanor said. 'I apologise if Nadia's a friend of yours, but I can't stand her. Her smile never reaches her eyes.'

I thought, I can't slag off Cassie's PA to my boss. I said instead, 'She's not my friend.'

'Did you know she used to be an actress?' Eleanor said.

'So I've heard.'

'She only ever did walk-on roles, but on set she used to behave like a diva. She upset so many directors that no-one would cast her. In the end, her agent dropped her.'

'That, I didn't know.'

'Don't look so surprised, Lucy. Listening to showbiz gossip is a vital part of our job. And now I really am leaving. I have to pick up my daughter from a birthday party – six years old and she has a better social life than I do. I'll see you on Monday.'

I stayed by the open front door long enough to satisfy my curiosity about which type of car Eleanor drove (a Volvo), and then I took a deep breath and went back out into the garden. Daniel and Owen, game of tennis abandoned, were sitting on the grass, talking with Cassie and Ryan. Nadia had appropriated Eleanor's deck chair.

As I joined them, I heard Ryan say, 'So that's the situation. At least we have the rest of the weekend before the newshounds descend on us.'

'Why would the press turn up here?' Owen said. 'Won't they get all they need from *Snowdrop's* production office?'

'You obviously have a lot to learn about showbusiness, Owen,' Nadia said. 'If you ever have any real success as an actor, you should take a media training course.'

'Or you could do what I do,' Daniel said, 'and rely on your natural charm.'

I sat down next to him on the grass.

Cassie had been staring at the ground, but now she lifted her head and said, 'How can I be too old to play Princess Snowdrop?'

'Oh, I'm sure it isn't just you that's too old,' Nadia said. 'Princess Daffodil turned thirty last year. Princess Rose has two school-age children. Prince Ash has a receding hairline.'

I glared at her.

Ryan said, 'That's really not very helpful, Nadia.'

'*I* am Princess Snowdrop,' Cassie said.

'No, you're not,' Ryan said. 'You're Cassie Clarke.'

'If I'm not Snowdrop, I'm nothing.' Cassie was still unnaturally pale, and I could see a film of sweat on her brow.

'You're an actress,' I said. 'I know you're upset, but -'

'You must be devastated,' Nadia said.

Ignoring her, I went on. 'You will get other roles, Cassie.'

'How? How exactly am I going to get cast in another show?'

'The same as every other actor on Reardon Haye's books,' I said. 'You audition.'

'I can't,' Cassie said. 'I never went to drama school like Daniel and Owen. I can't compete with

265

all those actresses who know about Shakespeare and the Method.'

'You've years of experience in front of the camera,' Owen said. 'I'd say that gives you the edge over someone who's only performed in their graduation showcase.'

'In my opinion,' Nadia said, 'the whole audition process is a nightmare.'

'Not if you get the part,' Owen said.

'You should try and think of an audition as an opportunity to show a casting team what you can do,' I said.

'What would you know about it, Lucy?' Cassie snapped.

I opened my mouth to remind her that I'd been a theatrical agent for nearly a year now, and did actually know rather a lot about what actors went through at auditions, but thought better of it.

'I've always rather enjoyed auditions,' Daniel said. 'Not that I have to do them anymore. Since *Fallen Angel,* casting directors know exactly what I can do.'

I shot him a disapproving glance, but he didn't notice.

'You don't need to think about any of this right now, Cassie,' Ryan said. 'Get through next week's filming and then –'

'Just one more week of *Snowdrop.*' Cassie shrugged Ryan's arm off her shoulder. 'You must be delighted, Ryan. At least we won't have to get married.'

266

Ryan gaped at her.

'I know you only asked me to marry you because of Princess Snowdrop's *reputation*,' Cassie said. 'But I'm not Snowdrop any more – as you keep telling me. There's no need for us to get married.'

'Our marriage has nothing to do with a TV programme,' Ryan said. 'I want to marry you because I *love* you and because I want to spend my life with you.'

'But I don't want to marry you,' Cassie said.

'You're going to be my wife. '

'No.' With a terrible finality, Cassie slid her engagement ring off her finger and pressed it into Ryan's hand.

'Cassie, don't do this,' Ryan said.

'How can anyone know that they're going to want to spend their whole life with just one person?' Cassie said.

'Do you love me?' Ryan said.

Cassie didn't answer.

'I see.' Ryan stood up slowly. 'In that case, I'm out of here. There's no reason for me to stay.' Without another word, he stalked off into the house.

Daniel said, 'What the f–?'

There was a long, agonising silence. I stared at Cassie in disbelief. I thought, does she know what she's just done?

'Go after him, Cassie,' I said.

'Don't tell me what to do.'

'If Cassie has ended her engagement,' Nadia said, 'I think we should all respect her decision.'

'For goodness' sake!' I scrambled up off the grass and ran after Ryan.

I found him in Cassie's bedroom throwing clothes into a holdall. I thought, this is absurd.

'Ryan, don't go,' I said. 'Talk to Cassie.'

'What's the point? She's made it perfectly clear how she feels about me.' He walked into the en-suite bathroom and came back with his razor and toothbrush, which he also shoved into his bag.

'You say you love her, and yet you're going to give her up that easily? You're just going to walk away?'

'I do love her. I'll always love her. But she doesn't love me.' The pain in Ryan's face was unbearable to see.

'She does love you,' I said. 'She's upset and angry, and she's lashing out. I think she may be in shock.'

'Lucy, I'm sure you mean well, but please stop. You wouldn't know, but things haven't been the same between me and Cassie since we got engaged - she's not been happy. I thought it was just pre-wedding nerves, and once we were married we'd be fine, but obviously I was wrong.' Ryan picked up the holdall, and walked out of the bedroom. I followed him down the stairs. He opened the front door.

Looking back at me, he said, 'Take care of her, Lucy.' Then he went out, closing the door quietly behind him.

Well, I'd tried. My temples throbbed with the beginnings of a headache. I rested my forehead against the door and shut my eyes.

A male voice said, 'Has Ryan gone?'

I swung round to see Owen watching me anxiously from the other end of the hall. I nodded.

'He looked so hurt,' I said. 'He's convinced Cassie doesn't love him.'

'She did just give him back her ring.'

'She's not herself,' I said. She'd certainly given me no indication she was having doubts about her and Ryan.

Daniel came into the hall. 'Cassie's most insistent that we all have lunch together. She's sent me to find out what's happened to the lettuce and tomatoes.'

'Oh, yeah,' Owen said, 'I'm supposed to be fetching the salad.'

'I'm told there's garlic bread in the oven,' Daniel said.

'Would you two stop talking about frickin' food,' I said. 'I'm worried about Cassie.'

'I know you are, babe,' Daniel said.

'She's in a bad place.'

'She's got herself in a state,' Daniel said, 'but she'll be fine. She might be out of work, but she's hardly going to be short of money. And she's still an A-lister.'

'I'm really not interested in Cassie's celebrity status,' I said. 'It's her relationship with Ryan I care about.'

'They're not the first show business couple to break off an engagement,' Daniel said. 'By the time the next issue of *Goss* hits the news-stands, they'll

269

have found someone else.'

I stared at him. *Il est tres superficiel.*

'Where is Ryan, anyway?' Daniel asked.

'He's gone,' I said. 'Cassie told him to go and he went. It's all such a mess. I wish I could think of a way to make it right.'

'You can't *make* her love him,' Owen said, quietly. 'She has to decide she wants him herself.'

'What Cassie wants right now,' Daniel said, 'is barbequed steaks and salad. I suggest we go and join her in the garden...'

The steaks, which Ryan had been cooking on the barbeque, were inedible. Daniel and I, and Owen, sat at Cassie's garden table, pushing bits of charred meat around our plates, while Nadia told us exactly what she thought of the producers of *Princess Snowdrop* (if she'd voiced her opinions to anyone else, she would have been arrested for slander). Cassie didn't eat much, but she drank almost a whole bottle of wine, and laughed too loudly at anything Nadia said. Even when it wasn't funny. Everyone studiously avoided looking at Ryan's empty chair.

'I think I'm going to sell my house,' Cassie said, suddenly.

'Why would you do that?' I said.

'I don't want to live in it anymore. Did I ever tell you that I only bought it because it reminded me of your dolls house?'

'Yes, you did.'

'How ridiculous is that?' Cassie said. 'Almost as ridiculous as a twenty-five year old woman skipping

270

round a magical kingdom in a white puff-sleeved dress.'

'Would you like me to phone an estate agent for you?' Nadia asked.

'Please, Nadia. First thing on Monday. While I'm at the studios getting fired.'

'You're not being fired,' I said. 'The show's been cancelled. There's a difference.'

'Is there?' Cassie pushed away her plate. 'Do you guys have plans for tonight? Maybe we could all go to a club?'

She's lost her job, I thought. She's broken off her engagement. And now she wants to go clubbing?

I said, 'Is that such a good idea, Cassie?'

'I'm single now,' Cassie snapped. 'I need to get back out there.'

Not tonight, you don't, I thought.

'You'll come out clubbing with me tonight, won't you, Owen?' Cassie said.

'I can't tonight,' Owen said. 'I've told a friend that I'll go and watch her band.'

'Viper?' It seemed an age since I'd seen them play in Camden.

'Yeah,' Owen said, 'they're one of the support acts for Blaze at the Sound House.'

'That's a step up from the pub circuit,' I said. I'd never heard of Blaze, but I recognised the Sound House as the venue whose stage had hosted the early performances of several bands, Silver Dollar among them, who'd gone on to acquire managers and record deals (and presumably roadies who didn't have a different job to go to in the morning).

'It is,' Owen said. 'I'm sorry Cassie, but it's not something I can get out of.'

'No, of course not,' Cassie said. 'You can't let down your friend.'

'I'm not doing anything tonight,' Nadia said. 'I have to go shopping this afternoon, but only for a couple of hours.'

'Aren't you seeing Leo tonight?'

'No, he's gone camping this weekend with some of his tedious colleagues.'

'In that case, we should have a girls' night out,' Cassie said. 'You, me and Lucy. You don't mind if I borrow her this evening, do you Daniel?'

'Of course he doesn't mind,' I said.

Daniel looked taken aback, but he said, 'No, I'm cool with that. Lucy and I hadn't made any definite plans.'

He does mind, I thought. Well, he's going to have to get over it, because Cassie needs me a lot more than he does right now.

Daniel turned to Owen. 'How about I come with you to this gig tonight?'

'Sure,' Owen said. 'I'll give Jess a call – she'll get you a backstage pass.'

I was shocked by the unexpected feeling of possessiveness towards Owen that suddenly shot through me. He was *my* friend, not Daniel's, and now they seemed to be embarking on a bromance. Almost immediately, I realised how juvenile that would sound to anyone else.

Telling myself to get a grip, I said, 'Say 'Hi' to Jess for me.'

'Do you want to go to Owen's friend's gig, Lucy?' Nadia said. 'Don't feel you have to come out with me and Cassie if you'd rather go out with the guys.'

Did Nadia seriously think I'd abandon Cassie, in the state she was in, to go to a concert? Unbelievable. 'It's OK, I'll catch Viper some other time.' I locked eyes with Nadia and gave her my brightest smile. 'We haven't had a girls' night out in months. It'll be fun.'

'Great.' Cassie said. 'We'll go to Attitude. Nadia, if you'd arrange for a car to pick us up at nine... And now I'm going to spend the rest of the afternoon lying in the sun. Princess Snowdrop can't get a tan, but Cassie Clarke can do whatever the hell she wants.'

CHAPTER 26

A muscular guy in his mid-twenties stood in front of me, blocking my view of the dance-floor. 'Wanna dance?' he said.

'Thanks for asking, but no,' I said. 'I'm here with my boyfriend, and he doesn't like it if I dance with other men.' My mother had taught me that I never had to do anything with a guy that I didn't want to, but that didn't mean I couldn't let them down gently.

'Fair enough.' The guy moved off, and approached another girl at the other end of the bar.

I returned my attention back to the crowded dance-floor where Cassie was dancing with an older man (he had to have been over forty), gyrating her hips and tossing her hair. The music changed to another track, and she spun away from him, dancing next to a young actor from one of the soaps. He moved behind her, pressing his body against her, and slid his arms around her waist. They writhed together, vaguely in time to the pounding house music. The crystals on Cassie's dress glittered in the club's flashing lights. As the dress was flesh-coloured, she looked as though she was naked, with the gems stuck strategically onto her skin.

I felt a tap on my shoulder and turned my head to find myself face to face with goalkeeper Fabio Rossi. The thunderous expression on his face told me that he was not about to ask me to dance.

'You are Lucy Ashford, yes?' he demanded,

raising his voice so that I could hear him above the music. 'You are here with Cassie Clarke?'

'Yes,' I said. 'Yes, I am.'

'My name is Fabio. I am a friend of Ryan Fleet.'

'I know,' I said. 'We've met.'

'Have we? I do not remember. I see your photo in a magazine. Where is Ryan?'

'I've no idea. He…didn't come out with us tonight.'

Fabio gestured angrily towards Cassie and the soap actor. 'She makes the fool of Ryan. How can she do this?'

On the dance floor, Cassie twisted around in the soap actor's arms and kissed him on the mouth. I actually felt sick. Fabio said something in Italian. I'd no idea what it meant, but I was pretty sure it wasn't very complimentary about Cassie.

'È ubriaca,' Fabio sneered. 'She is drunk.'

'Yes' I said. 'She is.'

The queue to get into Attitude that Saturday night had stretched down the street and around the corner, but Cassie's celebrity status, and mine for once, if I'm honest, had got us straight in the door, and secured us a table in the roped-off VIP area. From there, we could look out over the main dance-floor, where the usual motley crew of models, footballers and soap stars were rubbing shoulders with City boys, Essex girls and several of the more disreputable scions of the aristocracy. Cassie had immediately ordered us a round of cocktails, and then another, downing her second Long Island Iced

Tea while I was still sipping my first. She'd then moved on to shots, before dragging me out of the VIP area and into the heaving throng on the dance-floor. She'd spent the next few hours throwing vodka down her throat and dancing with increasingly uninhibited abandon. I'd shuffled and jerked next to her, trying unsuccessfully to remember how I'd managed to match my movements to the music when I'd danced at the Star Gazer Gala with Owen. Nadia (who'd returned from her afternoon's shopping expedition in such a good mood that I suspected she'd been with some guy who wasn't Poor Leo) had danced with us for a while, but then the attractions of a TV Reality Show Contestant offering to buy her a drink had proved irresistible. I'd last seen the two of them making their way through the crowd towards the rest rooms. Disgusted with Nadia, worried about Cassie, who was apparently determined to get completely and spectacularly wasted, I'd retreated from the dance-floor to the bar, bought myself an over-priced mineral water and wondered just how long it would be before I could persuade the pair of them to call it a night.

That was before Cassie had decided to play tonsil hockey in front of five-hundred clubbers with cameras on their mobile phones.

Fabio said, 'She behaves like a slut.'

Considering that Fabio had been all over me when I'd met him in BarRacuda, I thought this remark was completely out of order. Then I remembered that as far as he knew, Cassie was marrying his friend and team-mate.

'Cassie and Ryan split up,' I said. 'Excuse me, Fabio, I need to get her out of here.'

Turning my back on Fabio, I texted Nadia to let her know that we were leaving – it was up to her if she ditched the Reality Show Contestant and came with us. I debated phoning for a hire-car, but decided we could make do with a taxi. Then, to a disorientating backdrop of relentlessly pulsating sound and light, I went up to Cassie and the soap-actor, whose faces were still glued together, and put my hand firmly on her shoulder.

Cassie started, and broke away from him. The heat of the club had made her mascara run and her lipstick was smeared around her mouth.

'We're going home,' I said. 'Now.'

The soap actor leered at me. 'Whatever you say, baby.'

'Not you.' Fabio Rossi had followed me onto the dance-floor. He positioned himself between me and Cassie and the soap-actor, who took one look at the goalkeeper's biceps and backed away.

'Fabs!' Cassie lurched towards him, lost her balance, and if Fabio hadn't caught her, she would have fallen to the floor. 'Fabio... Fabulous Fabio. That's what *Goss* magazine calls you, isn't it?'

'We get you home now, Cassie.' Fabio put his arm around her and started to walk her through the jostling dancers towards the club's exit. She took only a couple of stumbling steps before once again she almost fell.

'I don't feel too good,' she said, slumping against Fabio's chest.

'That is because tonight you drink too much,' Fabio said. Holding Cassie firmly about the waist, he guided her off the dance-floor. I followed after them, conscious of the number of people watching us with undisguised interest, and drawing their friends' attention to us as well. The days when Cassie could dance in a club unrecognised were long over. Her engagement to Fleet Feet had brought her a whole new fan-base.

At the edge of the dance-floor, one of Attitude's trademark female bouncers, (black leather jumpsuit, scarlet lips and nails, rumoured to be expert in karate), planted herself in our way. At around six feet tall, she was exotically beautiful, but also incredibly scary.

'Do we have a problem here?' she said to Fabio. 'Is medical assistance required?'

'No, *grazie*, we are leaving,' Fabio said. 'My friend is tired.'

'I'm ver' tired,' Cassie said.

The bouncer gave her a long look and then, apparently satisfied that she wasn't about to pass out before she was off the premises, nodded and said, 'I'll escort your party to the door, Sir.' With the bouncer clearing a path before us, Fabio managed to get Cassie to the club's entrance without further mishap. Nadia was waiting for us in the foyer.

'There you are at last...' Nadia's petulant voice trailed off and her eyes widened as she saw that

Cassie was barely able to put one foot in front of the other. 'Oh my God, she's completely pissed.'

'Hey, Nadia,' Cassie slurred. 'Thish ish Fabio. He's taking me home.'

'Well, it's good to know that you have someone responsible looking out for you.' Nadia smiled at Fabio. To me, she said, 'Honestly, Lucy, how could you let her get in such a state?'

I saw red. 'How exactly was I supposed to stop her?'

'That's what friends do on a girls' night out,' Nadia said. 'You've really let Cassie down.'

I thought, *I* wasn't the one having sex and/or snorting cocaine in the toilets.

'Because you're such a great friend to her?' I snapped. 'At least I was with her most of the evening. Where were you?'

Nadia raised her eyebrows. 'You're very aggressive tonight, Lucy. Are you drunk too?'

'*Basta!*' Fabio said. 'Enough. We are leaving. *Subito!*'

I wasn't quite sure who'd put him in charge, but at that moment, I really wasn't feeling up to giving him a lecture on feminism. The bouncer had been talking to one of her equally glamorous colleagues, but now she re-joined us.

'There are a lot of photographers outside,' she said. 'My co-worker and I will accompany you to your transport.'

With Fabio keeping Cassie upright, flanked by the bouncers, we left the club. And were met outside by a solid wall of flashing lights, hand-held mics and rabid paparazzi. A photographer crouched in front of us and aimed his camera straight up Cassie's skirt. The bouncers manhandled him away. A reporter from *Celeb* magazine thrust a mic in Cassie's face.

'Word is that your TV show is cancelled,' he said. 'Any comment?'

Cassie shrank back against Fabio, as we were surrounded by mic-wielding reporters shouting her name.

'Cassie, is it true that you've been fired from your TV show?'

'Over here, Cassie.'

'Cassie, is it true that you've broken off your engagement with Ryan Fleet?'

'Did Ryan dump you, Cassie?'

'Are you and Fabio Rossi dating now?'

'Is it true that Ryan dumped you because you slept with Fabio Rossi?'

Fabio went rigid, and his eyes blazed with anger. He snarled at the reporters in Italian. They surged closer. A camera flashed directly in front of my eyes and I was momentarily blinded. I felt a growing sense of panic.

Then more bouncers piled out of Attitude, leather-clad glamazons and herculean men who formed a human barricade around us. With them holding back the press, we were able to move away from the club's entrance and head towards the line of cabs drawn up at the taxi-rank a short distance along the street. Their drivers, who presumably saw scenes like this outside nightclubs every Saturday night, looked on with bored indifference. One of the bouncers opened the back door of the first taxi in the line.

Fabio said, 'Get in the cab, Cassie.'

A female reporter, who wrote a column for one of the tabloids and was almost a celebrity in her own right, ducked past the bouncers.

'Cassie,' she said, holding out a microphone. 'Is it true that when you were a child you were taken into care?'

Cassie stared dazedly at her.

The reporter said, 'Is it true that your father was a drug addict and your mother a prostitute?'

Cassie leant forward as if to speak into the mic. And collapsed in a drunken sprawl in the gutter.

CHAPTER 27

The taxi drew up outside Cassie's house. Nadia jumped out, ran up the front steps, opened Cassie's front door, and went inside. Fabio got out and handed the driver a fifty pound note.

'Wait here,' he said. He helped Cassie out of the cab, and led her up the steps and into the house. I followed, carrying her clubbing purse, which she'd dropped on the floor of the cab, as well as my own. Nadia switched on the hall light. As soon as Fabio let go of Cassie, she slumped down onto the stairs and shut her eyes.

'It's so kind of you to see us home, Fabio,' Nadia said. 'Can I offer you a coffee?'

'No, *grazie*.' Fabio looked at me. 'I will say goodnight. Unless you need my help -' He gestured at Cassie. 'Her bedroom is upstairs? Maybe I carry her?'

'Please, Fabio,' I said, 'I don't think Nadia and I'll be able get her up there on our own.'

Fabio lifted Cassie up in his arms and with her head lolling on his shoulder, carried her up the stairs, with me and Nadia bringing up the rear. Since we'd left the club, Cassie had been a very docile drunk, but as we reached the first landing, she started shrieking.

'I feel awful,' she wailed. 'I'm going to throw up.'

'Bathroom?' Fabio said.

'This way.' I hurried past my, Nadia and Owen's

rooms, and flung open the door of the family-sized bathroom at the other end of the landing.

Fabio set Cassie down on her feet. She immediately sank to her knees in front of the toilet and was violently sick in the bowl. I stood behind her and held back her hair as she heaved.

From the landing Nadia said, 'This isn't in my job description.' A moment later I heard the slam of her bedroom door. What a terrific friend you are, Nadia, I thought.

Fabio was hovering just outside the bathroom. 'Is there anything I can do?'

'No, I can manage now,' I said. 'Thanks, Fabio, for helping me get her home. You're a star.'

'Ryan is a good friend of mine.' Fabio sighed. 'I must phone him in the morning and tell him what happened.'

Cassie moaned. I stroked her forehead.

'There were many photos made of us tonight,' Fabio said. 'They will be on the internet. They may be there already. I do not want Ryan to think that I have been with Cassie.'

'I'm sure he'd never think that.' I was well aware that one of the rules of male friendship was that you never *ever* got with a mate's girl. Even after they'd broken up.

Fabio fished his mobile out of his jacket. 'What is your number, Lucy? I would like to call tomorrow and know that Cassie is OK.'

I told him my number and he keyed it into his phone.

'I will go now,' he said. '*Ciao*, Lucy. *Ciao*, Cassie.'

'Goodnight, Fabio,' I said.

Cassie didn't say anything. Fabio walked down the stairs. I heard the front door open and close.

'Feeling any better?' I said to Cassie.

'I feel *terrible*.' Cassie's eyes brimmed with tears. 'What have I done? What have I done?'

I thought, Long Island Iced Tea, Tequila Sunrise and vodka shots, mainly.

Owen's bedroom door opened and he stepped out onto the landing. His blond hair was tousled, his eyes were heavy with sleep and he was wearing just a pair of jeans.

'Did we wake you up?' I said. 'Sorry.'

'Don't worry about it,' Owen said, taking in the scene in the bathroom. 'Is Cassie alright?'

'She's drunk,' I said.

'Yeah, I get that,' Owen said, as Cassie once again threw up. He came into the bathroom and sat on the side of the bath. 'Looks like you girls had *quite* a night out.'

I rolled my eyes. 'I've had better.'

Cassie stopped puking, and before I could prevent her, lay down on the bathroom floor. I grabbed her shoulders and tried to make her sit up.

'G'way,' she said. 'G'way, Lucy. I'm tired.'

'Then you need to get into bed.'

'Sleepin' now,' Cassie said.

'Come on, Cassie,' Owen said, 'you can't go to sleep here.' He bent down and picked her up as

284

easily as Fabio had done.

I thought, that's the second time tonight a man's had to come to my rescue. My mother would not be proud.

'Hey, Owen,' Cassie said, drowsily. 'Did anyone ever tell you that you have great abs?'

'Frequently,' Owen said. 'Where do you want her, Lucy? Her room, I guess?'

I nodded. Owen carried Cassie up to her bedroom on the second floor and laid her down on the bed. I took off her shoes, and with Owen's help managed to get her out of her dress and under her duvet. I found some make-up wipes on her dressing table and used them to clean her face. She moaned, rolled onto her stomach, and instantly fell asleep. I went to her window and closed the curtains. Outside it was already light.

'What's the time?' I asked.

'I don't know,' Owen said. 'Four or five maybe.'

'I think we can leave Cassie to sleep it off.' I was too hyped-up to think of sleeping myself. 'I'm going to make tea, if you'd like some.'

'There's nothing I'd like more right now,' Owen said. We went downstairs to the kitchen, and I made us two extra-large mugs of tea.

'I've never seen Cassie wasted like that.' I sat down next to Owen at the kitchen table, kicked off my high-heeled shoes, and undid the side-zip on my dress.

'We've all been there,' Owen said.

'Not Cassie,' I said. 'She might have an

occasional glass of wine, but she doesn't *ever* get drunk. I'm worried she's having some kind of breakdown.'

'She's had the worst day,' Owen said. 'I think that in the circumstances, overdoing the alcohol is entirely understandable.'

'I should have stopped her. She was behaving completely out of character. And the worst of it is that the press were there to record it...'

I described to Owen what had happened inside the club and how, when we left, the press had surrounded us.

'It was horrible,' I said. 'Daniel and I get papped all the time coming out of nightclubs, but we smile for the cameras, Daniel says something amusing that the columnists can quote, everybody's happy, and we go merrily on our way. Tonight was frightening. It was like they were after our blood.' I thought back to the ugly scene on the pavement outside the club. The cameras flashing as soon as we set foot outside the entrance. The reporters and photographers chanting Cassie's name. 'They were waiting for Cassie. They knew she was in the club last night.'

Owen drank some tea. 'I doubt that. Attitude is overrun with celebrities. I'm sure the paparazzi prowl around outside all the time.'

'You don't understand. They asked if it was true that her show had been cancelled. Someone has to have told them.'

'Maybe they did. Eleanor's producer friend perhaps? Or someone else from the production office?'

'They also knew about Cassie breaking up with Ryan,' I said. 'The only people who could have told them about that were Cassie, Ryan himself, me, you, Daniel or Nadia.'

'Cassie gets legless and totters out of a club clinging to a guy who isn't her fiancé,' Owen said. 'You don't have to be an investigative journalist to work out that she and Ryan are in trouble.'

'There was more. Private things that Cassie never talks about…'

Is it true that when you were a child you were taken into care? Is it true that your father was a drug addict and your mother a prostitute?

I remembered the night Cassie had told me about her awful childhood. At the time I'd wondered if Nadia had been eavesdropping. Now I was sure.

'It was Nadia,' I said. 'She told the press that Cassie had broken up with Ryan and… the rest. I can't prove it, but I *know* it was her. This afternoon when she went out, I reckon she was tipping off one of her media contacts.'

Owen leant back in his chair. 'That's quite an accusation. I don't see what Nadia would gain by talking to the press about Cassie's private life.'

I thought, everyone has their price. Nadia had said that. 'Money,' I said. 'Or perhaps she just did it for spite.'

'That seems unlikely. Even for Nadia.' Owen looked thoughtful. 'Are you going to say anything to Cassie?'

'I feel I ought to warn her about Nadia, but I don't

see how I can. She'd never believe me without some sort of proof. I'll just have to watch her back.'

'How will you do that?' Owen said. 'Tell Nadia she's grounded and confiscate her mobile?'

I sighed. 'Do you think I'm being paranoid?'

Owen smiled. 'Maybe a little. But then, I'm not a celebrity. I don't have to worry that my friends are going to sell their souls and my secrets to the media.'

'It's not all bad being famous,' I said. 'Daniel isn't complaining.'

'So I've noticed.'

'Ah. How was your night out with my *celebrity* boyfriend?'

'It was surreal,' Owen said. 'I know other actors who occasionally get recognised by the public, but going to a gig with Daniel Miller is something else.'

'He does get a *lot* of attention.'

'I could have understood it if we'd been sat in the middle of the audience,' Owen said, 'but we watched the bands play from backstage. Even the roadies were staring and nudging one another. When I introduced Daniel to Jess, she was completely tongue-tied. He complimented her on her singing and all she could do was giggle. *Not* very rock'n'roll.'

I laughed. I'd had a terrible day and a worse night. I was worried sick about Cassie. But after talking to Owen, I felt a whole lot better.

'Thanks Owen,' I said.

'What for?'

'For being my friend.'

'You're welcome.'

'I don't know why so many people think a guy and a girl can't be close, without fancying each other in the slightest.'

'Me neither.' Owen yawned. 'I think I'll head back to bed.'

'I guess I should try and get some sleep,' I said. 'I'll join you.'

'Again, you're welcome. But Daniel might object – even though we're just good friends.'

'Ha, Ha.' I grinned. 'Daniel wouldn't care. He's not the jealous type.' In a companionable silence, we stashed our mugs in the dishwasher, and went upstairs. On the landing, Owen put his hand on my arm.

'I know you're worried about Cassie,' he said, 'but I'm sure she and Ryan can work things out.'

'I hope so.'

Owen bent and kissed my cheek. 'See you later, Lucy.'

He went to his room. I stood alone on the landing, holding my hand on my face where he had kissed it, and thinking how lucky I was to have him as a friend. Then I went into my room, slid out of my clothes and, careful not to wake him, because he'd probably want to have sex, and I really wasn't in the mood, climbed into bed with Daniel.

CHAPTER 28

I thought, Princess Snowdrop doesn't do hangovers, but Cassie Clarke sure does.

Despite not going to bed 'til dawn, I'd been woken up after just a couple of hours by Daniel singing in the shower. Deciding that I wasn't going to get back to sleep, I'd jumped in the shower with him, and while we got dressed, I filled him in on the events of the previous night. I told him my suspicions about Nadia, but annoyingly, he wouldn't take me seriously.

'Come on, Lucy,' he'd said, 'she's got a right cushy job as Cassie's PA, she's not going to risk that for a few thousand pounds from the tabloids.' I wasn't about to have an argument with him because of Nadia, so I'd left it.

We'd gone downstairs to find Cassie and Owen already up and in the living room. He was lounging on the sofa, reading a script. By his feet, there was an open laptop. Cassie sat curled up in a chair, her knees drawn up to her chest, her arms wrapped around her legs.

'How are you, Cassie?' I said.

She groaned. 'My head is pounding. My tongue feels like it's covered in fur.'

Owen looked up from his script. 'Yeah, a hangover'll do that to you.'

'I wouldn't know,' Cassie said. 'I've never had one before.'

'Really?' Daniel said, genuinely interested. 'How come?'

Cassie shrugged. Then winced. Her face was devoid of make-up and her skin looked grey, except for her nose which was red with sunburn.

'Have you taken anything?' I said.

'No,' Cassie said. 'But there are plenty of postings on the internet about me being out of my head on coke last night. Although one rather sweet blogger thinks my drink was spiked.'

Relief surged through me. Cassie might look and feel rough, but at least she was no longer in complete meltdown.

'I meant have you taken anything for the hangover?'

'I gave her aspirin and milkthistle,' Owen said. To Cassie he added, 'Drink some more water. You need to re-hydrate.'

Spotting a glass of water on the floor by Cassie's chair, I picked it up and passed it to her.

'About last night,' she said, between sips of water. 'I'm so sorry. I know I made a total exhibition of myself in the club. Thank you for getting me out of there. If it hadn't been for you and Fabio, and Nadia…'

Like Nadia was any help. 'Forget it,' I said. 'I'm just glad you're yourself again.'

Cassie's eyes filled with tears. 'I'm so ashamed.'

Daniel said, 'Don't beat yourself up. You're not the first girl who's drunk too much tequila.'

'Lucy told you what I did last night?' Cassie said.

'Yes, she did,' Daniel said. 'And believe me, it was *nothing* compared to some of the things that go on in nightclubs. I should know.'

I shot him a look. Let's not go there Daniel, I thought. To Cassie, I said, 'You were pretty far gone last night. What do you remember?'

'I don't remember anything that happened after I got home,' Cassie said. 'But before that, I remember plenty. And anything I don't remember is up there on the internet to remind me.' She wiped her eyes with the back of her hand.

'It can't be all that bad,' I said.

'It's terrible,' Cassie said.

'It's what you'd expect,' Owen said. 'See for yourselves.' He put down his script and reached for the laptop. Daniel and I sat down on either side of him, and he brought up the most popular internet sites for showbiz gossip, the on-line magazines and newspapers, the links to TV shows, and the blogs. Photos of Cassie were everywhere. Blurred photos of her dancing in the club, obviously taken on mobiles. Photos of her with the soap actor. Photos and videos of her staggering out of Attitude with Fabio, and photos of her collapsed at the side of the road. There on the internet, for anyone to read, was the news of the demise of her TV show and the end of her relationship with Ryan-he's-so-Fleet. Along with the fact that, having slept with most of the players in Ryan's football team, she was now living with goalkeeper Fabio Rossi. Several of the newsfeeds mentioned in passing that she'd had a deprived childhood, but none of them went into detail.

'Seen enough?' Owen said.

I nodded. Owen closed the laptop.

'Last week I was the Nation's Sweetheart,' Cassie said. 'Now I'm a nymphomaniac with a drink problem.'

'You are so not,' Daniel said. 'Believe me, I've met a few.'

Thanks for that, Daniel, I thought.

Nadia came bustling into the living room.

'Oh, you're all here,' she said. 'Right, Cassie, Louella just called and offered to come over and do some damage limitation –'

'I told you, I'm not seeing anyone today,' Cassie said.

Nadia pursed her lips. 'Yes, and that's what I said to Louella. She said to call her back if you change your mind.'

'Who is Louella?' Owen asked.

'Technically, she's my publicist,' Cassie said. 'Although she's actually employed by the *Princess Snowdrop* production company. Which means that in five days' time she's out of a job. Just like me.'

Nadia perched on the arm of Cassie's chair.

'I'm sure you won't have any difficulty getting work,' she said. 'Not while you're all over the internet like you are right now.'

Cassie flinched. 'I know you're trying to be kind, Nadia, but I doubt that videos of me falling down drunk in the street are going to encourage anyone to employ me as an actress.'

'It's *publicity*,' Nadia said. 'All we have to do is take charge of it and tell your side of the story.'

'How can we do that?' Cassie said.

'I have some contacts in the media,' Nadia continued. 'I'm happy to set up an interview for you with one of the showbiz magazines. Or, better still, a national newspaper.'

'You want me to give an interview to a tabloid?' Cassie said. 'After what happened last night? *Absolutely not.*'

'I know you're upset,' Nadia said. 'You have every reason to be. The way the press behaved outside Attitude was despicable. But if you gave an exclusive interview to a newspaper, you'd be in control.'

I knew it, I thought. Nadia has made some sort of deal with a reporter. 'Do you think any of your press contacts would be willing to pay Cassie for an interview?' I said.

'Absolutely. That is… I can find out.'

'Don't do it Cassie,' I said. 'You might think you're in control, but you won't be.'

'I beg to differ,' Nadia said. 'This is a marvellous opportunity, Cassie. If you were to give an in-depth exclusive interview to the right journalist, you could make a great deal of money.'

I thought, a great deal of money for who?

'With your life story, you could make a fortune,' Nadia went on. 'You'd probably get a book deal.'

'My life story?' Cassie sounded bewildered.

'Deprived childhood. Teenage celebrity. Role

model. Wag. Heartbreak… You can use that to make a whole new career for yourself. You might even get a Reality Show.'

'You know nothing about my childhood,' Cassie said. 'If you did, you'd understand why I don't give interviews about it. As for my relationship with Ryan – I'd never do that to him. I wouldn't sink so low.'

Nadia, you've just shot yourself in the foot, I thought. I wanted desperately to talk to Cassie about Ryan, but decided now was probably not the best time.

'I should think not,' I said. 'I know the tabloids can offer a small fortune for the right story, but there are some lines that just can't be crossed. Don't you agree, Nadia?'

Nadia's eyes narrowed. 'Yes, Lucy, of course I do. But if Cassie were to tell her own story in her own words -'

'I'm *not* doing any interviews,' Cassie said.

Nadia looked as though she was about to implode. My phone rang. I checked the screen, saw that it was Fabio calling, and hit the answer button.

'Hello, Lucy,' Fabio said. 'How is Cassie this morning?'

'She's hungover.'

'That does not surprise me. Has she spoken to Ryan?'

'No.' I glanced at Cassie. 'We haven't discussed that.'

'She can hear what you are saying?'

'Yes.'

'OK,' Fabio said. 'I talk, you listen. I call Ryan this morning. I tell him what happen and what *not* happen last night. I tell him call Cassie, or see her, but he will not. He want her, but he say he not beg her to come back to him. *Lui e un idiota.* You make her call him, yes?'

'I'll try.'

'OK.' There was a pause, and then Fabio said, 'There are photographers outside my flat. Maybe they come to Cassie's house also?'

I went to the front window and peered out from behind the curtain. Apart from a teenage girl talking on her mobile, and the woman from two doors down walking her Irish Wolfhound, the sunlit street appeared to be deserted.

I said, 'I can't see any media types outside Cassie's place right now.'

'That is good,' Fabio said. 'You check again, if you go out, yes?'

'Yes, I will.'

'OK. *Ciao*, Lucy.'

'Bye.' I ended the call. 'That was Fabio Rossi. The paparazzi are camped outside his flat.'

'Oh, no,' Cassie said. 'That's because of me.'

Daniel stood up. 'I'm going to head off. I've a brunch meeting, and I really can't be late.'

For a moment I couldn't think where he was going that was so very important. Then I remembered that he was having brunch with an American producer who was only in London for the weekend. Whether or not the semi-social meeting led to work now or at some future date, he still needed to make a good impression. I followed him out into the hall.

'Will I see you later?' I said

'Yeah. We'll go out tonight, and sleep at mine.'

'I'd rather stay in,' I said. 'I don't want to leave Cassie on her own. I know she's a lot more together than she was yesterday, but she still seems very down.'

Daniel raised his eyebrows. 'She's an adult, Lucy. You don't have to babysit her.'

'I just feel she could do with a bit of support right now.'

'She's got Nadia with her. And Owen.'

'She hardly knows Owen, and Nadia only ever thinks about herself.' Suddenly, for the first time in months, I found myself thinking of the previous summer, when I'd discovered that Lawrence was married. There had been days when I'd felt so wretched that I could barely drag myself out of bed. Then Cassie had turned up on the doorstep…

I said, 'Cassie was there for me when I needed a friend. I owe her, Daniel.'

'OK, babe, we'll sleep here tonight.' He pulled me to him and kissed me very thoroughly. 'To be continued,' he said, with a leer.

'I'm counting on it.' I shooed him out of the front door. Back in the living room, Cassie had taken my place by the window.

'There's no-one out there, Cassie,' I said. 'No film crews, no paparazzi.'

'There will be,' Cassie said. 'They'll come for me.

297

It's only a matter of time.' A tear ran down her face. 'I can't face them again, I really can't.'

'You don't have to,' I said. 'There's no reason for you to leave the house before your car picks you up to take you to the studio tomorrow morning.'

'There's no way I'm going in tomorrow.'

'You're not going in to work?' I said. 'Why not? You've only got another week.'

'Exactly,' Cassie said. 'For the last ten years I haven't missed a day on *Snowdrop*. I've never rocked up late or rung in sick. I've always known my lines and hit my mark. And now the production company is firing me.'

'They're not *firing* you,' I said.

'They're *ruining my life*,' Cassie said. 'So I've decided that they can shoot the final episode of *Princess Snowdrop* without me.'

'How can they do that?' I said. 'You're the star.'

'Oh, they can always use a double or... it's really not my problem. I need to take some time for myself.' Cassie turned back to the window. She didn't make a sound, but I was fairly sure that she was crying.

I might have told her to pull herself together and stop acting like a diva, if I hadn't remembered how it felt to *know* that your life is in ruins, and you'll never *ever* be happy again. At least I hadn't had my worst moments posted on the internet. It occurred to me that if Cassie had a family like mine, she'd be with them now, and they'd let her stay as long as she liked, without asking questions (well, not that many), and give her some space to get her head together.

'Cassie,' I said, 'how would you feel about getting out of London for a while?'

'That's actually a rather good idea,' Nadia said. 'Why don't I book us into a spa hotel? Somewhere discreet with good security.'

Us? I don't think so, Nadia. To Cassie, I said, 'I was thinking you might like to spend a few days at my mother's place. The paparazzi wouldn't find you there.' And if they did, I'm pretty sure my mother would send them packing.

Cassie turned around. Her face was wet with tears.

'That would be wonderful,' she said. 'If Stephen and Laura wouldn't mind my descending on them. But it might not be convenient.'

'Of course they won't mind,' I said. 'They'll be delighted.' I thought for a moment. 'I'll come with you. It's far too long since I've seen my family. If I can get the time off work, I'll stay a couple of days. If not, I'll come back here tonight.' A few days in the non-celebrity and (relatively) rational atmosphere of my mother's house would give Cassie a chance to get her head straight and me a chance to talk to her about Ryan.

'What about Daniel?' Cassie said. 'Shouldn't you check if he's made plans for next week before you leave him on his own?'

'I'm sure he can cope without me for a few days,' I said. 'I don't want to worry you, Cassie, but I think we should leave as soon as we can. If you want to avoid the press.'

'I'll go and pack. Nadia, will you phone for a car? Oh…' Cassie had started to look a little less miserable, but now her face fell. 'I can't go anywhere. If I'm hiding from the paparazzi, I can't have some random driver knowing where I am. Everyone has their price.'

'Well, you certainly can't travel by train,' Nadia said. 'You'd be recognised. You'd probably get mobbed.'

I thought, how can it be this hard to transport one woman forty miles up the M1?

Owen, who'd taken no part in the conversation until then said, 'I'll drive you, if you like.'

'You don't have a car,' I said.

'No, but I can ask Michael if I can borrow his.'

'Michael has a car now?'

'Yep. He has a serious relationship, a mortgage *and* a car. I suspect he's trying to make me feel inadequate.'

'Do you think he'd let me drive his car?' I said.

No,' Owen said. 'Not a chance.'

'Are you talking about the journalist?' Cassie said.

'What journalist?' Nadia said.

'We're talking about my friend Michael,' Owen said.

'You have a friend who is a *journalist*?' Nadia said. 'Is he paying you to get him access to Cassie?'

'Don't be ridiculous,' Owen said.

'Is he planning to sell a story about Cassie Clarke to one of the nationals?' Nadia went on.

'I'm going to pretend I didn't hear that,' Owen said.

'Pot. Kettle,' I muttered.

Nadia started to say something, but evidently thought better of it and subsided into silence.

Cassie said, 'Sorry, Lucy, I didn't hear you. What did you say?'

'Nothing,' I said, 'I was just thinking aloud.'

'What would you like me to do, Cassie?' Owen said. 'Shall I give Mike a call or not?'

Cassie glanced from Owen to Nadia in an agony of indecision, her need to get out of London vying with her innate fear of anyone connected with the press.

'Phone him,' she said. 'That time I met him, he seemed like a nice guy – even if he is a journalist.'

CHAPTER 29

'That's my mother's house,' I said. 'A bit further. There - just beyond the post box. You can park on the drive.'

Owen brought Michael's Fiesta smoothly to a halt, next to my mother's Peugeot and Stephen's Nissan.

Cassie, who'd slept for most of the journey, opened her eyes and said, 'Oh, we're here.'

'Yes, Cassie, we're here,' I said. *Finally.*

Even after Owen had taken a cab to Michael's, picked up the car and driven back to Cassie's, it had taken us another hour to get on the road, most of which was time I'd spent on the phone. Firstly, I'd called my mother to warn her to expect us, saying only that Cassie needed to lie low for a few days, and I'd explain why when we arrived. Then I'd phoned Eleanor, interrupting a family outing to the Natural History Museum, and as she was too busy looking at dinosaurs to trawl the internet, gave her an abbreviated account of our disastrous girls' night out. She was all for my taking some time away from the office to act as Cassie's minder, reminding me that when I'd first started at Reardon Haye, she'd told me that sometimes we had to hold our clients' hands.

'I'll tell the *Snowdrop* people that Cassie is unavailable next week and they'll have to re-schedule,' Eleanor had said, 'but she *will* have to film that final episode in time for it to go out on air.'

Rather more confident of my ability to persuade Cassie to get back in front of the camera than I was myself, she'd added, 'I'm sure you can make her see that. It's understandable that she's upset, but the show must go on.'

I'd also phoned Erin the housekeeper to tell her that she didn't need to come into work while Cassie was away from home. This would have been a task for Nadia, but Cassie had told her to take the week off too. Then I'd tried to call Daniel to let him know I was going to my mother's. He was presumably still in his meeting, as his phone went straight to voice mail, so I left him a message. I'd tried to reach him again once we were out of London and heading up the motorway, and I'd texted him. And I'd called him half an hour later, but still got no reply

While Cassie went and knocked on the front door, and Owen lifted her massive case and my small one out of the boot of the car, I tried Daniel's number again, and once again got his voice mail. Realising that I was acting exactly like the sort of clingy girlfriend that no man would want to live with, I ended the call without leaving a message this time, and got out of the car. The front door opened to reveal my mother, with Stephen and Dylan close behind her. A wonderful smell of cooking drifted along the hall from the kitchen.

'Laura! Stephen! It's so good to see you.' Cassie flung her arms around them. They both looked rather startled, but Cassie didn't notice.

Stephen was the first to recover. 'We're glad to

have you here, sweetheart,' he said, hugging her back.

'You know you're always welcome in this house,' my mother said. She smiled at me. 'Hello, Lucy.'

'Hi,' Dylan said.

'Hi,' I said. Briefly, I wondered if I should break with years of family tradition and demonstrate how pleased I was to see my parents and brother with hugs and air-kisses. I decided against it.

My mother turned to Owen. 'Hi, I'm Laura Ashford.'

'I'm Owen Somers.'

'Stephen Harrington,' Stephen said.

'Dyl,' Dylan said.

'Well, come in all of you,' my mother said.

'Where shall I put the cases?' Owen asked.

'Oh, just leave them by the door.'

Cassie and Owen followed my mother along the hall to the kitchen. Stephen put his hand on my arm.

'Cassie looks terrible,' he said in a low voice. 'What's wrong with her? You said something to Laura about needing to get her away from London?'

I thought, how can he not know? Hasn't he read the tweets? I reminded myself that not everyone found it necessary to follow whatever was trending on the internet.

'Cassie's TV show got cancelled,' I said, 'and that sent her to a really bad place. She broke off her engagement, which *I* know is a huge mistake even if *she* won't admit it. And she's being hounded by the media. She's a mess. She needs some time out to clear her head.'

'Then we'll see that she gets it,' Stephen said firmly. 'You were right to bring her here. I'm sure a few days away from the limelight will give her some perspective.'

'I hope so.'

In the kitchen we found Cassie and Owen already seated at the table, and my mother making a salad to go with the chilli con carne simmering on the hob, while Dylan dropped tea bags into mugs and filled the kettle. I slid onto a chair next to Owen. Stephen stood next to my mother and helped himself to pieces of chopped tomato when she wasn't looking.

'So, Lucy,' my mother said, 'you and Cassie are *lying low* for a few days? Should Stephen and I be worried?'

'Only if you see a photographer with a telephoto lens lurking in the bushes,' I said. 'The press have been giving Cassie a hard time. This seemed a good place to come to avoid them.'

Cassie said, 'I - my private life - is headline news at the moment. But I'd rather not talk about any of it.'

My mother nodded sagely, as though celebrities took refuge from the media in her house on a regular basis. I saw her glance slide to Cassie's left hand, but she made no comment.

'What about you Owen?' she said. 'Are you also in hiding?'

'No, not me,' Owen said, smiling. 'I'm just the guy with the car. Well, the guy with the friend with the car.'

'The getaway car,' Dylan said.

My mother shot him a withering glance. 'You're still very welcome to stay,' she said to Owen.

'Thanks,' Owen said, 'but I should get back to London. I've an audition tomorrow.'

'Oh! Your audition!' Cassie said. 'I was supposed to go through the script with you.'

'Don't worry about it. I've gone through it myself so many times, I'll be over-rehearsed if I practise it anymore.'

'But you will at least stay for a late lunch?' my mother asked.

'Thank you.' Owen grinned. 'I was hoping you'd invite me to eat. It smells splendid.'

'I used to come here for Sunday lunch when I was a child,' Cassie said to Owen. 'One time, Dylan made me sit at the table for a whole hour after we'd all finished so he could paint my portrait. He can't have been more than seven. Do you remember that painting, Dyl?'

'I don't, sorry. Was it any good?'

'It was brilliant. I kept it for years. I wish I knew what happened to it.'

'He probably only did it to get out of doing the washing-up,' I said.

'Ignore my sister.' Dylan studied Cassie's face. 'I'd really like to paint your portrait again, Cassie. Maybe I could do some preliminary sketches over the next few days while you're staying with us? I promise you won't have to sit still for more than... three hours at the most.'

'I'd be very happy to sit for you,' Cassie said. 'But I get to keep the painting.'

'Fair enough,' Dylan said.

'You're an artist?' Owen said to Dylan.

'Art student,' Dylan said. 'Well, from next month. When I start at art college.'

'I'd love to see some of your work,' Owen said.

'Well, there are a couple of pieces I'm quite pleased with in my Dad's studio. If you'd really like to see them. If there's time before lunch.'

As there was still a good half hour before lunch would be ready, Dylan, Stephen and Owen all trooped off upstairs to Stephen's light-filled studio at the top of the house. Knowing that my mother never tired of looking at Stephen and Dylan's paintings, I offered to finish making the salad and put the rice on, so that she could go too.

'If you're going to sit for Dylan, you need to insist on the occasional break,' I said to Cassie, once we were alone. 'When he's drawing or painting he loses any sense of time. He'd forget to eat or sleep if someone didn't remind him.'

To my dismay, Cassie gave a little sob. 'What have I done?' she said.

'Don't upset yourself,' I said, quickly. 'You don't have to sit for Dyl. I'll tell him you're not up to it.'

'But I want to sit for Dyl. It's the only thing I've got to look forward to.' A single tear ran down Cassie's pale face and dripped off her chin.

Spotting a box of tissues on the worktop, I passed it to her. She wiped her eyes and noisily blew her nose.

'You won't want to hear this, Cassie,' I said, 'but the cancellation of a TV show does not mean the end of civilisation as we know it. I get that you're upset, I really do –'

'I *don't care* about the frickin' show,' Cassie said. 'No, that's not true. I do care, but I'm not *distraught* about it like I was yesterday. It's Ryan…'

'Ryan…?' I prompted.

'I love him,' Cassie said, 'and I've lost him. I made the worst mistake of my life when I sent him away.'

Cassie has just admitted that she was wrong to break up with Ryan, I thought. Because it would have been a little insensitive when she was so obviously wretched, I managed not to punch the air.

'You know you made a mistake, so put it right. Call him.'

'What can I possibly say to him?' Cassie said. 'I hurt him terribly. I can't just phone him and tell him to forget it.'

'Tell him you *love* him. Tell him that you were so traumatised by the show being cancelled that you didn't know what you were doing or saying.'

'That's not what happened. Ryan and I - It wasn't the same after we got engaged.' Cassie paused to gather her thoughts. 'When Ryan came back from Spain, I knew that I was in love with him, but it never occurred to me to wonder if we'd be together in ten or twenty years' time. I certainly never thought about *marrying* him. Or anybody else for that matter. I've never seen the point of marriage. I mean, Laura and

Stephen aren't married, and they've been together longer than any couple I know.'

'So why did you say 'yes' when Ryan asked you?'

'You were there, Lucy. You saw how he sprang it on me. He didn't give me a chance to think.'

'But you seemed so happy that night. We had champagne.'

'I just went with the flow,' Cassie said. 'I knew Ryan was fed up with hiding our relationship from the press. I didn't want to lose my job because it came out that Princess Snowdrop was shagging a footballer. A ring on my finger solved a lot of problems. Then suddenly we're this celebrity couple. With a centre-page spread of photos in every tabloid. And interviews in *Celeb* and *Goss.*'

'The Nation's Sweethearts.'

Cassie grimaced. 'It was all so false. I was engaged to a guy who'd only asked me to marry him because of my *image*. Our wedding would be nothing more than a publicity stunt.'

'Did you say any of this to Ryan?'

'No, I should have, but I didn't. Our relationship had gone so *wrong,* and I didn't know how to put it right. It was such a farce, that I wasn't even sure if I wanted to put it right. Then Eleanor turned up out of the blue and announced that *Snowdrop* was cancelled. That was devastating, but at the same time, it gave me a way out.' Cassie raised stricken eyes to my face. 'How can I have done that to Ryan? How can I have been so cruel?'

'You weren't yourself.'

'Ryan is the love of my life,' Cassie said. 'I know that now. Now that he's gone. When I woke up this morning, I reached for him and I couldn't understand why he wasn't there. Then I remembered what I'd done, and I just felt so *empty*. I love Ryan. I love him so much it hurts. I *ache* for him.'

'Then he's the one you should be talking to. Not me. Call him, Cassie.'

'I can't.'

'Why not?'

'I just *can't,*' Cassie said. 'I'll only make things worse. I'll wait for him to call me.'

'And what if he doesn't?'

'If he wants to get back with me, he'll call.'

Not according to what Fabio told me this morning, I thought. 'Well, you know him a lot better than I do, but –'

'Yes, I do,' Cassie said. 'And I'm not calling him. So don't ask me to.'

She needs to call him, I thought. At a loss as to what I could do or say to convince her, I picked up a knife and took out my frustration on a cucumber.

For a few minutes, Cassie sat silently staring into space, then she said, 'I must look a state. I'm going to go and wash my face.'

'OK, hun,' I said. 'When you've done that, would you go up to the studio and tell the others that I'm just putting the rice on?'

'Sure,' Cassie said.

Relationships are complicated, I thought. Friends shouldn't interfere.

I waited until the sound of Cassie's footsteps told me she'd gone upstairs to the bathroom. Then I fished my mobile out of the back pocket of my jeans, and called Ryan Fleet.

CHAPTER 30

'Is anyone still hungry?' my mother asked. 'We've eaten all the rice, but there's more chilli, if anyone would like it. Owen?'

'Yes, please, Laura.'

My mother ladled a second helping of chilli con carne onto Owen's plate. 'Anyone else?'

There was a chorus of groans and 'It was delicious – but I'm full,' and 'It was amazing, but I couldn't eat another mouthful.'

'Well, if you change your minds,' my mother said, 'you can help yourselves.'

Various conversations sprang up around the kitchen table. Owen, between mouthfuls of chilli, talked to my mother about auditions, rehearsals, and first nights. Stephen told Cassie a long, involved and very funny story about the discovery by a fellow artist and friend of his, of what he thought was an unknown painting by Picasso, which turned out to be a fake. Dylan mentioned to no-one in particular that a group of his friends were going to Ibiza next summer, and he was thinking about going with them. Stephen smiled wryly and said that a summer abroad would no doubt be of great benefit to his development as an artist, as the light was very different in the Med, especially in the beach bars. I let the talk flow around me and (1) wondered if my phone call to Ryan would have the result I wanted, and (2) worried that I should never have made the call. My mother started to collect up the empty plates. There was a knock on the front door.

The table fell silent. Cassie froze in the act of handing her plate to my mother, a look of terror on her face.

'The press are here,' she said. 'They've found me.'

'That's not possible, Cassie,' Owen said. 'No-one knows you're at this address. Lucy didn't even tell me where we were going until we were on the motorway.'

I thought, I didn't give anyone this address, except Ryan.

Dylan said, 'Shall I see who it is?'

'I'll go,' I said, quickly. I hurried out into the hall, and opened the front door. An unshaven, wild-eyed Ryan Fleet stood on the doorstep.

'Hello, Ryan,' I said.

'Lucy.' He raked his hand through his hair. 'What you said on the phone about me and Cassie, and one of us having to make the first move. I decided it might as well be me.'

I stood aside so that he could come into the hall.

'Where is she?' he said.

'Through there.' I was going to add that she was with my family and Owen, but Ryan was already striding past me into the kitchen. I shut the front door and trotted after him.

If he was taken aback to find himself facing a room full of people, three of them strangers, all of them gaping at him, he didn't show it.

He said, 'I'm Cassie's footballer.'

Stephen said, 'I rather thought you might be.'

'Ryan…' Cassie's voice was scarcely louder than a whisper. 'Why are you here?'

'I *had* to see you,' Ryan said. 'You and I need to talk. Please, Cassie. Is there somewhere we can talk?'

My mother rolled her eyes. 'Cassie,' she said, 'why don't you take your… young man out into the garden?'

I flung open the door that led to the back garden, where my and Dylan's old sandpit, now filled with earth and planted with herbs, still stood on the lawn. Cassie slowly got to her feet. Ryan held out his hand. She took it, and they went outside. I shut the door behind them.

'I'm not one for gossip,' my mother said, 'but I'm guessing the Nation's Sweethearts had a lovers' quarrel and are now in the process of making up?'

'Something like that,' I said. 'At least, I hope they're making up, since it was me who told him she was here.'

Five minutes or so passed in which the silence was broken only by the ticking of the kitchen clock. It seemed a lot longer. Dylan went and stood by the kitchen sink, and peered cautiously out of the window.

'Dylan!' my mother said. 'Get away from there. They'll see you.'

'No they won't.' Dylan looked back over his shoulder, grinning. 'I'd say the *making up* is going pretty well.'

Owen and I hesitated for about two seconds before joining him at the window.

Out in the garden, bathed in the soft golden light of a summer evening, Cassie and Ryan were locked in an embrace, arms around each other, eyes shut, her head resting on his broad chest. He stroked her hair. She tilted up her chin towards him, and he bent his head and brushed her lips with his. They both opened their eyes. Ryan let his arms fall to his sides. He took a step away from Cassie, and knelt down on one knee on the grass.

'We shouldn't be watching this,' I said.

'No, we shouldn't,' Owen agreed.

My mother and Stephen came and stood behind us.

'What's happening?' My mother said. 'Oooh.'

'We should so give them some privacy,' I said. Nobody moved.

Ryan reached into the pocket of his jeans, and brought out a small red box. He opened it, and the rays of the setting sun caught the diamond within and turned it to liquid fire. Ryan said something to Cassie, and she smiled, almost shyly, and nodded her head. He slid the ring onto the third finger of her left hand. Then he stood up and crushed her to him, his mouth on hers, holding her close as though he'd never let her go.

'I *think* she said "yes,"' Dylan said.

'Another lamb to the slaughter,' my mother said, but she too was smiling. We all were.

* * *

Over an hour later, the back door opened and Cassie and Ryan came into the kitchen hand in hand. The rest of us, seated demurely at the kitchen table, looked at them expectantly.

Cassie held up her left hand so that we could see her ring and said, 'We're getting married!'

There followed several minutes of shrieking (me and Cassie) hugging (me, Cassie and Ryan), manly shaking of hands (Ryan, Owen, Stephen and Dylan) and warm congratulations from my mother.

'Marriage doesn't suit everyone, Cassie,' she said, 'but if it's right for you and Ryan, if it's what you both want, then I wish you every happiness.'

Stephen opened a bottle of Cava to toast the happy couple which, it seemed to me, tasted a lot better than the champagne I'd drunk the first time Cassie and Ryan had announced they were getting married. Owen said he wouldn't have a drink, because he had to drive back to London, but then changed his mind and said he might as well stay the night and drive back first thing in the morning. Cassie and Ryan drank a glass of fizz, talked about cabs and hotels and then decided that they too would stay. My mother produced fresh French bread, numerous cheeses, and grapes, which we all devoured. Dylan fetched his sketchpad and sat at the kitchen table scratching away with a stick of charcoal. Stephen put on some music. Owen dragged me to my feet and danced me around the kitchen. My mother opened another bottle of wine and re-filled everyone's glasses. Even Cassie had a second glass.

Late in the evening, Cassie and I went out into the garden to get some air.

'I'm going to be Ryan Fleet's *wife*,' Cassie said. 'When people ask me my name, I shall say 'I am Mrs Fleet'. And it's thanks to you, Lucy. If you hadn't phoned him…'

'You'd have called him, or he'd have called you, eventually.'

'Perhaps. Anyway, it doesn't matter, because you got us back on track.' Cassie smiled happily. 'I wanted to ask you something, Lucy. Would you be my bridesmaid?'

'Oh, Cassie, I'd love that!'

Cassie beamed. 'It's going to be a very quiet wedding, just us and a few close friends and family. We're determined not to have any more *celebrity couple* nonsense.'

'What? No photo shoots? No magazine deals? Are you sure you and that footballer are getting married?'

Cassie laughed. 'We are *so* getting married. Ryan proposed to me and I said "yes". And this time it was for all the right reasons.'

'You can't live without each other? You want to grow old together? You want to make babies? You love each other to bits?'

'All of the above. Plus Ryan's really *hot.*'

Dylan came out into the garden carrying a sheet of paper.

'This is for you and Ryan,' he said, handing the paper to Cassie. 'An engagement present.'

'Oh, Dyl, it's wonderful,' Cassie said. 'Thank you so much.'

'You're welcome.'

Enough light was spilling out of the house for me to see that Cassie was holding a charcoal drawing of her and Ryan seated next to each other at the kitchen table, hands clasped, gazing into each other's eyes. Anyone who saw that drawing would know that it was a portrait of a man and woman deeply in love.

'Your brother is seriously talented,' Cassie said to me.

'Yeah, he is,' I said. 'I forget that sometimes. What with him being my brother. Don't tell him I said this, but I think he could be famous one day.'

'As long as he's famous for his art, and not for getting drunk in nightclubs,' Cassie said. 'I had a phase of getting drunk in nightclubs, but I've grown out of it now.'

'Falling out of nightclubs drunk is *so* last year,' I said.

Dylan grinned, and wandered back inside the house.

'Ryan and I are going to have to be up early tomorrow,' Cassie said. 'We want to get back to London before the rush hour.'

'Laura and Stephen wouldn't mind if you stayed on a few days. If you wanted to give the media frenzy a bit more time to die down.'

'Oh, I'm not bothered about a few photographers. Tomorrow morning, Ryan is driving me to the *Snowdrop* studios, and if the press are lying in wait

318

for me, I'll just smile at them and say "no comment". So what if they invent a few stories about my love life? I really don't care.'

Who are you, I thought, and what have you done with my friend Cassie? Aloud, I said, 'You're going to the studios? You've changed your mind about not working next week?'

'I've not missed a day's filming in eight years. I'm not about to let everyone down now that there's only one more episode of the show left to film. I'm not a diva, even if I did behave like one yesterday.'

'You're a star, Cassie, a real star.'

'I'm a professional actress who's had a lead role in a children's TV show, and is now looking to audition for her next job.'

'And you're *getting married.*'

'Yes, I am. Anyway, what about you, Lucy? What are you going to do?'

'Oh, I expect I'll get married one day. If anybody ever asks me.'

'I meant, what are you doing tomorrow? Will you stay on here, or would you like a lift back to London?'

I thought for a moment. Much as I enjoyed visiting my family, they wouldn't be free to spend time with me tomorrow as they'd all be working. And with Cassie's life sorted, and Ryan driving her to the studios, I'd be rattling round my mother's house on my own. If I travelled back to London tomorrow morning, I'd have the rest of the day to catch up on a few chores and the next day I could go into Reardon Haye at my usual time.

'I may as well go back to town tomorrow,' I said, 'but I'll get a lift with Owen. He won't have to leave quite so early in the morning as you, and he can drop me at your house before he takes the car back to Michael.'

Cassie smiled. 'I knew you wouldn't be able to stay away from Daniel much longer.'

Daniel. 'Absolutely,' I said. I hadn't thought about Daniel all night. What sort of girlfriend was I? 'Actually, I think I'll give him a quick call now. I left my phone in the kitchen.'

Cassie and I went back into the house, and I located my mobile on the kitchen worktop. I had one missed call from Daniel, but no voice messages or texts. Racked with guilt that I hadn't called him sooner, I hit his number on my speed dial, but his phone rang out and went to voice mail. I left yet another message for him to call me, said I'd be driving back to London in the morning, and would call him when I got there if I hadn't heard from him. I texted him as well. Then, before I could think of a reason why I simply *had* to be at my desk, I texted Eleanor, telling her that all was well with Cassie, but I'd like to take the rest of the week off as holiday. That would give me more than enough time to devote to Daniel.

By now it was gone midnight. My mother and Stephen had already gone to bed, and Cassie and Ryan and Owen vanished soon after, their status as guests allocating them the other bedrooms, leaving my brother and me to fight over the sofa and a blow up mattress.

Dylan had left his sketchbook on the kitchen table, and while he went off to fetch us pillows and blankets, I idly flicked through the pages. There were some studies of inanimate objects, but mostly he'd drawn people, Laura and Stephen, girls and boys his own age, some I recognised as his friends, and men and women in the street. Towards the end of the book I found the sketches he'd done that night, a picture of all of us sitting around the kitchen table, several unfinished sketches of Cassie and Ryan, a drawing of Owen and me laughing, Owen pouring me a glass of wine, Owen and me dancing close together, his hand on the small of my back as he kept me moving in time to the music.

When Dylan came back into the kitchen, laden with bedding, I said, 'I've been looking at your sketchbook. You've drawn some great pictures of me and Owen.'

'I draw what I see,' Dylan said.

I studied the picture of Owen and me dancing.

'This is such a good likeness of both of us,' I said. 'The only thing is, the way you've positioned our heads, it looks like we're about to kiss.'

'Yeah, sorry about that,' Dylan said. 'You'd better not show that picture to your boyfriend.'

'Oh, Daniel wouldn't care,' I said. 'He's knows he doesn't have to be jealous of Owen.'

'He should be.' Dylan grinned. 'Admit it, Lucy.

You and Owen are more than just good friends. Anyone can see it.'

I sighed in exasperation. Dylan might be an artistic prodigy, but he was still my annoying little brother.

'You are so wrong,' I said.

CHAPTER 31

'Your family are great,' Owen said to me, as we sped south on the motorway.

'They are,' I agreed. 'They liked you too.'

Owen had got on really well my parents and Dylan. I really ought to get around to introducing Daniel to them as well, I thought. And I should meet his family at some point. He didn't talk about them very often, but I knew that he had a brother and a sister who still lived at home with his parents. All they knew about me was what they'd read in the gossip columns.

Owen said, 'I usually get on fine with other people's parents. It's my own I have a problem with. I could never turn up at their house with a bunch of friends at short notice. I only visit them myself when I get a formal invitation and my sister tells me I can't refuse.'

'I might take Daniel to meet my family the next time I visit,' I said. 'I'd like them to have a chance to really get to know him, and forget that he's a celebrity.'

'Your family didn't seem particularly overawed by the international footballer,' Owen said. 'I'm sure they'll cope with the film star. Have they seen *Fallen Angel?*'

'Yes, we all watched the DVD together last Christmas.' Suddenly, I remembered how uncomfortable I'd felt watching the film alongside my parents and Dylan. 'Now I think about it, I wish they hadn't seen it. Especially the love scenes. It's going to be kind of weird introducing him to them after that.'

Owen laughed. 'That awkward moment when your parents realise that they've seen your naked boyfriend having simulated sex…'

'Not helping, Owen.'

He was still laughing

'Would you be happy to get your kit off for a film? I'm asking as your agent?'

'If I thought the part called for it, and I was being paid enough, I wouldn't hesitate.'

'What about a stage play? Would you find it intimidating to be naked in front of a live audience?'

'No, I really wouldn't. I have great abs, remember.'

Suddenly, ridiculously, I was embarrassed. To cover my confusion, I switched on the car radio, which was tuned to a sports channel. Not my ideal choice of listening on a car journey, but Owen was keen to hear yesterday's results. At least it prevented further discussion about his abs.

We made good time along the motorway. Even when we reached London, the traffic was relatively light, and it was still only half past nine when we turned into Cassie's road.

'I don't see anyone loitering with intent to take compromising photographs,' Owen said, as he parked the car in the first available space.

I looked up and down the street. The yummy

mummy who lived opposite was pushing a buggy in the direction of the park. A toned, lycra-clad jogger ran past, her ponytail swinging from side to side. A man in a leather jacket caused me a moment of concern, but then I recognised him as the surgeon who lived on the corner. Usually he wore a pin-striped suit. It was the leather jacket that fooled me.

'I think the coast is clear,' I said.

Owen and I got out of Michael's car. I retrieved my case from the boot, and we strolled along the pavement towards Cassie's house.

'Isn't that Daniel's car?' Owen said.

I followed his pointing hand. Daniel's Ferrari was parked a few yards further down the road.

'Yes it is. That's odd. I wasn't expecting him to be here. I was going to call him when I got back to London.' I checked my mobile. There was a reply to my text last night from Eleanor giving me the go ahead to take the week off, but no messages from Daniel. He hadn't returned my last call. 'I guess he must have decided to surprise me.'

Owen was still gazing at Daniel's car. 'Your boyfriend is one very fortunate guy.'

'Owen! I'd no idea you were into fast cars.'

'What? Oh, I'm not. Not particularly.' Owen turned his back on the Ferrari. 'Here, let me carry your case up the front steps.'

I was actually perfectly capable of carrying a small canvas holdall up a short flight of stairs along with my shoulder bag, but it seemed churlish to point this out. I handed Owen my case, ran lightly up the steps, opened the front door, and went into the hall.

'Daniel?' I called. 'I'm back.'

The house was silent. I checked the living room and the kitchen. Both were empty. I went back into the hall, where Owen was collecting up the morning's post from the mat.

'Daniel must be in my room,' I said. My boyfriend was in my bedroom waiting for me to come home. So that he could *ravish* me. My stomach turned a somersault. I climbed the stairs two at a time.

'Lucy,' Owen said.

'Yes?'

'Shall I bring up your case?'

Like I was thinking about luggage right now. I made myself smile at him. 'OK. Thanks, Owen.'

With growing impatience, I waited on the landing between my room and Nadia's, while Owen carried my case up the stairs.

From behind Nadia's bedroom door, her voice came to me quite distinctly.

'Do you really have to go so soon? Isn't there *anything* I can do to persuade you to stay?'

Then I heard another voice, male and agonisingly familiar.

'Shut up a minute, Nadia. I think I heard someone coming up the stairs.'

Nadia spoke again. 'There's no-one here but us.'

I took one slow step towards Nadia's room and then another. My heart was thudding in my chest. My hand reached out towards the bedroom door, and closed around the handle. I pushed the door open.

The two of them were sprawled on Nadia's bed, naked, half-covered by a sheet. Various articles of clothing were scattered about the room; his shirt was on the floor, her bra was hanging from the corner of her mirror. They stared at me standing in the doorway, and I stared back at them lying on the bed. Daniel's eyes were wide with shock. Nadia's mouth lifted in a sly, spiteful smile. *Daniel and Nadia.*

I thought, this *isn't* happening. This *cannot* be happening.

Behind me, Owen swore under his breath.

'How could you, Daniel?' I rushed to the foot of the bed. 'How could you *do* this to me?'

'You weren't here,' Daniel said. He got out of bed and put on his jeans. Even then, even when I knew that he'd just spent the night with another woman, I marvelled at the perfection of his body. He was quite simply beautiful. *My Fallen Angel.* My throat felt very tight.

Nadia said, 'He didn't take much persuading, Lucy. Just so you know.'

'You *bitch.*' I spun on my heel and walked stiffly out of the room, nearly colliding with Owen on the landing. I veered around him and went into my room, shutting the door behind me. My legs were shaking, so I sat down on my bed. Dimly, as if from a long way off, I heard shouting and the slamming of a door. Then there was silence.

My bedroom door opened, and Daniel, fully

dressed now, appeared in the doorway.

'Lucy.'

'You know we're finished, right?' Of *course* he knew we were finished. We both knew that as soon as I walked in on him and Nadia.

'Yeah. I thought you'd want me to give you back my key.' He came further into my room and put his key to Cassie's house on my nightstand. 'Could I have the key to my place please?'

At some point, my bag had slid unnoticed from my shoulder, and was lying on the bed. I opened it, found my copy of Daniel's key and tossed it to him.

'Why did you do it, Daniel?'

He shrugged. 'I don't know. Because I could.'

'I thought we were happy.'

'We were doing OK.'

'We were *happy,*' I said. 'So how could you *cheat* on me? And with *her.*'

'Listen,' Daniel said. 'I didn't turn up here yesterday with the intention of shagging Nadia. She came on to me.'

'Oh, well, that's all right then,' I said. 'Why did you come here at all? You knew I'd gone to stay with my family. I left you enough messages.'

'I drove straight back here after my meeting without checking my phone. I didn't get your voice mail until after I'd arrived. Nadia told me you'd all be gone for days.'

'I texted you that I'd be back this morning.'

'Did you?' he said. 'I never read that text.'

'What if I hadn't come back today? Did you think

you and I would just carry on as if nothing had happened?'

'I can't answer that,' Daniel said. 'Last night, I wasn't thinking that far ahead.'

'I don't understand why you'd throw away everything we had for a night with a slut.'

'I wouldn't have chosen to end it this way,' Daniel said, 'but it's not like you and I were going to be together for ever. It's not like we were *serious.*'

'But - we were going to live together -'

'What?' Daniel frowned. 'Why would you think that? When have I *ever* said anything to you about us living together? Our relationship was about sex and having a good time. Don't pretend it was anything more.'

'How can you say that!'

'Oh, grow up, Lucy, why don't you,' Daniel snapped. 'I never promised you undying love. One night we went to a club, you came home with me, and we had sex. It was good, so we kept on having sex. And now I've had sex with someone else.'

You cheating, lying fuckwit, I thought. 'I'd like you to go,' I said. My entire body was shaking. 'I'd like you to leave this house. Right now.'

For a moment he hesitated. 'I'm sorry I hurt you,' he said. 'For what it's worth.'

'Just go, Daniel,' I said.

He left.

I heard his footsteps receding down the stairs. Before I could stop myself, I ran to my bedroom window and watched him walk to his car. He stood

329

on the kerb for some time, and I thought he would surely look back up at the house, but eventually he opened the car door, got into the driver's seat and drove away. I looked out at the sunlit, tree-lined London street and thought, Daniel doesn't love me. He *never* loved me. I was hurt and humiliated, but mainly I was angry: with Daniel, with Nadia, but most of all with myself. I'd got it all *so* wrong.

A floorboard creaked. I spun around to see Owen observing me anxiously from the doorway.

'I take it that you and Daniel are over?' he said.

I nodded. 'I can't be with a guy who cheats on me.' My eyes brimmed with tears.

In two strides, Owen was across the room and gathering me in his arms. I buried my face on his chest.

'This is when you're supposed to tell me not to cry because Daniel isn't worth it,' I said.

'He isn't worth it. But you can cry all you want.'

I did cry then, but not for very long.

'I knew what Daniel was like,' I said, wiping my face with the heel of my hand. 'I should never have let myself fall for him. I'm such an idiot.'

'You,' Owen said, 'are a beautiful, intelligent *gorgeous* woman, and he's the idiot for cheating on you and losing you.'

The front door slammed shut with enough force to shake the whole house.

'What the...?' Letting go of me, Owen raced to the window. 'That was Nadia making a hasty exit. She's just got into a minicab, with three enormous suitcases. Looks like she's moving out.'

'Good. Because one of us had to.' There was a part of me that wanted to hate Nadia, but somehow I couldn't find the energy. She was beneath my contempt.

I sat down on my bed. Owen sat next to me and slid a comforting arm around my waist.

I rested my head on his shoulder. 'It's all such a mess.'

'Break ups always are.'

'It's not just about me and Daniel. Lord knows why, but Cassie's very fond of Nadia.'

'That may change,' Owen said. 'I'm guessing that celebrities tend to take a dim view of staff who do the dirty with their friend's boyfriends.'

'True. But that doesn't mean Cassie won't be upset.' A worse thought came into my mind. I raised my head and looked up at Owen in horror. 'Daniel is one of Reardon Haye's most important clients. If he has a problem with me working at the agency, if he's uncomfortable seeing me every time he comes into the office, I could lose my job.'

'This is the Fallen Angel we're talking about. If he was *uncomfortable* whenever he saw one of his exes, he'd have to retire from showbusiness.'

I smiled at that. 'Breaking up with him could still make my working at Reardon Haye very awkward for everybody. Me especially.' The thought that Daniel could turn up at my workplace at any time made me feel slightly sick, but I wasn't going to let him destroy my career as a theatrical agent. 'I'm supposed to be on leave, but I need to go into the agency this afternoon.'

'Today?' Owen said. 'Are you sure you're up to it?'

'I'm… OK.' The hurt of Daniel's betrayal was still there inside me, a tight ball of pain, but I was *not* going to let him turn me into an emotional wreck. 'I want to prove to Eleanor – and Maria and Adrian – that the end of my and Daniel's relationship isn't going to affect my ability to do my job.'

'Beautiful and intelligent,' Owen said. 'And tough.'

'I'm sure I'll feel a lot better if I'm at work phoning casting directors and getting actors auditions than if I'm at home feeling sorry for myself… *Owen!* What time is your audition?'

'It's at one o'clock.'

'It's half past twelve now!' I sprang up off my bed. 'Why are you just sitting there? You need to get to your audition.'

'I'm not going,' Owen said.

'What? You have to go. I know they're only seeing you for a small part, but it's exactly the sort of role that gets an actor noticed.'

'There's no point. I can't possible get there on time, and they won't see me if I turn up late.'

'They might.' I'd made him late. He could be missing out on a break-through role because of me. 'And you could still get there in half an hour if you take Michael's car.'

'Lucy, I'm nowhere near ready. I haven't shaved.

I'm still in the clothes I was wearing yesterday.'

'This is all my fault,' I said. 'If I hadn't cried all over you.'

'Don't worry about it. My incredibly talented agent will get me seen for other parts.'

'Your agent is going to be mad at you if you don't at least try and get seen for this one,' I said. 'Forget about shaving and changing your clothes. Just get to the audition as soon as you can. And if you're late tell them – I don't know – you're the actor – improvise.'

'OK. I'll think of something.' Owen looked unconvinced, but he got to his feet. My mascara was smeared over the front of his shirt, but I decided not to mention it.

'Best of luck.' I hugged him. 'Break a leg and all that.'

'Thanks, Lucy.' Resting his hands on my hips, he bent his head and kissed the side of my face. Then he kissed me on my mouth.

Almost immediately, he leapt away from me, leaving me gasping. 'Oh, God - Lucy, I'm sorry - I'm so sorry. I should never have done that. I just – I just couldn't help myself.'

Owen had kissed me. All I could do was stare at him. He'd kissed me and it'd felt good. More than good.

Owen's very blue eyes anxiously searched my face. 'Lucy, talk to me. Please.'

I stuttered, 'Y-You kissed me.'

'I'm sorry. It was wrong.'

'It was just a kiss,' I said. 'Stop apologising. And go to your audition.'

'Are we OK?'

'Yes, we're fine.' I wanted him to kiss me again.

'I'll see you later?'

'Yes. Now *go*.'

Owen seemed about to say something more to me, but evidently changed his mind. Looking thoroughly wretched, he walked out of the room.

I thought, I can't let him go off to an audition in that state. 'Owen, wait!' I pelted out of my bedroom and down the stairs.

Owen was half-way out the front door, but he spun around to face me, and I cannoned into his arms. My heart hammering in my chest, I put my hands on either side of his face, drew down his head, and kissed him, sliding the tip of my tongue between his lips. He kissed me back, softly at first, and then demanding and hard, his tongue probing deep into my mouth.

When we broke apart, both of us breathless, he said, 'Don't go into work this afternoon.'

'I won't.'

'You'll definitely be here when I get back?'

'Yes,' I said. 'Now go to your audition.'

Owen ran down the front steps.

'Just so you know,' he called to me, over his shoulder, 'that was not a stage kiss.'

CHAPTER 32

I closed the front door and leant against it, my pulse racing, my thoughts jittering around in my head. Daniel and I were over. Owen had kissed me. I'd just broken up with my long-term boyfriend. Owen was wrong to kiss me. And yet he and I had kissed. And it'd felt so right.

My legs shaking, I walked slowly back upstairs and on a sudden impulse went into Nadia's bedroom. A number of her belongings, a hairdryer, an alarm clock, several handbags and magazines, were still there, but an inspection of her wardrobes and drawers showed me that all of her clothes, shoes and make-up were gone. She really had moved out. There was no reason why I'd ever have to see her again.

It was unrealistic to think that I might never see Daniel again – not if I wanted to go on working at Reardon Haye – but I could at least rid Cassie's house of any unwelcome reminders of his presence. I went across the landing, and retrieved his toothbrush and razor from my bathroom, and his shirts, socks and underwear from the drawers I'd cleared for him. In my wardrobe, I found two pairs of his jeans, and one pair of inordinately expensive trainers. The toothbrush and razor went straight into a rubbish sack, and after a moment the clothes and shoes followed. As an act of revenge this could be viewed as somewhat pathetic, but I knew that he was very fond of those trainers. The dress he'd brought back for me from New York and a bottle of perfume he'd given me went into the trash as well. And I changed the sheets on my bed, because two nights ago I'd slept between those sheets with him. It occurred to me to wonder, in a detached way, if he'd cheated on me before, if not with Nadia, then with someone else. I'd loved him, but if I was honest, I'd never trusted him.

I took the old sheets down to the kitchen and shoved them in the washing machine. Then I poured myself a glass of lemonade, made myself a sandwich, and took them out into the garden.

I sat at the table on the terrace and thought, Daniel and I are over. I was with him for eight months, and it was good for much of that time, whatever he says, but now we're over.

The prospect of not having Daniel in my life left me curiously unmoved. I pictured him and Nadia lying in her bed, the expression of shock and surprise on his face when I opened the door. I'd been hurt by the depth of his betrayal, but now, all I could think was how *ridiculous* he was. The Fallen Angel. The movie star who can't keep his trousers on. Daniel Miller, A-lister, serial womaniser. The man was a walking cliché.

And Owen had kissed me.

I raised my hand to my face and touched my mouth, reliving the moment when Owen's lips had met mine. It was not a stage kiss. It was not the kiss of a friend. And I had no idea what was going to happen between me and Owen when he came back from his audition. That thought scared me just a little.

A noise made me turn my face towards the house. Cassie stepped through the French windows, starting when she saw me. She waved, and walked over to where I was sitting.

'Hey, Lucy.' She sat down opposite me. 'I didn't think anyone was home.'

'It's just me here,' I said. 'Owen's gone off to howl at the moon.'

'Oh, right, he's auditioning to be a werewolf.'

I thought, I have to tell her about Daniel. I have to tell her about Daniel and Nadia.

'You're back from the studios very early,' I said.

'Yes, we didn't do any filming today,' Cassie said. 'After all the rubbish about me on the internet, most of the cast and crew already knew that the show was being cancelled. The producers came on set before the cameras had started rolling, confirmed the rumours, and told us to take the rest of the day off. We all went straight to the nearest pub – Ah, here's my fiancé.'

Ryan came out of the house carrying two mugs of coffee. He set them down on the table and took the chair next to Cassie.

'I made yours extra strong,' he said to her. To me, he added, 'She's been drinking again and I need to sober her up. We're going to see my parents this evening to discuss our wedding, and I don't want them thinking I'm marrying a lush.'

Cassie grinned. 'I had a long talk with your

mother on the phone about the press coverage of my drinking habits, and she told me that any girl is allowed to act a bit wild when she's about to settle down to married life. She also wants an invitation to my hen night.'

'You and my mother on a girls' night out,' Ryan said. 'What a terrifying thought.' They both laughed.

'So what are you doing sitting out here on your own, Lucy?' Ryan said. 'Where's Daniel?'

'I've no idea,' I said. 'He and I broke up.'

Ryan froze in the act of drinking his coffee.

Cassie gaped at me. 'You and Daniel - But why? I don't understand. What happened?'

'He cheated on me,' I said. 'He slept with Nadia.'

'*What?*' The colour drained from Cassie's face. 'Are you sure? How do you know?'

'Owen and I arrived back here this morning and found them together, naked in her bed. So, yes, I'm sure.'

'Oh, Lucy -' Cassie's hands flew to her mouth.

'I told Daniel to go and he went. Nadia's gone as well. She went off in a taxi with most of her stuff. I don't know where.'

There was a long silence.

Eventually, Ryan said, 'Shite, Lucy. I don't know what to say to you.'

'How could they,' Cassie said. 'In this house - in our *home*. What were they *thinking*?'

'I'd imagine Daniel was thinking with his dick,' Ryan said.

'I thought I was the Girl who tamed the Fallen

Angel,' I said. 'I thought he'd changed since he'd met me. I was so wrong.'

'Even for the Fallen Angel,' Cassie said, 'this has to be an all-time low. As for Nadia, I'd never have believed it of her. She's worked for me and lived in my house for three years. I thought I knew her.'

Ryan put his hand over hers. 'Nadia is a sly, manipulative bitch.'

Cassie seemed about to protest, but then she nodded her head. 'She's certainly played me for a fool. I trusted her completely, and now she's betrayed me. What am I saying? This isn't about *me*. Lucy, I can't imagine what you're feeling right now, but I want you to know that Ryan and I are here for you.'

'We'll get you through this,' Ryan said.

'We'll stay in with you tonight,' Cassie said. 'Or take you out, if you'd prefer... Whatever you want. Ryan, would you phone your mum and dad and tell them we can't make it this evening?'

'Yes, of course.' Ryan produced his mobile.

'That's very sweet of you,' I said, 'but you really don't need to change your plans because of me.'

'It's not a problem Lucy,' Ryan said. 'My parents will understand.'

'We're not leaving you here on your own,' Cassie said. 'Not after what happened.'

'I'm OK,' I said. 'It was awful at the time – walking in on them, I mean – but now I just feel – I don't know – strange, but OK.'

'We're your friends,' Cassie said, 'and friends

339

look out for each other. Like you looked out for me this last weekend.'

Ryan said, 'No-one should have to deal with a break up on their own.'

'But I won't be alone tonight,' I said. 'Owen'll be here.' Much as I valued their support and concern for me, I realised that I'd actually prefer it if Cassie and Ryan went out. I didn't know what was going on between me and Owen, but I did know that tonight I wanted him to myself, so that I could find out. 'He'll be home soon.'

'Will he?' Cassie said, doubtfully.

'Oh, yes. He didn't want to leave me on my own either. I practically had to frogmarch him out of the house.' I thought, do I tell them about me and Owen? What do I tell them about me and Owen? What *is* there to tell?

'Well, we won't go 'til he's back,' Ryan said.

Cassie's mobile, which was on the table, trilled with the first notes of *Princess Snowdrop's* title music, telling her she had an email.

'I really need to change my ringtone.' She glanced at her phone, and then frowned and picked it up. 'You've got to be kidding me. This is *unbelievable*.' She passed the phone to Ryan, and he passed it to me.

The message was from Nadia: *I am no longer prepared to work long anti-social hours in an environment where I am patronised and unappreciated. I resign forthwith. You owe me one month's salary, plus two week's pay in lieu of*

holiday. Any item of mine remaining in your property
should be forwarded to ...

An address in Battersea followed.

'The nerve of the woman!' Cassie said. 'Patronised? Anti-social hours? I took her clubbing and introduced her to A-list celebrities! And she can't resign – I'm firing her.'

'Doesn't Leo live in Battersea?' Ryan said, 'I'm guessing she's decided to inflict herself on him full time, and this message was for his benefit as much as yours.'

'Poor Leo,' I said.

Suddenly, Cassie said, 'I just thought of something. I'm not saying they're going to turn up on our doorstep anytime soon, but once it becomes known that the Fallen Angel and his girlfriend are no longer together, there could be some... interest from the media. You need to be prepared for that, Lucy.'

'I guess you're right. But I'm not going to worry about it until it happens.'

Ryan said, 'Owen's back.'

I turned my head to see Owen striding towards me across the sun-scorched grass. He looked at me questioningly, and then gave me a tentative smile. My heart leapt, and I couldn't help but smile back.

'Hi, all,' he said, sitting down beside me.

'Lucy's been telling us about her and Daniel breaking up,' Cassie said. 'I'm still having trouble getting my head around it.'

'Er, yeah. Bad times.' Owen arranged his face into a suitably grave expression. 'How are you doing, Lucy?'

'I'm doing OK,' I said. 'Apart from regretting the time and tears I've wasted on my emotionally retarded ex-boyfriend, I'm actually doing fine.'

'I – I'm glad to hear that,' Owen said. 'That you're OK.' We were both smiling now.

'So how was your audition?'

'It went well, I think,' he said. 'They want to see me again next week, so I must have done something right. Oh, and they told me to be sure not to shave.'

'I thought there was something different about you,' Cassie said. 'It's the stubble.'

'Yeah.' Owen stroked his chin. 'Apparently werewolves, even in human form, are hairy guys. Or so I'm reliably informed by *Alpha Male*'s casting director.'

'It suits you.' I suppressed a sudden urge to reach out and touch his face. 'It makes you look ruggedly handsome.' I felt myself blush and could only hope that neither Cassie nor Ryan noticed.

'Is that so?' Owen said. 'You may never see me clean-shaven again.'

Ryan glanced at his watch. 'Cassie, you and I ought to be leaving about now if we're still going to my parents.' To Owen, he added, 'We didn't want to go out and leave Lucy on her own after the rough time she's had, but now that you're here...'

'I'll always be here for her,' Owen said.

I felt such a rush of affection for him that it took my breath away.

'I'll be fine with Owen,' I said. 'Really I will. And you two do have a wedding to organise.'

After a further ten minutes reassuring themselves that I really was *totally* fine about their going, Cassie and Ryan said their goodbyes, and went off to talk flowers and table plans with his parents, leaving me alone with Owen.

It was late afternoon now, and the sun was low in the sky. I heard birdsong, and the drone of bees. In the house next door someone started playing a clarinet, the music drifting out to us through an open window. Sitting there in the garden, the sunlight fading into dusk, it came to me that I'd fallen out of love with Daniel, my beautiful, shallow, selfish Fallen Angel, a while ago. Even if it had taken another man's kiss to make me realise it.

'Lucy…'

I turned my head to face Owen. His blue-eyed gaze searched my face. I felt as though I was melting inside.

'I can't be your friend anymore,' he said.

'I – I don't want you as a f-friend,' I said.

'Will you have dinner with me tonight?'

'You mean… like a date?'

'Not *like* a date. A date.'

'I'd love to have dinner with you tonight,' I said.

His smile was dazzling. 'I'll pick you up - from your room - about eight?'

'I'll be ready.' I willed him to lean forward and kiss me again.

'I need to go and get changed,' he said, 'I can't take a beautiful girl out to dinner in yesterday's T-shirt.'

With another smile, he stood up and headed off into the house. Leaving me in the garden, feeling distinctly light-headed, and aching for his kiss.

CHAPTER 33

An hour and a half later, showered, hair blow-dried and straightened, legs shaved, face made up, and nails varnished, I stood staring at my open wardrobe, wondering what to wear. My wardrobe and my chest of drawers were overflowing with clothes, from ridiculously short, sequined dresses to jeans and T-shirts, to flimsy skirts and strappy tops. Nothing seemed right. In the end, I settled on a sleeveless, low-cut top, red, scattered with black roses, and black skinny jeans. And my apricot-coloured silk bra and thong – I'd no idea how the evening was going to end, or even how I wanted it to end, but I needed to know that I looked good, whatever happened. After that, shoes and bag were easy (black high-heeled sandals and black leather clutch), and I kept my jewellery simple with a pair of silver earrings and a silver chain.

Scrutinising myself in my full-length mirror, I was pleased with what I saw. Hopefully, Owen would be too. Honestly, Lucy, I thought, you're behaving like a girl going on a first date. Then I thought, I *am* going on a first date. I've been out with Owen often enough, but this is the first time I've gone on a date with him. Suddenly, my legs felt decidedly weak. I told myself I was being absurd. It was *Owen* I was having dinner with, for goodness' sake.

Without warning, my head reeled. What was I doing going on a date with Owen, when it was only a few hours ago that I'd broken up with Daniel? It was way too soon for me to be even *thinking* about getting involved with anyone else, let alone putting on my best silk underwear. What if this was all a huge mistake? Lord knows I'd made enough mistakes with men.

Then I remembered the way I'd felt when Owen had kissed me…

'Owen.' I said his name aloud. I thought of all the times we'd been out, or stayed in together. How we always had so much to say to one another, how he made me laugh, even when I was feeling down. He was the only man I'd ever wanted to dance with… We'd been friends, close friends, but over the last weeks and months, however much I might not have wanted to admit it, even to myself, my feelings for him had grown from friendship into... something else. A delectable shiver ran down my spine. I wasn't sure what it was I felt for Owen, but whatever happened tonight, we couldn't go back to the way we were before that kiss.

There was a knock on my bedroom door. Quickly, I sprayed myself with perfume. 'Come in, Owen,' I said.

He opened the door. 'Hey, Lucy. I've booked us a table at that new restaurant opposite the station, so if you're good to go…' His voice trailed off and his gaze travelled appreciatively and unashamedly up and down my body, and back to my face. 'You look terrific. That red colour really suits you.'

'Thank you. You're looking pretty good yourself.'

He looked *gorgeous* in dark jeans, and a blue and white striped shirt that I'd not seen before.

We went downstairs and out into the street, and he took my hand, lacing his fingers through mine. I became conscious of a pleasurable fluttering in my stomach.

'I think I'm going to like not being friends with you,' I said.

The restaurant had a garden, its stone walls covered in honeysuckle that filled the night air with its scent. We sat outside at a wooden table for two, a candle flickering between us. The waiter came to take our order and Owen asked him to bring us a bottle of white wine. We ate, and drank, talking easily about anything and everything as we'd always done, but all the while I was wondering when he was going to kiss me again. The waiter came back with the dessert menu, but neither of us could eat another thing. We had coffee, just sitting there together, without the need for talk. Owen rested his hands on the table, his fingertips just brushing mine.

'Would you like another drink?' he said. 'Or shall we make a move?'

'I don't mind,' I said. 'It's up to you.' My stomach was clenched so tight that it hurt.

Owen signalled to the waiter, who brought him the bill. I was about to ask how much was my share, when he took some notes out of his wallet, and told the waiter to keep the change. I reminded myself that tonight we were not two friends meeting up in a bar after work, but a man and a woman on a date. And even in the twenty-first century, there are still guys who expect to pay for the meal if they ask a girl out to dinner.

I thought Owen might kiss me once we were outside the restaurant, but all he did was put his arm loosely around my shoulders. We strolled back to Cassie's house, with my heart beating so furiously that I was sure he must be able to hear it. We arrived home and I got out my key, but my hand was shaking so much that I couldn't get it in the lock. A smile playing about his mouth, Owen took the key, unlocked the front door, and stood to one side, so that I could go into the hall. He slowly closed the door. I was trembling all over now, but somehow I managed to return my key to my bag.

Owen laughed softly and put his hands on my waist, drawing me close. I melted against him, feeling the heat of his body through his shirt as he folded me in his arms. I slid my arms around his waist, and tilted up my face. He brushed a strand of hair out of my eyes.

And then at last, he bent his head and kissed me, his tongue exploring my mouth, desire lancing through me as his hand glided under my top and stroked my bare skin. We kissed for a long time before he lifted his face from mine.

'Are we going to spend the night together?' he said.

My body felt as though it was on fire. 'Yes,' I whispered. 'We are.'

'Are you sure?' His voice was hoarse. 'Because

there's nothing I want more right now than to take you to bed, but if it's too soon, if you need more time, I can wait.'

'I've never been more sure of anything in my life,' I said. To let him know exactly how sure I was, I took off my top. Then I reached behind my back and unhooked my bra, sliding it down my arms, and letting it drop to the floor. Owen groaned and crushed me to him, and I could feel that he was hard, even through his jeans. He kissed my neck, a hand cupping my breast. Then he swept me up in his arms and carried me upstairs, kicking open his bedroom door, before setting me gently down on my feet next to his bed. The curtains were open, and the room was flooded with light from the newly risen moon. I noticed that the bed was made with freshly laundered sheets.

Owen started to unbutton his shirt, but then reached over his shoulders and pulled it off over his head. He slid his feet out of his shoes, and stripped off his jeans and boxers, and I took off the rest of my clothes. We stood facing each other, naked, our bodies bathed in silver moonlight. He reached out a hand and traced the line of my jaw. I looked at his hard, muscular body, his chest rising and falling, and I wanted him very badly.

'You are so beautiful,' he said softly.

I lay down on the bed, and he lay down next to me, holding me close against him, so that I could feel his heart beating next to mine. He kissed me on the mouth and at the base of my throat, and then he kissed my breasts. He trailed a hand down my body, and I moaned and gasped as I felt his touch between my thighs. He gathered me to him, and there was more kissing and caressing, our bodies and limbs entwined, his erection hot against my stomach. He reached under his pillow and brought out a condom. I smiled to myself. Fresh sheets and a condom under the pillow. He may have been happy to wait a while before we had sex, but he'd obviously hoped he wouldn't have to.

He turned away from me for a moment, and I opened my legs so that when he turned back, he could position his body between them. He lowered himself until he was lying on top of me, supporting his weight with one hand, and guiding himself gently inside me with the other. For a moment we lay still, looking into each other's eyes, and then he began to move, his hips rhythmically rising and falling. Desire, a craving hot and insistent, surged through me, and I raised my knees, gripping him with my thighs, and he thrust deeper, faster, harder. An intensity of heat and passion was building deep within me, and cascading through my body. Owen's eyes were shut now, and he was breathing harshly, and my hips were moving with his, and then I felt his body jolt and arch towards me, and both of us were gasping as wave after wave of ecstasy crested within us and flooded our senses …

Owen brushed my forehead with his lips. Then he raised himself off me and lay on his back next to me on the bed, one arm under his head. I draped an arm over his waist and a leg over his legs, and settled my head on his shoulder. I breathed in the lingering scent of his cologne, and a gloriously masculine scent that was just him.

'Lucy Ashford,' he said, 'you are a really great theatrical agent.'

'And you, Owen Somers, are my favourite client.'

He put his arms around me. I could have lain there forever, safe in his arms.

'How would you feel if I stopped telling people that you're my agent, and started telling them that you're my girlfriend?'

'I'd like that Owen,' I said. 'Very much.'

I was drifting off to sleep, when he said, 'It's so good to hold you. You can't imagine how many times I've wished that you were there beside me.'

'You have?'

'I'd have asked you out months ago if you hadn't been involved with another guy.'

'Really? You told me you wanted to be my *friend.*' I was wide awake again now.

'I was attracted to you the moment I first saw you,' Owen said, 'but it would have been a little unprofessional of me to hit on you when you were auditioning me for the agency. Or the first time you came to see me perform on stage. I was planning to – ah – make a move at the Reardon Haye Christmas party, but I could see that I didn't stand a chance with you that night.'

If I hadn't only had eyes for the Fallen Angel, I thought, Owen would have asked me out that night.

351

If I hadn't gone to that club with Daniel…

'I wanted you, Lucy,' Owen said. 'I wanted to be *with* you. I told myself that you and I were never going to happen, and I would settle for being your friend, but it was never enough.'

'I'd no idea you felt that way,' I said.

Owen smiled ruefully 'I'm a good actor.'

'Until today I really did think of you as my friend,' I said. 'But for a while now… let's just say that I'd noticed you have great abs.'

'And there was I thinking you fell for me instantly after just one kiss.'

'That kiss may have had something to do with it,' I said. He held me just a little tighter. I sighed contentedly and shut my eyes. Whatever mistakes I've made in the past, I thought, I'm with the right guy now, and that's all that matters.

I was almost asleep again when he whispered my name, 'Lucy? Are you still awake?'

'Just about.'

'Do you remember the day we went rowing on the Serpentine?'

'Yes, of course. It was lovely.'

'I realised something that day – I nearly told you –'

'What was it?' I said.

'I love you.'

My heart brimmed over.

'I love you too, Owen,' I said.

EPILOGUE

A year later...

I arrive at the restaurant, to find that Daniel has got there before me and is already seated, sipping a glass of wine and studying a menu. I make my way towards him through the crowded eatery, conscious of the sidelong glances of the other diners. I arrive at his table, and one woman actually takes our picture on her mobile phone. Four girls of about my age stop drinking their spritzers, nudge each other with their elbows, and whisper to each other behind their hands.

'Lucy. Hi.' He smiles at me, a little uncertainly.

'Hello, Daniel.' I sit down opposite him, and lean back in my chair. It's strange, being here with him after all this time. I can see that his face is still beautiful, if rather more tanned than the last time I saw him, but I'm no longer physically attracted to him. I don't feel anything for him at all. It's as though I'm looking at the photo of a beautiful stranger in a magazine.

'Would you like a glass of wine?' Daniel says.

I nod my head. I plan to go back to the agency after this lunchtime meeting, but one glass of wine won't affect my work.

'It's good to see you,' Daniel says, 'I thought you might stand me up.'

'I wouldn't do that to anybody.'

'You didn't come to the premiere of *Fallen Angel II*. I know everyone at Reardon Haye had tickets.'

'I didn't come because I didn't want photos of *Daniel Miller's ex-girlfriend* on the red carpet all over the internet. Is that why you asked me here? To complain that I didn't come to a premiere?'

'No, of course not. I –'

He breaks off as a waitress comes to our table, and the next few minutes are taken up with her writing down our order. I watch, half-amused, half-irritated, as she lavishes attention on Daniel, explaining various dishes to him, while I'm left to interpret the menu on my own.

'I'd forgotten what it's like being out in public with you,' I say to him, when the waitress has gone.

He grins, a flash of white teeth in his sun-tanned face. The four girls at the next table give a collective sigh. His eyes flicker towards them.

'Daniel – I know you have trouble focusing on just one woman, but I've only got an hour.' I sound much more acerbic than I intended. I'm not sure why I agreed to meet him, but it wasn't to give him a hard time.

Daniel doesn't take offence. 'Owen Somers must get recognised as often as I do these days,' he says.

'Not really. Well, he has been recognised a couple of times, but only when he hasn't shaved. Which suits him just fine.' Even a year later, I feel absurdly pleased and proud that Owen was cast as the lead in *Alpha Male,* rather than the lead's brother. The show is extremely popular, and another series is planned. I tease Owen that he only got the part because of his designer stubble (and, crazily enough, this is partly true), but we both know that it was his talent as an actor that got him the Best Newcomer award at the Baftas.

Daniel says, 'Cassie told me about you and Owen.'

'I know,' I say, 'I remember you phoned her before you went to the States.'

A few days after we broke up, Daniel had phoned Cassie and asked how I was. Having berated him for precisely twenty-two minutes and forty seconds (Ryan was with her when she took the call, and he'd timed her), she'd told him that I was doing a lot better than he might have expected after the way he'd treated me. In fact, I was doing great, because I was with Owen, and the best thing he, Daniel, could do was stay out of my life. Which, to be fair, he had done. But then, it was only a week or so later that he'd got the call from the American producer he'd met in London inviting him out to LA to star in his first Hollywood movie, so it hadn't exactly been difficult for him. Even before he'd left for California, my fears that breaking up with one of Reardon Haye's star clients might affect my position at the agency had proved groundless. On my first morning back at work after my holiday, I'd announced that Daniel and I were over and I was fine about it. Eleanor had merely commented that she knew I was a thorough professional who would always leave my personal issues at the door of the workplace. Neither she nor Maria had seemed particularly surprised when after an interval of about a month, I'd let slip that I was dating Owen. Adrian had remarked that he'd thought he was working in a theatrical agency, not a dating agency, but he'd smiled as he'd said it (and he'd done the sandwich run that day), so I'd forgiven him.

Daniel had visited England several times since then, but we hadn't run into each other. While I knew that our paths would probably cross at some point, it'd been a shock when he'd phoned me out of the blue, informed me that he was in London for a few days and asked me to have lunch with him before he flew back to the States. I couldn't imagine why he would want to see me after all this time, and had no particular desire to see him, but he was most insistent, and somehow I'd found myself agreeing to meet him.

'So,' Daniel says, breaking in on my thoughts. 'You and Owen. How's it working out?'

I hold up my left hand so that Daniel can see the diamond ring on my third finger.

His eyes widen in surprise. 'You're getting married?'

'Yes,' I say, happily. 'Next year. In the spring.'

'But that's great, Lucy. Congratulations. Many, many congratulations. To both of you.'

'Thank you,' I say, taken aback that Daniel's reaction on learning of my and Owen's engagement is almost as enthusiastic as that of our friends. My parents and Dylan are delighted that Owen is going to be a part of our family. To my surprise, because she's never been the least bit interested in fashion (or weddings, for that matter), my mother is enthusiastically trying on mother-of-the-bride outfits, including hats.

'How did Owen propose?' Daniel says. 'Did he do the whole down on one knee thing?'

'He did. Both knees, actually.' I've no idea if Daniel is genuinely interested or if he's just making conversation, but I'm always happy to talk about Owen's proposal. 'We'd been to see a show in the West End and were walking through Piccadilly Circus to get the train home – we've been living together in our own place for a couple of months now – and as we went past the statue of Eros, Owen staggered and said the god of love had shot him with an arrow in the heart, and collapsed onto his knees on the pavement. I thought he was just messing about, but then he reached inside his jacket and brought out a ring...'

I'm melting inside just thinking of that moment.

The waitress returns with my salad and Daniel's risotto. She spends an inordinately long time ensuring that he has enough parmesan and black pepper, and I have to admire the way she manages to hold a pepper grinder in a manner that can only be described as suggestive. Daniel thanks her, reading her unusual name off her name-badge, and asking her how she pronounces it. She returns to the restaurant kitchen with an exaggerated sway of her hips. I think, I have more important things to do this afternoon than watch my film-star ex-boyfriend flirt with a waitress.

Aloud, I say, 'Daniel, why did you ask me to have lunch with you? What was it you couldn't say to me on the phone?'

Daniel swallows a mouthful of risotto and lays his spoon and fork down carefully on the side of his plate. His brown eyes lock on mine.

'I've been thinking a lot about the day we broke up,' he says. 'I wanted to tell you again how sorry I am that I hurt you. I really am sorry, Lucy.'

This is so unexpected that I stare at him, speechless.

'What I said to you that day –'

'The day I found you in bed with that slutty girl who sold her story to the press?'

Daniel winces. As well he might. Nadia's kiss and tell, 'I Fell for the Fallen Angel,' had been shockingly explicit, (I'm sure she made most of it up - he certainly never did those things with me) and had brought her the proverbial fifteen minutes of the fame (or notoriety) that she presumably craved. What it hadn't done was resurrect her acting career, and her descent from the giddy heights of a centre page spread in a Sunday tabloid to total obscurity had been swift. As the wronged girlfriend, I'd been papped a couple of times, but my own brief moment of celebrity as the girl who'd failed to tame the Fallen Angel was fortunately soon forgotten. Strangely enough, I'd spotted Nadia once, just a few weeks ago, walking along Oxford Street with Poor Leo, looking bored. And, no, I did *not* feel any sympathy for her when I saw her pinched, miserable face. Why

Poor Leo was still with her after her antics in the media, I couldn't imagine. Maybe he was being punished for something terrible he'd done in a previous life.

'Yeah, *that* day,' Daniel says. 'When I said that you and I were just about sex… it wasn't true.'

'Is that so?' *Where is he going with this?* I have absolutely no desire to discuss my sex life with my ex.

'Oh, sex with you was always great,' Daniel says, 'but I liked spending time with you outside the bedroom as well as in it. And I don't just mean that I liked walking into an event with you as my arm-candy. I liked it when it was just the two of us watching a movie, or sunbathing in the garden on a summer afternoon. I liked you, Lucy, but I wasn't in love with you, and I never thought we'd be together forever. I'm sorry if I said or did anything to make you think otherwise. And most of all, I'm sorry that I cheated on you.'

I'm sorry too, I think. Sorry that I was stupid enough to let myself fall for you when I knew what you were like.

'The thing is,' Daniel says, 'I'm a bit of a shite.'

'Only a bit?'

He runs his hand through his hair. 'You're angry with me. Well, I don't blame you.'

'I'm not angry with you, Daniel. I *was* angry with you, but I got over it – over you – pretty quick.' In a matter of hours. But you don't have to know that. 'It's hard to stay angry with your shite of an ex-boyfriend when you're in love with another guy.'

Daniel risks a smile. I find myself smiling back.

He says, 'So, while I'm back in London, if we happen to turn up at the same showbiz event, you won't be throwing a glass of champagne over me?'

'I'll try and restrain myself. I hate wasting champagne.'

He laughs, and then he says, 'Lucy, I know I messed up, but we had some good times when we were together, didn't we?'

'Yes,' I say. 'We did.'

And suddenly we're chatting to one another. He tells me about his life in California, his mansion in Beverly Hills ('Yes, of course it has a pool.'), his cars ('No, Lucy, I don't walk anywhere. I don't usually drive myself either. I have a driver. I have a PA and a publicist as well.'), the A-listers he hangs out with, and his next Hollywood film. I tell him about Owen and my terraced house in North London, Cassie and Ryan's wedding ('She looked like a fairy-tale princess, but don't tell her I said that.'), and Cassie's performance as Nora in a West End production of *A Doll's House* ('She was terrified she wouldn't be able to pull it off, but she was really great.'). I don't tell him that Cassie's pregnant, because she and Ryan have only told their closest friends. He tells me about his trip to the Cannes film festival. I tell him about the weekend Owen and I spent in Paris with Michael and Annette.

The waitress comes to clear our plates, favouring Daniel with a beaming smile. I roll my eyes. Daniel grins, and asks if I'd like a coffee.

I shake my head. 'I should make a move. I've a ton of emails waiting for me back at Reardon Haye.'

Daniel asks the waitress to fetch the bill. He phones his driver and tells him to bring the car round to the front of the restaurant. He pays for our meal, and we leave the restaurant together. A sleek black limo draws up by the kerb. A man in a dark suit gets out of the passenger seat and holds open the door to the back.

'Who's that?' I ask Daniel.

'My minder.'

'You have a minder? Anyone would think you were a Hollywood star! Oh – you are.' He has the life he wants. And so do Owen and I.

'Thanks for meeting me, Lucy,' Daniel says. 'It was good to clear the air.'

'Yes, it was.'

'Would you like a lift back to the agency?'

'Reardon Haye is literally just round that corner. I'll probably be able to make it on foot. It's not like I'm a celebrity.'

He smiles self-deprecatingly.

'Goodbye, Daniel,' I say. 'Safe journey back to LA.' I turn to go, but he puts his hand on my arm.

'Lucy,' he says, 'I don't suppose there's any chance that you and I…'

He has got to be joking. I jerk away from him. Why am I shocked? I know what he's like.

'I'm not going to sleep with you, Daniel, so don't ask me.'

He raises his eyebrows. 'I wasn't planning to. Even before I saw that ring on your finger.'

'Oh. OK. Good. Sorry.' I can only hope my face is not as flushed as it feels. 'So what were you going to say?'

'I was going to say, do you think you and I could keep in touch? I'm going to be based in the States for the foreseeable future, but maybe we could email sometimes?'

I'm taken aback by this. 'I don't know, Daniel...'

'It's OK, Lucy, I understand.'

'Oh, why not.' I realise, with some amazement that despite everything, I like Daniel Miller. He is *incorrigible* – but what you see is what you get. 'Email me a photo of your pool and your cars that you don't drive. I warn you though, I have no intention of being impressed. And if I see something in the media that makes me think you're behaving like a louse, I'll tell you.'

We exchange air-kisses, and Daniel gets into the back seat of his limo. As the car pulls out away from the kerb, he lowers the darkened window, leans out and waves. I wave back, until his car is lost in the traffic.

I fish my mobile out of my bag and text Owen: *Lunch better than expected. Will tell you all tonight. Love you. xxx*

I smile. Only a few more hours and I'll be with him.

Still smiling, I head back to work.

362

ACKNOWLEDGEMENTS

Massive thanks to Hazel and the team at Accent Press, and to my editor, Caz.

And to all my writer friends who have been so generous with their advice and support.

And last but not least, to Guy, Joanne, David and Sara, for putting up with having a writer in the family, and of course, Iain, Laura and Marc.

Proudly published by Accent Press

www.accentpress.co.uk